THE NIGHT WATCH

Julian Dinsell

TINDERBOX
The Moving Book Company

THE NIGHT WATCH

This edition (2021) is published by Tinderbox Films Ltd in association with TVC Books (an imprint of TVC Films Ltd.)

ISBN: 978-1-9168808-3-2

"When men shall say peace and safety, then comes sudden destruction."

Paul's Letter to the Thessalonians

"There will be a new world revolution, not of the ragged masses but of those with money vision, and power"

Golkov

"Where does the dark go when the light comes on?"

Kloptik

"I prefer the kind of bullshit you can smell."

Murphy

With love to Brenda, whose inspiration and generosity of spirit made *The Night Watch* possible.

Special thanks to Simon Dinsell at Tinderbox Films and Sandra Martin, Editor Extraordinaire.

For Jan Harlan, whose enthusiasm and great wisdom has guided *The Night Watch* since its inception.

Contents

1

Before The Beginning

Kloptik was afraid. It was a primitive, animal fear, the kind that sharpens the senses to the limit of endurance. He caught the bitter odour of adrenaline on the palms of his hands as he pulled up the collar of his old overcoat and lowered his head into the freezing wind. So close to the end of his journey, he had expected that fear would have been left behind. But the terror that had driven him from Central Europe and out across the dark Atlantic pursued him still; down this long, dark, empty American street. His slight body struggled to keep an even pace in the face of ferocious blasts of air. Like a threatening crowd, gusts of frozen air jostled him across the sidewalk and he lurched forward with uneven steps. Litter washed in and out of darkened doorways Like wet seaweed on a receding wave, an old newspaper wrapped itself around his leg. He tried to shake it free but it clung tenaciously to him and he had to turn his back to the wind to rid himself of it.

Kloptik's first hour and a half in America had been a shock. He was in one of those parts of the inner city that had been surrendered to the vandals. The fight was over; everywhere graffiti proclaimed the triumph of the new rulers. He did not understand much of what he read but as a scientist his instinct was to analyse and to classify. It seemed to his central European academic mind that the slogans were in celebration of a culture whose supreme achievement was dereliction. Places that had once been redoubts of family pride – Fink's Auto Store, The Haven Deli and Mario's Dry Cleanery – had long since been abandoned. Empty windows framed burnt-out roofs against the night sky. He wondered if anyone would ever live here again.

On the crumpled map in Warsaw, he had memorised the walk from the docks to the rendezvous. It looked so simple, so easy to remember. Unlike the tangled city centres of Europe, here the streets were numbered and laid out in a grid pattern. But neither the map, nor anything else, had prepared him for what looked like a war zone. As a distraction from the cold, he let the strangeness of such self-inflicted wounds engage his imagination; was this another ancient Rome? A civilisation that imploded like a supernova and sucked barbarians into its empty core? He sensed that this was different. No foreign enemy had done this. No Mongol horde, no band of Visigoths, not even a Communist conspiracy had destroyed the neighbourhood and driven out the population. There were no answers, only more questions. Struggling on against the angry cold, he wiped his streaming eyes on the rough sleeve of his coat. Perhaps only a nation of plenty and power could indulge in such destruction? He struggled on, his shallow breath condensing into ice crystals that froze on his moustache.

He admitted defeat. The answer to this bizarre landscape lay buried deep in a way of life foreign to his understanding. Yet the madness of it all was strangely reassuring. It made the warning he carried seem somehow more normal, more believable.

Less than a kilometre. His memory of the map had become distant and anxiety rose as the distance shortened. It was not a simple fear of death; that was a mere detail. It was a fear of losing control, of collapsing under the weight of it all. That was the greatest terror. Yet somehow part of him retained a strange detachment; a second personality that was a passionless observer of the frightened creature he had become.

Over and over, his mind forced his memory to replay the Warsaw experiments. In the terrified faces of the laboratory animals, eyes and ears searching an environment they did not understand, he saw a mirror of himself. It was then that the numbing wind became a comfort. He let the icy air flow through his mind and it froze his remembrance of what had followed into suspended animation. But the price of an anaesthetised memory was a cold that ate into the soul. His core body temperature was falling rapidly and he knew that he could not go much further.

* * *

Five blocks away, Murphy was waiting and he was furious. His broad build, heavy features and red hair made his anger seem all the more formidable. A fool's errand on this night of all nights, he thought. The call from London, two hours earlier, had dragged him away from his son Tad's graduation party; a heart-warming expression of solidarity in what was often a dysfunctional family.

Murphy bitterly resented the intrusion. There were guests from all over the country: San Diego, Fort Worth and Chicago, even cousin Largo from Virginia. His announcement that he had to leave had left them stunned. None of them understood and some were openly hostile. His wife Mary went into one of her silent stoic moods. It was her way of trying to cope. She wanted to understand, but a world of urgent secrecy and occasional danger was so far from her own experience of life, that she remained a permanent outsider. They barely spoke as he left the crowded room. In the hallway, Murphy managed a few words with Tad, short sighted, tall and narrow faced, he looked entirely unlike his father. Their physical difference also seemed to describe the emotional distance between them. Even as he spoke, Murphy knew what he said sounded like a platitude, but could think of no better way of putting it.

"Son, you know there's no place in the world I'd rather be than here tonight."

Without aggression, Tad asked the obvious question.

"Then why are you leaving?"

After their many screaming rows of recent years, Tad's gentleness was unsettling and it provoked Murphy to have an unusual moment of frankness. "If I really knew the answer to that, I'd have explained it to your mother twenty-five years ago." Now was not the moment for a deep discussion. A Grade Nine call was only one level below a warning of imminent armed attack. He took the car keys from his pocket and moved towards the door.

"I just have to go, that's all. If I was any good at self-justification, I'd have been a politician."

Tad made no reply until Murphy was halfway to the door. Then the dam burst. "I did it for you." The point did not get home. "The study, the degree and all, I did it for you." The rebuke hit Murphy like a freight train.

It was the first time he realised how little he understood. Forty years of rigid self-control began to implode and he swallowed hard against the threat of tears.

"Son, we have to talk and I have to go."

Mary, tall and slender like her son, came into the hallway. Silently she put her arm around Tad's shoulder and guided him back into the crowded room, where he merged into a morass of bright chatter about his future. Largo appeared at Mary's elbow and asked to use the secure phone in the spare room.

* * *

Five miles away, on the other side of the river, Kloptik steadied himself against an unlit street lamp. With great effort, he resisted collapsing under the folly of it all. Why was he on his way to meet a man he did not know, on a derelict street corner, in the hope that it would lead him to the only person in the world he believed he could trust? With one final effort, he pushed himself into the wind and lurched on.

* * *

Belfast, Berlin, Baghdad, Prague, Potsdam, Riyadh, Hong Kong. Across the world, for a working lifetime, Murphy had waited for frightened fugitives in shadowy places. On this bitter night, he had been in street-craft mode for more than an hour. He stood in a children's playground, on a vacant lot between two empty apartment buildings. The meeting point was at an intersection, which formed a jagged frontier between the district that was still inhabited and the wasteland that stretched away to the docks. In daylight, the bright playtime colours of the school yard were the highlight of the block; the flagship of RAD – Residents Against Dereliction – as the action group called itself. In the dark space beyond the children's swings, Murphy was sufficiently out of the way to avoid casual observation, but had the necessary line of sight to identify the contact. It was something he had done so often that he'd taken up the position almost without thinking. He stood motionless; his only concession to the cold was to move his toes in an attempt to prevent what felt like frostbite. Time, like the air, seemed frozen.

Across the river stood the crystal-sharp lights of Manhattan and he felt a distant sense of outrage at how quickly the skyline without the twin towers had again become familiar. But it was impossible to stay angry in this much cold. Bitterness at having to leave home at so important a moment slowly deflated into sullen boredom. He heard a car several blocks away. It was a battered Cadillac and as it cruised slowly by, he saw that it contained four heavily-built black men.

Murphy heard the muffled thump of Heavy Metal from inside the car. He stiffened; they seemed to be looking for somebody. He knew Mantoni, in the first-line backup vehicle, would have seen them and he was concerned that he might overreact. The Cadillac stopped; the occupants seemed to be having an argument. Then, with squealing tyres, it suddenly shot away. Murphy watched the tail lights fade and eventually disappear as the car sped down the hill towards the river.

A false alarm; the moment of tension passed, boredom returned and he began to get toothache.

Murphy was not a deep thinker, more of a cheerful cynic; he was everybody's idea of New York–Irish. From a distance, people often said that he looked and moved like Gene Hackman. Minutes before the call came he was having a loud, good-natured political argument with Largo. "When politicians make public declarations of high ideals they always involve private dealings on some dark street corner. Believe me, I've been there." But there was something more than usually curious about this particular street corner.

Who in their right mind would choose this piece of urban desolation, with the unnecessary complication of muggers or even a snatch squad from the Drug Enforcement Agency? Either it was the work of a complete amateur, or someone was playing a very deep game indeed. He was not to know that he was right on both counts.

Kloptik could no longer feel either his feet or his hands. Two blocks, just two blocks to go. Murphy stood stony-still in half-concealment. The cold was getting dangerous rather than just painful. The hastily snatched Donegal tweed overcoat was a grave underestimate of the temperature. It felt like 20 below and he knew that he would soon have to move. Then he saw him; a small figure with a jerky stride; even in the poor light it had to be him. As Kloptik slowly came closer, the anxious face, the grey hair and the gaunt eyes were unmistakable. Murphy stepped out of the shadows.

"Welcome to the United States of America," he said.

The old man was startled and then he felt a surge of relief. He took a step closer and delivered the code word with dignity.

"Kloptik."

"Great, let's call a cab."

Murphy pressed the bleeper in his deep overcoat pocket and the dusty brown Chevy with the hot engine rumbled around the corner of the block. Kloptik was stiff with cold. Like a corpse, Murphy thought as he eased him into the back of the car. He spoke to the driver.

"Tell them they can split, five-minute intervals. Mantoni knows what to do, he'll tail us, but nobody else through the tunnel, that's ours."

It was two thirty a.m. as the three other nondescript vehicles made their devious ways home. Half a block behind, the shadow car kept pace with them. Murphy felt the pain of frozen limbs coming back to life. He could only guess what the old man was feeling.

But Kloptik said nothing and Murphy didn't break the silence. It was not until they were approaching the tunnel that Kloptik spoke.

"You must appreciate, I am most unsuited to this work. You will listen, I will explain. The old weapons, nuclear, germs, chemicals … all they can do is kill…"

Murphy interrupted sharply. "I don't collect information, buddy. Just people."

"But at least I must introduce myself. I am Professor Josef Wolski…"

Murphy cut him short. "I'm only the doorman. It's my job to take you to the management."

Kloptik lapsed into frustrated silence as the car sped through the almost empty tunnel beneath the river; a giant catacomb of dirty white tiles. The car's headlights, bouncing off the fractured reflective surface, strobed across Kloptik's anxious face. Murphy thought of fairground ghost-trains at Coney Island when he was a kid and tried to lighten the mood.

"Looks like the longest public John in the universe,"

Kloptik said nothing, but he knew he had reached the end of the beginning.

2

Kloptik

The cold wouldn't go away. Kloptik closed his eyes and waited for the welcome pain of returning circulation, but felt nothing. Not knowing what was ahead, he tried to make sense of what lay behind. At university and in academic life, he had excelled. In a kinder age, or if he had been more politically orthodox, he might have been recognised as one of Poland's most notable contributors to science. He had even become well known in academic circles in the West, and late in the Cold War, during one of the recurring periods of 'détente' with America, he had appeared on the cover of Newsweek. The magazine said he was: 'In the tradition of Marie Curie, who discovered a new element and named it Polonium – for her native land'. The parallel was disturbing. Discovery and death were woven together from the very beginning of her work. While the world marvelled at X-ray images of bone beneath flesh, nobody understood that the power that produced them was lethal.

Concerning himself, he understood the truth. He had grown used to veneration by his academic peers and, from time to time, the ominous word 'genius' had appeared in print.

But he knew better. What they saw as an outstanding talent, he knew to be merely uneven development, like that of a physical giant with a mental handicap. Though he possessed a remarkable intellect, he often experienced the emotions of a timid child. To each of his small circle of friends he was a different person.

Some knew him as a colleague with a reputation they could never hope to equal, others perceived him as shy and lonely and found his vulnerability reassuring. None of them saw the whole man. As for the scientific and political establishments, he allowed them to think of him as an austere academic, a public image that produced an aura of moral and scientific authority. Since everyone seemed to take these characteristics at face value, in rare moments of relaxation he jokingly referred to maintaining this persona as his 'Newsweek strategy'. The scientist in him thought how predictable it was that under stress, his mind should retreat over seven decades in search of some perfect moment when he had been completely happy. It was always a fruitless endeavour. Childhood held few warm memories. Aunt Lisa had dutifully tried to be father and mother to him. But duty was no substitute for love. He filled the void with reading. Books were the garden where he played childish games, the gymnasium for the growing mind and later a defensive perimeter against a world full of ever-threatening emotions.

The car emerged from the tunnel into the sparkling Manhattan night. Nothing had prepared him for this.

3

Murphy

For an apparently uncomplicated man, Murphy had a very tangled history. Most people who knew him thought of him as a bluff New York Dubliner and most people were wrong.

Murphy's father, 'The Old Man' as the family called him, had been a mail-plane pilot in his youth. Flying was a passion that overrode every other part of his life. When war broke out in Europe, he borrowed money from an uncle and took a ship from Boston to Liverpool. For six weeks in 1940 he had tried to join the Royal Air Force. It was a lonely experience. As an American citizen, he was breaking US law by trying to join the armed forces of a foreign country

Back home, the America First Movement drew hundreds of thousands to rallies in support of keeping the country out of the war. Their star turn was Charles Lindbergh, the All-American Boy who made the first solo flight across the Atlantic and who later became infatuated with the Nazis and their formidable new air force. Such was the mood of the time, that when President Roosevelt promised America that, 'Our boys will not fight in foreign wars,' he was a hero to all but a few.

Nor were the British any more welcoming. The political complication of having neutral nationals fighting on the front line was something that nobody in the British establishment seemed willing to contemplate. "Dead Americans in British uniforms would be a positive embarrassment, old boy," was how one civil servant had put it.

It was a time that became known as The Phoney War. There was little fighting. The Germans called it Sitzkreig, the Sitting War. But suddenly, Sitzkreig became Blitzkrieg – Lightning War. German Panzers and aircraft overran the allies with a speed that no one believed possible. A large part of the defeated British army escaped; 360,000 men were ferried back from the beaches of Dunkirk.

As the fortunes of war changed, so did those of Old Man Murphy. France surrendered and Hitler, now master of Europe, began to plan the invasion of Britain. Pilots were desperately needed. Escaped Polish airmen were taught to fly Spitfires and Hurricanes in a matter of days. And, to the Old Man's delight, the Eagle Squadron was formed, for Americans wanting to fly with the RAF. Britain was running perilously short of everything needed to fight a prolonged war. Winston Churchill was now Prime Minister and one of his highest priorities was to mobilise American support that was vital to national survival. It was no easy task. Joseph Kennedy, father of the future President, was US Ambassador in London. He expected a swift Nazi victory, told Washington so and was widely believed.

It was in those desperate days that Old Man Murphy became famous. Though his first name was Sean, inevitably he became known as 'Paddy' Murphy. He fought not so much out of idealistic fervour but a sense of adventure and a passion to fly Spitfires, the best fighter aircraft in the world.

He revelled in the notoriety, flying by day and at night being feted by the rich, the powerful and the fashionable.

At a party in Belgravia, he met Caroline, the shy, slightly clumsy daughter of a wealthy family. The bombing of London had begun. It was the first time that a city had ever lived with a nightly ritual of destruction. No one knew who would be dead by morning. Such uncertainty drove them together and they were married within a month. A 'Whirlwind Romance', the gossip column of Vogue called it. Caroline kept the cutting of the official announcement in a tattered scrapbook:

> The Times. London, 28th November 1940
>
> Married. Miss Caroline Kilrea, daughter of The Honourable Arthur Kilrea and the late Lady Kilrea, to Flt Lieutenant Sean 'Paddy' Murphy, son of Mr and Mrs Gerald Murphy of New York, at St George's Church, Hanover Square, London.

Caroline worked in a dismal office at the Ministry of Information, in the soot-laden streets behind Waterloo Station, dealing with the ever-increasing number of foreign journalists reporting the war from London.

* * *

For almost a year, while the air war raged over southern England, the couple met only fleetingly; a day here and there, and sometimes the luxury of a whole weekend. They planned for a future when they would get to know each other. Both talked of long holidays in the sun. He recalled the Big Sur coast of California, and she the French Riviera. And so it almost was.

When the Nazis surrendered, Caroline believed that for both of them the war was ended. But Murphy volunteered for the continuing conflict against Japan. For Caroline, it was a terrible blow. Yet it was not in her nature to complain and once more she quietly endured the pain of parting and the anxiety of waiting.

Then suddenly, there were the atomic bombs. The Japanese surrendered and it was all over. Murphy was back in London six weeks later. On an impulse, he resigned his commission and the couple took over the top floor of the Jacobean manor house in the Cotswold Hills of Oxfordshire that was the Kilrea family home. For eight glorious weeks they had the honeymoon that had been delayed by half a decade of war. Then came peacetime reality. For three years Murphy unsuccessfully tried his hand at all manner of jobs. Restlessness and despair pressed in on him. A future without flying seemed unthinkable. But opportunities for ex-aircrew were few. During a visit to the nearby airfield at Benson, he heard of the sudden need for pilots to fly in the Berlin Airlift.

West Berlin was an island of the Western allies almost two hundred miles inside the Soviet Zone of Occupation. The Russians had blockaded the city with the aim of starving it into the Communist sphere of influence. In response, the Americans and British organised a massive airlift to supply the city with the essentials of life. Nothing like it had ever been attempted before. Round the clock there were continuous flights carrying everything from coal to chocolate. Murphy was back in his element. Aircraft landed nose to tail at Tempelhof, the crowded city airport, which was one of the most fog-bound in Europe.

Caroline found she was pregnant. Then three weeks later, on 28th October 1949, a glorious late-autumn morning, the telegram came:

'I regret to inform you.. aircraft.. collision.. fog…'

It was a strange grief. At first she could not contain her sense of outrage. It seemed so brutally unjust that someone who had survived so many years of aerial combat should die in such a mundane, inglorious way.

As time passed, she struggled to hold the whole man in her memory, but found she possessed only part of him. There were so many gaps; so much she did not know. Young Murphy was born the following July. In the warmth of high summer, the hurt very slowly began to fade. As the boy grew, his mother began to rediscover her husband. The infectious laugh, the quick temper, the generous spirit; all stirred memories that were painful yet which built an understanding of the person she had loved but never fully known.

Young Murphy's upbringing was the cause of an unlikely friendship. Caroline's father, the Honourable Arthur Kilrea, was from a family who traced their ancestry back to the Protestant ruling class in Ireland during the reign of Elizabeth I in the 16th century. The Scotch–Irish as the Americans called them.

The Murphy family had altogether different roots. During the Great Hunger, the potato famine of the 1840s, when Ireland lost more than half its population to starvation and emigration, their forebears had escaped to America on board a stinking disease-ridden ship. Many died, but the Murphy's survived. Amid the wheeling and dealing of Tammany Hall politics, their keen business sense built them a modest fortune and immodest political ambitions. Though he never sought office for himself, Gerald very effectively wielded power through others.

'America's answer to Warwick the Kingmaker', The Washington Post once called him.

Gerald arrived to see his grandson just two weeks after he was born and his friendship with Arthur began almost at once. 'The Grandfather's Club' they called themselves.

After Gerald returned to New York, the two men corresponded at length about young Murphy's future, and especially about his education. Gerald returned every summer and, with Arthur and the boy, walked for hours over the Cotswold Hills and the Wiltshire

Downs. It was a landscape with a story to tell, and in the evenings the child would repeat to his mother vivid tales of Bronze Age hill forts and mediaeval knights, and how, above the village of Uffington, they had stood at the very place where St George slew the dragon.

The boy did not understand much of the men's conversation, but he sensed they both had a deep affection for Ireland. They spoke of 'The Old Country' much as he had heard countrymen talk about a well-loved hound, a creature with great charm, delinquent habits and an uncertain temper. Only years later did Murphy see how unusual this friendship between a member of the landed gentry and a third-generation Irish Republican was. It flowered in the eye of a storm, the lull between two eras of violence. A generation earlier, or later, the talk would have been about bombs and terrorism, not music, horses and whisky.

Caroline loved these summer interludes. She watched with pleasure as the boy grew into a teenager. 'Young Murphy', everyone called him. Even close friends used just the one name. It fitted him so accurately that a first name seemed unnecessary. Arthur used his well-polished network of personal relationships to set young Murphy on the privileged path of an English aristocratic education: the Dragon School at Oxford, then on to Winchester. By the end of the 1960s Murphy arrived at Oxford to read Economics. 'The Swinging Sixties' were over and protest was receding from its high water marks in Grosvenor Square and on campus at Berkeley. Disdain and lassitude were high fashion and there was the stale taste of aimlessness in the air. As Dean Acheson, the Mandarin of American foreign policy, put it: 'Britain had lost an Empire and not yet found a role.'

For a birthday gift, Gerald paid for a course of lessons at the flying school at Kidlington, an airfield on the edge of the city.

While his fellows marched occasionally and drank continuously, Murphy found his escape in flying. Though the Chipmunk trainer was no Spitfire, it touched his emotions like nothing else. Navigating between the towering nimbus clouds that populated the uncertain spring climate of southern England, he discovered an understanding of his father that he could never put into words. Between grandfather and grandson the bond grew stronger. Murphy's long and thoughtful letters to Gerald never made direct mention of his father, but they both knew that this was what they were about. When Gerald invited Murphy to New York for the summer, he leapt at the chance.

Manhattan had a strange effect on him. Though he had never been there before, it was like coming home. The accents, the street talk, the body language, all were oddly familiar. As he wandered the high-ceilinged, tall-windowed rooms of the family Brownstone in Greenwich Village, it seemed strange that he could not recall what had taken place in each of them. The absence of memory in a place that felt so familiar was oddly disturbing.

He spent days walking the streets: Midtown, the Lower East Side, Little Italy and the Financial District. He would sit for hours over a succession of cups of coffee in the 7th Avenue Deli, observing New Yorkers of every kind. Occasionally he had the curious notion that he might catch a glimpse of himself as a stranger on some busy sidewalk, or come face to face with himself on a park bench or in a crowded subway train. He never knew whether it was this strange game that he had invented, or some deeper impulse, that made him decide to acquire a New York identity. Whatever the motivation, he quickly discovered that language was a surprisingly effective disguise. Soon he was testing himself by replaying accents and mannerisms; trying the patience of an assistant in Brentano's by searching out an obscure book, swapping stories with students in a bar near NYU, or cheering amid a sea of Yankee fans.

Very quickly he had assembled a Manhattan personality that those he encountered took for real. By the time he embarked on the Queen

Elizabeth for his final term at Oxford, the game had become a secret obsession. Gerald had noticed none of it, and the New York episode wilted in the hothouse of undergraduate life, and might have been forgotten completely, but for a chance meeting with a friend of Arthur's during a weekend visit to the manor house.

4

Thornhill

In the rose garden, the elderly Arthur Kilrea sat under a huge apple tree, like a tribal chieftain holding court. Jack Thornhill arrived as the housekeeper was serving tea and delicate salmon sandwiches. "Excellent sense of timing, you young villain," Arthur said to him as the tea was poured. "The tea is Darjeeling, but the salmon's canned I'm afraid. Come and meet my grandson, young Murphy; he's a student of Oxford and the streets of Manhattan."

"An interesting combination," Thornhill replied.

"Thornhill was two years ahead of you at Oxford," Arthur said by way of introduction. "Then he went on to Cambridge; languages wasn't it?"

"Just one language actually," Thornhill replied.

"Which one?" Murphy asked clumsily.

"Russian. He works in Whitehall now," Arthur said as if to take charge of the conversation. "He's a rising star. A keen mind and good Russian will take a man far in his profession." Arthur's brisk manner constrained Murphy from asking what profession that might be.

Thornhill was dressed for the weekend in well-worn corduroy trousers and a wool shirt in need of darning. Yet despite his casual appearance, or perhaps because of it, Murphy sensed an inner edge, a tension that prevented relaxation. They shook hands and exchanged the ritual "How do you do?" of the English middle class. 'Prickly', Thornhill's fellow students called him. Though his sharp temper made the nickname inevitable, few were bold enough to use it in his hearing. Thornhill wandered away in a haze of small talk with other guests. It was a blissful day, warm and heavy with the scents of summer. Murphy laid full length on the grass. The sun shone through the fine Wedgwood china as the housekeeper set a plate of thinly cut crustless sandwiches and a cup of fragrant tea on the grass beside him.

"America?" Thornhill asked as he sat down next to Murphy.

"Perhaps our paths have crossed. I spent some time at Harvard after I came down from Cambridge and I was in New York from time to time."

Murphy sat up; there was something about Thornhill that commanded respect and he had to make a conscious effort to avoid calling him 'Sir'. For the first time, he found himself talking about his American game. Thornhill listened quietly, his silence drawing Murphy on.

His interest was more than polite curiosity. He had come upon an ability which his professional training told him was rare. Murphy was flattered by Thornhill's interest and the afternoon passed quickly as he revelled in the game; recreating characters from the Brooklyn Navy Yard to the New York Athletic Club. As Thornhill left, he suggested that they stay in touch. Murphy took the suggestion to be no more than a formal courtesy.

As Thornhill crossed the garden and drove away in a well-polished MG TD. Arthur, who had listened a lot and spoken little, stood beside Murphy.

"Like St George," he said. Murphy was puzzled. "Jack Thornhill," Arthur repeated, "he's like St George. A slayer of dragons."

On the eve of Murphy's graduation, Thornhill was true to his word. A postcard in a flowing copperplate hand arrived at his rooms. It proposed that they meet for lunch at the Randolph Hotel in Oxford. Murphy's career with The Service had begun.

5

Westminster

Westminster chimes. It amused Thornhill to keep the clock on the window sill in exact synchrony with Big Ben across the Thames. It was one of several exacting eccentricities; small defences against a violently unpredictable world. Decades in a high-stress profession had turned his wavy hair grey and kept him thin. For a man devoid of vanity, he took an uncharacteristic pride in his ability to get into the bespoke tailored suit in which he was married more than thirty years previously. People who said he looked like an Edwardian cabinet minister would have been reinforced in their view had they seen him stood with his hand resting on the clock feeling the minutes tick away. It was eight a.m., three a.m. in New York, and still there was no news. Another half-hour and he would be sure that something had gone wrong. From the outset, he had decided not to use the satellite link. It would have provided continuous communication but this operation was too sensitive for that. Doing a snatch from under the nose of an enemy was one thing, from an ally entirely another. The call was to come from a pay phone, during the switch of vehicles in an underground parking garage in Battery Park City at the tip of Manhattan.

Still standing sentry beside the mantelpiece, he watched the grey winter sky lighten over the Houses of Parliament. At eight twenty-six the phone rang. It was Murphy.

"Kloptik," he said.

"You have the wrong number," Thornhill replied testily and put the phone down. The relief was immense. For the first time since the operation began, Thornhill allowed himself to think of something else. His eye travelled across Westminster Bridge to the riverside skyline and the great dome of St Paul's. He could not count how many times in the last decade, by this same window, he had weighed heavy problems in his mind. Like the comforting presence of an old friend, the cityscape seemed to help.

"Earth hath not anything to show more fair...", Wordsworth had written of the view from the bridge a century and a half before. In a rare act of self-indulgence, Thornhill allowed his thoughts to wander for a few minutes longer. Of the same perspective, Shelley had written, "Hell is a city, much like London," and there, thought Thornhill, was the heart of the problem. Who to believe? What picture do you construct from the evidence before you? Sounding an alarm would be severely unwelcome. All political, military and strategic eyes were on terrorism based in the Islamic world. Nobody wanted distractions. Moreover, as the spectre of retirement drew nearer, his own influence was waning. Already he had wangled one extension, but was far from confident of securing another.

A month ago, a formal letter from Buckingham Palace had arrived, offering a Knighthood; another step in the ritual dance that he dreaded, For Thornhill, the prospect of retirement was like a terminal illness.

It could have only one outcome. He took a grip on himself and snapped out of his lapse into the gloom. Like other luxuries, pessimism was strictly rationed. He crossed the room and sat at his neatly ordered desk. It gave him a sense of being in control.

* * *

With great care he began to measure what was soon to become the most important decision of his professional life. From the perspective of a working lifetime, it seemed no more than yesterday that everyone had been euphoric at the end of the Cold War and the collapse of the tyrannies that went with it. In the semi-darkened satellite viewing room, Thornhill had watched the death of a political system; poisoned by the malignity it had itself devised. Tanks in the streets of capital after capital across Eastern Europe proved no match for people fired with a longing to be free. But for Thornhill, it had been a period of supreme unease. 'Fear of redundancy', friends had joked, and to a few he admitted that they might be right. But privately his reading of the events was at a radical variance from conventional political wisdom. 'A triumph for democracy', the politicians had called it. But he believed he saw something else. Often in the small hours of the morning, frame by frame, he studied the anger and the raw courage of the crowds and towards the end, he saw the light of victory in their eyes. Within a year, Communism was declared dead and the nations of the Soviet Empire rushed to bury the corpse. While CNN hailed: "The march of freedom", for Thornhill, the most important thing was what the viewer did not see and which no political commentator pointed out.

The victorious crowds in the streets were not a conquering army, but a people marching into a vacuum. Not long afterwards, he was invited to deliver the Churchill Memorial Lecture whose purpose was to look into alternative political and social futures for the Western world in the 21st century.

* * *

"Peace without purpose is all too often a void into which new conflicts are drawn," was how he had tried to sum up his misgivings. "Political structures may come and go, but the human condition remains unchanged..." Speech making did not come easily and he had laboured long to make his thoughts sound less reactionary. Now as he spoke, he quickly realised how far out of tune he was with an audience high on political euphoria.

"In Russia, the revolution before this one started with the overthrow of a thousand years of authoritarianism alleviated only by periods of tyranny. The reformers lasted a matter of months, then the Bolsheviks took over and one age of oppression seamlessly followed another. Significantly, all that happened to the secret police was that the name was changed – several times. The new state was more efficient than the old one. It industrialised the means of controlling the population."

Of course, they had heard it all before and could see no reason for it to be said again now. Thornhill was glad that the end was in sight.

"Whatever comes next will be the child of our times; times in which the predominant force is not political or national ambition, as it was with the Bolsheviks or the Nazis, but economic power in a moral vacuum." Thornhill could read the audience's faces. None were engaged with his thesis.

"In the West, democracy has become the servant of economics. In the Islamic world, to our great puzzlement, we have seen a violent tide of rejection of these principles." The argument needed passion and he knew he did not do passion well. He ended: "In the face of this changing world, our economic superiority is both fragile and insufficient. At best, it can only solve economic problems. The dangers that we face now, most especially in Eastern Europe and the Middle East, lie not at the frontiers of nation-states but deep in the nature of humankind."

They had listened politely and applauded briefly. In retrospect, Thornhill realised that the response was inevitable. Though his definition of the problem was sharply resolved, he could supply no better answers than anyone else. He was not used to feeling inadequate, and remembered the experience with discomfort.

Not long afterwards, Kloptik's first message came; newspapers and television news were full of speculation about a world summit, possibly in Geneva. 'A World Without War' was the slogan. In the face of global terrorism, it felt as if the world's major powers were 'getting the wagons in a circle' as Thornhill put it. There was much speculation about a Treaty of Friendship: something new in the history of the world, bringing together the nations of Western Europe and North America with the new Russia, and the other states that had emerged from the former USSR. 'From the Rockies to the Urals', the Daily Telegraph said.

"How wise to leave out California," Thornhill remarked to a friend as he left the office at midday.

6

Bach

"The van from Moss Bros is here," Jane was cautious about intruding into Thornhill's private space. The fact that he was at home, rather than at the office during the working day, was always a sign that he was grappling with some issue of special complexity. He sat at his desk, wearing an expensive hand-tailored shirt and a scruffy cardigan badly in need of darning. There was no computer, the workspace was empty, except for two sheets of notepaper crammed with disciplined handwriting. Thornhill turned towards the door. "So the time has come, he said with deliberate overstatement."

"Yes I'm afraid it has. I'll get them to put it all in the living room."

"I need a few minutes more and then I'll be out."

The hired formal long-tailed morning suit, with Dove Grey waistcoat and matching top hat, lay draped across the sofa. The whole notion of dressing up for anything, even a trip to the palace, was alien to Thornhill. "It's OK for you, you can wear the dress you got for Susannah's wedding. I have to wear the penguin suit.

With that, and all of the pomp and circumstance that goes with it, It's very difficult to keep a straight face."

"Well it's you that's getting the knighthood, so you have to wear the shining armour" Jane said with mock seriousness.

"You don't get away with it that easily madam. This is your last night of freedom, from tomorrow, you'll be Lady Jane."

"Only because you're Sir Jack."

"I've a small surprise, Thornhill said, I've booked a table for dinner, we're going to celebrate."

Jane was surprised, they very rarely ate out together. "But we're going to the Savoy Grill tomorrow, after the investiture."

"That's for the family, this is just for us."

"So, where are we going?"

"To Marie's Café"

"Marie's!" Jane was delighted. It was a place they used to go to as students, when an extravagant night out was cheap seats at the Old Vic and Marie's afterwards; a sandwich bar by day, that did Thai home cooking night. They embraced for a long time, but neither of them felt the need to speak. Their shared memories said everything. Then Jane had a sudden thought. "I mustn't let you forget to put these in your pocket in the morning."

"What are they?"

"Pins, the palace briefing says you have to wear them otherwise there's nowhere to hang the decoration."

* * *

Once every two weeks, Thornhill allowed himself a visit to the lunchtime concert in St John's Smith Square, a deconsecrated baroque church used by the BBC as a music-recording studio. It was there that he was confronted with half-forgotten encounters from the past.

His routine began as normal. He bought a salami sandwich and a double espresso from the Italian café in Vauxhall Bridge Road and ate along with an attentive audience of office workers from the Department of Transport and nurses from Westminster Hospital, both less than five minutes away. The music was joyful, the Bach Suite No. 2 in B minor for Flute and Orchestra. As the audience moved slowly through the door and out into the angular winter sunshine, Thornhill remained preoccupied with the memory of the music.

"Kloptik says you will understand." It was a female voice on the steps behind him. The code name, even after so long, had the power to stop him dead. Thornhill was used to controlling impulses. Not wanting to display surprise, he turned slowly. She had the fair hair and blue eyes of someone whose family history lay in the Baltic. He was certain he had never seen her before, either in person or in the endless videos that London Briefing supplied to Section Heads. Almost all the comings and goings of the numerous former Eastern Bloc embassies, trade missions and cultural organisations strung out across London were on tape. But she was a newcomer.

"I am called Anya," she said, as if her name explained everything. Thornhill recovered his composure and smiled as if to a favourite niece.

"How very nice to see you again. Do you have time for a stroll?" He moved off without waiting for an answer.

As they reached the bottom of the steps, he deliberately walked through a bed of leaves fallen from the many plane trees in the square.

They felt soft underfoot and exposed a spectrum of mellow colours as his polished brogues ploughed through them.

"London can be beautiful at this time of year, don't you think?" He wanted to keep up the small talk until they reached the main road a hundred yards away. He sensed her nervousness, but she seemed to understand. They crossed Vauxhall Bridge Road, turned left and walked towards the river. If they were being monitored, the sound of heavy traffic on the Embankment would make the task of the listeners difficult or, with luck, impossible. She spoke first. Her English sounded as if it was not used often. Her accent was Slav, Thornhill thought.

"Things are not what they seem. The great meeting…" she said with urgent uncertainty.

"You mean the summit?" asked Thornhill.

"Yes, in Geneva. It is not reality."

Thornhill played for time. "Of course not, there's no fixed date for it yet."

She continued as if he had not spoken. "The reality is otherwise. It is very destructive.

It is fatal. It is what he told you about a long time ago."

Thornhill said nothing. "He said you would understand," she added with rising anxiety. But Thornhill did not understand, and it was important not to let her realise it." I need to speak to him," he said.

Beside the river, they walked on in silence; Thornhill knew that she was deciding whether she could trust him with the next part of what she had been told to say. It was clear that she was disturbed by his non-recognition of the message.

He judged it prudent to say nothing. The traffic roared by, covering the fallen leaves with a layer of grit and diesel soot. Eventually, she made her decision.

"He is travelling to see you."

"When?"

"Soon. Give me an address. I must reach you personally. The office is not good."

Thornhill gave her the address of the safe house in Lambeth.

"I'll have him met at the airport," he said cheerfully.

"No." Her reply was firm. "Air travel is too easy to trace."

Nobody in Europe had talked like that for a long time. Was it paranoia? They turned away from the river and drew closer to Pimlico underground station. She turned to go inside. At the top of the escalator she spoke again.

"Tell him: 'I will bring reality with me.' He told me to say that."

Keen not to betray his lack of comprehension, Thornhill hesitated.

"How can I reach you?" She did not reply, and in a moment was gone.

Should he have tried to stop her? Could he have discovered more? He examined his decisions carefully. The answer to both questions had to be no. He was sure that she did not yet have the information that she had spoken of. Holding on to her would only separate her from the source. He strode quickly back to his office. As he entered the building, he passed by Sergeant Willis without his usual greeting. But his haze of preoccupation was penetrated as he passed the transport office at the end of the corridor. One of the drivers was talking.

"Old Prickly has taken to chatting up the birds. I saw him with this blond at lunchtime, a right looker she was…"

So they were being watched. Thornhill smiled as he walked on. When he got to his office, he cleared the desk of everything: the computer terminal, files, letters and trays of documents. He took a pad of plain unlined paper and with his battered Waterman began, piece by piece, to re-construct what happened when he first met Kloptik. The one thing that had kept the encounter alive in his memory was that, even now, he did not know if what had happened was accidental or planned. If it was not coincidence, the degree of insight into his character had been astonishing. The event had to be the result of pure chance or great precision, one or the other; the facts did not fit anything in between.

He had come upon Kloptik during one of his regular visits to Hamburg, on this occasion to resolve a squalid dispute between field personnel that had led inevitably to the red light district of St Pauli.

"Another triumph of the late-lamented German economic miracle, Europe's most efficient hypermarket for the sale of human flesh." He was trying to get a smile out of Koenig, the humourless signals officer, as he left the office for a day of meetings.

Coming up for air, in the late afternoon, he had more than an hour and a half to spare before his next appointment. It had been raining heavily, but now the air was clear and he decided to walk towards the Alster lakes in the centre of the city. It was a walk he always enjoyed. 'For anyone with prejudices about the German national character, Hamburg is a great day out,' someone had said at an Embassy party the previous evening. He was reminded of the observation as he watched a procession of overweight and overdressed elderly couples perform their afternoon ritual: a promenade past the windows of banks, each with a display of video screens showing the rise and fall of shares and commodities on the world's major markets. Nothing that happened in Tokyo or New York was without interest, so long as it had an effect on share values. One large couple, complete with a small dog on a long lead, looked so much like the creation of a cartoonist that Thornhill's natural courtesy was overcome and he laughed out loud. They did not notice. Like lovers, their concentration was total, not on each other, but on prices.

Thornhill came alongside the St Michaelis Kirche, whose spire is to Hamburg what St Patrick's twin spires are to Manhattan, or Westminster Abbey is to London. A large billboard offered an organ recital. Thornhill knew it was an instrument with an international reputation. He hesitated, weighing up how he should invest the next hour; reflectively by the lake, or listening to Bach? The opening notes of a fugue drew him inside. The elaborate, pews were carved from solid oak. By habit, he chose the first row from the entrance that already had an occupant. He wanted to be close enough to the door to leave without being noticed, yet be less conspicuous than he would be by sitting entirely alone.

Thornhill believed that it was such matters of detail that separated the excellent from those who were merely good at the job. Slowly he turned to look at his neighbour, a small grey-haired man in a creased raincoat, damp from the recent downpour. The old man sat rigidly upright, with his hands holding a shapeless hat that rested on his knees.

The interior of the church was like nothing Thornhill had seen before. Protestant builders in this northern city, being denied the religious imagery of the Catholic south, had carved what looked like a sea fantasy. The centrepiece was the pulpit, a giant oyster shell borne on the pinnacle of a breaking wave, all in amber marble. Thornhill supposed that the preacher, or perhaps the preaching, was intended to be seen as a pearl. It was only the beauty of the materials and the quality of the craftsmanship that saved the work from looking like Disneyland. He recoiled at the thought of what the result might have been, if fibreglass and plastics had been in the architectural lexicon of the 17th century.

The music was magnificent, all possessing. Thornhill closed his eyes and listened. The preposterous marble seascape now put him in mind of the real thing. The sound swept into the mind, like surf breaking on a rocky shore, seeking out and filling every empty crevice. At the end, he sat for a moment in the echoing silence, eyes still closed. As he rose to his feet, the aisle was blocked with people talking about the performance. He turned to leave the pew in the other direction and saw that the small, dignified man with the grey hair was crying. He sat perfectly still, his dignity strangely enlivened by tears. Thornhill was flushed with English embarrassment at the sight of a grown man weeping. As he went to step past him, the man spoke without turning his head.

"Here is reality..." He looked directly at Thornhill. "The rest is vanity."

With the music still ringing in his ears, Thornhill had some feeling for what he meant. The man fumbled for a handkerchief, wiped his eyes, smiled and continued.

"I am an expert in vanity. Would you care for a consultation?"

Thornhill was intrigued and he still had half an hour to spare. Was the old man an eccentric? A defector perhaps, or just lonely? Thornhill felt conspicuous and sat down.

"That would depend on the fee," Thornhill said. The man looked him directly in the eye and spoke very deliberately.

"I am not a merchant, I am a student."

Thornhill said nothing. Early in his career he had learnt that, sometimes, silence is the most probing form of question.

"I am called Kloptik," the man said, extending his hand, "a student of human frailties."

Thornhill shook the outstretched hand; it was small and bony but had a spring-like resilience. He looked around to see if they were being watched, but the church had emptied. Together, they began a slow circuit of the interior.

The man spoke slowly and with care. "I said I am an expert, and so I am. My home is Poland, so I have had a front-row seat in the theatre of vanity. We Poles have observed many virtuoso performances: Hitler and the Nazis, Stalin, the Red Army and the Workers' Paradise that they brought with them. And now..." His voice trailed away, and then he changed tack. "And you, my silent friend, what of you?"

Thornhill thought fleetingly that only foreigners, usually Americans, used the word 'friend' in that way.

"Me? I'm just an administrator."

"An administrator?" The man turned the word over carefully like a jeweller holding a fake gem up to the light. "I have known many administrators. Yours is a sinister profession." The Pole suddenly laughed and Thornhill half-heartedly joined in.

"Let us see the last of the daylight. The moments before nightfall are always to be savoured, don't you think?" The man said.

Thornhill didn't reply but moved in the direction of the door. The older man followed. In the street he gestured to a café across the busy street.

"A game of chess perhaps? The chess café is close by and they serve excellent coffee."

"No," said Thornhill.

"Don't you play?"

"Yes, but I haven't time."

Some service to perform, something to administer?"

"Yes." Thornhill didn't like being interrogated, even in minor matters.

"This evening perhaps?"

Thornhill thought of the alternative – another Embassy reception and then Wagner.

"Very well, eight thirty?"

"Eight thirty it shall be."

Thornhill shouldered his way through the rush-hour crowds to the office behind the Kunsthalle. He went to the third floor in the ornate brass and wrought-iron elevator. Behind his borrowed desk, he went over the incident carefully from start to finish. If he had not known he was going to end up at the recital, how could anybody else have predicted it? He chose to sit where he did. The Pole was already in place; how could it be a set-up?

He checked the registry and called London on the secure line.

While waiting for replies, he remembered a chance remark made by a wise old soldier:

'Nothing ever happens by accident'. But for that to be true there was someone out there who knew Thornhill better than he knew himself. Someone who knew he would choose the recital, rather than a walk by the lake; someone who even knew where he would sit. It was unnerving.

His thoughts were interrupted by the sound of the network printer in the next office. Koenig, the Duty Signals Officer, came in with the brief message: no trace. Koenig was a short, well-groomed man with a reputation for being none too bright.

"Anything I can help with, sir?" he asked over-eagerly.

"Do you believe in accidents, Koenig?"

"Depends on who they happen to, sir." Not so dim after all?

* * *

Eight-thirty found Thornhill at the chess café. The Pole was already seated at a small corner table.

"You came!" he exclaimed with mock surprise.

"Yes," Thornhill said curtly as he sat down. 'Always say less than your opponent,' was advice he frequently gave to others. Now he remembered it himself.

The waiter came and the Pole ordered a beer for them both.

"Do you play well?"

"No," he replied truthfully.

The game began. "You enjoy Bach?" The man across the table continued without waiting for an answer. "In Warsaw we have a Bach circle – academics and scientists."

Thornhill wondered which his opponent was, an academic or a scientist. The Pole continued. "In my experience, if you share a love of Bach with someone, you share a regard of many other things; certainly that is how it began for us in Warsaw."

"Who in Warsaw?" Thornhill interrupted.

"For us, The Night Watch."

The conversation seemed to be moving towards fantasy and Thornhill could think of nothing to say that would not sound incredulous. The Pole seemed offended and studied the board. Then he moved a knight to threaten a bishop that Thornhill had left exposed.

"You have been to Amsterdam," the man said without looking up, "and you have visited the Rijksmuseum." It was more of an accusation than a question.

"Some years ago," Thornhill admitted cautiously.

"That's not important," Kloptik said impatiently. "The Night Watch by Rembrandt; what you have seen you have not forgotten."

It was an accurate prediction. Thornhill remembered the picture well. It showed a group of wealthy merchants self-consciously setting out to do ceremonial civic duty. They were all elaborately dressed and stared at the artist, much as the subjects of Victorian photographs stared at the camera.

"That's how it began, our own Night Watch. I was young then, but many of the others were older and they knew they would not see the dawn." As Kloptik developed the analogy, Thornhill was beginning to understand. "How naive we were when we began. We had not the slightest understanding that the Burghers of Amsterdam had a vastly easier task than ours. You see, securing the City Gate is one thing, defending the Mindgate is entirely another." The analogy was baffling, but Thornhill did not interrupt.

The Pole continued. "There were fifteen of us at the start, all of us people of prominence or promise in our chosen professions." His prim manner was devoid of arrogance.

"Those were days of despair. In America they had McCarthy, witch-hunts and Rock and Roll. You had the Coronation and delusions of Empire. We had Stalin in the Kremlin and tanks in the streets."

* * *

Thornhill stood up and paced across the office. Though the conversation had taken place long ago, it was sufficiently unusual for him to remember it in forensic detail. It was the mood and feel of the time that his opponent at chess described which was much more difficult to recapture. The defunct Soviet Empire was fast becoming as remote from the realities of daily life as the empires of Britain or Spain. The grey days and dark nights of Eastern Europe were all but forgotten. Now, everything had changed. But back then, such hopes were only for the most private of dreams. Thornhill circled the room as his memory continued to play back Kloptik's story.

"None of us were heroes, we did not protest. Who would have listened? You must understand that at a time like that, a time from which there is no escape, both the oppressed and the oppressors live in an equilibrium of fear. Those without power fear those with it. And those with power fear losing it. The child of such fears is silence; a silence which only the prospect of liberty, or final desperation, can break. We watched and we remembered, it was our substitute for hope." The chess game was forgotten; they had made no more than a dozen moves.

"As time passed, our numbers gradually grew. We had no organisation and sought no recruits. We grew organically. As we encountered like-minded people, they were drawn into the circle. When the Soviets went home, we all thought it was over. But then everything was for sale and a new Imperialism arrived. He who has the most dollars wins."

Thornhill recalled that it was at this point that he began to wonder if had a big fish on a thin line. Kloptik kept talking

"Dollars are not the currency of a single nation but a language, the Esperanto of our time, the world's first universal tongue. Many big people have a wide vocabulary in this language; many dangerous things are devised with it. So the Night Watch continues and if we live long enough, we may make history, Mr Administrator Thornhill."

Was this a fantasy or was he being presented with a gold mine? He remembered vividly what the Pole went on to say. "And why do I speak to you like this now?" He answered his own question. "Because we know our value, but we are not for sale; in turn, we know who you are and will not disguise the value you could be to us."

"I need to know what you mean," Thornhill replied.

"We will not spy for you, Mr Thornhill, but there will come a moment when we must speak, a moment when we will be of great importance to you."

"When?" Thornhill remembered trying not to sound impatient.

"I can't tell you. Maybe soon, maybe never. None of us ever sought martyrdom. But even in those dark early days we all secretly realised that hope, despair or danger might one day force action upon us."

What kind of action?" Thornhill needed clarity.

"An alarm, a fire alarm in the night, but the moment never came and we thought our task was done."

"What's changed?" Thornhill asked sharply.

The night may be over, but have you ever wondered where the dark goes when the light comes on?"

"Are you going to tell me what you mean?"

"Not yet, but when that time comes, we will be your ally. Will you be ours?"

"Perhaps. What do you want in return?"

"Credibility. Who will listen to a fire alarm at dawn? It somehow lacks the urgency of midnight, doesn't it? We have to know that we will be believed without delay, because you may need to respond very quickly."

The chess pieces had remained untouched for too long. A waiter came to the table and they ordered more drinks. Thornhill moved his second knight. "How soon?" he insisted.

"Not yet."

"How may we keep in touch?"

"We shall not, that is why I speak to you now. Just remember; 'Kloptik', a childhood nickname of no consequence, but that is the name I shall use when the time comes." He continued briskly. "My question is, are you powerful enough to serve our purpose?" Of course," Kloptik added, "you will understand that this is a question I have to ask, just as surely as I understand you cannot answer it."

Kloptik was wholly unlike any potential recruit Thornhill had met before. Indeed it was unclear who was recruiting whom. Kloptik pushed away the chessboard with its unfinished game and sat upright, as if preparing for a speech.

"Now, Mr Thornhill, your instincts will be, as the Americans say, 'to check us out' with your computers and to make vigorous enquiries in London. This could be dangerous to us. Will you promise not to do it?"

Thornhill had replied without hesitation. "No, I won't give you any such undertaking, and if I did, you wouldn't believe me."

For the first time, Kloptik smiled and laughed out loud. "Excellent! I do believe we understand each other. However, I think you will be disappointed if you imagine you will find out much about us from such sources…"

* * *

Thornhill's desk was beginning to fill up. He reached for the file sent up from the registry; he had wanted to test his memory first. Carefully, he went over the notes he had made at the time. There was nothing more; the imprint on his memory had been remarkably complete.

He thought hard. What unfinished business could there be for The Night Watch, now that the night had passed? Where, indeed, did the dark go when the light came on? As he closed the file another thought struck him. What if it was not unfinished business but new business: a threat of a different kind?

His dilemma was acute. Raising an alarm about a threat to the summit, if it were to have any value, would have to be communicated to all of the governments involved. If false, it would destroy both him and his department. Most alarms were false and he was expected to exercise his judgement.

"Trust," Kloptik had said at the first meeting. "We have to know that we will be believed."

Thornhill sat and stared into space, wishing he had the comforting view of the river to help focus his thoughts; to help him decide between Wordsworth and Shelley. He lifted the phone and spoke to Lloyd-Emlyn in the outer office. "Robert, make an appointment with the Minister, please. You may tell the Permanent Secretary that it is a matter of urgency."

He put the phone down. The die was cast.

7

Bermuda

"ExecAir Fyfer One Seven Niner, cleared to taxi." The La Guardia controller's voice came through the crowded chatter of New York air traffic.

"Worse than Grand Central on Thanksgiving," said Murphy as the elderly HS 125 rolled slowly forward to join the long line of aircraft inching towards the end of the runway for take-off. Nobody responded to his attempt at conversation. From several rows back, Latchford, the Embassy doctor, sized up his fellow passengers. Unless there was an emergency, his job was to do nothing. There were eighteen seats, only five were occupied. He studied the elderly Pole who, gaunt and grey, sat in near catatonic stillness. Latchford thought how like delivering a baby an operation like this was. You could never tell whether the central figure would turn out to be a hero or villain, the cause of triumph or disaster, and only very occasionally did you ever find out.

Anwar Darzi was a high-flier from a humble background. His parents, when they arrived in Manchester from Pakistan, had opened a corner shop. The family of six only had two downstairs rooms. In recognition of his need to study, he was given one of them. His parents, three brothers, numerous friends and the TV were crowded into the remaining room.

It was an investment that paid off in a succession of scholarships that propelled Darzi to a prominent position in psychology at Cambridge.

Across the aisle sat Morag, whose usual working day involved 'research', which was as good a euphemism as any for searching vast quantities of scientific papers, trade journals and industrial statistics. 'Like stoking the boilers of the Titanic' was how she described feeding the voracious appetite of the Cray super-computers deep beneath the flashy new office block on the south bank of the Thames.

Morag was a woman with a sharpness of mind overlaid by a dullness of appearance, which those who knew her well realised was a defence against casual intrusion into her private space. The satellites could tell you what was happening; Morag could tell you why it was happening. As an analyst, she had no experience of work in the field and had been drawn into the operation almost by accident. As ever, the new Russia was causing a lot of travel among those whose business it was to assess risk and predict outcomes. She had been in New York, on a visit to Columbia University, when she was called back to the office in Midtown where she was given a fifteen-minute briefing and sent to 5th Avenue with a roll of dollar bills and instructions to get dressed for the part. Ostentation was foreign territory and it showed. Her impatience with Gucci and expensive perfume made them seem like the disguises that they really were.

You've got to want to turn heads before you can do it, Latchford thought. But, the result was better than anyone might have expected. The unintentional double bluff of a see-through disguise succeeded magnificently. She really did look like a bright young PhD from a wealthy family, who had been persuaded to spend a few days at a seminar in Bermuda with her Austrian professor. And together the group would pass for a team of academics whose travel was paid for by a multinational think-tank; the cover story hastily devised before departure.

Murphy sat next to Kloptik, his rumpled bulk like a giant teddy bear beside a nervous child. He knew it was important to stay close. They were at cruising altitude before Kloptik spoke. To Murphy, his mannered English brought back a flood of memories of Oxford professors and tutors whose language was of another age.

"I would deem it a favour if you would call me Josef."

"Sure," Murphy replied, not offering his Christian name in return. That would be a card to play later in the game.

Kloptik continued. "I am Professor Josef–"

Murphy cut him short; he was about to hear something that he did not need to know. "Josef," he said, using the newfound influence of the name, "why don't you get some sleep? There's a lot of talking to do tomorrow, when your friends from London come visit us."

To pre-empt a response, Murphy got up, tossed one of the skimpy airline pillows into Kloptik's lap and shambled to the rear of the aircraft. He filled a paper cup with indifferent coffee from the urn and took two doughnuts from the big paper bag beside it. He didn't offer anything to anybody else.

Darcy was the team leader. He was in his mid-thirties and looked and dressed like a merchant banker. Savile Row suits, designer shirts and handmade shoes were possible because he had no family to support and useful because they were a most effective set of props. Everyone welcomes a man with money to invest.

Recently, he had begun to wish he were the real thing, rather than working in what everyone could see was a declining industry. Having climbed close to the top of his chosen pyramid, he found it slowly deflating beneath him. 'Three years of Russian and Slavic studies at Cambridge and a Doctorate in dark alleys and deceit in Warsaw and

Moscow aren't the career credentials that they once were,' he often complained. But this 'little caper', as he thought of it, was something different; more like old times.

The hurried departure from La Guardia had gone without a hitch. The cover story was plausible and the oncoming weekend fortuitous. Dozens of private jets left New York every Friday night. Getting into the United States could be a problem, getting out rarely was. His chief disappointment was Morag. Darcy thought of himself as having a way with women and history supported his opinion. But Morag simply seemed not to notice him and he found it unsettling.

He moved across the aisle and sat next to Kloptik. His Polish was good enough for casual conversation.

"Less than two hours to Hamilton, then you can get to bed," he said, thinking that the use of his native language would help the old man relax. Instantly he realised that this was a mistake. He recognised 'The Bulgarian Jam Syndrome', common in Eastern Europe before the fall of Communism. In those days, East Bloc consumer goods were universally appalling, but Bulgarian jam was a shining exception, much sought after by eco-fashion-conscious customers in the supermarkets of Kensington and White Plains. But anywhere east of the Elbe it was rejected as a poor substitute for the highly coloured, additive-laden Western imports at five times the price of the local product. So it was with Darcy's Polish. Those with power spoke nothing but English.

Kloptik looked on Darcy's expensive suit and silk tie as the uniform of a concierge at a fancy hotel and he spoke as if he was rebuking a minor factotum. "This diversion is both unnecessary and unacceptable; this matter is of the greatest importance. Sir Jack should be here." Darcy was surprised that the old man knew about Thornhill's new knighthood. It seemed strange that he was so well informed.

Darcy judged that Kloptik's secret, and his dignity, were the only two things he had been able to bring with him.

Yet there was more to it than that; the old man had a natural magnetism that was intriguing. Darcy waited for a moment before replying.

"Sir Jack will be here in the morning, he's flying out from London. I'm his Deputy. My speciality is Eastern Europe. He asked me to look after you."

"Young man…" Kloptik began. It was a long time since anybody had called Darcy that, but somehow, coming from Kloptik, it didn't seem strange. "I am flattered, but I do not understand. Why are we not flying directly to London? Why go to this tiny island?"

"Tiny islands have their advantages," Darcy replied.

"Why?" Kloptik asked sharply.

"Because right now, suspicion is very unfashionable. Everyone wants to be inside the circle of the rich, the powerful and the ruthless; they're all climbing over each other. That's what the summit is all about. Very few questions are being asked. So the market for the sort of trouble you seem to be bringing is a difficult one."

Kloptik thought for a moment, taking in the implications of the information. "So I am unwelcome?" He suddenly sounded vulnerable.

Darcy decided to be direct. "In a word, yes. A political inconvenience."

Kloptik looked out at the night sky. Sirius, the Dog Star, followed Orion the Hunter as he climbed over the horizon. He spoke thoughtfully, as if to himself. "In the Roman Empire they used to kill the bearers of bad news…"

"Dreadful manners, the Italians," Darcy said.

Two rows back, Bullivant, a broad-shouldered figure, was immersed in isometric exercises, tensing and relaxing his muscles in slow succession.

He heard the conversation but did not understand a word. An ex-para corporal, he was the firepower of the team and he felt redundant.

* * *

"Who is Kloptik?" the Minister asked with an edge of impatience in his voice. Thornhill knew the man well. Arnold Braithwaite had been an MP for twenty years and this was his first cabinet appointment. He brought with him political cunning, a gift for self-protection and very little else. His instincts were to keep the infection of unwelcome news at a distance.

"I cannot reveal that," Thornhill replied with the cool exactitude that senior British civil servants have used for centuries when dealing with truculent political masters. Braithwaite was really angry now. It was his turn to use formality as a weapon. He was careful to use Thornhill's new knighthood with a politeness close to mockery.

"Then what, Sir Jack, is the point of this meeting? I have to brief the Prime Minister in less than an hour. The most important summit in history is close to being agreed upon. I cancelled two important working sessions to see you, and all I get is some fantasy character whose identity you won't reveal, or more likely don't know."

Braithwaite was dangerously close to the truth. Thornhill felt a flicker of doubt and hesitated for a moment. The sound of traffic in Whitehall rumbled through the dusty windows and mingled with the cold sunlight that fell across the desk between them.

Thornhill spoke with deliberation. "The purpose of this meeting is to warn Her Majesty's Government of an attempt to sabotage the summit about which you are to give your briefing."

He was trapped; there was no other way to put it. Until he could reach Kloptik, he knew no more, and if he were to get the Minister to take the threat seriously he could express it in no lesser terms. The diversion to Bermuda had been a calculated risk. It ensured that the debriefing would take place with minimum interference, but it lost time – a valuable twenty-four hours.

Braithwaite's mocking tone was unremitting. "Do you mean another terrorist attack – Islamists?"

"No, I'm certain of that."

"Then who, and above all why?" Braithwaite said with rising exasperation. "The Russians the Ukrainians the Poles, one way or another, by force or complicity, are all attempting to move into the land of capitalist plenty. The Americans, after the mauling they've just had, want out from the responsibility of world policemen. The Germans want to be left alone to get on with taking over Europe… and the Japs are looking over their shoulders at the Chinese." The Minister was not a man of ethnic subtleties. "Everyone has something to gain from a treaty."

"I suspect not quite everyone," said Thornhill.

"And how is this attempt on the peace of the world to take place? Political treachery, physical attack…?"

"Perhaps neither," Thornhill replied.

"Perhaps neither," the Minister mimicked Thornhill's evasiveness. "Don't talk in riddles, man, I haven't the time for your kind of subtlety."

Thornhill paused for a moment, wondering how he could convincingly explain the radical idea he had only that day begun to formulate. "Minister, with respect, thinking in national terms may now be out of date. There are powerful interests which transcend national and political boundaries."

Braithwaite's pride in speaking bluntly continued to exert itself. "Don't try and give me a geo-political history lecture. I know as well as you do where the threat comes from. Islamic fanatics. We've had enough lessons; even the liberals understand that now."

"This is not about Islam. At least not directly." Thornhill knew it was going badly.

"Well is it or isn't it? What do you mean, man?" Braithwaite looked at the large wall clock with Roman numerals. "I've got less than fifteen minutes before Cabinet. Explain yourself, if you can."

"By not directly, I mean not instigated by them but made possible by their impact on public opinion." Thornhill felt the conversation slipping from his grasp. He'd almost lost Braithwaite.

"So are you talking about some other sort of cross-border conspiracy?" It was an accusation, not a question.

Though conscious of the ticking clock, Thornhill took the luxury of a moment of silence, then tried to present a world view in a few sentences.

"Look at the facts. Since time immemorial, every state has viewed potential or actual threats to its safety as coming from three sources: other nations, terrorism or subversion from within. But consider the world that is now emerging. Superpower confrontation may be on hold, but what about the huge void that the collapse of the Eastern Bloc military and economic power has created? Vast amounts of money and very powerful technologies have no home. What we can be certain of is that this black hole will suck in all manner of things. The witch's brew that it may produce could be perilous in the extreme."

"That's your problem, isn't it? A witch's brew; you've no real idea what's in it,"

"Minister, I fear that it is not just my problem but our problem.

The whole world is terrorised by terrorism, and is ready for anything that appears to offer an answer."

Braithwaite had little regard for theory and wanted to take control of the conversation. "Interesting notions, but no more than that. You can prove no linkage between them."

"There doesn't need to be a linkage, just a coincidence of timing. Just look at what happened with Al Qaeda and Iraq," Thornhill said.

The Minister, ever anxious to get to the point, was in danger of missing it. "So what are we talking about? Eastern Europe being taken over by American drug barons while we're all hunting Islamic terrorists?"

"Of course not," Thornhill said, annoyed at a second interruption. "The analogy is imperfect. All the drug cartels in South and Central America have produced is money and a ruthlessly protected distribution network. The possibility I'm talking about is something quite different, something much larger and more dangerous. I believe we may have had our first warning, perhaps our only warning. Frankly we need your help."

Braithwaite was alert to the hint of some political advantage. "How so?"

Thornhill continued. "It's a matter of recognising the importance of the opportunity. Let me present you with another analogy. Just before the Second World War, two Poles smuggled a machine to London. It became known as Enigma. It was a device of the type used to encode all German military signals: Wehrmacht, Luftwaffe and Kriegesmarine. As you know, for most of the war, from the Blitz, through the Battle of the Atlantic, to the D-Day landings, we knew almost everything of importance that the German High Command sent to their forces in the field and could act accordingly. Understanding the importance of what those two Poles brought with them almost certainly saved the Western world from defeat."

Braithwaite looked pointedly at the clock and Thornhill knew he'd used too many words. "And the relevance of those events to this situation?"

"I believe we may be in the process of being offered something of similar magnitude."

"A machine?" Braithwaite was far from simple minded, but he did have a tendency to be over-literal.

Thornhill controlled his exasperation. "No, Minister, not a machine, not another Enigma, but something with the ability to put at risk the new accord. 'From the Rockies to the Urals.' I believe that was the phrase you used in the House this week?"

Braithwaite did not appreciate having his own words quoted back to him and stood up as if to emphasise his authority.

"You will be aware, Sir Jack, that I have little affection for your trade, and it will be no secret to you that I have frequently opposed your department in committee in the House of Commons." He got up, walked to the window and looked out across Whitehall. He spoke without turning to Thornhill. His political instincts led him to the heart of the matter. "What you are telling me is either the delusion of a few cold warriors who face being pensioned off, or it really is important. How am I to know which?" He reached out to wipe away the dust from one of the windowpanes, but the grime was on the outside.

* * *

"What's the difference between a hedgehog and head office?" The owner of the champagne-modulated voice was too intoxicated by the brilliance of his own wit to wait for answers. "A hedgehog has the pricks on the outside!" he shouted in triumph and then collapsed in a fit of girlish giggles. Thornhill sat in silent anger amid the mindless chatter of a group of photocopier salesmen. Incentive travel, he had been told, a long weekend in Bermuda for the sales region's superstars and their wives or girlfriends. The business section of the 747 was simply another stage on which to perform.

"Performance is what this business is all about, darlin' ...know what I mean?" One of them leered at the stewardess as she served yet more champagne. Thornhill concentrated on the Atlantic sky and tried to isolate his mind from the noise around him.

The curvature of the earth stood out sharp against the light, just like the end of the world in which the ancients believed: 'go too far and you fall off the edge'. The thought set Thornhill to wondering, was he approaching the end of his own world? Were suspicion, imagination and anticipation any longer enough?

The salesmen ranted on. Thornhill put on a sleep mask and went over the ground again. The encounter in London with the woman called Anya; a pseudonym, he supposed. Then the near disaster with the second message.

It came on the back of a postcard mailed to the Fulham safe house whose address he had given her. The message was brief – a street number and the avenue with which it intersected in a rundown area across the river from Manhattan. The coordinates were followed by a date and a time. A five-day postal strike in South London had delayed the arrival of the message. Mrs Matthews, the Fulham housekeeper, rang Lloyd-Emlyn in Thornhill's office to warn of its arrival, but out of long years of habit, she did not read it. A courier was immediately organised and the card arrived thirty-five minutes later. Lloyd-Emlyn signed for the package and left it on his desk while he continued a difficult phone conversation with Sally, his almost ex-girlfriend.

It was a relationship with an uncertain future; Sally talked a lot and Lloyd-Emlyn became restless. While half listening, he broke open the seals on the envelope, slid out the card and froze. In one movement he slammed down the phone, launched himself towards Thornhill's office door and burst in.

Thornhill was in a long and difficult meeting with a senior official from the Treasury to negotiate the coming year's budget. Lloyd-Emlyn saw Thornhill's anger at the interruption and spoke first, cutting the Treasury man off in mid-sentence.

"Sir Jack, we have an emergency." The Treasury official swept his papers off the desk, stuffed them untidily into his briefcase and left the room without another word.

"Bad timing..." Thornhill began.

Lloyd-Emlyn interrupted again. "It's Kloptik; there's a meeting in under two and a half hours – on a street corner in New Jersey."

Thornhill took the card and read it twice. "Call Murphy, grade nine alert. Then organise whatever back-up you can; he may need protection."

Lloyd-Emlyn was thinking ahead. "What about the Americans? Surely we must operate within the inter-services agreement; it's on their turf after all. And we'll need to use the satellite if we want to know what's going on."

"No." Thornhill spoke sharply. "That way we'll lose him."

"But the Foreign Secretary signed the agreement personally," Lloyd-Emlyn insisted.

"Get on the phone, man, you're wasting time." Thornhill knew exactly the professional risk he was taking. If things went wrong, they would be after his head for giving the Americans a justification to operate an open-season hunting licence in London; something that the Foreign Office had been trying to contain for years.

* * *

The aircraft droned on and Thornhill sank deeper into thought. He could find no way to understand Kloptik's unnecessarily mysterious journey across the Atlantic.

Looking back on the first meeting in Hamburg, he felt like a character trapped in a script somebody else had written. The difficulty was that he didn't know who the other characters were. Intellect told him that to stake so much on such slender evidence was irrational, but instinct told him otherwise. He understood himself well enough to know that his reputation among colleagues for 'a sure touch' rested on an ability to make precise judgements between the competing values of acute analysis and instinctive insight. Now everything rested on his judgement of Kloptik. He tried to sleep but couldn't; wondering how many times the future of nations had turned on the look in a man's eyes.

The sleep mask was no protection against intrusion. "Do you know…?" The voice of Thornhill's neighbour shouting into his ear was heavily inebriated; it stumbled and began again. "Do you know that we're travelling a mile every time you breathe in and out?" The voice waited for acknowledgement, and receiving none, moved on to the next wonder-fact. "As fast as a Colt .45 bullet, that's how fast we're going."

"Then let's hope you don't get ahead of yourself," Thornhill replied irritably.

The salesman tried to grapple with the thought but lost interest and sank into semi-consciousness. Thornhill closed his eyes again and, without success, tried to close his ears.

* * *

The sun shone blood-red through Kloptik's eyelids as he lay listening to the surf. He felt cheated that in all his life he had never experienced anything like this before.

This was no East European sun that skimmed across a cold landscape like a pebble on a lake, a sun that never touched the soul of the nation. On this fragment of limestone seven hundred miles from the American coast, the sun was not a fleeting visitor but master of everything it fell upon. The sea was warm, the sand hot and, after sunset, the rocks radiated back the heat they had soaked up during the day. Warmth suspended animation and he lay torpid, like a lizard, on the sand. A shadow passed across the light. It was Darcy.

"The plane's landed. He'll be here in half an hour."

Guiltily leaving his reverie behind, Kloptik rose uncertainly. He felt self-conscious wearing nothing but unfamiliar bathing shorts, and the sand made him feel unsteady on his feet. He attempted to regain his dignity before he spoke.

"Very well, I shall go and change," he said as he began to tread cautiously across the hot sand. "I shall meet him in the hotel."

* * *

Thornhill had decided to deal with the first encounter alone. When he arrived, Darcy left the room. Bullivant sat in the suite across the hall with the door open. Morag had set up her computer, the modems and the miniature satellite dish on the balcony of her room next door. Murphy operated the recorder. Latchford went to the bar to watch for new arrivals.

The meeting was an emotional moment. Thornhill found himself in an extravagant Slavic embrace.

Despite years of European socialising, he remained embarrassed by displays of physical affection between men and took half a step back to avoid the full force of the gesture.

Kloptik spoke first. "I knew you would come," he said with the charm and self-assurance that Thornhill remembered from their first encounter in Hamburg, but he was in no mood for charm.

"You knew damn well I'd come, you've been trying to manipulate me since we first met. So let's get to the point; why all the melodrama?"

Kloptik smiled, but it was a theatrical gesture, without humour. "Ah, so you are angry. I thought you must be angry to have brought me here instead of London."

"I brought you here so I could find out how much of a fool I'm making of myself before unleashing you upon my masters."

"Or to ensure that you remain in control once you have heard what I have to say?"

Thornhill spoke sharply. "I had a message from you concerning a threat to the summit. That's all I know. That's why you're here, that's why I'm here. So let's get on with it."

"Almost correct, but not quite." Kloptik made the point as if identifying an error in a student's thesis.

"You know about me, you know about the Night Watch and, most importantly, you know that I understand you well enough to have been able, as you put it, to 'manipulate you'. An ugly term, but it is your own. Now, I suspect that such 'manipulation' is something unusual and perhaps unique in your experience?" Kloptik paused for a moment. "That is why you are here, and that is why I am here, rather than in London."

Thornhill drew breath to reply, but the Pole broke into a smile, stretched out both his arms and said, "But I am not here to listen to your confession, but you to mine. It's a long story."

"Then begin at the beginning, go on to the end and then stop," Thornhill said irritably.

"Alice in Wonderland … The Duchess?" Kloptik said with obvious pride at catching Thornhill unconsciously using a quotation. He expected some recognition, but received none.

"Get on with it." Thornhill immediately knew that he had reacted too sharply. He was tired and jet lag was beginning to show. Kloptik didn't seem to notice. He moved away and lowered himself into one of the big armchairs. Thornhill thought how incongruous he looked; a small, intense man in borrowed clothes, sunk into a morass of garish Hawaiian fabric. He took the matching chair opposite and waited.

"First, my name. I am Wolski, Professor Josef Wolski."

Next door, Morag keyed the name into the terminal that was linked, via the dish on the balcony, to the London computer database.

The response was instantaneous but brief: a list of the scientific papers that Wolski had presented to academic conferences over the previous decade, the article in Newsweek, but nothing more.

Wolski's professorial manner, married to an orator's turn of phrase, made Thornhill wonder whether he had remembered the man as completely as he had imagined. "You recall the Night Watch, our small effort at recording the events of our long national night?"

"Yes, I remember."

"I told you we never intervened, rather we vowed to record, so that one day the truth would be remembered; a limited objective, but perhaps a noble one.

'A Testament for Humanity' someone called it, I don't remember who it was; delusions of grandeur no doubt. But you must understand that those dark days were also days of innocence. We thought that being witnesses for the prosecution would be sufficient, that somehow this would separate us from the wrongdoers."

He faltered and Thornhill saw that whatever was to come next was going to be difficult to say. There was a long pause. Then close to tears, Wolski spoke haltingly. "In my case at least, that was wrong. I am no longer just a witness, I stand among the ranks of the guilty."

"What happened?" Thornhill asked quietly.

"What happened?" Wolski repeated with rising volume. "What happened? The Night Watch could not secure the Mindgate. You have understood nothing," he added accusingly.

Wolski was right, Thornhill did not understand. The Mindgate? It was the first time he had seen Wolski angry, or was he just raving? What was it that he was expected to understand? Perhaps the truth was that there was nothing to understand, except that Wolski was insane.

Wolski's mood changed; he seemed detached, looking around the room as if waking from a dream and seeing it for the first time – the carpet with hair long as rye grass, the expensive split bamboo wall coverings, the pinks and lime greens of the furnishings. It was an alien environment. His eyes locked on Thornhill and with difficulty he pulled himself out of the large, soft armchair and moved to the writing desk. For an instant Wolski saw himself in the mirror over the desk and Thornhill noticed how sharply he turned away to avoid eye contact with his own reflection.

He took the hard upright chair from the desk and carefully placed it at the centre of the balcony window that gave a view of the sea.

He sat for some time with his back to Thornhill, his silhouette set against the bright sky outside. The rising wind was blowing towering heaps of white cloud across the sky. It was past high water and the ebbing tide was throwing up sharp, steep waves as it collided with the onshore wind.

"Do you remember Wilfred Owen?" Wolski asked. Without waiting for a response, he answered his own question.

"One of your people, an English soldier in the First World War; the best poet of his generation. Month after month, year after year, he recorded the horror of it all. Then, just days before the armistice was signed, he was killed. I always thought that was especially cruel."

Thornhill was careful not to respond, and it was some time before Wolski spoke again. His grip on reality seemed to be failing fast.

"I feel like that, a soldier fatally wounded in the last moments of the battle. I am dead and will never live again. It seems unjust, but how can the guilty plead for justice?"

"What do you mean?" asked Thornhill softly.

"For years we watched through the night, we saw terrible things. For those who did not resist, there was little persecution; in the physical sense at least. But the price of safety was moral surrender. People closed their minds to hope. Children grew to middle age knowing no alternative." He faltered, and Thornhill, sensing the rising level of stress, did not interrupt. "Then at last, as all the world knows, the first light crept over the horizon and with it came the collapse of the old order.

Millions rejoiced in the streets…" Wolski buried his face in his hands and breathed deeply. Thornhill had to listen carefully to catch the words. "But it was a false dawn; with the light came a new vileness, less visible; more dangerous…" His voice trailed off and he sat silently, head in hands.

"New business, not unfinished business?" Thornhill asked quietly.

"What did you say?" Wolski asked, seeking some reassurance.

"Nothing important, I was just thinking out loud," Thornhill said.

Looking beyond Wolski, out onto to the breaking surf, he was unaccountably angry that the waves beyond the window were silent and that all he could hear was the low hum of the air-conditioning. Any thought was easier to deal with than the completeness of their dependence on each other. Thornhill knew that this moment would come, but its arrival was still alarming. Now there was no retreat.

He went to Wolski's chair, put his hand on his shoulder and eased him into an upright position. "I think you should begin at the beginning," he said.

"Alice in Wonderland?" Wolski asked, turning to face Thornhill with the flicker of a smile.

"Yes, Alice in Wonderland: 'Begin at the beginning, go on to the end and then stop'.

Let's get in touch with reality," Thornhill said as he slid open the balcony window. The sound of the sea rushed into the room and the wind blew an art deco vase off the dresser. It didn't break; it was made of plastic and hit the carpet with a dull thud.

8

Warsaw

The Institute in Warsaw was a flamboyant building in Imperial style, put up during the nation's last flowering of optimism in the second half of the 19th century. In those days, the country was more than twice its present size. Russia, to the east, was concerned with the turmoil of its own affairs, while in the west, Germany was becoming a single nation for the first time. For three-quarters of a century, the Institute was home to some of the most respected academic minds of Central Europe. Then in 1939 Blitzkrieg came. Panzers rolled across the Polish Plain and from the air, the Luftwaffe struck a largely undefended population. It was all over in less than a month. The Nazis were everywhere victorious. In a city so heavily devastated, the Institute survived comparatively well. At the end of the war, along with other historic buildings, it was lovingly restored. But things were not what they appeared to be.

The victory over the Nazis had been a Soviet, not a Polish, triumph. In its own way, this left deeper scars than those inflicted by enemy action. The restoration of treasured pre-war architecture was political propaganda, empty of serious scientific or intellectual content. Everything worth having was removed and shipped to Moscow. In scientific endeavour, the rich and powerful academic institutions of the West raced ahead, with the Soviets keeping pace only in military and aerospace hardware.

Central Europe became a technological backwater. But with the death of Stalin, the grip of Moscow gradually slackened and the Institute slowly recovered.

But outside the Institute, the Soviet-dominated state continued to intrude in every part of life. The secret police were omnipresent and, from time to time, there were political murders that the authorities made little attempt to disguise. Arrests, for the slightest expression of opposition were common. Families had children removed from them, careers were blighted and international travel was restricted to government officials, performers and contestants at major sporting events.

Almost out of sight, in the privileged environment of the Institute, Wolski was one of the fathers of an academic renaissance. Fighting discreet political battles for resources, he carefully built a reputation that attracted the best of a new generation of would-be research scientists. Despite the struggle, or perhaps because of it – he sometimes wondered which – Wolski was comfortable at the Institute; it was home. He developed a talent for advancing its international reputation and nobody was surprised when, though still young, he was appointed to one of the three Deputy Directorships, a post that was the limit of a scientist's advancement. The Director was a political appointee. Wolski's job suited him well; it meant out-thinking his Western peers. His skill lay in identifying specialities not already monopolised by others in the USA, Western Europe or Japan, and in developing them with a fraction of the resources available to his Western counterparts.

Institute staff were shielded from the harshness of life among the population at large and it was in this protected atmosphere that the Night Watch met every month.

Each arrest, each intimidation, each threatening speech and act of censorship was discussed and recorded in a journal: 'The Testament', as it became known.

At the end of each meeting this was passed to a different member for safekeeping. Though their purpose was serious, the meetings were not sombre. Vodka was always plentiful and even in the most difficult times, someone in the group had contacts that enabled them to bring a delicacy to accompany the copious supplies of black bread which were always available: a jar of herrings, some German sausage, fresh mushrooms and occasionally caviar, bartered with some visiting Soviet academic; there was always something special. For Wolski, the Institute and the Night Watch were the two most important things in his life. One exercised the intellect and the other the conscience. It was the perfect combination, the kind of atmosphere that, in an earlier time, a monastery might have provided. Then Golkov arrived.

* * *

In the Soviet days, Russians were common visitors, mostly raiding parties of technicians and commissars who, in the name of fraternal collaboration, were looking for anything worth stealing. They earned the nickname Carrion Crows from the long black Zil limousines that ferried them about.

The Institute's senior staff became skilled at protecting their best work while appearing to offer the cooperation that political pressure demanded of them. Some even came to enjoy the game of cat and mouse.

Then with a suddenness that nobody would have dared to predict, the Carrion Crows were gone. Soviet power collapsed in a matter of months.

Everyone at the Institute supposed they were now free, but nobody was sure what that meant. Nothing in their past dreams and speculations had prepared them for living out the reality they had all hoped for. Neither were they at all prepared for the way in which power changed hands, not just in the change of government, but also in all the layers of power between government and the governed.

As in so many revolutions, the power of corrupt influence simply passed from one set of hands to another. Golkov was living evidence of the new reality. His masters were not the Moscow Politburo; who they were was a matter of much speculation. Golkov was smoother and sharper than any of the other Russians that Wolski and his colleagues had come to know. He possessed a quick mind and an unknown quantity of power. Mysteriously, he also appeared to have a wardrobe of American business suits. 'Brooks Brothers', one junior professor claimed to have seen on the label inside a jacket left on the back of a chair during one long, hot meeting. Everyone was cautious; they smelt danger.

* * *

Six weeks after Golkov's arrival, Wolski was summoned to a meeting; 'invited' was the word used, but there was no opportunity to decline. When he arrived at the Director's office, Wolski was surprised that none of the other Deputy Directors were present. He was immediately uneasy. The Director of the Institute sat at his desk, and by the glass-fronted Gothic bookcases that lined an entire wall stood Golkov. The Director, a small man with a legendary reputation for pomposity, rose while simultaneously motioning Wolski to a seat.

"Comrade Doctor Golkov wishes to speak to you." The Director used the old Communist title by force of long-learned habit. "He wishes to speak to you alone," the Director added, stiff with resentment. Wolski could not disguise his surprise as the Director left the room. Golkov said nothing. He took the Director's big chair behind the wide desk and smiled a warm, insincere smile. Just like an American politician, Wolski thought; a notion reinforced by a well-tailored dark-blue suit, a gold Cross pen and an Italian silk tie. Instinctively Wolski tried to think of a way to avoid becoming the only person to hear what Golkov had to say. Hard-won experience had taught him that secret information was the most dangerous kind.

"Professor, I am glad to meet you. I have asked to speak to you alone because what I have to say is for your ears only. That is also why during the past twenty-four hours, for the security of us both, I have had this room swept for electronic listening devices."

In the old regime nobody talked of such things. Wolski realised that this opening was not intended to reassure but to establish Golkov as a man with the power to control the world in which he operated and the lives of others who were summoned into his presence. From the pit of his stomach, Wolski felt a rising tide of fear. He tried to disguise it with a joke that might level the ground between them.

"So the only ones remaining are your own." It was a misjudgement.

Golkov ignored the remark and continued in the same self-confident tone. "First let me introduce myself. I am Doctor Vladimir Golkov. From Moscow." He added the name of the city as if it were an explanation, which in a way it was.

Wolski was becoming annoyed at Golkov's superior manner.

"Thank you, Doctor, I already know who you are, but I would like to know what you are."

Golkov's shallow affability vanished and the conversation continued with academic formality. "Professor, there are those who might consider such curiosity unsympathetic."

Wolski understood the warning and waited for Golkov to speak again. It was an ominous beginning. "History teaches that the prizes go to those who can see furthest," Golkov said cryptically. Wolski doubted the truth of the observation but continued to listen. Like everyone else at the Institute, he had long lived partly in the present and partly in hope of a future free of Russians. Golkov seemed to have thought of the same possibility.

"In the new Russia, there are those who can see that things as they are now will not last much longer. The present democratic reforms are simply Band-Aids on a corpse." Wolski wondered what Band-Aids were. There seemed a curious rhetorical quality to Golkov's way of speaking. It was as if he were addressing a large and expectant audience.

"There will be a new world revolution, but this time it will not be a revolution of the ragged masses but of those with vision, money and power. We shall join forces with others of like mind in the United States and across the world. Why should we continue to endure terrorist outrages and the tedious demands of those without the imagination to better themselves?" The enormity of the proposition left Wolski speechless. Golkov continued. "Already in the think-tanks around Washington they are talking about the collapse of the old order and 'A One World Alliance' to enable civilised nations to protect themselves against the rest. Soon the phrase will start appearing in presidential speeches, the media will pick it up and it will become everyone's expectation."

Wolski was puzzled to know why this seemed like good news to Golkov. He spoke quietly. "Why do you tell me this, and what have you to gain from such expectations?" Golkov paused and Wolski, now sick with anxiety, regretted asking the question. It was clear that Golkov was deciding how much to reveal.

"We have everything to gain. The Bolsheviks in their revolution had to destroy the establishment. We need destroy nothing; chaos will do it for us."

Wolski searched for some evidence of the fanatic or lunatic in the man, but found no such comfort. Nor could he think of a prudent reply and it was a relief that no answer seemed to be required.

"Why do I tell you all this?" Golkov answered his own question. "Because we want your Institute to join us."

"Then why not speak to the Director?"

"The Director is a bureaucrat, he will do as I instruct; he can be coerced. You, on the other hand – you are different. I would prefer your willing cooperation."

"To do what?"

"To do what you are best at, competitive science, in a field where you can lead the world." The notion seemed childishly simplistic, but Golkov spoke too rapidly to allow interruption. "Don't concern yourself with the technicalities, everything will be formally arranged; a research contract between the Institute and the sponsor. In reality you will work directly for me, as Moscow's representative." For a dangerous moment, the professional in Wolski was intrigued.

"Why come here? There are many more resources in Moscow."

"And many more prying eyes," replied Golkov.

The Moscow Mafia? Wolski thought, trying to anchor the conversation in some part of the real world. His mind was racing, trying to make sense of what he was hearing. Organised crime seemed too easy an answer.

Golkov continued in a tone of prim reasonableness. "Here we can work without arousing curiosity and we can conduct field tests more discreetly."

"Field tests?" Wolski seized on the term. "What kind of field tests?"

Golkov shook his head in mock dismay. "Have you no wish to change this sad world?"

Wolski knew there were many precedents for doing sensitive scientific trials in out-of-the-way places where the locals could not complain too loudly if things went wrong. Oral contraceptives tested on women in the Third World; 'miracle' treatments on Romanian orphans. Was this what Golkov had in mind? "You will need to tell me what you mean," he said stubbornly.

"I have confided enough in you for you to make a decision. I want a commitment from you before I tell you more."

"That's quite impossible. It's all too vague; I must know to what I am agreeing."

Golkov stood and leaned forward across the desk aggressively. "I am disappointed. I offer you an outstanding scientific opportunity and you quibble like a bureaucrat." He paused, staring into Wolski's eyes, and as if saddened by his lack of enthusiasm, sighed and shrugged his shoulders. He withdrew back across the desk, paused for a moment and went to the opposite side of the room where he hesitated again, then spoke with studied courtesy.

"But of course you are right, I must tell you more." On a side table lay a stainless-steel briefcase. As Golkov undid the combination locks and swung the polished lid open, Wolski noticed that it reflected the ornate plaster ceiling. He was to remember that reflected image for years afterwards.

As Golkov shuffled through the papers inside the case his tone became relaxed, with a hint of warmth. "Perhaps I can reassure you. We have common interests; you are fond of Bach I believe, and of painting?" Wolski's mouth was dry; he nodded. Golkov took a folder from the briefcase and, as if to avoid formality, sat on the edge of the desk beside Wolski. His closeness was deeply disturbing. "I too am a lover of art. I think every effort should be made to preserve great paintings, don't you?" He took a postcard from the folder and, with another of his brittle smiles, handed it to Wolski. As he took it, his hand began to shake. The picture was The Night Watch by Rembrandt. Golkov pretended not to notice Wolski's distress. "It's terrible what people will do to such fine expressions of the human spirit.

Did you know that the picture, as it now hangs in the Rijksmuseum in Amsterdam, is only part of the original?"

Wolski was too shocked to speak. Golkov kept talking. "Yes, a great barbarity. One of its early owners cut off the edges so that it would fit between two doors; such short-sightedness, but such finality." Golkov would not stop. "And only recently it was damaged with a sharp instrument by a man out of touch with reality. I believe that he was taken into care, for his own protection, of course. You are not out of touch with reality, are you, Professor?"

Wolski turned and met Golkov's gaze with a look of fear and contempt. Golkov fell silent. For Wolski, the impact of the discovery of the Night Watch was massive. Here was the crudest of all forms of coercion, the threat of violence. A rush of indignation overcame anxiety and he shouted his reply. "The old days are over, we are a free people. You can no longer threaten us."

"Oh, but I can and I do. Is it necessary for me to arrange for one of your 'free people' to have an accident for me to convince you? Which one should I choose? Perhaps you can advise me?"

Wolski could find no words for the fear and disgust that was welling up inside him. Golkov was unstoppable.

"Ask yourself how much your 'freedom' is worth. Who can you run to for help? Politicians? The police? They are commodities who are bought and sold every day." Golkov returned to his chair, leant back and put his feet on the desk; he spoke in a menacingly relaxed manner.

"The reality is that power is an equilibrium with three components: money, knowledge and people. Those whom I represent have unlimited quantities of all three. I am merely a technician with the task of maintaining that equilibrium, which is why I shall ensure that you do as we wish." Golkov let the message sink in. "The reality is quite simple; I am more powerful than you, Professor Wolski.

Denial of that fact is like denying gravity; it can only bring you and your friends great grief."

Wolski was totally outclassed and knew it. His mind was reeling and the only thing he was certain of was that he needed time. Time to think, time to plan. Time to escape?

"I ask you again, Professor, are you in touch with reality?"

"I understand the reality of this situation."

"I take it then, that you agree to join us?" Wolski nodded.

"Good. If things go well, there could be a Nobel Prize in this."

It was a measure of Wolski's mental turmoil that he could not tell whether Golkov was serious or merely taunting him. The one thing that was certain was that Golkov had won.

Briskly Golkov brought the meeting to a close. "Tomorrow, I shall brief you in detail." He snapped the metal briefcase shut and picked up the postcard that Wolski had left on the desk.

"Please keep the picture; think of it as a memento of our understanding."

Wolski could think of nothing to say in reply. He slid the postcard into his breast pocket and, head bowed, moved towards the door. In deep shock, he walked along the familiar echoing corridor, with its grand sweeping arches and lancet windows that poured shafts of light onto the marble and bronze statues of his predecessors. Junior staff greeted him with their usual respect.

But his world had changed. He was frightened, very frightened, but the humiliation of being a prisoner in his own professional home was worse than the fear.

* * *

Sitting in the crowded tram at the end of the day, he was oblivious to his surroundings. The difficulty that he faced was much worse than a problem; problems have solutions. This was a dilemma; there were no answers, only alternatives and each of them offered the prospect of disaster. The tram rattled on and the crush of people became denser as home-going workers got on at the stops in the city centre.

But Wolski wasn't conscious of the pressure of bodies upon him. He struggled with the options. To warn the Night Watch would alert Golkov and bring about reprisals. Yet to let them continue would be an act of betrayal. The tram crossed the river, and the passengers began to thin out until Wolski was left almost alone in a haze of body odour and stale cigarette smoke. Eventually, the tram ground to a halt at Wolski's stop.

* * *

Who was Golkov? What power did he represent? Was there any way in which he might be stopped? There were no answers; the only fact Wolski was sure of was the threat to the Night Watch. About that, he had no doubt at all. He walked to the tall terraced house that had once belonged to an importer of French wine.

Now it was divided into apartments. Wolski's was on the second floor. He climbed the stone stairs, opened the door and turned on the lights. Inside, everything was the same, yet everything was changed. The once comfortable refuge filled with books and well-used furniture was now contaminated by nauseous anxiety and self-loathing.

He turned out the lights. Sitting in the dark somehow made thinking easier. For a long time, he listened to the trams clattering by. Occasionally, a blue flash from the overhead power cables lit the room like lightning. The tide of commuters receded and in time was replaced by late-night revellers: 'The Vodka Cosmonauts', as everyone called them.

Eventually, the street became quiet and for most of the silent hours of the night Wolski applied his mind to analysing the new reality. There seemed only two possibilities. Either Golkov must have an informant within the Night Watch, or he had the meetings bugged. Either way, the damage had been done. A warning would achieve nothing; there was nowhere to escape to.

He could not rid his mind of what Golkov had said about the postcard: 'A memento of our understanding'. The implication that if he cooperated, the Night Watch would be protected, and that if he did not, it would be destroyed.

* * *

In the darkness he could see them all clearly: Jakob with his fierce humour; Stefan, devoted to his wife and twin daughters; Ignace, who had such a keen eye for detail that it almost constituted a photographic memory; Arthur and his trail of adoring women; Krystian the linguist, and the many others. Alone in the dark, for the first time he realised who this unlikely collection of people really were; they were his only family and he loved every one of them. Silently, he wept. Never before had he been conscious of love for anyone.

Sometime around four in the morning, his decision was made. He must tell them nothing. Even more painfully, he would have to find reasons to separate himself from them, in the hope that they would not become infected by whatever he himself was being contaminated with. It was not much, but it was the best he could do. As he thought long and bitterly about Golkov, the second realisation of the night came upon him. This was the first man he had ever truly hated. A shallow sleep crept up on him and with it came impulses of love and disgust that pursued each other through his semi-consciousness. By first light, he was gaunt-eyed and dry-mouthed.

* * *

He was at the Institute early for his meeting with Golkov. He first went to his own office and, on an impulse that he did not wholly understand, tidied the files on his desk and sat with arms folded waiting for the phone to ring. He did not have to wait long.

It was a woman's voice; Golkov had acquired a secretary. The uncertainty of the new power structure was obvious from the tone of her voice. "Professor; Doctor Golkov asks if you will please come to his office?"

Golkov had installed himself in a large corner office, with windows on two sides. Previously the room had been inhabited by a group of statisticians. Wolski wondered where they had been banished to. The room looked strangely bare; there was none of the usual academic clutter, no untidy piles of papers, no books, nothing on the walls. Golkov had managed to acquire a large antique desk, the room's only concession to status. A Japanese laptop computer on the desk was the most prominent article in the room. It was of a kind Wolski had not previously seen in the Institute but he chose not to notice it, and without being invited took a seat across the desk from Golkov. From his expression, Golkov made it clear that he saw the manoeuvre for what it was and Wolski felt as if he'd been caught out in some childish misdeed.

Golkov spoke with cold, formal courtesy. "Professor, we shall never be friends but perhaps we can avoid the barrenness of mutual contempt? What we are attempting here is too important for such trivialities."

Wolski ignored Golkov's appeal. "If I am to be useful, I need to know more."

Golkov studied him for a moment and then began an explanation. "Consider the world of science. In the West, if research is not for military purposes, it is ruled almost entirely by commercial objectives.

Capitalism demands a bottom line that shows a profit. Of course, vanity can also be a motive. If an obscure university in the USA wishes to become well known, it will establish a centre for the study of something or somebody ignored by everybody else. That will get the name of the institution into the papers and sometimes onto television – always good for fundraising. Don't misunderstand me, Professor, while I may abhor capitalist motivation, I envy its success. We in the East, on the other hand, have always pursued research for political reasons, to strengthen the power of the state. And we were very effective at it. Let's not forget our successes. The Soviet Union grew from a near-mediaeval peasantry to a superpower in less than a single lifetime."

"But at what price?" Wolski was outraged. "Stalin killed twenty million of your people; more than Hitler. Moreover, he carved up my country with the Nazis."

Golkov was unmoved. "You may not approve of Comrade Stalin but nevertheless you must recognise that he was a genius. In a choice between tyranny and chaos, the Russian people will always choose tyranny. The Czar, who people in the West call 'Ivan the Terrible', every Russian schoolchild knows as 'Ivan the Formidable'. You should remember that."

Wolski's outrage emboldened him. This was the type of argument he had long ago believed would never again be necessary. "Are you saying you admire Stalin?"

"I simply observe life as it is," Golkov replied. "The past is irrelevant. The Communist system is finished, exhausted. It has served its purpose and now it's dead."

"Everyone knows that," Wolski said for want of a better reply.

Golkov ignored him. "The present system in Russia, the weakling orphaned child of Communism, will soon follow its parent to the grave." Golkov seemed smug with the completeness of his vision.

"What does this have to do with your being here at the Institute?" Wolski asked.

"I explain these matters to you because your willing cooperation is more useful to us than mere compliance with our instructions," Golkov replied.

Wolski chose to ignore the point. "Nothing you have said explains what you're trying to achieve," he insisted.

Golkov took time to choose his words. Eventually, he used only one. "Power."

Wolski looked quizzical; Golkov took this as a sign of interest. "Technology expresses power, it always has, from the flint axe to the forty thousand nuclear warheads which we and the Americans possess but have no idea what to do with. Until now, such technologies have always been deployed by one bloc to dominate another. The costs of doing things in this way are, of course, colossal. The spending match with the United States in weaponry destroyed the Soviet Union. The ideas of the Stone Age have lasted too long. Nuclear weapons, biological weapons, all of them belong to the past.

Why, you may ask," Golkov had a habit of answering his own questions, "I will tell you why. All such weapons are capable of destruction and it's no longer necessary to break down castle walls. We do not need wasteful efforts of siege or destruction. We shall have a point of entry where there is no resistance." For a moment he studied Wolski's incomprehension. "I like to call it 'The Mindgate.'" He delivered the phrase like someone unveiling a statue of a hero. Wolski found the total absurdity of the idea reassuring, and it showed.

Golkov kept talking in a tone of cold calculation. “Your own visible disbelief is valuable.

You don’t believe us, and in turn nobody will believe you, should you be foolish enough to think of sharing with others what I am about to tell you.”

Wolski’s moment of lightness was extinguished and what he heard next made him sit still as stone.

“I will come directly to the point,” Golkov said. “You are going to help us find out what makes humans act as they do. Our work on the electro-chemical components of the brain that govern behaviour is well advanced. Now we need to complete our understanding without delay and we have chosen you for the task.”

Wolski was rigid; he sat looking at the blank wall to avoid eye contact with Golkov. His mind rang with a clamour of emotions; fear if Golkov was right, fear if he was mad. He spoke with difficulty. “Your objective is better addressed to a theologian than a research scientist.” It was his last act of open defiance and it appeared to be entirely lost on Golkov.

“I will show you something,” Golkov said, as if speaking to a junior member of class. From behind the desk, he lifted the metal briefcase that Wolski had seen the day before. He dreaded what it might contain this time. The catches snapped open; Golkov took out a DVD and walked to the battered cupboard that once housed over-stuffed boxes of statisticians’ forms. He opened the door to reveal a disc player and television monitor. The screen slowly came to life. The image was a copy of a scratchy black and white film from some time in the silent movie era. Wolski quickly recognised the figure of Charlie Chaplin. The scene was a boxing match. Charlie, cheered on by the heroine, reluctantly entered the ring. His opponent, a villain of huge proportions, followed. Charlie managed to dodge a few blows but was on the ropes as the bell sounded.

Between rounds, the heroine slapped a gas mask on the face of the big boxer. Unsteadily the camera tilted down to see 'Laughing Gas' crudely painted on the cylinder. The bell sounded again and the villain, for all his fury, could only laugh as he took clumsy swings at the dapper Charlie. The film was assembled into a continuous loop that repeated the comedy of the big man's despairing struggle to maintain his aggression against the effects of the gas. Wolski was transfixed. It was one of the most sinister things he had ever seen.

The shock on Wolski's face made Golkov laugh. "Don't be too literal, Professor, that's the most common failing of the scientist. We don't intend to conquer the world with laughing gas, it's simply our little demonstration reel, a parable if you like. Control the mind of the enemy and you control his intentions and his abilities."

"And who is the enemy?" Wolski asked.

Golkov put the disc back into the briefcase and snapped the catches shut. The sound was like a weapon being cocked. "The enemy is whoever we choose the enemy to be," Golkov said with a sharpness that indicated the meeting was at an end.

For Wolski, the situation had the character of a terrible dream. To be talking about ways of controlling the world in a dusty former office of statistics in the capital of an economically exhausted and technologically backward country was bizarre. But Golkov left no space for thinking. "The first members of the team arrive in the morning. We shall be using the East Wing." Golkov picked up his briefcase and indicated that they should both leave the office.

The following morning, when Wolski got to the Institute, he was astonished to find builders bricking up the corridors that joined the East Wing to the rest of the building. In the early afternoon, armed guards in unidentifiable dark-blue uniforms appeared at the doors to the street and at the intersections between departments. A day later, groups of technicians arrived; each had a floor plan that identified the offices allocated to them. Golkov had done a thorough job.

By the end of the week, Wolski was issued with a pass by a dour Russian clerk who sat in a corridor that was rapidly filling up with filing cabinets and racks of computer drives.

To anyone used to Eastern European bureaucracies with their built-in lethargy and muddle, the speed and efficiency of the operation was breath-taking. Wolski wandered through the laboratories and lecture rooms that he knew so well and was mesmerised by the speed with which they were being transformed. In a matter of days, all the years of theft from the Institute were being repaid with interest.

During the second week, a convoy of sealed trucks arrived. They drove straight into the courtyard of what had once been the stable block and were unloaded beneath a tarpaulin canopy that prevented anyone in the main building from seeing what they carried. As the crates were unpacked, against all his earlier impulses Wolski experienced a surge of excitement. For decades, research of most kinds in Eastern Europe had been held back by a US government ban on the export of computer equipment. Now Wolski stood before eighteen shrink-wrapped mainframe computers that appeared to have come directly from the manufacturer in California.

"Our methods and their money." Wolski was startled; Golkov had an unnerving ability to come upon him silently.

Who are 'they' and who are 'us'? Wolski wondered, but did not ask.

The men who came with the computers were handpicked enthusiasts; hard-eyed and short-spoken. They seemed to have no interests beyond their machines and each other.

As the novelty of their presence ebbed away, the most surprising thing was not the high-intensity Western-style operation that had arrived apparently from nowhere, but the speed at which the main body of the Institute forgot the East Wing and what was going on within it. The two staffs did not meet and curiosity in the face of a brick wall soon faded. It was not long before life adjusted to the new normality.

Wolski anxiously waited to discover what was required of him. He kept a tiny hope alive. If he remained unobtrusive, perhaps he might be forgotten. Because frequent all-night working was anticipated, he was provided with a room to sleep in on the top floor in what had once been the servants' quarters. He liked the pitched roof and the little dormer window that looked down upon a broad avenue. It was a view that held a strange fascination for him. He had a distinct childhood memory of this same avenue, lined with tall trees and ornate buildings as grand as the Institute itself. But the war had intervened and now the picture was different. The trees and the fine buildings were gone and the thoroughfare was flanked by ranks of crumbling workers' flats in grey weather-stained concrete.

Alone in his small room he wrestled with the painful dilemma of the Night Watch. Should he carry on attending the meetings as if nothing had happened?

He dismissed the possibility, knowing that would infect them with the poison of Golkov. In the end, he could not escape a choice was between two kinds of betrayal: the dangerous treachery of pretending that nothing had happened, or the pretence that he was no longer a believer. He wrote a letter of resignation, the first one that the Night Watch had ever received. There were a few phone calls to which he responded in a deliberately offensive tone. He half believed that they would understand his tactics. But the people he was trying to protect were far too innocent to recognise the warning.

* * *

After a week of painful inactivity, Wolski was summoned to Golkov's office. Across the large room, a long conference table had been set up. A dozen people sat round it; all of them were in their late twenties or early thirties. Golkov was at the far end. At first, Wolski assumed that those at the table were also Russian, yet in the buzz of conversation he was certain he heard fragments of English.

"Professor, join us." Golkov's phrase hung between an invitation and an instruction. Without replying, Wolski sat at the opposite end of the table from Golkov, who began what sounded like a carefully prepared speech. Out of sight, below the table, Wolski gripped the sides of the chair in an attempt to counter the spinning sensation inside his head.

The main points of Golkov's oration registered with Wolski through a haze of detail. "Honour … speciality … report to Wolski … ground-breaking research … security … speak to each other only about work … Russian … co-ordinate … USA … importance … cellular … build from components … timescale … targets."

As Wolski began to build a mental picture of the project, he was all but overwhelmed by his own place at the centre of it. The meeting drew to a close but none of the participants spoke to him. Somehow, they seemed to regard his presence as a tiresome necessity. This did not trouble him; he had grown to be emotionally self-sufficient and was not disturbed by being treated as an outsider. Golkov was the last of them to leave and Wolski remained at the table. "You will find the papers in your office," Golkov said as he closed the door.

The office assigned to Wolski was furnished in a bizarre combination of fine 19th-century craftsmanship and shoddily made junk from the Soviet era.

But he noticed none of it and sat on a bent metal chair behind a grand baroque mahogany desk that was covered with blue hardback-bound computer printouts. It was the kind of prospect he had always relished and now there was the added incentive of isolating his mind from what was going on around him. He locked the door, drew the shutters, turned off the room lights and switched on the small spot lamp on his desk, and began to work.

In the days that followed, his submersion in the task became complete. Day after day, he studied the files and interrogated the computers. The long hours at his desk provided another advantage – a genuine justification for withdrawal from the Night Watch.

A vast amount of advanced theoretical work had been done but there was no obvious source material and each line of exploration terminated before a conclusion. It was the strangest collection of research material he had ever encountered.

* * *

Everyone involved with the project gradually came to live an island existence. The canteen was well supplied with German and American delicacies. They got used to the teams of watchers, the security checks and the permanent guard on the photocopier room. On the streets outside, there was a transition from lines of people with wads of money trying to buy goods from empty shops, to shops packed with goods and people with no money to buy them.

But Wolski noticed none of these things. The intensity of the work, and the retreat from the outside world, began to have an unanticipated effect. He became intoxicated by the task. Fear and moral reservations seemed to float away on a sea of data. Even his hatred of Golkov faded to a dull acceptance. It was like recognising time, space and gravity as facts of life.

Then, without warning, the adrenaline that fuelled his flight from reality ran out. The black despair was paralysing and he fell to earth with terrible speed.

He could not rid his mind of Golkov; he became an obsession, all-powerful; dominating every avenue of thought, blocking all attempts at escape. For some time, he struggled with thoughts of self-destruction.

Then for no apparent reason, it was as if he awoke. Like a dream, the terror was gone and he found himself laughing out loud. Only slowly did he understand why. Somewhere beneath conscious thought he had discovered a flaw in Golkov's judgement. With a sense of liberating shame, he realised that Golkov's threat to the Night Watch was a blunder. This awareness transformed Golkov from a giant with impenetrable armour, to an adversary diminished to human proportions.

Wolski treasured this realisation of Golkov's fallibility, like a convict finding a file in his prison cell and concealing it against an opportunity to escape.

* * *

"You see, we have powerful friends abroad."

It was no more than a chance remark by one of the Russian technicians when the second consignment of computers arrived, but it set Wolski on a path of action. It was in that instant that he realised that unless he too had 'powerful friends abroad' he would be crushed and with him any hope of influencing whatever it was that Golkov's masters wanted him to produce. He needed a plan, but had no notion of what to do or where to begin. Taking shelter in his tiny room high up in the East Wing he sat wakefully, deep into the night. He opened the window and stared down the long grey avenue that seemed to be awaiting a triumphant procession that somehow never arrived.

In the feeble pools of streetlight between the apartment blocks, a pair of hungry cats hunted for mice.

9

Jakob

Wolski was fasting; food was an intrusion, and he savoured the sharpness that hunger brought, as he searched the crevices of his mind for some way out of his dilemma. Just before first light, an answer came. It was triggered by the recollection of a half-remembered conversation, some years earlier, with Jakob, the only Jewish member of the Night Watch. He wondered whether he had subconsciously suppressed the memory of their brief exchange because Jakob had seemed to be moving towards confiding a secret, and secrets were dangerous. The two of them had first met shortly after Jakob returned from a conference in Germany. At the time, Wolski wondered if Jakob had been recruited by the West Germans, as they were then called. It was safer not to know the answer. They had met several times after that, at the Night Watch or in the company of mutual friends, but as if by some unspoken agreement, Jakob's visit to Germany was never mentioned again. But now it was time to take risks.

The next evening, Wolski boarded a tram to the Amama district and called Jakob's flat from a public phone. He tried to sound drunk and spoke in German with an attempt at a Silesian accent. There was a chance that any listeners might not understand. "I was passing your door and I have a bottle of Scottish whisky. Do you have any glasses?" His attempts at subterfuge sounded inept and he hoped Jakob recognised his voice.

Thankfully, Jakob was in good humour. "How much do you have left, old friend? If you can still manage the stairs, come up."

The climb to the fourth floor was further than Wolski had remembered and he collapsed, breathless, into a large old-fashioned armchair upholstered in threadbare William Morris fabric. It was one of Jakob's treasures.

"Glasses, you said." Jakob put two Czech crystal tumblers on the table.

Wolski pulled an unopened bottle of Glen Fiddich from his overcoat and broke the seal. Jakob was impressed.

"The best; you must have generous friends. A celebration?"

"I hope so." Wolski took a pen from his pocket. Feeling self-conscious, he wrote in the margin of the newspaper on the table: 'I need to talk to you'.

Despite his caution, he was alarmed when Jakob took the gesture seriously. He wrote: 'Unwise here. Sunday 10.30 – Café Mozart?'

Wolski nodded.

"Well, it's good to see you a happy man, Josef Wolski. Tell me about your life."

They talked boisterously, and swapped jokes and sad stories for several hours. Jakob was an easy man to talk to.

* * *

Jakob sat waiting. Café Mozart was in a leafy park beside the river – an attempt to import the Danube to the Vistula.

It was not an idea that appealed to Jakob and he spoke with loud mock-anger as Wolski sat down.

"Why Café Mozart? Why not Café Chopin — a good Pole?

That's the sadness of this country – everything worth having we have to import."

The waiter arrived and they ordered coffee and Viennese pastries. The interruption gave Wolski a chance to think of a reply.

"But Chopin escaped and lived in the Mediterranean sunshine," Wolski said with as much irony as he could manage.

Jakob stared at him thoughtfully. "And what is on your mind?" he said. "Imports or escape?" The moment had come quickly; there could be no avoiding it. He had to trust this shambling friendly bear of a man.

"Both," Wolski said.

Jakob again lapsed into one of his thoughtful silences. When he spoke, it was as if he had not heard Wolski. "What a strange time this is. You wish to speak to me in confidence. In my home I cannot be sure that this is possible, yet here in public we have a good chance of speaking in private.

A very special kind of madness, I think." He burst into a ready peal of laughter of the kind that is a refuge for people with little to laugh about. Wolski tried to get the conversation back on track. "When you were in Germany, I gained the impression that you formed, shall we say, an alliance. You began to speak about it once and I stopped you."

"Why should you wish to speak of such a possibility now?" Jakob asked guardedly.

Wolski ignored the question, pressing his original point. "Did you? Did you make friends in the West - reliable friends?"

Jakob replied sharply. "No! I do not believe in, as you put it, 'alliances'." He used the word contemptuously. The conversation was halted as the waiter brought their coffee and cream-filled Windbeutel.

It was clear that Jakob wanted to make his own pace. "Here we sit by the river, not any river but the Vistula, drinking good coffee and eating imitation Viennese cakes…" Jakob lapsed into silence; his mind seemed to drift away and his gaze became fixed on the middle distance. Wolski waited patiently.

When Jakob spoke, his mind was in another time. "The very worst of them were Austrians. Did you know that? I wasn't here then of course, not then… I was a child at the time, my father sent me to Turkey, my uncle ran part of the family carpet business in Istanbul." As any Pole would, Wolski knew exactly what Jakob was talking about. "Even now, more than sixty years later, I feel guilty for being absent.

I survived not by having courage, nor skill or resistance, but simply by being somewhere else. In the Ghetto rising, when more than three hundred thousand died, I lived comfortably abroad. Can you imagine how it must have been on the streets near here? Three hundred thousand people killed." He repeated the fact. "Three hundred thousand, here in a tiny part of this city. Can you possibly imagine it?"

Wolski knew the facts well but had never appreciated the depth to which they touched Jakob, who always seemed to live in a haze of goodwill and joviality.

"And while this slaughter was going on, here beside this very river our 'allies', the Red Army, on Stalin's orders, sat and watched, waiting for the Germans to exterminate us so that they would be saved the trouble. A couple of Russian generals protested but they were liquidated. And how did it all begin? With our other 'allies', the British. Though they had the decency to declare war when Hitler invaded us, they were totally powerless to help. They watched while our cavalry charged the Panzers, and the Luftwaffe destroyed Warsaw and machine-gunned refugees."

Wolski was overwhelmed by the torrent of emotion his question had unleashed. But Jakob was not finished yet.

"And when Auschwitz, Birkenau and Treblinka were making their contribution to six million Jewish dead, our 'allies' in London and Washington simply chose not to believe it. And you talk to me of 'alliances'." Jakob stopped suddenly and Wolski did not know how to respond.

He began clumsily. "I'm sorry–"

Jakob cut him short. "Don't be, there has been too much sorrow beside this river." He emptied his cold coffee cup. Without taking his eyes off the grounds that remained in the bottom, he said, "Yes, I will answer your question. They did approach me. Not the Germans, the British. I said no."

"Will you tell me about it?"

"Your coffee is getting cold," Jakob replied.

Wolski drank and attacked the giant cream cake. Jakob did the same, and then spoke slowly and thoughtfully.

"Confession, they say, is good for the soul, but in this city, even today, it can be very bad for the health."

"I am not a priest, I'm someone looking for a guide," Wolski replied. "I'm trapped in something that I'm being forced to create; some fearful game being played by the Americans and the Russians, or to be more exact, some Americans and some Russians. They want a test-bed for their fantasies and they have chosen to set it up here..."

Jakob interrupted. "I think it best that you tell me no more. I will confide just this. There is a man, his name is Thornhill."

Wolski nearly wrote down the name but instantly realised the folly of doing so. "I met him in Hamburg. It was when I delivered my last lecture at the Academy of Arts. They put on a concert for the speakers – Bach Viola Sonatas. I remember it clearly; music to move the soul. He also had a passion for Bach, this man Thornhill. There was a reception after the concert; that's how we began talking."

"You spoke to him more than once?" Wolski was beginning to betray his eagerness.

"Yes. I met him again just before I left. I was invited to a cocktail party arranged by the British Council. We talked for a long time. He made it plain that he wanted to make me an offer. They were looking for 'honest eyes and ears', he said."

"How did you reply?" Wolski asked.

"I told him that 'honest eyes and ears' working for him would be a contradiction in terms. He laughed and told me to contact him if ever I should come to another view. I refused to take an address or phone number but I recall that, though he was based in London, he had responsibilities in Germany and used an office behind the Kunsthalle in Hamburg."

It was an anti-climax. Wolski was disappointed. He had confided much and in return had got nothing usable.

"Shall we walk?" he said as he waved at the waiter to bring the bill.

"What will you do?" Jakob asked.

"I don't know what I can do. I only know what I need to do."

"Go on."

"I need to establish credibility, to find somebody of influence on the outside so that, if and when the time comes, I can act quickly. But it's essential that I do this without strings. I'm already the servant of one puppet master and will not become tangled up with another."

"Difficult," Jakob said. Silently, they walked beside the Vistula. In the dappled spring shadows, the new green of the trees stood vividly against the sky and windowpanes across the river glinted with reflected sunlight. But the river remained untouched by the uncertain spring warmth. Its source was too far into the cold interior to yield to so transient an influence.

"Can I help?" Jakob asked.

It was an offer Wolski had not expected and he was unsure how to reply. "Perhaps."

"Marriage is a wonderful institution, one which you have never entered. I, on the other hand, have passed through its portals twice."

For a moment, Wolski resented Jakob wandering off into a story that he was sure would be full of self-pity, but instinct told him that this was Jakob's way of explaining something important. Wolski had never thought of Jakob as married and was puzzled as to why he brought up the subject now. They walked with the sun at their back and it cast long shadows across their path.

"Hannah, my first wife, left me. It was me or Israel," Jakob said. He waved his walking stick across his portly shadow on the gravel path. "How could I win?" It was some time before he spoke again.

"She has an apartment in Tel Aviv and teaches history. Very happy, I hear."

He stopped for another long moment and then spoke more quickly, as if not wanting to let his mind dwell on the details. "Not long afterwards, I met Natasha. She is, she was, Lithuanian, lectured in musicology here in Warsaw. That's where we met. Her husband…" He paused. "He was a psychopath, or at least he behaved like one; a failed violinist, I believe. He frequently beat her senseless and eventually they were divorced. But he couldn't come to terms with it and still appeared at her flat from time to time, full of rage and hate. Once he nearly killed her. So there we were; I was lonely, she was afraid, not just of him, but of life. That's how we came together." He halted, leaned on the parapet overlooking the river and lapsed into silence. "Cold and grey," he said when he eventually spoke.

Wolski had learned not to interrupt.

"That was the end of her; the end of us," Jakob said, staring into the water. It was a riddle that Wolski did not understand.

Erratically the story came out. "She was drowned, swimming in the sea … we were on holiday … the Baltic that she loved. Endless sand dunes and ceaseless wind, but it was home to her. It was the water, the cold water, it gave her cramp. I saw it happen but I could do nothing. I never learnt to swim. All I could do was scream for help. Scream, scream, scream." He repeated the word, softly pounding it with his gloved fist into the unyielding granite of the river wall. It was an expression of such helplessness that Wolski was left without words. Jakob turned away from the river and looked directly at Wolski with an ironic smile.

"So you see, I know what it is to call for help."

Wolski was touched that Jakob should reveal so painful a secret but disturbed by the comparison with his own position, and it was a relief when Jakob's solemn mood slowly changed to one of deliberate cheerfulness. "Why do I tell you all this?"

He strode on without waiting for an answer and Wolski had to walk quickly to catch up with him. "Because what is left is Anya, Natasha's daughter. You must meet her." He spoke emphatically and Wolski was unsure how to reply.

Wolski couldn't see how meeting this woman would help and was cautious about being drawn into the tangle of Jakob's emotions, but he was given no opportunity to express his doubts.

"Come here again; Café Mozart, lunchtime next Sunday," Jakob said, and hurried away without further explanation.

As the low sun began to lose its grip on the afternoon, Wolski wandered alone among the departing crowds. Without conscious thought, he found himself again overlooking the broad river where Jakob had stood. The light began to fade and as an icy east wind arose, his mood congealed into cold sadness.

Jakob, though loveable, was unstable. His help was impossible to accept. He had chosen the wrong man.

10

Cortexean

In the week that followed, everything changed. Wolski recognised that until meeting Jakob he had unconsciously believed that, despite his acute anxiety, nothing truly terrible could happen in so public a place as an academic institution in the centre of a major city. It was a phrase from the long conversation with Jakob that destroyed such comfort: 'The Nazi's prototype concentration camp was in Dachau, a suburb of Munich. It was there that they devised everything that was to follow: medical experiments, gas chambers, everything. But nobody noticed; outside the wire, life went on as normal.'

Jakob's insight lay heavily on Wolski as he arrived at his office that Monday morning. More files were waiting for him. He gathered them up and took them to his small bedroom with its now familiar sloping ceiling at the top of the building, where he had managed to have a computer terminal installed. He sat for a while with the printouts stacked neatly in front of him. He sensed that they would provide a revelation, but feared to begin.

In the street below, a woman from the workers' flats was pushing a pram that had a buckled wheel. With one hand she attempted to keep it in a straight line, while with the other she tried to control two rebellious children, who both looked under three years old.

It was an uneven struggle and the woman was close to the edge of her ability to cope. She stopped and shouted at them.

When neither took any notice, she lashed out. They both began to cry and she shoved them forward. As the children resentfully moved on, the misshapen wheel collapsed. It was some sort of final straw; the woman crumpled over the pram and started to sob. The children, now alarmed by their mother's tears, clung to her long shapeless skirt and cried along with her. Wolski felt a surge of envy at the humanity of the little tripod of figures. Eventually, the woman pulled the pram backwards on three wheels towards the graffiti-covered doorway of the flats. The children followed, knuckling the tears from their eyes. Wolski opened the first of the files.

The title page read:

CORTEXEAN – Section 1

A Briefing on the Development of Psychological Control Mechanisms for Political and Sociological Purposes.

By Major R. T. Doubleday
US Army Medical Corps.

The first section was an extract from a US Congressional Committee hearing dated November 1952.

Report of the Psychological Condition of Prisoners Following Internment at Fu Chin Interrogation Centre, North Korea.

Wolski scanned the pages.

> The broadcasts and appearances on news film of US military personnel, though obviously under the psychological control of the enemy, or perhaps because of this fact, have had a significant impact on the morale of our forces. Investigations into Chinese techniques show that this success was achieved very simply.
>
> At no time was any attempt made to influence the psychological state of the main body of the prisoners. In the first days of captivity, the Chinese observed the behaviour of each group of men. This allowed them to identify the actual or potential leaders who were then separated from the main group, and subjected to sleep deprivation and disorientation techniques. All but the mentally strongest rapidly became compliant and readily suggestible to the enemy's viewpoint on a wide range of political and social matters.
>
> The few who did not go under were subjected to a device that the Chinese claimed never failed. It consisted of a small, brightly lit room, the walls, floor and ceiling of which were made of stainless-steel mirrors. The victim could not at any time look at anything but himself. Insanity, either temporary or permanent, often resulted.
>
> With the leaders gone, the enemy found it no longer necessary even to mount a guard over the remaining prisoners...

Wolski stopped reading and closed the file. The idea of a prisoner in a box of mirrors brought on a panic attack. It was of a kind he had experienced several times since Golkov arrived at the Institute but this was much worse than before. He tried to analyse what was happening to him. It was more than a physical fear. It was terror at the prospect of his own mental disintegration.

Desperately he looked down into the street, half hoping to see the woman with her broken pram and crying children, or anything. that would offer an image of humanity to set against the dread that threatened to overwhelm him. But there was nobody there.

With great effort, he made himself sit quietly until the sharp edge of fear subsided into a dull feeling of nausea. He swallowed hard and began reading again.

The next items were case histories: experiments with hypnosis, LSD and other mind-control substances by various agencies of the US government and the scandal that followed these secrets becoming public in the 1970s.

More up to date was an analysis of the development of Smart drugs and the arguments for and against their use in expanding functional intelligence, learning capacity and memory.

The page read:

CORTEXEAN
2 – Objectives (deleted)
3 – Formulation (deleted)
4 – Compounds
5 – Trials
6 – Results

Wolski did not understand why sections of the document had been deleted. He read with increasing speed and growing disbelief. By the end of the afternoon, it became clear that he was faced with a proposition even more alarming than any he had earlier imagined. He was looking at a technological blind alley, abandoned during the opening stages of the Cold War. He knew enough to realise that now, computers, genetics and bioengineering could open a catacomb of madness that had been sealed off half a century ago. He closed the files and tried to empty his head. For some reason he could not understand.

One of the many stories Clara had told as a child came to mind: 'You shall be as Gods.' It was the promise the Serpent made to Eve in the Garden of Eden.

He felt an urgent need for fresh air, opened the window and breathed deeply. But the room still seemed to bear in upon him. He hurried out onto the landing, down the back stairs, past the guard and into the street. It had begun to rain, but it was some time before he noticed. The slow, steady drizzle made him feel cocooned from the stream of umbrella-carrying office workers hurrying home at the end of the day. He wandered far, and it was after dark, in an unfamiliar part of the city, that he finally came to a decision.

* * *

"I cannot continue," he said in Golkov's office. A taxi had brought him back to the Institute, cold and shivering.

"You are soaking wet, Professor." Golkov stated the obvious in a tone heavy with contempt at Wolski's emotional condition.

"I have been thinking–" Wolski began, as if to explain his sodden state.

"You should be working, not thinking," Golkov interrupted sharply.

Wolski would not be diverted. "What you demand is outrageous. I am asked to construct a set of field trials from a series of unknown compounds, unknown because you have deleted the information about their formulation. There are eleven of these compounds, which means that the variable combinations of each run into tens, perhaps hundreds of thousands. The whole thing is preposterous – totally unscientific."

Wolski's anger seemed not to touch Golkov. "And the final section of the data, with what does that deal?"

Wolski thought for a moment, half hoping that as a non-scientist, Golkov could somehow be misled. He hesitated before answering. "The final section? It's a computer model of the chemistry in the human brain relating to changing mood states."

Golkov replied sharply. "So your task is not to blunder in the dark but to identify the compound profiles which match the patterns in the analytical software."

"In plain language, to play God with the human mind," Wolski replied coldly.

"Now you understand," Golkov said, as if to a slow-learning child.

"It's unscientific, it's unethical and I won't do it."

"Unscientific?" Golkov was genuinely incredulous. "We stand on the brink of a great scientific advance. How can you call what we are doing unscientific? And as for being unethical, don't be pedantic, people have always manipulated the emotions of others: coffee, music, speeches, drugs, sex, alcohol. All we are doing is trying to locate the volume control."

"Why?" asked Wolski.

"That is not a question for you," Golkov replied. "You are a scientist, not a philosopher and certainly not a politician."

"I am a human being; that entitles me to ask."

"Yes, yes, yes, of course." Golkov had a rare ability to transform himself from a tyrant to the voice of unassailable reason. "But why should we argue?" He spoke almost sorrowfully. "Look at the opportunity; we both have serious responsibilities, but in the end I am merely a manager. But you…" He made a gesture like a conductor acknowledging a virtuoso soloist. "You are a creator." The flattery only added to Wolski's rising nausea.

Golkov continued in full flood. "And here is the biggest challenge of your career. This is world class, this is fame, this is power; this is a chance to change the future." Wolski was appalled to find, for a fleeting moment, there was a measure of attraction in the proposition. Was it possible to negotiate a way out? No. "It is damnation," he said in a whisper.

Golkov seemed not to hear. "Think of all this as a meeting of East and West, our methods and their money." It was the second time Wolski had heard Golkov use the phrase. "It's a way of making peace, without the need for a war first. An end to destruction," Golkov added.

Wolski tried to confront Golkov's insincerity. "Then why the secrecy, the threats?"

"The secrecy? That, surely, must be obvious. A vast sum of money, several billions of dollars, has gone into the project. An investment of that scale must be protected."

"And the threats?" Wolski asked.

"Merely a tool of management; as you know, a highly efficient one. Tell me a more effective way of avoiding leaks or delays that we simply cannot afford?"

The fear and anger that had fuelled Wolski's revolt had run out. He couldn't think of a reply and sat looking blankly at Golkov. He was exhausted and Golkov knew it.

"It is essential for us to be sure of the full support of key people. If you are with us, you have nothing to fear, and we need never talk of such matters again." He smiled one of his cold smiles that didn't reach the eyes. "You have a great objective and the resources to achieve it, resources you would have to fight for years to get in one of those self-important places like Stanford, MIT or Oxford. What more do you want?"

Wolski wasn't listening. He had a question which had puzzled him from the beginning and again, he sought an answer. "Why here, why this country? Why not Moscow, California, the Third World, anywhere but here?"

"Freedom," Golkov said flatly.

"Freedom!" Wolski was astonished.

"Yes, of course. Here we are free to do as we please. California is too public for this stage of the work, the Third World too primitive or too unstable. And as for what was the Soviet Union, the facts speak for themselves. Here things are almost perfect, even if the weather is sometimes unkind," he said, with a sorrowful look at Wolski's shapeless, waterlogged clothes.

"We are an independent nation now, you cannot behave as you used to," Wolski said with indignation.

"That is exactly the point," Golkov replied. "When you were part of the Warsaw Pact and COMECON, there were committees, local Soviets and constant interference from the Ministry of Foreign Affairs. Now, you follow in the footsteps of your first anti-Soviet President – a good man, a Catholic who went to Mass on the way to the office at seven a.m. every day. But what do such presidents rule? Just the top five centimetres of the country," Golkov said, measuring the space between finger and thumb. "Below that, if you stay out of sight, you can buy what you like. Sometimes we pay in money, that's the cheapest way. Sometimes in power or ambition, and in other cases, we use the currency of fear – it's more expensive, but has remarkable purchasing power." Golkov's explanation left Wolski with no ready reply. "So you see, it's a free market now. A set of contracts between buyer and seller. The capitalist system at its simplest, at its purest."

Wolski could all too easily see how the pieces fitted together and felt a welcome surge of fury. He tried to hold on to the strength of his anger but it died away. Like a man trapped in a fast-flooding cellar, he felt defeat rising all around him.

It was only the realisation that he must not allow Golkov to sense the scale of his victory that made Wolski continue to sound defiant. "And what if your calculations are wrong? What if the individual whose cooperation you want to buy refuses to sell?"

The hard edge returned to Golkov's voice. "In our experience, that is simply a matter of price. A person making such a decision would be forcing someone else – friends, colleagues and perhaps their families – to pay for such self-indulgence. Most reasonable people would see that as too expensive an option." He paused for effect, and then walked round the desk to stand over Wolski as he drove the point home. "It really is just a matter of price," he said. "You are a reasonable man, Professor, and will do what any reasonable person would do; use your influence for good, rather than cause others to make sacrifices on behalf of your conscience." Golkov smiled again.

"That is evil." Wolski's voice was thick with emotion.

"It is practical," Golkov replied. "After all, in this of all countries you should know the result of the cavalry charging the tanks."

Wolski looked away so as not to let Golkov see that he was fighting back tears. "I am cold, I need to change, and there is a lot of work to do."

11

The Bialystok Road

Time passed; was it weeks, months or years? Wolski neither knew nor cared. The anaesthetic of work made the pain bearable. In the nation outside, there was chaos as the last traces of the old system faded into oblivion. From crude oil to crude sex, the invisible Barons of the new prosperity fought over monopolies in every kind of human need and want. But none of this intruded upon Wolski's monastic existence.

Then, one Sunday night during a violent rainstorm came another turning point. It was sometime between midnight and one in the morning when a battered panel van, with headlights off and wheels spinning, lurched towards a large log-built house, half a kilometre down a cart track off the main road to Bialystok, capital of the former Soviet Republic of Belarus. The vehicle's destination had once been the weekend Dacha of some senior Russian bureaucrat. Now, without its tenants and their access to government funds, it had suffered severely from the ravages of long frozen winters and short blistering summers. At the edge of the vast forest of birch encircling the house, a pair of huge Russian trucks was hidden.

In the back of the approaching van sat two men, deafened by the cacophony of the rain pounding on the roof. The van driver got out, slipped on the soft earth and fell onto one knee. He swore and made an attempt to wipe the mud off his new American jeans, but quickly realised it was hopeless. The men in the back of the van watched with sullen amusement as the driver struggled through the mud to the nearest of the trucks. He opened the door and climbed in.

"I've got them," he said to the two silhouetted figures in the cab. "Fifty US dollars apiece."

The smaller of the two pulled an envelope from an inside pocket, slit it open and counted out the money.

"And fifty for me, that's what we agreed," the driver added, as if uncertain that the bargain would be kept.

The man counted out five more ten-dollar bills and said, with a heavy Russian accent, "they are to be there by three, unloaded and away by four thirty and back here by seven. There's help at the other end to unload. We're leaving now; wait five minutes, then move."

The two Russians climbed out of the truck and picked their way through the mud to a Zil limousine parked deeper among the trees.

"So the price of silence remains affordable," the Russian said as he took the envelope from his coat and divided the remaining dollar bills with his colleague. The Zil started reluctantly and drove slowly forward to the centre of the track where the ground was hardest.

"Silence is all that's worth buying in this country," the second man said.

As the limousine departed, the van driver opened the rear doors and waved a ten-dollar bill at each of the men inside. "Out. Ten dollars now and ten more when you get back – if you're on time. If you're not, you'll have the Russians to answer to."

The two men got out of the van and traded exposure to the downpour against an opportunity to stretch their stiffened limbs. Like a pair of bad-tempered dogs, they tried to shake off the rain as they plodded and slid across the mud to the trucks. The van driver disappeared into the trees. Moments later he reappeared at the wheel of a four-wheel-drive Audi that disappeared at speed towards the main road.

"Lucky bastard," one of the men said.

The truck engines were warm and started easily. The big heaters, designed for Siberia, began to do their work and both drivers started to relax. The mood did not last long. The rain and unaccustomed traffic had churned the track into a quagmire. The Polish drivers, unfamiliar with the heavy Russian-built vehicles, had difficulty in controlling them. As they inched forward, the rain grew heavier and the noise of it on the bare metal roofs of the cabs made their ears ring and drowned out thought. In the lead truck, the driver reached for the vodka bottle inside his jacket. It was a badly timed move, because at the same moment the truck began to slide sideways off the track. The driver cursed and slammed the gear lever into reverse, but the wheels spun and dug deeper into the mud. He tried going forward again, but the wheels continued to spin and soon the truck became completely bogged down. His first thought was to stay in the cab, keep the heater running and wait for daylight. It was fear of their Russian paymasters that drove the drivers out into the rain with fire axes taken from the back of the cab.

They spent hours hacking down birch branches to give the wheels grip. Metre by metre the trucks moved forward until they regained firmer ground where the trees began to thin out at the edge of the forest. By the time they got to the Warsaw–Bialystok road, they were cold, wet, angry and hours behind schedule.

* * *

Wolski was up early that morning after a rare weekend of retreat from his own apartment. At the island tram stop in the middle of the street there was no shelter from the rain and he joined the sullen line of waiting people. Everyone was listening for the tell-tale metallic sound of the tram from round the bend in the road that would rescue them from the drenching rain. Nobody spoke. It was as if after the riots marking the fall of Communism, the tens of thousands who had shouted slogans in the street had run out of things to say. The dreary reality of daily life spoke for itself. Traffic sloshed by, throwing up sheets of dirty water. Rain dipped off the brim of Wolski's hat. Using a trick learnt in childhood, he let his eyes focus on the droplets, reducing his vision of the street to a distant watery blur. It helped him think.

A week previously, Golkov had made an offer of a car and driver. Now, in the merciless rain, Wolski wondered if he had made the wrong choice.

He told himself that he had turned the offer down out of pride, which was true, but not the whole truth. More important was the fact that he didn't want to give away information about his movements. A car and driver would make private meetings impossible.

The insidious damp was seeping through his old overcoat before the ancient red and cream tramcar rounded the bend. He arrived at the Institute a little before seven thirty. As he neared the steps to the entrance of the East Wing, two mud-covered trucks splashed and thumped along the rutted road and through the gate that led to the central courtyard. Wolski hurried to his office. Draping his soaking overcoat across the tepid radiator beneath the window, he watched the vehicles being unloaded.

First came cages of animals; rabbits in a motley collection of colours, agitated by the strangeness of the journey. Then came a succession of crates, boxes and six brightly coloured containers that

Wolski recognised as housing mainframe computer drives. He went downstairs to the laboratory where the cages were being noisily stacked in the holding area. Seizing the opportunity to gather information, he approached the drivers. They were covered in mud. Instinct told Wolski it was important not to appear surprised.

"Coffee and a shower, something to eat?" he asked affably.

The larger of the two men answered for them both. "Coffee and vodka. No time for anything else, we are already late."

Wolski led them to the kitchenette behind the lab where he produced coffee and a half bottle of vodka from the supply that the lab technicians kept hidden in the equipment store.

"How far behind schedule are you? Do you need to use the phone?" Wolski enquired helpfully.

"No, there's no phone, we just have to get back." The driver was beginning to sound nervous. "We should have been away more than three hours ago."

"Very well," said Wolski. "You'll find what you need in there." He stepped into the outer room and, hidden from their line of sight, he could hear them talking in low voices. Though he couldn't catch the whole conversation, he heard an argument about the road to Bialystok and kilometre post one twenty or one twenty-five. Wolski opened the door again and the men stopped speaking.

"I have to go now. Is there anything for me to sign?" he asked cheerfully.

Back in his office, Wolski put the pieces together. It was an operation designed to eliminate any direct contact between the point where the cargo originated and its destination. The drivers were probably black market heavies recruited for just the one job. Since they arrived at seven thirty and were more than three hours late, they were obviously intended to be away long before any of the Institute staff arrived. It must have been the mud that delayed them, and that mud was probably somewhere near kilometre post one hundred or one hundred and twenty-five on the Bialystok road. The radiator showed no sign of heating up, and more in hope than expectation Wolski draped another part of his wet coat across the top of it.

He tried to discipline his thoughts. If Golkov's people had taken such precautions to avoid anyone finding out where the trucks were coming from, it was clearly dangerous to be seen asking questions. Fifty-four kilometres further down the Bialystok road lay the border with Belarus.

Wolski still thought of it as the Soviet frontier and with justification. The Republic was notorious as the least reformed of all the former Soviet territories.

Laboratory animals had always made Wolski feel uncomfortable. Though he would witheringly dismiss sentimentality in others and not admit it in himself, years of constructing experiments and teaching students to carry them out had not hardened him to the emotions that the creatures showed. After the noise, darkness and strange movements of the journey they were terrified. Walking between the cages, he heard Golkov's voice on the other side of the lab.

"Professor, a word if you please."

Golkov had never before been seen in the storage area and it was unlikely that the animals were sufficiently important for him to check on their arrival personally. Wolski wondered about the other cargo the trucks had brought. They walked to the far corner of the loading bay to escape the noise of cages being dragged across the uneven concrete floor.

"Time is getting short," said Golkov.

"Life is short," replied Wolski. He was in a bitter mood.

"Shorter for some than others," Golkov said in an almost friendly way, before launching into a list of instructions.

"There is a lot of work to do. The first trial is scheduled for Friday. You will need to analyse the data that has just arrived and report your detailed recommendations to me no later than Wednesday evening. You may have as much computer time as you require. The staff have been instructed to offer you every assistance." Wolski nodded and began to move away, but Golkov wasn't finished.

"One more thing. You will see from the printouts that the data is divided into modules. You will have access only to those that concern experimentation, not formulation." In a tone deliberately calculated to mock Wolski, he added, "Information is power, as comrade Stalin said."

"And incomplete information is dangerous," Wolski snapped. He wanted to hide the value of what was being handed to him.

Almost without interruption, for four days and most of four nights, Wolski worked in the inner lab. With a kind of reverence, the staff watched from a distance. Only Nina would occasionally venture inside with a cup of coffee and the offer of something to eat, which was usually refused. Even Golkov stayed away, keeping in touch with progress through Petrovitch, the leader of the Physical Experimentation Team.

Eventually, Wolski gave in. He took his notes and printouts up to his attic room, laid them on the narrow bed and began to assemble them into a logical order. It was a task he couldn't complete. Fully clothed, he collapsed on top of the papers.

When he awoke, he didn't know what time it was or how long he had slept. A great weight of fatigue still bore heavily upon him, and he was only half-conscious when there was a knock on the door. It was Nina.

"Professor, Doctor Golkov wants to see you." There was no answer. "Now, without delay," she said cautiously, unsure how far Golkov's delegated authority should take her.

"Ten minutes." Wolski hauled himself off the bed, turned on the tap at the small hand basin and splashed cold water onto his face. The world slowly came into focus as he tried to gather the thoughts that had forced their way into his exhausted sleep. Nina hammered on the door again.

"Coming," he said, and picked up the papers from the bed. They were compressed where he had lain, and still warm with damp body heat. It seemed absurd that they could contain something of so much importance. In Golkov's office, Wolski handed over the documents.

"Give these to Petrovitch, they're what he needs to start the trials.

The discs are in the computer room; the cross-references are all listed. He should have no difficulty." With that, he turned away without waiting for an answer. Though his mind was still crying out for sleep, he was desperate to get out of the building.

In the street, the recent rain had washed the atmosphere clean of the pollution that usually overlaid the city. Not far from the Institute, he came to a small park that had become a gathering place for market gardeners who met there before venturing further into the city to sell their produce. In the far corner was the more permanent population of the garden, the raw vodka drinkers who had begun to appear on the streets in ever-larger numbers. Wolski lay down on a bench in the unaccustomed sunshine. He fell into a half-sleep among a comforting babble of voices talking about the onion crop and the prices that their tomatoes and celery would fetch. Like a corpse rising from a coffin, a prostrate drunk clutching an empty bottle sprang half upright.

"God save Walesa," he shouted, and fell back into a horizontal stupor, but nobody noticed.

When Wolski finally woke, his mind was full of disconnected images, words and ideas. The park was empty and the only trace of the drunk was the empty vodka bottle. Wolski picked it up and dropped it onto the mound of rubbish overflowing from the bin near the gate. When he got back to the Institute, there was intense activity.

Petrovitch was behaving like a Beach Marshal at an invasion, giving orders for equipment and cages to be moved into a new configuration in the main lab.

"Today," Petrovitch pronounced, "today we begin." Everyone stopped to listen.

There was a shining enthusiasm about the man that, despite his Slavic features, put Wolski in mind of the triumphant young Storm Troopers, whose faces were among his first childhood memories. Perhaps that's what these people are, he thought, the Storm Troopers of a new age.

The first experiment began in an atmosphere of tension. Despite having given strict instructions for everyone to be on time, Golkov was himself nearly twenty minutes late. Wolski guessed that he had been on the phone to whoever it was that was waiting for the results. He guessed accurately.

"Time is pressing. I have undertaken that we shall produce the first observations by the end of today," Golkov said. "Mr Petrovitch..."

Petrovitch stepped forward to address the little group. He spoke like a sergeant major and Wolski had the absurd notion that he was wearing medals and regimental insignia on his stiff white lab coat.

"These are the first live tests of CORTEXEAN. The formulations that we will now test are those constructed by Professor Wolski, according to the computer models. Each of them has a predicted effect profile. The purpose of these tests is to verify the accuracy of the computer predictions of behaviour, before we move on to the next phase of tests on larger mammals." Wolski was a silent spectator as the first group of rabbits was prepared for the tests.

The technicians set the instruments, and the video and audio recorders were started.

"Each specimen will be injected within a timeframe of one minute." This was a moment that Wolski had hated since he was a student. The trusting creatures were about to be betrayed by their masters.

The first injections were given and the time clock started. Nothing happened and nobody spoke. The animals seemed completely unaffected. Five minutes passed, then ten. After half an hour, Nina appeared with bitter black coffee and a few biscuits. There was a jar of American coffee whitener on the tray, but nobody took any.

Wolski broke the silence. "The test suggests an error in the computer model. The prediction is for noticeable effect in less than five minutes."

"You mean you have made a mistake, Professor?" Golkov asked coldly.

"Perhaps, but I don't believe so. It is much more likely to be in the original data on which the predictions were made."

"So what do you suggest?"

"We must check the data," Wolski said.

"How long will that take?" Golkov asked.

"Ten days, perhaps as little as a week. We have massive computing power here," Wolski said optimistically.

"Totally impossible; we must proceed with what we have," Golkov said dismissively.

"No. We can't do that. It would be like depending on figures when you don't know if someone has added in the date."

Golkov ignored Wolski's protest. "Mr Petrovitch, we shall continue. Double the dose."

But Wolski would not be so easily silenced. "You must realise that it could be dangerous. Quite literally, we don't know what we're doing."

"You may not know what you're doing, Professor. I know exactly what I'm doing," Golkov snapped. Wolski drew breath to protest further.

"Enough," Golkov said, like a teacher short of patience. "Unless you remain silent, I shall have you removed."

Wolski said nothing. His first impulse was to walk out, but like Golkov, though for different reasons, he needed to see the results. The second group of animals was injected and the recorders started. A mood of anti-climax had descended on the watchers; they expected nothing. Then it happened. The results were almost instantaneous. It was in the animals' features that the change was first noticeable; a look of ferocity possessed them. The log showed that it was at one minute and twenty seconds that the killing began. The rabbits tore into each other. Blood, fur and cries of pain were mixed in a convulsing heap. After less than three minutes a single animal remained alive. Its entrails were exposed and it died while tearing at the carcasses of its mates.

"We have it, we have it," Golkov shouted.

Wolski dashed to the kitchen and vomited into the sink, which was full of Nina's coffee grounds.

12

Hamburg

When Sunday came, Wolski sat alone in Café Mozart at a corner table overshadowed by trees. He should have asked Jakob what 'lunchtime' meant. He felt exposed and tried hard to control his anxiety. It was one forty-five and he had been waiting since twelve thirty. Twice he had held off an impatient waiter with orders of Pilsner. Just before two, they appeared. An unlikely pair, he was squat, dark and Central European, she tall with long, fair hair and the severe, elegant looks of the far North. Jakob was in a generous mood and made no mention of their late arrival. They sat down opposite Wolski.

"My dear Josef, here is my beloved daughter Anya. We grew up together. She, as you see, to womanhood and me to equanimity."

Wolski became even more certain that he had made a serious mistake. He was about to accept help from a man who was at best an eccentric, and his daughter who was of such striking appearance that, if questioned, anyone, man or woman, was certain to remember her. The waiter appeared, anxious at last to get an order. Jakob waved aside the offer of a menu and without consultation ordered for them all: Rhamschnitzel with noodles and rotkhol and a bottle of Bull's Blood. A dark Hungarian red wine.

When the waiter was out of earshot he spoke again. "I have a plan," Jakob announced with conspiratorial pride. The declaration made Wolski try to think of some polite form of rejection, but it was Anya who spoke next.

"You are a remarkable man, Mr Wolski; you have brought my father back to life."

Jakob corrected her. "Professor, my dear, he is Professor Wolski." He continued with rising excitement. "what my daughter means is that I had begun to think my existence was at an end, at least as far as doing anything significant was concerned. Now you offer me a renaissance of the soul," he said with a large, expansive gesture.

It was exactly the kind of emotional entanglement that Wolski dreaded, and all his life had struggled to avoid.

"It may be that I am offering you death," Wolski said. Jakob looked at him with the steady penetrating gaze that was slowly becoming familiar. Very deliberately he said, "Sometimes life and death are the same thing."

Wolski surrendered. "Tell me what you have in mind."

Jakob was eager to oblige. "First we must recognise that we are amateurs. This means that though we lack experience, we have the advantage of surprise. Anyone we approach will not know who we are. This Thornhill, Jack Thornhill, the person of whom I spoke; contacting him at the Hamburg office could be dangerous. But I remember he told me he sometimes had business in the St Pauli district, usually a couple of times a month. I didn't want to listen then; I didn't want to become involved."

Anya interrupted. "Why should this be so difficult? Why not simply telephone the Embassy from a phone booth?"

Jakob answered. "Because we must not act like helpless supplicants. We must appear to have substantial abilities, so that our target will believe that we are his equal. If we want him to act to our advantage, it is essential that he should put a high value on what we say to him. Only in that way can we retain control of what happens. The contact must be a mystery. It must intrigue him, and to do that we need to capture his imagination not just professionally, but personally. If we can manage that, we shall have his undivided attention."

The logic, Wolski thought, was sound, but Jakob spoiled its effect by what came next. "And besides, I like mysteries," he said with his odd, disturbing laugh. Wolski's doubts grew firmer. The food arrived and immediately Jakob began to eat ferociously.

Anya looked embarrassed and Wolski poured the wine. Jakob looked up.

"If in your life you had ever been truly hungry you would know that it forever changes your attitude to food."

"I'm sorry," Wolski said quietly. "I didn't realise..."

Jakob cut him short. There was more than a hint of anger in his voice. "There is much you don't yet realise, old friend."

Wolski lowered the tension. He lifted his glass. "To understanding," he said. They each touched glasses and together began to eat.

"Then let us begin with the essentials," Jakob said between mouthfuls of noodles. "If we need to meet again, we can't do it here. Twice is more than enough. My front door is often watched, especially when my business has been less generous than usual in its contributions to local police bonuses.

Call on Lotte; she is an ancient and hugely distant relative who has a flat in the street behind mine.

Look for the green door. That will be easier than remembering an address. We share a basement storeroom. You can get to my flat from there."

Wolski began to realise how little he really knew Jakob.

"Give me a name she will know you by."

"Kloptik," he immediately replied; Aunt Clara's nickname for him was a reminder of a past before innocence was lost.

"Now to more immediate questions," Jakob said. "A journey to Hamburg; could you justify one to your masters?"

Wolski did not reply immediately. Could he convince Golkov that there was something they needed? Analytical software, perhaps? The kind that would have to be purchased secretly from one of the shadowy figures who traded illegally in material restricted by the US government's ban on the export of strategic goods. He had been indirectly offered such packages in the past but had always turned them down.

"Perhaps," he said cautiously.

"At short notice?"

"More difficult, but perhaps not impossible."

"Good; here is what I have in mind."

Anya and Wolski waited for him to continue, but he did not speak again until he had finished his schnitzel.

He pushed the plate away and topped up his wine glass without offering any to his audience. He seemed to be addicted to the process of feeding, which was closer to refuelling than eating.

"Anya is a traffic supervisor with LOT, our esteemed national airline, and Hamburg is one of its most important destinations, so she has reason to travel there quite often. Moreover, she has access to the computer and airline passenger lists." Jakob delivered this last point with a sense of triumph.

"There is no reason to suppose that Thornhill does not travel under his own name. He uses it openly enough, and since he travels frequently among people he knows, petty camouflage would be more likely to attract attention than avoid it. So, it is possible for Anya to know when he next arrives in Hamburg."

Wolski made as if to interrupt. "Is all this really necessary? Surely there must be some other way of doing this?"

The question drew a flash of indignation from Jakob. "Is what you told me true? Are you serious about this?"

"Yes," Wolski said.

"Then beware of comforting explanations."

"You're talking in riddles," Wolski replied.

"Then I'll speak plainly. Learn the lesson of history."

Sensing that some inner pain prevented Jakob from coming to the point, Wolski said nothing. Jakob leaned across the table as if to shield Anya from what he had to say.

"We are dealing with the British. They have a history of welcoming comforting explanations. When the truth is too difficult to deal with, they seek alternative explanations that require them to do nothing. When they were first told about the camps, Auschwitz and Treblinka and all the rest, there were aerial photographs of the buildings, the gas chambers and crematoria. But they chose to devise a more comforting explanation. That's what politicians do, they devise comforting explanations, and that's why we have to reach someone who will believe us."

Wolski spoke calmly, as if to counter Jacob's passion. "That may be a definition of the problem, but what of the answer?"

"As I said before, we begin with the man," Jakob replied impatiently. "Remember that everyone is an egotist. If we can flatter this man with our apparent knowledge of him personally, he will want to know more. In short, he will respect what we tell him later if we are right about him now."

"So what kind of confidence trick are you proposing?"

"Not a confidence trick, that would be too ambitious; merely a piece of theatre," Jakob said. "You will play the lead."

"Go on," Wolski replied cautiously.

"Choosing the place of the meeting is especially demanding," Jakob said. "But we have a lucky advantage, my nephew, Roland. He is a taxi driver. For reasons I won't go into now, he feels he owes me a great deal. He is of course correct."

"When does all this happen?" Wolski asked helplessly.

"You will hear from us when everything is ready, not before." Jakob had no more to say. Briskly he got up and led Anya away. The sudden end of the meeting left Wolski in a confused state of mind. Once again, he wandered thoughtfully beside the river. The uncertain sky vacillated between winter and spring, lightening and darkening every few minutes. The pattern matched his mood. Who to trust? What to do? There were no answers, and the questions seemed to fade into the grey evening mist that began to gather among the trees on the far side of the river.

* * *

In the days that followed, nobody at the Institute noticed Wolski's retreat into isolation. By now it seemed entirely usual behaviour. He felt no emotion, not even fear, only a numbing sense of emptiness. He watched himself from a great distance, as if a spectator of his own actions, and wondered what this distant self would do next. There were moments when he felt he had come to the brink of mental collapse. Yet some deep-buried sense of purpose drove him on. Then, late on a Tuesday afternoon, ten days after the meeting at Café Mozart, the call came. He recognised Anya's voice at the first syllable.

"Professor Wolski?" she began tentatively in German.

"Yes."

"Professor Josef Wolski?"

"Yes, yes," he replied with feigned impatience. He realised that they had not agreed any form of code, which was an obvious and foolish mistake.

"Forgive me, but I am unfamiliar with Polish names and I thought there might be more than one person at the Institute with yours."

Wolski was impressed by the tactic. Anyone listening would not immediately guess that they knew each other.

"Who's speaking?"

"I'm calling on behalf of Herr Doktor Dornhugel. He will be in Hamburg and could discuss your software enquiries on Thursday or Friday." The transliteration of Thornhill's name into German lacked caution, but he admired her style.

"Is it convenient to travel here tomorrow?"

"Yes, that will be entirely convenient."

As he put the phone down, the dam broke. A great tidal wave of panic hit him, his knees began to shake uncontrollably and he gripped the edge of the desk in an attempt to steady himself. Yet the mental anguish came as a welcome relief from the eerie unreality that had tormented him since the last meeting at the café. Feeling fear again was like a reunion with an old friend.

He sat still and silent, waiting for the panic to subside. When he picked up the phone, his hand was steady, though his stomach felt as if it had turned to water. He called Golkov's office; his secretary answered at once. As he started to speak, his voice was uneven. He disguised it with a cough and began again.

"Excuse me… Maria, please book me a flight to Hamburg, as early in the morning as you can, with a return on Saturday, and make me a reservation at the Europäischer Hof." It was the only hotel he could think of. From his only other visit to the city, as a graduate student, he remembered with affection the tall old-fashioned barn-like building opposite the Hauptbhanhof. "Oh, and inform the administrator; Dr Golkov's office will need to authorise the expenditure."

Earlier in the week, Golkov had accepted Wolski's proposal that a software verification programme should run in parallel with the tests. Wolski had become convinced that Golkov did not want to let his backers sense any hint of trouble. He guessed that proposing this initiative would simultaneously ease Golkov's concerns about the delay and also appear to be Wolski's final capitulation. The keenness with which the suggestion was taken up suggested that Wolski's estimate had been correct on both counts. For the rest of the afternoon he made himself deal with a pile of papers on matters of routine administration.

Just before six, he was surprised by a visit from Golkov. He hadn't noticed him standing in the doorway and was startled when he spoke.

"Off to Hamburg in the morning, I hear. A city with more money than culture, I'm told. Certainly, I know of no Rembrandts there, but then it's never wise to confuse personal interests with business, is it, Professor?" Wolski was strangely glad to be reminded of the threat to the Night Watch. It helped concentrate the mind.

* * *

As the aircraft broke through the heavy Central European cloud at just over twelve thousand feet, Wolski felt a moment of exhilaration. The sunlight hit him with a force that made him sit upright in his seat. He was flying in one of LOT's new Boeings. Even the plastics and fabrics smelt new. When he asked, the stewardess told him proudly that the aircraft had been in service less than a week. How different, he thought, from the shabby Ilyushins, with their broken cabin fittings and threadbare seats, which used to be the backbone of the fleet.

A little over three and a half hours after leaving Warsaw, Wolski was checking into the Europäischer Hof. Twenty minutes after that, he was doing the same thing at a rundown commercial hotel in a side street behind the station. He needed a room with a phone where he could set up base. The man at the desk was a Berliner who looked like a nightclub bouncer gone to seed. He was fat, with dark porcine eyes and greasy hair grown long to compensate for advancing baldness. He looked like a school bully who had only partly grown up. Ideal, Wolski thought; nobody is easier to bully than a bully.

He needed to get the room without using his passport to register. It was essential not to give the man any feeling of power. He spoke as if to a janitor at the Institute. "A room, for two, perhaps three nights." The man slid a registration card across the counter. Wolski had two one-hundred-euro notes concealed in the palm of his hand. He covered the card and slid it back.

This was the part he was least confident about. If the amount were too small, he would lose the advantage of authority, if too large, the man would smell danger.

"Formalities are inappropriate; I am here on private business. A young lady…" He hesitated for effect. "My niece is joining me shortly. I am sure you understand." He lifted his hand from the counter to reveal the money. The man looked surprised; Wolski had almost overdone it. With one hand he pocketed the cash and with the other pushed a key across the counter.

At that moment, a woman's voice barked from a back room. "Klaus, telefon…"

From the expression on his face, Wolski realised that he had been right. The man was used to being bullied.

He replied meekly over his shoulder, "Ja … Schon da. Turning to Wolski, he said, "Room seventeen, breakfast at eight."

"I shan't need breakfast," Wolski said as he began to climb the stairs.

"You don't get a reduction," the man called after him.

The room was depressing. In his experience, many places had atmospheres; Some cathedrals exuded sanctity and sometimes houses reflected generations of family happiness. Here, in the smell of stale cigarette smoke, he sensed the despair of an army of salesmen down on their luck. But felt safe. It was a luxury he had not known for a long time.

He sat on the sagging bed, lifted the phone and called Anya.

"I'll be there in an hour, perhaps less," she said.

* * *

Wolski lay on the bed feeling grateful, old and foolish. He had forgotten how striking she looked. As she stood in front of the window, the light made a halo of her fine blond hair. When they met before, there had been the powerful personality of Jakob overshadowing them both. Now, alone with her for the first time, he felt clumsy, as he often did with women, only this was worse. The difference in their ages made him feel as inept as a teenager.

"Only you and the doorman know I am here. I'm booked in at the Europäischer Hof," he explained, "I said you were my niece." The absurdity of the situation struck them both at the same time. She sat on the bed beside him; it creaked and they both giggled like schoolchildren. For the first time since the nightmare had begun, Wolski felt happy.

"I must tell you what is arranged," she said.

* * *

Roland sat in his spotlessly clean Opel taxi with the engine running. He was fifty metres from the office behind the Kunsthalle where Thornhill worked. He had the flag down and the stereo turned up. He beat the steering wheel in time to Dolly Parton and hoped to convince anyone watching that he had been hired by a fare who had gone into one of the nearby shops.

He enjoyed acting, and periodically would ostentatiously look at his watch and then at the meter with a satisfied shrug.

The message from Jakob had been welcome. It was Jakob, his mother's brother, who had kept the family together after his father died. Roland had come West when the Wall came down. The best of the memories of what he had left behind in the East all featured Jakob. He especially enjoyed the summer visits to Warsaw that Jakob, by some mysterious means, had been able to arrange. Jakob was full of irony, philosophy and tactics for what he saw as 'the trench warfare of life'. And there were also the letters that for years arrived faithfully every week, full of humour, stern good advice and the occasional reproach for being such a poor correspondent.

Roland was ashamed of being a cab driver. With his degree in Philosophy, he believed he should have done better for himself, and if times were not so difficult he might well have done so. But the truth was that after a year and a half of trying, this was the only job he had been able to get. He felt as if he had let Jakob down. So far had he cast his mind back into the past, that he almost missed Thornhill. The fuzzy picture of him with Jakob and the Bach viola players, that had arrived the week before, was not ideal. But he picked him out nonetheless. Roland slammed the transmission into drive and the cab surged forward.

He pushed the flag up as Thornhill came to the kerb, but his initial slowness had let another cab into the stream of traffic ahead of him. Thornhill hailed it and got in. Roland hit the dashboard with his fist and a haze of dust settled over the car's instruments. He waited at the kerb to allow the delivery van behind to overtake and fill the space between the Opel and Thornhill's cab.

Again, he almost left it too late. An elegantly dressed woman laden with parcels reached out and opened the passenger door. He sped away with the door swinging open. In the rear-view mirror he saw the woman shouting, but her outrage was constrained by the need to hang onto her new possessions. Roland nearly collided with a beer truck as he leant over the back seat and struggled to close the door.

Trailing another vehicle clandestinely was a new experience for Roland and he began to enjoy the tingle of excitement. Carefully, he kept at least one vehicle between himself and Thornhill's cab. Only once did he have to act decisively, jumping a set of lights as they changed to red.

They entered the St Pauli district. The shabby streets around the Reeperbahn, Europe's most notorious red light district, looked as if they had a hangover from the night before. Thornhill's cab stopped outside a building that, like many others, had steel doors and sheet steel bolted over the windows. The whole exterior was painted matt black; the background for a vast illuminated sign that proclaimed: Blau Paradis. Roland had delivered passengers to this part of the city hundreds of times before, but only at night. It was not a place where daylight was welcome. There was a drab strangeness to it all. The steel-shuttered buildings, without the cover of darkness and with their gaudy illuminations switched off, looked like nuclear bunkers.

It was as if the outer edges of human fantasy had to be contained like some toxin destructive to life. Thornhill was expected. The door of the Blau Paradis opened as he approached. Roland wondered what to do next. He knew Wolski would be waiting and looked for a phone. There was a kiosk on the other side of the street.

Using a handful of coins from a bag between the front seats, he dialled the number Anya had given him. Wolski answered at once and listened to Roland's news without interruption.

"Take this number down."

Roland reached into his jacket but found nothing to write with. Angry at his own thoughtlessness, he fumbled through his pockets.

"Eine moment..." Eventually, he found a pair of nail clippers and carved the number on the cover of the directory, which, even in this part of town, Germanic civic pride had kept unvandalized. He tore off the cover and stuffed it into his jacket pocket. Perhaps to drown the embarrassment of having forgotten something as simple as anything to write with, the philosopher in him went to work on the surrounding landscape. What kind of place was it that kept telephone booths intact and vandalised people?

* * *

Wolski put the phone down and looked at the map again. The day before, Anya had carefully noted the numbers of all the public call boxes on the roads out of St Pauli. Wolski had read about how easy it was to trace mobile phones and he distrusted them. Calls between public phones would be much harder to trace. The number he had given Roland was at the Bismarck Memorial, a little garden with a clear view down the incline that led to St Pauli. It was a good place to wait. Anya sat in a hired Toyota parked by a meter at the other end of the garden. With little warning, it began to rain. Immediately Wolski saw the flaw in his plan.

An elderly man sitting in a public garden reading a newspaper, close to a phone booth, would normally go unnoticed.

In the rain he would be an object of curiosity. Reluctantly he decided to join Anya in the car. As he got in, she started the engine.

"Which way?" she said.

"Not yet. Do you have an umbrella?"

The rain brought Roland many would-be customers and he waved them away. He remained parked in sight of the Blau Paradis and was disguising his surveillance as a meal break with Brocwurst and a can of lager from the delicatessen across the street. The rain coursed over the windscreen, making it difficult to see. He wound down the driver's window a couple of inches and quickly began to get wet; it didn't matter. This time he was determined not to miss his man.

* * *

Wolski had found a place under a giant chestnut tree that broke the force of the rain. With Anya's umbrella, he felt effectively disguised as someone caught in a shower while crossing the park. He had always found rain a stimulant to thought; there was something about it that protected the mind from intrusion. Looking across the empty park and down the hill towards the port, he thought how like a sea battle before the days of radio the whole game was; trying to predict an opponent's movements by analysing his behaviour and so come upon him unawares.

Soon the rain stopped and, as so often close to the North Sea coast, bright sunshine and a cool wind followed. He went to one of the park benches and tried, unsuccessfully, to wipe away the water with the palm of his hand. He sat down and took out his copy of Die Welt. As he pretended to read, the dampness of the wooden seat soaked into his clothes and he began to shiver.

* * *

For an hour and a half Roland turned away angry customers, but this was not a part of town where he was likely to be reported to the taxi administration. The door of the Blau Paradis opened and a tall, heavily built man looked up and down the street as if to hail a cab. This was not something Roland wanted to happen. He turned away to avoid eye contact and lifted the can of lager to demonstrate that he was off duty. It was at that moment he caught sight of Thornhill in the doorway.

He dropped the can on the floor and started the engine. The beer soaked into the carpet as the cab surged forward. The big man was pleased to have succeeded in getting a cab for his boss. As he drew alongside, Roland heard Thornhill turn down the offer, choosing instead to walk. Now it was the big man's turn to avoid eye contact.

Not wanting to pay for hailing the cab, he went inside and slammed the steel door shut behind him. Roland kept the cab moving until he came to a phone. He called the number and became alarmed when there was not an immediate answer. Wolski had heard the phone ring and tried to move quickly, but was stiff with cold and was slowed by a sharp pain in his left leg. When he picked up the phone Roland's excitement was immediately obvious.

"He's walking up the hill towards The Alster."

"Which side of the road?"

"The right."

Wolski was annoyed at the imprecision of the answer.

"His right walking up the hill, or mine looking down towards him?"

"His right."

Wolski felt a moment of triumph, and with unusual discourtesy put the phone down without offering Roland any thanks. He opened the phone directory and laid the picture of Thornhill on it. To the outsider he would appear to be looking for a number. Unless Thornhill was not heading towards the centre of the city, he would pass by the spot where Wolski stood. He looked around. The place was too exposed for a contact. An alternative began to form in his mind. He stared at the poor-quality image, looking up occasionally until Thornhill came into view – a distant yet unmistakable figure, tall with an assertive stride. Wolski was a man renewed. The pain was suddenly gone. He hurried up the hill in the direction he believed Thornhill would take, glancing back to ensure he was not mistaken. When he approached Thornhill he wanted to be part of a crowd. That way he would stand a better chance of seeming to be part of a team, with supporters close at hand, rather than appearing to be an elderly crank in the park. At St Michaelis Kirche he climbed to the tall entrance doors and stood behind a pillar. A small stream of people was coming up the steps for the afternoon organ recital. Wolski looked over the arrivals as if waiting for a friend. Thornhill came into view about a hundred metres away.

Then two things happened simultaneously; a change in Thornhill's stride when he saw the posters announcing the recital and Wolski's memory of the Bach Circle where the picture with the viola players had been taken. In a decisive moment of intuition, he was totally certain of Thornhill's decision and he stepped quickly into the church.

* * *

In Bermuda, Thornhill had been listening to Wolski's story for what seemed like hours. He noticed that the wind had dropped, the tide had ebbed and the sound of the sea was more distant. In the pause in the conversation he had to suppress a smile at the picture of himself as an incipient egomaniac. The strategy had worked, but his voice betrayed nothing.

"So that's how you did it," Thornhill said.

"Yes; like most successful tricks it was simpler than it looked," Wolski replied.

"I'm not interested in tricks, however successful or simple. Time is running out," Thornhill snapped.

"Trickery and simplicity, what other weapons are there for the weak to use against the strong?" Wolski asked.

"Let's avoid the philosophy. I need to know what happened next," Thornhill said.

"I went to a sports shop." Wolski recalled that after the meeting with Thornhill, he hurried across the city centre to Lindeman's, a travel goods shop, where he bought a cheap nylon holdall. Ten minutes later, he was handing over Golkov's letter of credit at the Industrial Bank of Switzerland. He was shown into an oak-panelled back room. There, without comment or emotion, fifty thousand dollars were neatly packed in the nylon bag.

"A taxi perhaps?" was the only question asked when the transaction was complete.

At the Europäischer Hof, Wolski made a clumsy joke with the hall porter as he collected his key; anything to be remembered.

He made for the stairs, but the man at the desk called him back. "For you," he said, waving a postcard.

As he put out his hand to take it, Wolski instantly knew what it would show – the Night Watch. The card carried a Hamburg postmark with the previous day's date. Immediately questions flooded in on him. Was he being watched?

Had anybody observed the meeting with Thornhill? He was surprised that he no longer felt intimidated, only angry. Action had somehow made him stronger. There was a single typed line on the back: 'Thinking of you'. He crumpled the card and threw it into the ashtray at the bottom of the stairway. As he climbed to the second floor, it struck him that Golkov had miscalculated. The renewed threat had not worked. The effect was opposite to that which it was intended to have. It was not a big mistake, but reassuring further evidence of the enemy's fallibility.

Wolski sat on the bed for a few moments, enjoying his small victory. Suddenly he felt hungry, called room service and ordered the crab soup for which the hotel was famous. He added rye bread and Swiss cheese to the order and put the phone down. It rang almost at once. It was Altman.

"Room 209," Wolski said.

"I have a better idea," Altman replied.

The thought of food forgotten, Wolski headed for the lobby. On a sudden impulse, he paused at the ashtray at the foot of the stairs, picked out the crumpled postcard and slid it into his pocket.

For someone engaged in a clandestine trade, Altman was surprisingly conspicuous. He was tall, grey haired and dressed in a long black-leather overcoat. He made no attempt to introduce himself and turned towards the door. Wolski, carrying the nylon bag, followed him outside. He had expected a large Mercedes, but not one with its three-pointed star and door handles plated in gold.

"They think I run a whorehouse in St Pauli," Altman said when he saw Wolski's reaction.

"Who does?" Wolski said, feeling flustered.

"Everyone; it's the perfect disguise."

They drove in silence for a while.

"Ostentation is easier than discretion. Wasn't that what St Augustine said?"

"No, it was not," said Wolski curtly.

The car was soon out of the city centre traffic, heading for the Mexico Ring and its clusters of glass and steel buildings.

"Dead." Altman spoke with such force that Wolski was startled. Altman was like a taxi driver who felt the need to strike up a conversation with a silent fare. "No life in it, this place." He settled into a monologue. "Berlin, that was the place. There, everyone was alive. There were deals to be had on every street corner, but that's all over now, so here I am, an economic refugee."

Wolski was indignant. "Am I supposed to feel sorry for you?"

"Why not?" said Altman. "You look like someone who feels sorry enough for himself." Wolski was stung into silence and Altman's one-man debate continued. "Perhaps I should go East and get a piece of the nuclear surplus trade."

"What do you mean?" Wolski asked anxiously.

"I mean, turn some of those rusty nuclear spears into golden ploughshares."

Wolski resisted the impulse to ask more, and they rode on in silence. The car approached a steep ramp beneath an office block and they plunged into the darkness of an underground car park. "Welcome to the dealing floor," Altman said.

* * *

At Okecie Airport in Warsaw, Sedkov, Petrovitch's assistant, was waiting. He was unshaven, red-eyed and not inclined to conversation. With a curt nod at the silent officials, he led Wolski straight through customs and immigration. Even though an examination of his bags could prove dangerous, Wolski resented the unquestioned power that Sedkov represented and the arrogance with which it was exercised.

"Working late?" Wolski asked in the Polski Fiat as they drove to the Institute.

"Night and day. The large mammal tests have been brought forward to December."

Wolski wanted to know more. "What large mammals? What do you mean?"

"Look, Professor, I was sent to fetch you, not to brief you," Sedkov said. Then, with the same look of insolence that he had shown in the customs hall, he added, "My guess is that Golkov wanted you out of the way for a few days."

Instantly they both recognised that he had said more than he should and they continued the rest of the sixteen kilometres into the city without further conversation. The endless ranks of grey buildings rolled by and Wolski again began to feel fear again.

At the Institute, he went directly to Golkov's office. As he turned to close the door, Golkov spoke.

"Leave it open," he said.

"Everything went as planned," Wolski noted with a hint of pride. Golkov looked haggard. It was the first time Wolski had seen him ill at ease.

"Things have changed while you have been away. We are leaving out the intermediate tests and going directly to final trials."

"Why? When?" Wolski was full of questions.

"December."

"You can't possibly do that." Wolski was appalled.

Golkov ignored the remark. "Do you have the software?" he said.

"Yes," said Wolski, lifting the nylon bag onto the table. It was heavy with manuals and computer discs.

"Valentina!" Golkov shouted for an assistant, who appeared in the doorway. She was a young woman, uncertain of herself, and she looked worried. Golkov indicated the bag with an impatient gesture.

"Take this to Petrovitch and tell him to lock it in the safe."

"Tell me what's happening," Wolski demanded. "I must have access to that material."

"You'll do as you are told," snapped Golkov, "just like everyone else. "He stood up, and as he did so Wolski recognised one of the mood changes that he had come to expect. It was foreshadowed by his strange smile; the aggression was gone and he once more spoke as if appealing to reason. "You and I, we've been given an international stage on which to perform our debut. We shall play to the entire world. We will achieve something that nobody anywhere will ever forget," he said with rising enthusiasm. "I will have nothing to do with it," Wolski snapped.

"You will," Golkov insisted. "Indeed you have returned exactly at the time I intended. It would have been tiresome to have had you here earlier; certain preparations have been necessary."

"What's been going on? What are you doing?" Wolski's panic was uncontained. "I must be told."

Without replying, Golkov left the room. Wolski's sense of accomplishment at having deceived Golkov collapsed in on itself.

He had no more resistance, no more hope. Golkov was once again omnipotent, and Wolski began a final retreat into the work he despised, but which was his only refuge.

13

The Experiment

Time was a lost dimension. Wolski allowed himself no space away from the exacting confines of work. His mind paced the walls of a narrow cell that was formed by calculation, formulae, extrapolation and speculation. Mental confinement was a defence against realities too disturbing to contemplate. In the small hours of one especially dark morning he carefully considered the possibility of sabotage. Yet as dawn broke, he knew he dared not do it. Not for fear of discovery and reprisal, which he believed certain; rather it was the knowledge that science was the only thing he had to hold onto. If he let go of that, he would fall into the abyss of madness.

* * *

What he later was to remember as the worst day of his life, started with a surprise. It was snowing. The springtime conversations with Jakob beside the Vistula seemed at once like yesterday, and a lifetime ago. He went down to the courtyard and stood amid the falling snow.

"Thank you."

Wolski turned at the sound of a now familiar voice. It was Golkov. He was with Petrovitch, a dozen of the lab staff and a number of uniformed guards. They seemed completely oblivious to the falling snow.

"All your hard work has kept us on schedule." Golkov's gloating was expressed as patronising gratitude. "I admire such devotion, which is why you've been left alone. I gave orders that you were not to be disturbed." Wolski's despair was total.

Even his escape into work belonged not to him, but to Golkov. Both knew that nothing in Wolski's life was his own and Golkov savoured the moment. "This is your day, Professor, it is your achievement that we are about to witness," Golkov continued, with contempt thinly disguised as respect. Wolski stood speechless, trying to let the falling flakes of snow fill his mind. He began to shiver, but it wasn't the snow; he felt ice in his soul.

"What do you mean?" His mouth was dry and he swallowed hard.

"The large mammal tests," Golkov said flatly.

"No," Wolski said firmly. He managed only the one word before Golkov's anger broke on him.

"I've had enough of your petty indignation." Golkov spat the words at Wolski. Turning to the guards, he shouted, "Take Professor Wolski to the gymnasium gallery and keep him there."

The guards' large peasant hands clamped onto Wolski's thin wrists like steel.

"So it has come to this," he said, looking at his captives' hands.

"Yes," said Golkov, "it has come to this."

"Why?"

"I want you there, I want you committed. You helped create this, now you're going to see the results."

"There's months more work to be done. Do you have any idea what you are doing?" Wolski demanded.

"That's what tests are for, to find out."

Wolski struggled to find expression and was conscious of how feeble his words sounded. "This is outrageous."

Golkov's anger flared up again. "Your sense of moral superiority disgusts me. In the end, you obeyed instructions just like me, like the rest of us. All you've done is make a fuss about it. That doesn't make you different from any of us. Just more self-righteous." He shouted at the guards, "Take him away."

The gymnasium had been a gift from the Soviets, a showplace of Communist investment in young athletic talent. The glass-fronted gallery was soundproofed for use by radio commentators, talent scouts and favoured guests. As Wolski was led through the door, Petrovitch was giving last-minute instructions to the lab technicians who were hastily putting black duct tape around the edges of the windows. Golkov arrived with the rest of the team.

"Shall we begin?" Petrovitch asked.

Golkov spoke from the shadows at the back of the gallery. "Are both the holding area and gymnasium sealed?"

"Yes," Petrovitch replied.

"Proceed," Golkov snapped.

The video, audio and data recorders were switched on. "Large mammal skin absorption tests, stage one. Dosage Alpha," Petrovitch said for the benefit of the tapes.

Later, Wolski could not understand why he did not foresee what was about to happen, why he closed his mind to what 'large mammals' might be. When the college basketball teams came through the players' doorway the shock made him leap to his feet.

"No!" he screamed in horror.

The guards slammed him back onto the bench, knocking him breathless. As the teams lined up to play, Petrovitch continued speaking in the same steady tone. "The computer model predicts mild agitation thirty seconds after release." Wolski tried to bury his face in his hands, but he could not manage even that small comfort, as the guards' grip prevented him from moving his arms. Petrovitch zeroed the timer.

"Geneva, here we come," Golkov murmured.

Play began, and the large picture window filled Wolski's vision; there was nowhere he could hide his eyes.

He heard Petrovitch's voice. "The clock is zeroed and release will begin at ten seconds."

It happened very quickly. Within a minute the game collapsed into a heap of figures clawing and tearing at each other. Long buried childhood memories leapt to life; there were hundreds of maimed bodies on the streets of the city during the war, but he had seen nothing like this. Faces and eyes bled, hands gouged and teeth sank into bare flesh. Yet from where Wolski sat, it all happened in silence. The soundproofing of the gallery amplified the obscenity of what was happening on the floor below, transforming horrific reality into silent fantasy. Wolski's view became mercifully obscured as the watchers pressed eagerly towards the glass. He alone remained seated, pinned between the guards. Silence in the gallery was absolute. Wolski wanted to shout, to scream, but as in a nightmare, when he opened his mouth no words came.

On the floor below, the ball rolled away from the struggling bodies and left a smear of blood on the floor as it came to rest in the far corner of the court. The silence broke. There was a voice, high-pitched with tension. "Enough – stop it now!" It was Golkov, who was at the centre of the group of figures by the window.

"How can we?" Petrovitch protested. "It's not safe to go in there for at least another twenty minutes."

Golkov yelled at the two guards. "Go and open the fire sprinkler valve by the main door – drench the place."

They clattered off obediently and Wolski was free. Golkov swung back to the window, pounding his fist on the glass. Wolski could not see his face and could not tell whether the gesture was one of triumph or despair. He seized the moment, stepped quietly into the corridor and on into the labyrinth of passages that he knew so well. Soon he was at the old night porter's entrance, and then out into the street. He reckoned he had a minute, perhaps less, before the shock wore off and they came after him. A bus drew up at a stop close by and an elderly couple stepped painfully down. He dived behind them, almost knocking them over. He heard their shouted protests as he made for the back row and slid down low behind one of the high-backed seats. With agonising slowness the bus pulled away into the stream of traffic. He found a two-day-old newspaper under the seat in front of him and hid behind it. All afternoon, his only impulse was to keep moving. He changed from bus to tram and back to bus again, crossing and re-crossing the city. In deep shock, he sat immobile with the newspaper griped tightly in front of him. It was a wall between him and the rest of the world.

Then came the urge to think, the need to blot out what had happened and above all, the reasons why it had happened. Piece by piece, he tried to make sense of it.

Whoever the paymasters were, their timing had changed and what had begun as a textbook research operation had turned into a bloody shambles, probably through a miscalculation of the rate at which the vapour was absorbed through human skin. From the disaster a terrible knowledge had emerged, and the power, however crude, to amplify human aggression to the point of suicidal carnage. But what possible use could this bizarre ability have? Sending people mad as a weapon of war or politics appeared to offer no advantage over any other means of destruction. And above all, why risk so much investment for the sake of only a few months more work? He wondered why he had not asked himself any of these questions before. Simple moral cowardice, he told himself, and in that self-arraignment there was a certain kind of strength. Eventually, he lowered the newspaper. The private world created by its shelter could be sustained no longer. He felt the tingle of blood returning to his cramped fingers. The bus was passing through an industrial area. Tall chimneys billowed acrid smoke across the setting sun and the air tasted of grit. With unfocused eyes Wolski stared at the decaying landscape.

He tried to put together some of the things Golkov had said: 'Locating the volume control'; 'A world stage – something that nobody will ever forget.' And the unguarded remark about Geneva. His mind wandered on until he stumbled upon the realisation that they would kill him. The knowledge did not frighten him. Amid so much that was unknowable, this one certainty was oddly comforting.

"Far as you go," the tobacco-scarred voice of the driver croaked as the bus reached the end of its route.

"Yes, yes, that's exactly it. Thank you," Wolski said with academic courtesy as he stepped onto the broken pavement.

The driver was amused by Wolski's incomprehensible response. "Have a nice day," he wheezed in parody of one of the American soap operas that had become compulsive nightly viewing.

Wolski picked his way between sinister-coloured puddles that had collected in the ruts pounded into the road by the daily traffic of heavy chemical-laden trucks. He began to add up his only accessible assets: two thousand euros in cash and his passport, both of which he had risked mailing to Jakob's flat after the trip to Hamburg.

* * *

He found the green door in the block that backed onto Jakob's apartment, rang Lotte's bell and waited. He had almost given up hope when he heard shuffling feet in the hallway.

"Who is it?"

"Kloptik."

There was no reply, but Wolski heard the rattle of chains and the door slowly opened.

"You know the way," was all she said as she shuffled back down the corridor.

After what had happened at the Institute, Jakob's flat was like a reintroduction to the human race. Jakob splashed Napoleon Brandy into his prize Czech crystal.

"Act Two Scene One?" Jakob asked.

"This is not a game," Wolski said.

"Indeed not," Jakob replied. "Theatre is art; so much more satisfying than a mere game."

Wolski wanted to avoid analogies. "You once said that I offered you a new lease of life and I replied that I might be offering you death, do you recall that?"

Jakob seemed delighted that Wolski had remembered what he had said. "And I said that 'life and death are sometimes the same thing'. I thought it sounded rather clever at the time, but I'm not sure if I know what I meant by it." He laughed at his own obtuseness. "But I knew you'd come, it was only a matter of time. Where else could you go?"

"I am concerned that others might come to the same conclusion." Wolski wanted to introduce the prospect of danger gently.

"Perhaps our investment in coffee and caution at Café Mozart was worthwhile," Jakob said.

"If, thanks to Lotte, you weren't seen coming here, it may take your pursuers some time to find this address. They have a lot of money and, it seems, a lot of power. But that's not the same as being on every street corner like the KGB in the old days."

"You know more about that sort of thing than I do," Wolski said.

"Yes, I do," said Jakob, taking the remark as a compliment. "From what you have told me, I think your former friends are more likely to operate like gangsters than a secret police force."

"Is there a difference?"

Yes. You could always tell what the KGB would do, unless they were going through one of their less efficient phases. Your people are unpredictable.

They present a different kind of danger. They will not attempt to create a bureaucracy of watchers and heavies. They are more imaginative than that. With their money they will have bought their way into corrupt officialdom, the police, the Ministry and so on. But getting those wheels turning takes time, time which we must use well."

"I hope you are right," said Wolski.

Jakob got up from the sagging armchair with the threadbare William Morris fabric and walked slowly round the room as if measuring the distance. When the circuit was completed, he began another.

"You look like Joshua circling the walls of Jericho," Wolski said.

"And are you the one who sounds the horn which will bring them down?" Jakob asked. He stopped pacing and, towering over Wolski, said, "Are you going to tell me what happened?"

"No."

"Why?"

Wolski said firmly, "There is danger in knowing…" He faltered. "And, God help me, there is guilt in it too."

"Then why are you here?" Jakob was resentful at being shut out of Wolski's secret.

"As you said, Act Two Scene One. You scripted the meeting in Hamburg, you made the audience believe in us, now everything depends on the construction of the second act. "You must remain here until they have exhausted their initial panic in looking for you. Meanwhile, I have things to do and people I must see."

* * *

For forty-eight hours Wolski sat quietly and alone. The recollection of what had happened shut out the power to think or even to move. Eventually, he heard a key in the lock. The door opened and Jakob stood staring at him. He advanced across the room and dropped a newspaper into Wolski's lap. The headline read: Basketball Teams in Ferry Disaster.

"I take it that it would be prudent for you to be elsewhere than Warsaw?"

Wolski couldn't find words. With vacant eyes he scanned the newspaper story. Gas explosion … Sinking … Drowned.

"My information is that they loaded the bodies onto a ferry across some lake near the Belarus frontier and sank it. It seems that it will be some considerable time before the corpses are all recovered. No doubt the official verdict will be death by drowning."

With great effort, Wolski at last spoke. "I need to see Jack Thornhill again – urgently."

Jakob thought out loud. "That is a problem that is easily defined and difficult to solve."

"Yes," Wolski said with a hint of impatience at Jakob's didactic manner.

"We have to get you from here to London without your being noticed," Jakob said, as if announcing the answer to a riddle.

Sensation came flooding back into Wolski's brain. It would not have mattered to Wolski if Jakob had suggested going via the moon; the relief of hearing the difficulty reduced to a single sentence was enormous.

Jakob sat down again and the chair creaked a friendly welcome.

"Since you will not tell me your secrets, perhaps I should tell you mine. I have played other games, usually out of boredom and occasionally for a little profit. I change baubles into things that are useful; my own tiny gesture of welcome to our new free-market economy." His hands did as much talking as his voice. "But I am still ahead of the times in some respects; the state continues to take an unreconstructed view of such trade. A little silver, a few paintings, diamonds occasionally and in return I provide what people want most ; hard currency. I never see most of the goods, you understand. I merely make their arrival possible. A worthy public service, wouldn't you agree?"

Wolski was too surprised to respond and Jakob took his silence as a sign of approval.

"Why do I do it? I am a modest man with a modest ambition. I do not want to die here, not in this country where so many of us have died. I shall go to Israel. I have only remained here because of Anya, but I must leave soon. Another reward is that occasionally, for a short time, I have beautiful things to live with." He made a gesture that embraced the paintings that lined the walls. "So I am enriched in life by beauty and in death by geography!"

Wolski could not restrain his curiosity. "How do you do it?"

"With people I trust. With people who trust me. Everything goes to a gallery on 5th Avenue in Manhattan. None of the items is sufficiently well known, large enough or expensive enough to attract undue attention, but they sell for satisfactory prices. Most of the pieces you see here come from people with an ambition similar to my own. They know that I keep faith with them.

My 'cut', as I understand it is called, is small." He took a heavy volume of Goethe off one of the bookshelves and from it produced a sheaf of Bank of America statements.

"These are my clients' accounts. I distribute them each month, and this is mine." He handed Wolski a bank statement; it showed a balance of nearly eight hundred thousand dollars.

"You could get thirty years for this!" Wolski said.

"At my age that's an attractive proposition," Jakob said, and collapsed into convulsing laughter. He cleared his throat, wiped his eyes and spoke again, as if making a carefully calculated decision. "I shall not tell you everything, but I shall tell you two more things that are important for you to know. Natasha, my wife, she had a brother, an interesting man, a sailor, captain of a Lithuanian timber ship, mainly in the Atlantic trade. He comes into Gdansk every two months or so. That's where I met him. We were on holiday up there on the Baltic, Natasha and me.

It was the summer before she died. He surprised me. I always thought sailors were never out of the bar once they came ashore. But he was different; he dragged me all the way out to Oliwa to hear the cathedral organ. Eight thousand pipes – it has an amazing sound. It must be the biggest in the world. That's when it all began. On the way back, he started talking about the Metropolitan Museum in New York and how he tried to get there every time his ship docked. It was usually only a subway ride away. I was interested, as I had also visited the museum. That was more than half a lifetime ago. I was on an exchange programme with NYU. It is the only time I have been to America. One thing led to another and soon our little scheme was hatched..."

Jakob's attention seemed to wander and his eyes turned to a magnificent carriage clock that stood in a place of honour above the fireplace. When he started speaking again, it was as much to himself as to Wolski.

"He has lusted after that clock for the past two years. I've always resisted, it belonged to my grandmother, but perhaps now..." He paused and then, with one of the abrupt gestures with which Wolski was becoming familiar, he clapped his hands as if waking himself from a daydream and became brisk and business-like.

"The other thing you should know is that Anya is travelling to London in the next few days, I don't know exactly when…" He paused again, as if there was something he had forgotten; then he stood up. "Now I must use the telephone." He dialled a number, waited for a long time, then gave up and dialled another. He began speaking almost immediately. Wolski recognised the language as Lithuanian and was surprised by Jakob's fluency. Without explanation, Jakob tried the original number a second time.

"Anya?" Again he spoke rapidly in Lithuanian, though Wolski noticed occasional English words and place names. Jakob put the phone down triumphantly, reached across to Wolski and clapped him on the shoulders. Wolski flinched under the impact.

"You are going to America!" Jakob said proudly.

"America, why America?" Wolski was losing control of developments and wanted to protest.

"Why? I will tell you why," Jakob said. "We must assume it is unsafe for you to try and leave by air – airports are easy places to watch."

Wolski remembered the ease with which he was taken through customs and immigration on his arrival from Hamburg and did not argue. "The same is true of trains, and there are two frontier crossings between here and the West. As for going by road, I have no papers, and in any case, they will be expecting something of that kind, a conventional exit.

The script you asked me to write has to be more devious than that." Jakob was once more beginning to enjoy himself and Wolski felt helpless. "You are going by sea, and here is your ticket." With a flamboyant gesture, he lifted the carriage clock from the mantelpiece and set it gently on the table in front of Wolski.

"My brother-in-law shall have what he wants and you shall have eight days of sea air."

Wolski shook his head in disbelief. Jakob kept talking. "When Anya goes to London, she will contact Thornhill to tell him you are coming and to arrange for someone to meet you. I remember a piece of small talk when he and I met. There's a concert he goes to sometimes, in the middle of the day; you can hear it on the BBC World Service. I remember him saying that. I'll try and find out what it's called and Anya will attempt to contact him there. She'll be in London for several days, so a number of attempts will be possible. She will keep in touch with me so that I can pass on your sailing date to her. It's haphazard, but it's the best we can do."

Wolski choked back a lump in his throat. "Why? Why are you doing this?"

"Why? Revenge, of course."

"Revenge?" Wolski had expected some gentler motive, friendship perhaps. "Revenge on who?"

"Revenge on them all." Jakob's outburst was of a kind Wolski had not seen before. "All of them who have taken this country and twisted it into their own detestable image. Polish anti-Semites, Nazi supermen, Communist ideologues and now your friends, whoever they are, with their technology, their money, their arrogance and, no doubt, their lust for power like all the rest.

They carve their murderous ambitions out of the sufferings of ordinary people. I hate them all with a loathing that even you will never understand. Revenge, you see, is the sweetest and most powerful of all motives." With that, Jakob left the room and Wolski sat in a daze. He had not moved by the time Jakob returned from the kitchen with a pile of newspapers, which he dumped beside the clock.

"Wrap it up. I have to use the phone again."

Like a drunk trying to prove himself sober, Wolski began the task with cautious deliberation; he knew that if he moved more quickly, he would not be able to prevent his hands from trembling.

"Kinski is coming," Jakob announced as he put the phone down. "He helps with the distribution of our merchandise. He'll take you to Mlawa, about halfway to Gdansk. You can stay overnight with my cousin Freda; I'll warn her of your arrival. Remain indoors and wait for a call from my brother-in-law. He'll fix things at the docks; he also has 'acquaintances' at the American end, but you will have to risk the train from Mlawa to Gdansk on your own." Jakob went to the bookshelf and rummaged through an assortment of catalogues and guides; various loose pieces of paper floated unnoticed to the floor. Eventually, he pulled out a faded brochure in blue and white; it showed the bulbous shape of a 1950s Pan Am Stratocruiser and carried the slogan 'Visit New York with the World's Most Experienced Airline'.

"I kept it as a souvenir of my visit," Jakob said. He unfolded it to reveal a map of New York City and the surrounding area. "The ship usually docks somewhere here," he said, indicating the New Jersey side of the Hudson. "Let's decide on a rendezvous, somewhere near the docks."

Wolski formed a mental picture of long, busy streets ending in a forest of masts. Jakob took a magnifying glass to examine the plan more closely.

"The map is old, but I don't suppose things have changed very much," he said confidently.

14

The Judgement

The hotel room was quiet and it was dark outside. The magnificent view of the sea was long forgotten. Wolski, close to complete exhaustion, had been shepherded away to bed by Latchford. Nobody wanted to be the first to speak. "Hell or Hoboken by Christmas." It was Thornhill who broke the silence.

"What's that supposed to mean?" Darcy was looking unusually dishevelled. His normally well-groomed hair was a tangled mess and his voice was laden with impatience and fatigue.

"Stream of consciousness, I suppose," Thornhill said absent-mindedly. "It's what 'Black Jack' Pershing said to American troops sailing off to the First World War. Hoboken was close to where Wolski came ashore."

"What other good news is there?" Darcy asked tartly.

"He's still alive and it's not yet Christmas," Thornhill replied.

In the adjoining room, Morag sat at her computer waiting for any key word or phrase that the system could analyse. Nothing came up. Murphy was draped diagonally across the king-size bed behind her, listening through headphones. Morag thought, as she had so often before, how sharply people were defined when you could hear them but not see them. Darcy seemed tiresomely pleased with himself. But she felt differently about Thornhill; sensing an inner strength that she found strangely attractive. It was an emotion she found puzzling. It wasn't sexual attraction, or was it? Were intellectual attraction and sexual attraction two sides of the same coin?

Thornhill's voice broke into her reverie. "Case conference, Morag. Murphy, will you join us?" Thornhill knew that they would hear him on the sound recording system. "Let's try and get the essentials agreed before we turn in," he said, stretching his limbs as he lay back in the big chair.

Morag and Murphy came through the connecting door and Murphy sat on the arm of the sofa. Morag took Wolski's chair.

The hallway door opened and Latchford, not wanting to interrupt the discussion, eased himself into the room without a greeting.

"How's the patient?" Thornhill asked.

"Sleeping. Bullivant is staying in there with him."

"Let's get on then. Darcy, you first," Thornhill said.

"The story doesn't hold water," Darcy said. "On one hand, we are asked to believe in mega-computers, vast amounts of money, some sort of techno-Gestapo that experiments on humans and threatens the lives of anyone it takes a dislike to. On the other hand, the fruit of all these labours is the most spectacular cock-up. And…," he emphasised the word, "on top of all that, there is supposed to be a supra-national conspiracy to pull some kind of stunt at the summit. Doesn't that all sound ever so slightly paranoid? I recommend we give him to the Psychos, see what they have to say before we go any further."

"If all that is so, how do you account for Wolski's presence here?" Thornhill asked.

Darcy had a ready answer. "I account for it with the greatest possible caution. Somebody may be feeding us a line, perhaps our old friends from the former Soviet Union, the kind of people now engaged in every kind of squalid struggle for power in some glorious new Russian Empire. Or he may be just a plain nutter, I don't know. What I do know is that, either way, in the present political climate, if we get this wrong we'll all be out of a job."

"Thank you for your professional concern," Thornhill replied sharply. "Murphy, you saw him first…"

"The way I see it," Murphy, uncertain of his conclusion, responded slowly, weighing his words as he spoke, "it could be a scam, but who's in that line of business anymore? He could be crazy, but if he is, he's not like any other nut I've ever seen, and I've seen a lot. I think he's for real," he said with a shrug.

"Thank you; I'm inclined to agree," Thornhill said.

Morag, protective of Thornhill, sensed the scale of the disaster if he were persuaded to believe a fantasy. Uncharacteristically, she did not wait for an invitation to speak.

"Did you know that there are more than seventeen million items on so-called 'mind control' on the Internet? It's a crude phrase and may not present an accurate description of what we are being asked to believe. But the fact is that most people taking a sustained interest in this kind of thing are themselves crazy, at least in a small part of their lives."

"Maybe they're crazy with good reason," Murphy said. "It's on the record that the US government has spent billions on things not so very different from what the good Professor is talking about."

"You can't be serious, Latchford," interrupted.

Murphy shrugged. "Don't take my word for it, look at the Congressional Enquiry report back in the late 70s. The Enquiry found a so-called 'Truth Drug Programme', with all kinds of psycho experiments in prisons and mental hospitals. There was a programme called MK Ultra that proposed multiple kinds of madness for a whole decade in the Cold War. Then later, the CIA was out of control with craziness like throwing LSD-filled light-bulbs in the path of subway trains to see how far the effects would carry. Just for the hell of it they also tried spraying several different kinds of junk over cities from the air." Murphy continued in full flood. "Ever heard of 'National Security Brothels?' They were in business to develop sexual techniques for extracting information. Then there was something called the Law Enforcement Assistance Administration, a special favourite of the late and unlamented Richard Nixon. Among other things, they proposed a child screening programme to identify potential criminals while they were still in first grade. Nothing came of it, or so we're told." Murphy paused briefly. "Don't you see the point? If anybody came in here with ideas like that we'd say they were nuts, wouldn't we? But we'd be wrong."

Darzi joined the argument. "Murphy is right. There are claims about government money for proposals that could be regarded as psychotic: killing by eye contact, telepathy, even remote seeing; TV without the technology."

Latchford was incredulous. "Why didn't anybody notice? Murphy turned on him sharply. "Why didn't you notice? There are eighteen thousand pages of declassified information about this. What were you back then, a student? Students are supposed to get angry about this kind of shit." Nobody interrupted and Murphy continued. "You know what makes me believe Wolski's story? I'll tell you, it was the brick wall."

"Brick wall?" Darcy was genuinely puzzled.

"Yes, the brick wall in the East Wing. All this stuff was going on just one course of bricks away and nobody noticed. That's real life, that's why I believe it." Darcy was having none of it. "Think cautiously about this, it's also real life that there are people out there who believe that a million kids a year are snatched off the streets for brain experiments and are held in multi-storey cages like lab animals on Long Island and in disused missile silos. And there are others going around in tinfoil hats to ward off mind control messages from mobile phone masts. Then there are those that believe there is some kind of giant conspiracy to control thoughts by ultra-low-frequency sound waves. These ideas come and go like waves of hysteria in a henhouse."

Everyone saw the conflicting arguments for what they were and instinctively looked to Thornhill for a judgement. "Where better to hide a scorpion's egg than in a henhouse?" Thornhill said.

Darcy replied impatiently. "Sir Jack, with respect, I must ask you to consider the possibility that your own judgement is prejudiced. This man targeted you personally. He said so. They put a lot of effort into attracting your attention. Consciously or otherwise, that's flattering. Look at it objectively. You've been fascinated with the man ever since."

Nobody in the room had heard Thornhill being spoken to like that before and everyone wondered how he would react. He didn't dismiss the point, but neither did he dwell on it. "Thank you," he replied, "That needed to be said. I will so consider." Darcy said nothing. He shuffled in his seat and tapped his gold pen on the little leather notebook he always used at meetings.

Thornhill wanted to move on. "Latchford, you're the medic; is he a madman?"

"It depends on what you mean by mad. It's not a medical term. Sorry, but I can only offer an opinion, not a diagnosis, at this stage." Latchford's professional caution annoyed Thornhill. "Then may we have your opinion, Dr Darzi?"

"Some of the symptoms he exhibits may be signs of a psychiatric disorder. On the other hand, what sort of condition would you be in if you'd just lived through the sort of hell he's been describing? Only what you might call a 'madman' would be capable of appearing entirely sane. To come to a considered opinion I need time, several days, and expert help."

Thornhill did not comment on Darzi's views. "Morag, what do you think?"

She understood that coming to her last was a sign of respect, but she also noticed, as the only woman present, that she was alone in being addressed by her first name. Yet she bore no resentment, knowing that Thornhill's clubbable world simply had no instinct for the finer points of female emancipation. She spoke in the formidable style for which she had become well known.

"I note the opposing opinions on the facts set out by Darcy and Murphy and the fact that Dr Darzi cannot yet come to a view. However, with respect, these are expressions of personal judgement, and I will not compound the difficulty by adding my own to them. I am more concerned with the evidence. The facts on the computer are these. We know that Wolski has, or had at one time, a substantial professional reputation. So he is not an unknown crank off the street. He is also clever enough to have got us all here; that in itself should tell us something. Then look at the timing. The project begins at an even pace and then it accelerates. The events in Warsaw, as described by Wolski, follow almost exactly the chronology of the developments that led to the Global Summit being announced. I have more work to do overnight; by the morning I will have a comparative chart of events." She stopped as abruptly as she began.

"Please go on," Thornhill said, tempting her onto ground of which she was less sure.

This time she hesitated before she spoke. "A hypothesis, not a judgement you understand, which fits these facts is as follows." She paused, gathering her thoughts, and then began to express them with such precision that the improbable began to seem possible. "A powerful group of interests, or even a powerful individual, sees the recent radical changes in the balance of world power as an opportunity to establish themselves in a position of unique influence. They believe that they have the technological means to do this. Whether they are correct or not, for the purposes of this hypothesis, is not important. A programme of research is set up, drawing on the most advanced science that money can buy. But for their research they need a facility away from the intrusive eyes of the West.

That would be easy; dollars are very welcome in Eastern Europe, literally everything is for sale. All goes satisfactorily for them until they see a target of opportunity. The Summit changes their plans. It presents the possibility of coming in with a bang. It's then that things begin to go wrong."

Darcy snapped his notebook shut. "That's not credible. According to Wolski, they were running around like headless chickens. Nobody had any idea what to do when things took an unexpected turn. People who are supposed to be doing world-class science using the fire sprinklers out of desperation?"

Morag cut him short. "On the contrary, it's exactly what you might expect when a highly controlled management system with a distant final authority has an unexpected new element thrust upon it. The events that Wolski described are typical of what happens when such systems break down. Just look at the disaster of Chernobyl."

Darcy made no reply, and Morag moved on to the climax of her argument. "The tests, according to Wolski, began by direct injection into small animals and moved, with insufficient further work, to airborne particle tests on humans. These, according to Wolski, had catastrophic results. But what we regard as a disaster may, to them, be a success; the very breakthrough they were trying to achieve." Nobody responded and she continued. "Keep that in mind, and ask the question of how they intend to use the knowledge they now have." She hesitated and then allowed herself to do something unusual.

She made a guess. "In my estimation, we have only so far seen the crude early abilities of whatever it is that they are developing."

"I fear you may have it," Thornhill said quietly. "And if so, our difficulties are acute. Ahead of the Summit there is simply not time for the sort of prudent analysis which we would normally undertake: a research committee to tell us if any of this is possible, psychological profiles of the sorts of people we are looking for, consultation with the allies and so on."

Darcy interrupted, more gently this time. "Do you mean that you do not intend to share our speculations with our allies?"

"That, for the present at least, is a possibility," Thornhill said gravely. "Whoever is behind this must have a huge capital base and access to leading-edge technologies in computers, chemistry, biology and genetics. The USA is the only place in the world where sufficient money and science could be mobilised for a coup like this, and any organisation with that sort of power will also have intimate contacts with government and government agencies. So, until we know more, it's impossible to be sure that our colleagues at Langley and Washington are not compromised."

Morag spoke again. "As important as who, is why," she said. "What's it all for? The evidence suggests that the Summit is no more than a starting point–"

Thornhill cut her off in mid-sentence. "True, but first things first, we must identify who these people may be. Until we do that, we are flying blind." He looked at his watch and then at the exhausted faces around the room. "Let's sleep on it – meet here for breakfast at six?"

Everyone nodded and shambled off. Thornhill slid the balcony window open to feel the Atlantic breeze. He undressed and crawled between the vivid green sheets. As he fell asleep he could hear the distant clack of Morag's keyboard. Later, he could not tell how long, he sensed someone in the room.

It was Morag. Thornhill sat bolt upright. She stood in the balcony doorway, her hair and long white nightgown flowing in the stiff night air.

She stepped into a patch of moonlight by the open door and Thornhill could see a wild, sensual look of triumph in her eyes.

"It's November," she said.

15

November

"Give me ten million dollars and I'll make you rich." Calvin November made the now legendary proposition to Morton B. Grant at the end of dinner at the Grant mansion. The Scottish-Baronial cluster of granite towers and battlements stood at Grosse Pointe beside Lake St Clair, a dozen miles and an entire world away from the growing dereliction of downtown Detroit. Grant was an industrial Emperor of the dynastic kind. Grant Industries was one of the oldest and most powerful conglomerates in the United States. It was a company that the press cautiously referred to as 'controversial'. Editors were mindful of the destruction of at least two newspapers by Grant's devastating ability to sue and win. By contrast, November's position was less complex. After working his way through Harvard and having just completed a PhD at MIT, he was flat broke. All evening he had gone unnoticed by the grandees of industrial Detroit. The outrageous remark to Grant silenced the babble of deal making and overtures to seduction that had ebbed and flowed around the long silver-laden candlelit table. There was no suggestion of humour in November's challenge, but rather one of contempt.

Grant was a man with a genial manner, but those who knew him appreciated that this was a thin camouflage for a mind like a rat trap. The social destruction of the young upstart seemed imminent. Like statutory witnesses at an execution, everyone sat still and blank-faced. But Grant was amused, though cautious of an ambush.

"Son, there are some who'd say I was rich enough already." Nervous laughter rippled around the table.

"No, sir," November replied, "your grandfather was rich. You may have more money than he did, but you are merely wealthy."

"I suppose you intend to tell these good folks what you mean by that." Grant spoke with cold humour and an expansive gesture that embraced the expectant audience.

At the other end of the table, Morton Grant Jnr, heir to the Grant fortune, was aghast.

November had been his roommate at Harvard and during those years, their unspoken understanding was that money was never discussed. The invitation to dinner at the family home was intended to mark the parting of their ways; Grant Jnr to join the business that he would one day inherit and November to begin the task of climbing the corporate ladder wherever he could best market his skills.

"Yes, I'll tell you exactly what I mean," November said. "You are a steward, a steward of the fortune made by your grandfather. A very successful steward, but a steward nevertheless." Grant's face hardened. His eyes, which had been measuring the reaction on the faces around the table, now locked onto November. "Hector Grant became rich because he created a fortune out of his own genius, and the science of the time. All the things he is famous for, the high-speed insulation of cables, ductile iron for pressure vessels, dye technology for denim, all of them were the result of him seeing further than others. His riches lay in the power of his own imagination; only his money was kept in the bank. A fortune like yours is indestructible; you will always be wealthy, but without imagination you will never be rich."

Nobody round the table had ever heard a performance like it. Grant had grown used to celebrity in public and sycophancy in private. But there was something about the absolute self-confidence of November that was magnetic and Grant's natural indignation was tempered by a powerful curiosity.

"That's a romantic idea, son, but the end product of business is money. You see," he said with mock patience, "Grant Industries earns more on its investments on Wall Street than out of manufacturing. Why go to the trouble and risk of making money out of raw materials when you can make money out of money?" November's replied with a rebuke of unexpected intensity.

"Because the show is over. The players have left the theatre, but nobody's wound down the curtain. So the few that are left in the audience have mistaken the sceneshifters for the cast. Eventually, they too will leave and the lights will go out."

Grant, as November had already observed, was not an imaginative man. "What's all that supposed to mean?"

"It means that we, here in this magnificent house…" November somehow contrived to make the grandeur seem trivial. "We are sitting at the centre of the largest piece of industrial obsolescence in the world. From Philadelphia in the East to Chicago in the Mid-West, industries that made America great are in deep trouble, or will be in the next ten years."

Grant's silence encouraged November to continue and he swung both arms in a gesture towards the darkened windows.

"Your splendid lawn which sweeps down to the lake, how often is it mown? Every week in the summer? Just like backyards right across America. To do that you need gasoline, steel, design, engineering, manufacturing, marketing, distribution and a gardener. Soon you won't need any of that, just a different packet of seeds; grass that doesn't grow above an inch high. What is Grant Industries doing about that?"

Grant didn't want to lend credibility to November's thesis by entering an argument on equal terms. "I don't answer questions on game shows," he snapped, picking up his brandy glass. "Our guests are becoming fretsome." He used an antique New England term in an attempt to lift the feeling of embarrassment that had descended upon the table. He pushed his chair backwards and stood up. Others took their cue and began to gather in small groups, murmuring about November's outrageous behaviour. The man at the centre of their attention stood alone with his back to them, looking out into the shadowy space beyond the tall window that opened onto the lawn and the distant lake. Grant Jnr took his father by the elbow and led him into the study, a room lined with shelves of matching leather-bound volumes, all of them unread. Gibbon's History of the Decline and Fall of the Roman Empire, the works of Victor Hugo, Jane Austen and Washington Irving, stood side by side in virgin uniformity.

"Father, I'm sorry…" he began.

"It's okay, son. He knew he'd only get one bite at the cherry and I'm used to teeth marks. Tell me about him."

"He's unusual, you've seen that; he never had any real friends, not even me."

Grant Jnr found it difficult to explain what it was like to live alongside November. "He has the strangest abilities. He wasn't like some students who are just brilliant. You know the type – they goof off all semester, study the week before exams and get straight As for everything. He's obsessive. He was always studying – nights, weekends, vacations, he never let up. Not for a dance, not to meet girls or go to a movie, not for anything. He'd work away in his corner of the room for hours at a time. Sometimes I'd try to distract him, turn the stereo on real loud maybe or some stuff like that, but it made no difference, he didn't seem to hear. Then, for no reason at all, he'd come out with the weirdest things–"

"Weird? What kind of weird?" Grant interrupted sharply.

"I only remember some of the things he said: 'Wealth is a sign of weakness', and 'Power is the product of the mind, not of politics'. Another time, he said, 'You only think money, you don't think rich enough.' And then he'd set back to work without any attempt at explaining what he meant. It was like trying to talk to somebody who's sleepwalking; you couldn't wake him out of an idea."

Grant Snr was thoughtful. He slowly strode the length of the room, running his fingertips over a long shelf of books. The sensation helped him think.

"Mr November sounds like a troubled young man," he said as he turned to face his son. "How did you and he come to share a room?"

Grant Jnr thought for a moment. "That's strange, too. On the first day, when the allocations were made, I was there ahead of time, unpacking my things.

He came in and said, 'My name is November, and I have chosen you.' That made me nervous because, well, you know, because of the family name I thought he might be some sort of social climber. But he wasn't, and that was strange too, because most of the guys and a lot of the girls were, when they found out who I was. That's why I thought it safe to invite him here tonight; I even lent him a dinner jacket!"

"What did he do for his PhD?" Grant Snr asked.

"Bioengineering."

Grant Snr thought for a moment longer, and then made a decision. "Let's go talk to him."

November was standing where they had left him, in unselfconscious isolation. He did not turn as the Grants approached.

"Do you have answers as well as questions?" the elder Grant asked. On getting no reply, he reached out and pulled the cord that drew the curtains across the window, cutting November off from his view of the night. His concentration broken, November turned to Grant.

"Yes, I have answers."

"What are they, and what will they cost me?" Grant said.

"The answers are free, but to find out if you're asking the right questions will cost you the ten million dollars I asked you for earlier."

"Meet me in the library in the morning," Grant said.

November simply nodded. Father and son turned away towards the centre of the room where a group of guests quickly gathered round them. November was left alone.

The next time any of the guests took notice of Calvin November was when the New York Times called him: 'The World's First Eco-Billionaire'.

16

Galesburg Illinois

At Grade School in Galesburg, Illinois, Calvin November was an introspective child; his classmates thought him gloomy. 'When November comes, winter can't be far behind,' a spiteful teacher had once said, and the label stuck. Moreover his first name, that of a dour president well remembered for saying nothing, made him the butt many schoolyard jokes. It was his mother, Martha, daughter of a Lowland Scottish immigrant family, who was the secret behind the name. Calvin Coolidge, recent President and former Vermont lawyer, displayed a wintery aloofness from worldly entanglements that was much admired in a faithfully Presbyterian household. Yet there was also ambition in Martha's choice. John Calvin of Geneva was one of the fathers of the Protestant Reformation that had changed the world.

Hard times and heavy drinking by Walter, Calvin's father, forced the family to move repeatedly from one small Mid-Western town to another, ever in search of another job, cheaper lodgings or escape from growing notoriety. November's abiding memory of childhood was of a land with uninterrupted horizons and small communities, like islands in an ocean of prairie. Each had a welcome that ,sooner or later, wore out.

Choices for a growing child were many but few – many because every type of sport was available, and few because there was little to exercise the mind. Those for whom this was important tended to turn in on themselves. Often the results were unexpected, like small prairie towns producing a succession of Admirals who grew up without ever having seen the sea.

The first words November remembered learning to read were 'The Land of Lincoln', the state motto on the fender of his father's battered Ford pickup.

It was while still very young that November became obsessed with the idea of greatness. To his teachers, he was a learning machine. His ability to study the lives of people who had left their mark on the world was prodigious. He devoured the lives of Alexander the Great, Thomas Edison and John D. Rockefeller in the same way that others followed the careers of Babe Ruth and Jesse Owens.

Since he had no friends, his mother supposed that the boy must be lonely, but loneliness never occurred to him. His contemporaries simply did not interest him. In none of them could he see any trace of his heroes. He enjoyed the idea of being at a distance from people and took long solitary walks along the prairie skyline, knowing full well that the daily sight of a single figure in so large a landscape would imprint itself on the mind of the community.

* * *

One dusty Saturday morning, the county librarian and two policemen arrived at the front door of the small timber-framed house with peeling paint where the Novembers lived. The librarian was a short, energetic woman who was almost overpowered by the force of her own outrage. She hammered on the front door. "Your boy is an animal, a thief and a vandal," she shouted as Alice November cautiously opened the door. Though a forceful woman, she was dumb with astonishment. Faced with the librarian alone, she would have answered back, but ever respectful of authority, she was overawed by the two policemen. The librarian's fury knew no limits. "He has done the basest and most disgusting thing I have ever come upon in twenty-five years of public service."

The sergeant, a kindly man, tried to reduce the temperature. Stepping in front of the librarian, he said, "Mam, if we could just take a look in the boy's room?"

She nodded, and in a state of shock led them up the narrow stairs, past the open door to the teenage chaos of Jonathan's room. She stopped at Calvin's door and knocked. There was no answer. She tried the handle. "Sometimes he locks it," she said apologetically.

"I'm not surprised. We've been watching him, gathering evidence," the librarian said.

"Shall I bust it open?" the younger of the two policemen asked.

The sergeant turned to Alice and gently asked, "Do you have a key, Mam?"

"No, no, I don't believe I have." Alice's mind was numbed by thoughts of the nameless atrocity that her son was supposed to have committed.

"We don't like doing this; are you sure you don't have a key?"

By now Alice had recovered some of her normal sense of indignation. "Just tell me what you're looking for, and by what right you can come bursting into my home."

The sergeant ignored her. "Okay, Leroy, do it."

The doorframe offered little resistance, and the librarian strode inside at the head of the group and began to open the dresser drawers.

"Leave this to us, Mam," the sergeant said.

He began searching the dresser, but was interrupted by his partner who was reaching onto the top of the wardrobe.

"Hey, take a look at this." He held a bunch of scrapbooks that had been carefully bound by red cord into a single volume.

Alice dreaded what they might contain. The cluster of scrapbooks carried a title in large hand-drawn letters: A Strategy For My Life. The sergeant put it on the dresser and flicked it open.

"That's it," the librarian screamed. "It's obscene what he's done." The scrapbooks held a pantheon of heroes, with their name and achievements recorded in meticulous handwriting. Alice was appalled. Each page was covered with pictures and phrases neatly cut from library books.

"Two hundred books he's destroyed, two hundred," the librarian shouted.

* * *

Doc Stevenson's elderly Buick pulled up outside the Novembers' house. Stevenson had been the Novembers' family physician since their arrival in the town some years earlier. He knew Alice to be a woman of sober judgement and she was clearly in distress when she called.

As he put the phone down, he resisted the temptation to finish the excellent dinner of chicken gumbo that Clarissa, his wife of forty years, had prepared as a wedding anniversary reminder of their honeymoon in New Orleans. But he was resigned to interrupted meals and broken sleep.

When he knocked on the door at the Novembers' house he was more puzzled than resentful. Alice opened the door, and the doctor's perplexity grew as soon as she led him into the parlour and closed the door behind them. Saying nothing, she thrust a bundle of scrapbooks into his hands. He took them, looked for a seat and sat himself down next to the table lamp that illuminated a corner of the gloomy room. For a moment he fumbled for his glasses, and then began to read. Alice couldn't wait for an answer.

"He's sick, isn't he?" she said, as if willing the doctor to agree.

"Well, I..."

She cut him off in mid-sentence. "I know it's serious. There are Commies in that book, Marx and Lenin, real bad people. Why does a boy his age want to fill his mind with that sort of stuff?"

"There are plenty of other people in here besides Commies..."

Alice took a deep shuddering breath. Slowly her head sank to her knees and she began to sob convulsively. "Nine hundred and fifty dollars ... I don't know what we shall do."

"Nine hundred and fifty dollars for what?" the doctor asked, his patience wearing thin.

"The books he cut up. Over two hundred of them, and they say we have to pay nine hundred and fifty dollars, that's the State valuation. Nine fifty is more than Walter earned all last summer, leastways it's more than he brought home."

"Alice, this is not a medical problem," the doctor said sympathetically.

"Not a medical problem! A boy would have to be sick to do a thing like that," she insisted.

"Perhaps I ought to speak to him."

"Yes, you ought," Alice said firmly. "I'll go get him."

Frank Stevenson sat in the dimly lit corner of the room with his eyes half-closed as he listened to Alice's determined tread on the stairs. The sound of a door being opened was followed by a conversation, which was too distant for him to make out. Another thoughtless, selfish child, another father on the booze and another mother under more stress than she knew how to handle, a sad and familiar story. He thought of home. Clarissa, the abandoned dinner and the open fire waited for him fifteen blocks away. There were footsteps on the stairs again, two people this time. Calvin November stood in the doorway. There was something strange about him, but in the low light Stevenson could not decide what it was. The boy stood tall and self-assured, as if his early teenage frame was a disguise for a person of maturity. Stevenson found himself getting to his feet so as not to feel at a disadvantage.

He mustered his most authoritarian voice, the one he used for giving patients bad news.

"Young man," he said, "you've put your mother to a lot of grief. What do you have to say for yourself?" Stevenson remembered the reply he got for years afterwards.

"I'm going to discover the outer edge," Calvin November said.

17

44th Street

The traffic on 44th Street growled and snarled its way across midtown Manhattan. Twenty-two floors above the intersection with 2nd Avenue, Murphy put another cassette into the recorder and asked Goldman his next question.

Finding Goldman had been a masterstroke. At four thirty in the morning after Morag identified November, Thornhill had called another meeting in his room. Everyone wondered why? The tension of the previous night had drained away, leaving a collective of dull headaches, gritty eyes and coated tongues. Thornhill alone was showered and shaved. He sensed their resentment.

"Sorry to deny you your orange juice and croissants, but we need to move quickly."

It took Morag no more than five minutes to set out the profile of November.

"Sounds to me as if we are hanging a great weight on a small nail," Darcy said.

"He's the best candidate we have," Morag said flatly.

"He's the best candidate we have because he's the only candidate we have," Darcy said with unconcealed irritation.

Thornhill chose to ignore the exchange. "Morag has a direct route in," he said.

Morag spoke before anybody could interrupt. "There's a writer, his name is Art Goldman; he specialises in 'revelatory biographies'. His current subject is Calvin November. Goldman is known as a 'sleaze ball'."

She used the unfamiliar phrase like a technical term. "I know somebody at Columbia University who can get us to him."

"Great," Murphy said, bringing a large hand down with a thud on the arm of his chair. "Sounds like my kind of guy. Let me go talk to him."

"Very well," Thornhill said.

"I can be in Manhattan before lunch," Murphy said eagerly.

* * *

In Goldman's book-cluttered apartment, the windows faced the grimy brick flank of the building alongside. Murphy pressed the record button again.

"The Outer Edge, that's the name of the book?"

"Yeah, that's the title, unless I come up with something better," Goldman said huffily.

"It's original, it's what November said when he was a kid. The old doctor told me, the one I interviewed at Galesburg, out in Illinois. He's dead now."

"Sounds tacky, the title," Murphy said; he wanted to find a way through Goldman's self-confidence.

Goldman took the bait. "Look, I agreed to talk to you on a confidential basis, because an old friend at Columbia said it was important."

"And because we're paying you twenty grand," Murphy added.

Goldman ignored the remark. "Look, if you want to play at literary criticism, then you can wait until the book is published and read it along with everybody else."

"And pay $29.95 instead of twenty thousand." Murphy knew it was important to stay in the driving seat. "How much collaboration have you had from your subject?"

"I don't do collaboration, it cramps my style."

Murphy noticed that the absence of a view into the street also meant that nobody could get a shot into the apartment.

"I guess you must get scared some nights; these people you write about, some of them have a long reach."

"Ha!" Goldman snorted in contempt. "With what you don't understand I could fill several books. These guys, all of them, they threaten to sue, try to buy me off and yes, I get threatening calls – they feel they have to go through all of that. But underneath it all, they love it. Even if they won't admit it, even to themselves, they can't get enough of it."

Murphy stood up as if to stretch his legs and began a circuit of the small, cluttered room. The wall opposite the window was lined with rickety shelves crammed with research files, each dated and labelled in Goldman's careful handwriting. The sins and omissions of the high and the mighty were listed, indexed and numbered with academic exactitude. The last file was a catalogue of computer databases that gave access to newspaper articles and broadcast transmissions in Europe, the USA and Japan.

Sleaze it might be, thought Murphy, but it was very professionally managed sleaze. Murphy completed his tour of the room and turned to Goldman.

"A lot of paper," he said.

"Habit of a lifetime. When I started, there were no word processors. Besides, paper speaks to you like no computer screen ever can," Goldman replied.

"So you found this old guy, the doctor; what happened next?"

"Doc Stevenson?" Goldman replied. "Yeah, a remarkable old man, in his nineties but sharp as a tack. He died only a couple of months back. He was my way into November's early years. It seems that the young man made such an impression that the old doc tracked his progress for decades afterwards. He didn't go over the top – it was no kind of fan club; the old boy was too sensible for that kind of thing. It was more of a hobby, like some people watch birds or collect butterflies."

"So what kind of caterpillar was November back then?" Murphy asked.

"A very special kind of loner. He lived in a world where he saw other people as one-dimensional, like cut-out scenery in a one-man play. He didn't seem to understand that this was cruel to anybody who cared about him, though there were precious few of those."

"A lot of guys like that wind up in the slammer or go to the chair," Murphy said.

"No!" Goldman threw up a hand in protest. "You've got him wrong. November is different."

"What do you mean?" Murphy asked.

Goldman took a while to reply and the noises of Manhattan filled the empty space between them. "He was different because he was not driven by anger and frustration like so many kids who knock over a corner liquor store, but…"

He hesitated again. "Look, this is not easy to explain; it's the chapter in the book I am rewriting now."

He gestured towards the word processor on the overloaded desk across the room.

"Why's it so difficult?" Murphy asked, and was surprised when Goldman seemed embarrassed about the answer.

"Because I can't make it sound real," he said, as if confessing to some shameful failing. "Anything I write sounds like I'm describing Napoleon, or worse, someone who thinks he's Napoleon; like some common or garden loony. But this guy is certainly no loony, or if he is a head case, he's a very special kind." Murphy was careful to let Goldman keep talking. "This is how I see it. Behind everything he did, and probably still does, is a sense of merely being a transient, passing through on his way to a place in history that had somehow already been allotted to him. That's why he was never interested in people, only in progress – progress along the road to what he kept talking about as greatness. You see what I mean about making it sound real?" Murphy let Goldman struggle on. "Here's an example," Goldman said, leafing through a printout from a file on the desk. "He won a scholarship to Harvard. People were prepared to tolerate him because of his brilliance and because he was a local. Here's a cutting." He handed Murphy a column-length article from a local newspaper. It read: LONELY SCHOLAR WINS IVY LEAGUE PLACE.

"Now that was big news in a small town," Goldman said. "a grand send-off was planned. His father stayed sober all day, and his mother hired the fire house and announced a party for the whole street." Goldman went to the computer and read a draft chapter off the screen.

"It was her chance to emerge from lifelong self-effacement, her shelter from a deep fear of public humiliation.

At last, she had a chance to win without the fear of losing." He turned to Murphy. "But it didn't work out that way."

"What went wrong?" Murphy asked.

"The little bastard didn't show up, that's what went wrong. His father, for the first time in his life, did something useful. He tracked him down at the Greyhound Bus depot." Goldman read from the screen again: 'What do I tell your mother?' the father pleaded. 'Tell her I've moved on.'"

"Then what happened?"

Goldman continued. "The father didn't go back to the fire house but into the bar across the street and drank himself stupid. Alice, humiliated in front of the entire town, went home and cried all night. In the morning, she wrote a long, carefully worded letter to Doc Stevenson and took it to the mailbox on Main Street. Then she returned to the house, went upstairs and took all the sleeping pills in the bottle on the bedside table." Goldman turned away from the screen. "Calvin November didn't even come to his mother's funeral."

Murphy sat and wondered. What could all this have to do with the events in Warsaw and the frightened old man he had been sent to meet on a dark, bitterly cold street by the Hudson?

Goldman was a natural storyteller and seemed no longer to notice Murphy. "November put Grant's ten million dollars to spectacularly good effect. Of course, he didn't get the money all at once. It was a kind of capital development fund." Goldman took a folder from the long rank of shelving behind him. "Here; there's all kinds of stuff about it in *Scientific American* and *Nature*."

He handed Murphy the file. It contained page after page of cuttings, some from learned journals and others from the popular press: '*Rearranging the Building Blocks of Life*', one said. Others reported: '*Bugs Eat Garbage – Produce Fuel*'. '*Is Crop Spraying Obsolete?*' '*New Disease-Free Grain*'.

Murphy was impressed. "Looks like a good start."

"It got better, for November, that is. The recession in Reagan's time hit Grant's manufacturing industries hard."

"And then?" Murphy asked.

"By that time old man Grant was himself in bad shape. He had one heart attack and then another. He died just as the troubles were at their worst. According to the will and various trusts, Grant Jnr took over. But he couldn't hack it. Grant Industries needed cash in a hurry, and when November raised the money to buy out the bioengineering interests of the company, for a fraction of their true worth, his offer was accepted. Nobody outside the outfit knows how November got the money to do it, but that wouldn't have been too difficult for someone like him."

"Still, it must have been a lot of money," Murphy said.

"Not a problem. You've got to remember, back then Vietnam was a painful memory and the Cold War was a bloody mess. In those days, there was more than one superpower. And both sides were sending their teams of proxies into action all over the world. There was desperation to hit the Soviets everywhere from Angola to outer space. Everyone worked on the basis that 'my enemy's enemy is my friend'. That's how Bin Laden got his start; trained by the CIA. The same kind of thing was going on all over the world. Civil, or should I say very uncivil, wars were being fought between clients of East and West right across Africa.

Arms were secretly and illegally sold to our sworn enemy Iran to raise funds for a conflict by proxy in Central America. Here at home, the fog of war was thick over Washington. I expect you'll recall the bizarre scandals of the CIA and all the others. And on top of all that, here in the 'Home of the Brave and Land of the Free', we were building an illegal drug business bigger than the space programme and Medicare put together. With so much money and power out of control, who knows what kind of people November might have met. Then, as now, everyone had their own angle: money, power, ideology, megalomania or even do-goodery. Everything was out of whack."

As a bit player in the game, Murphy understood exactly what Goldman was saying. "So however it was done, November found a way to create his own Imperium," Murphy said.

"A good word that, Imperium. I'll use it," Goldman said, writing it down.

"You're welcome," Murphy said.

Goldman read from the screen again. "Those working for him were noted for being fanatical in their loyalty, as if to some mystical higher purpose."

"So what happened next?"

"His new backers made a lot of money," Goldman replied. "Plant genetics, medicines, any set of molecules capable of being taken apart and rebuilt. November was interested. Here's what he said in one of his very few TV appearances:

'My recreation is re-creation.' The interviewer thought he was joking."

"Some guy," Murphy said, just to keep the conversation moving.

18

The United States of Paradox

"Thanks, Gene, I owe you," Murphy said as he slid the New York Press Association credential into his wallet. Lunch at the 21 Club in Mid-Town Manhattan was convivial. Gene Stanton and Murphy had a long-standing trail of mutual favours behind them. For Murphy, 21 was a favourite meeting place. He always enjoyed the atmosphere; the oak panelling, leather furniture and sporting prints were strangely English for such a completely American institution.

"One of these times you'll get me busted," Stanton said from behind the menu.

"One of these times I'll get you a Pulitzer," Murphy replied.

"There are no Pulitzers for freelancers." Stanton let his eyes wander around the room crowded with the rich, the fashionable and those who had ambitions to be either or both. "We're just the beaters, we drive the game onto the guns. You need a by-line to get to hang the trophies on the living room wall." The conversation drifted into ritual pleasantries.

"How's Mary?"

"Fine, she's still has dreams of open spaces wider than Central Park."

"And Tad, how's he doing?"

"Great, Hunter's been good for him."

"You still flying?"

"Only just. I've still got half-shares in an old Cessna 180 over at Morristown. We let the flying club use it. That covers a lot of the expense, but I need to book some time soon. I've got to fly six hours before Labour Day or I lose my licence."

Murphy put the lunchtime edition of the New York Times on the table between them. The lead story was about a rally at Madison Square Garden. The headline read: *World Waits For November.*

"Why are you interested in this guy?" Stanton asked, as if protecting personal property.

"We think he may have interesting ideas."

"Interesting, like dangerous?"

"Interesting, like you'll be the first to know if any of it becomes publishable," Murphy said, running his index finger under the slogan on the masthead of the paper: *All the news that's fit to print.*

"We have a deal?" Stanton wanted to be sure.

"We have a deal. Tell me what you've got."

The waiter arrived, an unwelcome interruption. They both ordered as if on autopilot. Stanton continued speaking as soon as he judged that they would not be overheard.

"It's no news that he's one of the world's richest men; exactly how rich nobody knows. And maybe he's one of the smartest too."

"Rich I understand, but smart? That doesn't always go with the territory. Some guys who've made billions wouldn't know how to catch a bus," Murphy replied.

"Everyone will be doing big features on the back of the rally," Stanton said.

"So you've been digging?" Murphy asked.

"This stays between us, right?" Stanton hesitated. "Strictly background. OK?"

"We both know the rules," Murphy said.

"OK, I wish I had been digging. It's like trying to drive a spade into concrete. Everything's tied up in those weird domes down in the Nevada Desert," Stanton said.

"Tell me about them," Murphy said.

"November founded an outfit called Celestacom, to 'probe and prove the future', and housed it in two vast domes out in the Nevada desert.

He must have a couple of thousand people working out there. Strange sort of a place, very public yet very secret."

Murphy was disappointed. "Come on, Gene, you can do better than that. They're just some kind of Eco Disneyland. Bus tours, school trips, student study groups, the whole nine yards."

Stanton replied sharply, "That's what *National Geographic* might think, and Joe Public certainly does, but nobody really knows what's going on down there. Step off the tourist trail and the place is as tight as a duck's ass."

The food arrived but neither of them seemed to notice.

"So you have this irony; here's a guy with a massive profile in the public consciousness but when you look into it, he has no real profile at all. He just sits out there in the desert under his glass domes, when he could be walking with kings and presidents; maybe he thinks they're beneath him."

"How much have you been able to find out?" Murphy asked.

"About the past? Not much. There are no spin-doctors, no PR stunts. Despite that, or maybe because of it, media people like me are gagging for every crumb we can get."

"Is that genius or an accident?" Murphy asked.

"Who knows? Perhaps both. I'm more interested in the future than in the past."

"Why's that?" Murphy asked.

"Something that stuck in my mind. It was in one of the very few public speeches he's ever made; a commencement address at Harvard. I guess he must have been flattered by his Alma Mater asking him to return to the fold."

"So what did he say?"

"Well, along with all the usual onwards and upwards stuff you get at that kind of event, he said this." Stanton pulled a notebook from an inner pocket. "'Choose your time, choose your place. Choose well, for he who rules the moment rules the hour.'"

"A slogan," Murphy said dismissively.

"No, more of a mantra. Look at the strategy. He's succeeded by putting himself in the right place at the right time," Stanton said.

Murphy was unimpressed. "Come on, Gene, you could say that about anyone with mega-bucks, Howard Hughes, Bill Gates, any of them."

"And you might be right," Stanton replied, "but this is different, there's a pattern. Time and again he's chosen to back gateway technologies and through them gained a dominant position. But that's only the half of it. His other killer skill is in timing."

"So what are you saying?"

"I'm saying remember the mantra. 'He who rules the moment rules the hour'," Stanton said.

"Go on." Murphy sensed that there was something important to come.

"Here's the strangest thing. The people closest to him, the few we've been able to speak to, they're devoted to him. They're total believers. That place in the desert is the nearest thing to a mediaeval university there's been for the last six hundred years."

"Mediaeval university!" Murphy laughed. "He's really got to you, hasn't he?"

"I mean it," Stanton said insistently, "and I'll tell you why. Do you know why there are Bachelor degrees? Because once upon a time that's exactly what a graduate was, a bachelor married to science or art. To marry a woman, a bachelor needed permission from the university, and that was rarely given."

Murphy's cynicism rose in ratio to Stanton's enthusiasm. "Gene, you'll give hype a bad name."

"Don't underestimate what's going on down there, that's all," Stanton said, as if he wanted to close the conversation. They began to address the tepid prawn pasta in front of them. Murphy chose his moment. "So what's with this laser show at the Garden? Is he going to announce some new techno-breakthrough?" he asked.

"Maybe, but my guess is not."

"Not? Why not?"

"My guess is it's something political."

"Political? That's horseshit; he's not a loser. He's not going to get into a fight he can't win," Murphy said dismissively.

"Maybe he's got a new idea," Stanton said.

"There are no new ideas. Even with an ego his size, he's got to know it's a closed game. He's got no power base, no organisation and no workers. No deal," Murphy said.

"Of course that's true, but it's also traditional thinking. See it the way he sees it for a moment," Stanton said.

"How can you see it as he sees it?" Murphy asked.

"Stop asking questions and start using your imagination. If he does have a new idea, something truly radical, think about the market opportunity. Think about timing. Look at the mess we're in. We're near paralysed by what terrorism has done to us, look at Iraq. The greatest of nations are led by the smallest of men. The economy is going to hell in a handcart and what choice have we got? Right-wing sleaze, or left wing-sleaze. Mindless war or timid inactivity."

"It would have to be one hell'uva big idea," Murphy said.

"Only big enough to make people believe in it. That's what worries me," Stanton replied.

Murphy tried to lighten the mood. "Even that's not a new idea. You know what Marx said – not Karl, the other one? 'The two most important things in politics are sincerity and integrity, and if you can fake them, you've got it made.'" He shuddered with laughter at his own joke, but it fell flat.

Murphy's frivolity made Stanton's concern more intense. "Nobody is uncontaminated. Nobody has enough credibility to say the big words without sounding like Coco the Clown reading the Gettysburg Address. People want vision, that's why everyone's got so much hope invested in this summit in Geneva that everyone's talking about."

The connection of November with the Summit rang an alarm bell, but Murphy made sure it didn't show.

"Who's arguing?" he said dismissively. "But you know as well as I do, no amount of money or personal charisma from outside the established parties has ever come close to cracking the system. It's never been done, the whole world knows that," he said, trying to provoke Stanton into saying more.

"But what if this guy knows something we don't?" Stanton asked.

"Like?"

"Like what happens if the system implodes?"

"You mean caused to implode?" Murphy said sharply.

"Maybe. Want to tell me more?" Stanton asked cautiously.

"Like I said, however insane you think that possibility may be, you need to see it from his perspective," Murphy said.

"Okay, try me," Stanton replied.

Murphy waved at the waiter. “Bring us a bottle of Irish. My friend and I need to adjust our perspective.

19

Madison Square Garden

The laser show was super-spectacular, a Grand Canyon of light and sound. Murphy tried hard not to be impressed but failed.

"I remember when it was just searchlights, trumpets and Wagner," Stanton said from the back of the Press Box. In the auditorium, the silence that abruptly followed was as forceful as the sound and fury of the opening. A single spotlight followed Calvin November to centre-stage. For a moment he stood motionless. Murphy was surprised at how small he was. As a murmur rose from the crowd, November raised his hands and there was silence once again. From the back of the Press Box, Stanton voiced Murphy's thoughts.

"This guy gives me the creeps. Give me have an honest crook for a politician any time."

November's first words were level toned, their lack of emotion contrasting with the magnitude of the declaration they made.

"I stand before you at a moment in our nation's history where new possibilities rush towards us at exponential speed."

"How the hell does he expect people to understand exponential?" Stanton muttered.

"The world is witnessing the failure of the old ways. Communism has collapsed. Capitalism is buckling under the weight of its own greed and injustice. Terrorists strike at us and we hit out at shadows."

"He's not making himself any friends," Stanton said.

"And what do I say of America? What do you say of America?" November's voice and body language rose in intensity. "I hear the voices of your mind. We are the United States of paradox. We are an idealistic nation. We are a corrupt nation. We are a nation founded on freedom yet we have a history of ethnic cleansing, slavery and lynching."

There was complete silence in the Press Box and Murphy felt his mouth go dry.

"We are a wholesome nation yet we are the world's largest consumer of illegal drugs. We are a righteous nation yet we produce more pornography than anywhere else on earth. We are a nation of conscience yet we preside over sixty million on the breadline. That is a number greater than the combined populations of Belgium, the Netherlands, all four countries of Scandinavia, Australia and New Zealand put together. Our planet is precious to us yet our lifestyle consumes five times the resources per person of other industrialised nations. We are a great democracy, but the will of the people is perverted by a system shot through with avarice and self-serving mediocrity."

The crowd seemed stunned. November paused for effect, his eyes staring into the darkness beyond the circle of the spotlight.

"We have been cheated of our birthright." For a moment, November was still. In the Press box, Stanton wondered where all this was going.

"So who screwed Mother and stole the Apple Pie?"

"Shut up," snapped another journalist from the back row.

November spoke with growing passion. "And who is responsible for this?" He lowered his voice almost to a whisper. "You are responsible, I am responsible. We are responsible.

Why? Because we are America. Technology has led us to the brink of wonderful and terrible things. Things unimaginable even a few short years ago. Vast prizes and unfathomable dangers lie before us. Only by facing our past honestly can we face our future confidently. Therefore, let us glory in our greatness, bind up our self-inflicted wounds, seize the moment and rule the hour."

At that phrase Stanton and Murphy exchanged silent looks. Slowly the applause came. At first Murphy was willing to believe that it was stage-managed. But as the volume rose, he knew that November had the crowd eating from his hand.

Stanton's cynicism was undiminished. "Words, words, words..."

November raised his hands and the crowd were obediently silent. "Empty words, I hear you say. I reply – no. I give you substance. I give you the power to change America, to defend our nation against the squalid politics of here and now and the dark technologies of the future."

Even Stanton became attentive.

"How is this to be achieved? Not by redistributing resources like the socialists or by amassing wealth like the capitalists, but by beginning again, by releasing the power that is inherent in everyone; by being the best we can be. Today I put that power into your hands, the power to turn poverty into prosperity, despair into hope, goodness into excellence."

Stanton put Murphy's thoughts into words. "He's gonna need one hell'uva of a punch line to get himself out of that."

November did not disappoint.

"Today I announce an endowment of a hundred billion dollars to the people of America. I repeat, one hundred thousand million dollars, to the people of America."

The Press Box was a sudden blur of activity as keyboards clattered into simultaneous use. Most astonishing offer in the history of America ... If Calvin November can deliver, the world is a different place ... America is asking, is this guy for real? The flurry of instantly crafted headlines died down as November continued, and news desks across the globe stood by for more.

"I believe that there is no more useless substance on earth than money unused. This hundred billion dollars is not a gift, it is an investment, an investment in the genius of America. You are the shareholders, I am merely an officer of the company."

"This is getting scary," Stanton said.

"This investment will put within our grasp the keys to relieving disease, depravation and environmental degradation. And we shall demand that those in power allow us to unlock the doors. We are not a political party, we are more than that. We are the people." The crowd roared in response. November appeared to be unmoved. "To create a voice for all the people, I announce the formation of a Council for a New America. Who are its members? You are its members. I shall be advised by you, guided by you and answerable to you. In thirty days I shall stand before you again, here in this great gathering place, and announce the technology which will provide access for all, so that we may give reality to our dreams and advance confidently together to the outer edge."

The lasers cut through the darkness and the crowd went wild. November slipped away among the lattice of lights.

Cacophony broke out again among the reporters as they called their news desks or pounded their keyboards. Stanton was typing and talking simultaneously.

"The bastard is going to buy the country at a hundred dollars a vote."

Murphy was the only one not typing or talking into a phone and he made an unnoticed exit onto the street. He tried to let the reassuring clamour of 7th Avenue fill his brain but he failed. For the first time in the whole affair, he began to feel real fear.

20

Noplace, Nevada

"They dropped two atomic bombs on the Japs and let off nine hundred and twenty-eight, right here in the deserts of the good 'ole USA. Does that make any kinds sense to you? " Rocky was a large man with an even larger sense of irony. "Above ground, underground, every which way, nearly a thousand nukes" He paused, as if expecting some kind of response.

90 MILES FROM NOPLACE' – the sign over the door of Rocky's Desert Diner was a favourite with tourists, but there were none about at this time of year. Murphy was the only customer. Rocky was running on automatic, telling his own story and answering his own questions.

"They let off eleven of them at Yucca Flats, just a few miles from here. A good many of us died of cancer after that; in one town it was more than one in three. John Wayne, the all-American hero, he was killed by the all-American fall-out, right over there," he said, making a gesture towards the horizon. "Leastways that's what they said on TV, and who am I to argue? He made a picture about Genghis Khan out there in the desert."

Rocky pointed to a line of fading photographs on the wall. “Signed one of those pictures for me, he did. But the desert got him, radioactive sand and dust I say, and a lot of others say so too. Like I said, it was on TV,” he said, as if it was the final proof of his argument. Murphy nodded sympathetically and Rocky kept talking.

“This was a happening place back then – the movies, the stars, the rubberneckers. What they spent paid off the loan on this spread in three years, and I put some aside too. Now it’s only desert nuts like you that keep me from going under.” Murphy had been listening for an hour and Rocky was keen not to let him go.

“See that road out there? Runs direct from Noplace to Noplace.” Rocky was unstoppable. “Why do I stay?” he asked himself. “When you’re on the road to Noplace, there’s no place to go.” He let out a wheezy chuckle at his well-practised line.

Murphy had worked his way through a double cheeseburger with a heart of ice, the legacy of long interment in the massive freezer behind the counter. A truck roared by. The blue and white Celestacom logo, formed of two domes, was sliced into horizontal strips by the slatted blinds. “You get any business from those crazy domes down the road?”

"Nix. Everything’s trucked in and nothing and nobody comes out. Right by the gate there’s a container park. Truckers get no further than that, just drop off a full one, pick up an empty and turn right around.”

“Did you see November, the guy who owns the domes, on TV?”

Rocky was not impressed. “Guess he’s just trying to promote the place. It’s just like Disneyland, a world on its own. You can go on tours; did you know that?” he said incredulously.

“You been out there?” Murphy asked.

Rocky seemed astonished at the notion. “Me? Why would I go there? I’ve no reason to. Have no reason to do much else either,” he added morosely. "Mighty short on distractions out here. A man'd give a lot to be distracted once in a while."

* * *

Murphy had flown down to Las Vegas overnight. After the Madison Square Garden event, timing was critical. He wanted to get to Celestacom after the media satellite trucks had left but before the inevitable tide of tourists had time to make travel arrangements. At the airport shop he had bought himself an outfit of garish tourist gear, a baseball cap and large pair of Ray-Bans. He rented a 4x4 and set out to view November's empire before dawn. The huge domes stood out dramatically against the rising light. But reconnaissance revealed little. The only thing he saw close up was the electric fence. He guessed that it was alarmed and backed up by motion detectors, video recording and night image intensifiers.

Forty miles away, in the small desert town that had been coaxed back to life through the tourist trade generated by the Domes, Murphy checked into the Palms Hotel, two storeys of imitation Hacienda. Where in Spain there would have been a courtyard, there was the inevitable pool. Murphy was the only guest not to use it.

"How do I get on one of those tours to Celestacom?" he asked at the front desk.

"The bus comes right by the door at eleven fifteen a.m., gets to the Ecosphere around one thirty," the clerk said in a voice that sounded as if it was computer generated.

"You're lucky you can get a place; they've put on an extra two buses after that big show in New York. The tours leaving direct from the airport are booked all month."

Murphy joined the cluster of brightly clad figures waiting for the bus. He was looking for camouflage.

He chose a woman in her late 40s; she carried a backpack and a book. As he got closer he saw that it was an illustrated guide to snakes.

"Collecting?" he asked.

She gave him a cool, analytical look. "No, observing."

"Snakes or men?"

"Snakes mostly."

"Glad you think there's a difference. A lot of women don't."

They both laughed, and when the bus arrived it seemed quite natural that they should sit together. The woman opened her book. Murphy continued to talk. "Been on the road for ten days. Had some time due me. Thought I'd check it out round here for a while. What's your name? You don't mind me asking that, do you?"

"Carol. Carol Hirschberger from LA." They shook hands. Instinctively, Murphy avoided giving a name, even a false one.

"So, Carol, what brings you to the South West?"

"Snakes. I teach at UCLA. But after two weeks tracking reptiles I'm ready for a break."

Murphy laughed. "I know how you feel."

"Are you a cop?" she asked. The question was too close for comfort.

"You don't have to be a cop to recognise the failings of your fellow man."

"So what do you do?" Carol asked.

Murphy was angry with himself; a sloppy remark had resulted in him being interrogated when the purpose of the conversation was to provide cover, not exposure. "Leave me with my pathetic air of mystery, you'll like me better that way."

As if on impulse, he said, "Look, I was taking the tour because I didn't want to drive alone – I do that in real life. I'm on vacation now. What do you say we drive up there together? I've got a 4x4 in the parking lot. We could talk about snakes."

"Okay," Carol said.

They climbed out of the bus and walked to Murphy's Land Cruiser. They drove in silence for a while. Ah hour later, as they climbed a long hill, the domes came into sight. In the crystal-clear light they seemed to be etched on the distant red-rock skyline. There was a line of buses ahead; each trailed its own plume of dust. Carol pulled a guidebook from her bag and began to read. "We're now entering a twenty-mile straight road built to provide access to the domes. It's become known as 'The Highway to the Future'."

"Every road is a road to the future," Murphy said.

Carol didn't respond but droned on about size, scale, distance and number of visitors. Though the flawless blue sky looked like mid-summer, it was cold outside. Murphy calculated that the altitude was around seven thousand feet. He decided it was time to reanimate the conversation.

"We're on the edge of the largest inhabited plateau outside of Tibet," he said.

"How do you know something like that?" she said, looking up from the guidebook.

"Just something I read. Why are you so surprised?"

"You don't seem like a person who'd be interested in that kind of thing," she replied.

"I warned you, it's my pathetic air of mystery."

"Look, I'm sorry, that just came out the wrong way," she said apologetically.

They were both laughing as they arrived at the huge parking lot. At the visitors' entrance to the Domes, Murphy steered them into the centre of a group from New York City. Inside the huge structure there was an instant change of climate; the warm, moist air came as a shock after the sharp edge of the desert winter.

The hubbub of several thousand people was lost in the cavernous interior. A young woman in corporate uniform greeted them.

"Welcome to the home of Celestacom. Please step this way. I am your visit coordinator. My name is Sandra. I shall be with you at all times and will be pleased to try and answer any questions you may have."

The Dome was vast, far larger than anyone in the group had expected. The interior was laid out in a succession of interconnecting terraces. Each housed individually designed buildings surrounded by trees and forest plants. The group began to exchange expressions of wonderment. Sandra was programmed to pre-empt questions in the course of efficient visitor processing.

"The interior is inspired by the Hanging Gardens of Babylon, one of the Seven Wonders of the Ancient World. Each location has its own microclimate with tropical plants towards the top of the dome and temperate plants at the bottom. Please follow me to video registration and pass in single file through the entry point.

You will receive your souvenir pass, which will also show our group identity. We give each tour party an identifying name from the Greek alphabet. Ours is Gamma. Please remember this in case you become separated from the group."

As the group moved forward, Murphy wondered whether keeping the Ray-Bans on outweighed the attention they might attract inside He looked around the group and saw that two others had not removed theirs and he decided his would not look out of place.

Sandra led them to a platform set among stainless-steel sculptures and Caledonian Pines. Everyone stared upwards. She continued to speak like a corporate brochure.

"These Domes are the largest geodetic structures in the world. The one we're now in is Dynamos. This is the ancient Greek word for power; the word has the same root as dynamic. We like to think that this applies to the people who live here. Dynamos is our home and the place where we receive visitors. Our second Dome is our place of work. It's called Helios, named after the ancient Greek word for the sun – the source of all life. As you can see, the plastics from which the domes are made are easily bendable by hand." Sandra handed out samples to the group. "The strength comes from the design of the frame that locks the pieces together so that each braces the other."

While the group stared into the space above, Murphy bent down as if to tie a shoelace and slid one of the samples into the case of his Ray-Bans. "This design is a practical expression of the Celestacom philosophy of using a small amount of innovation in just the right place to achieve a spectacular result.

You will notice the difference between Dynamos, which is transparent - keeping us in touch with the world outside, and Helios, which has a mirror-like surface, turning our attention inwards to unlock the mysteries of our planet."

"Why are the Domes built so big? Why not make smaller ones?" a woman from the back asked.

Sandra had a ready answer. "They're not built large just to be the biggest, but to be the right size to maintain their own climate." She had a lot more ground to cover and another group was closing in. "Almost all our power comes from the sun and nearly everything is recycled. All domestic water is cleansed and used repeatedly. We get fresh drinking water from the condensation produced by the vegetation. At night, warm air rises and the moisture it carries collects in the upper dome. The diagonal slats you can see under the apex capture the moisture.

It's piped down again ready for use, much like rain in a temperate climate. Human waste has two uses. It is processed into fertiliser, for plants growing inside the dome, and into gas that powers the utility vehicles operating on the outside." The group had given up on interruptions. Like Murphy, they were hanging on every word.

"Helios, our other Dome, is also entirely self-contained. It houses all our research and industrial plant. We use a lot of power and we produce it all ourselves by synthesising hydrogen; the raw materials for that are water and sunlight." Sandra was enjoying herself. "And who can tell me what the main waste product of hydrogen power is?"

"Water," an eager school kid immediately shouted.

Sandra wasn't used to getting answers, and the intervention stole a moment of triumph. She quickly regained the initiative by passing on to another wonder-fact.

"Helios has the world's largest reserve of naturally produced hydrogen. We burn no fossil fuels here. If our planet is to survive, Helios must be the model of the future."

"Do we get to see inside Helios?" one of the teenagers asked.

"No. Helios is where we work; it's a very private place. To some of us it feels sacred.

Later, we'll show you some of the ideas that have emerged from Helios – innovations with the potential to change the world."

"Sounds like you got some mission, lady." Murphy didn't see who spoke, but the voice was male, elderly and from the Bronx.

For Sandra, saving the planet was not something to be polluted by irony. "We believe in what we do. All of us who work here have made a critical life choice – to leave the contamination of cities and to enquire into the fundamental mechanisms of life. Like Mr November says, 'Pure science in a pure environment'."

"Some crock of shit." Murphy spoke under his breath.

Sandra didn't hear, or chose not to. Without providing an opportunity for any kind of response, she led the group on.

"Is Mr November here now?" the Bronx voice asked.

"We don't discuss Mr November. It's our work here that we concentrate on," Sandra replied crisply.

"Like I said, some mission." Bronx was emerging as the person who liked to speak last in any conversation.

Immersed in mutual exchanges of awe, the group filed on. They arrived at the portal of another gallery.

"What kind of work do you do?" Bronx asked.

Sandra avoided the personal dimension of the question. "We all work to the rhythm of the sun. Our working day is five hours either side of noon, when the sun is highest. Before we begin work and after we finish, we meditate or do Tai Chi to retune our minds and bodies for the next phase of the day."

"I prefer a six-pack," Bronx said.

Sandra didn't know how to respond and stuck to the script.

"The last person to leave Helios has the honour of turning on the Great Laser that projects from the centre of the dome. In other places they haul down the flag at sunset. Here we raise ours as a light to the world. The Helios Laser can be seen from the Moon." She waited for a moment to let the idea sink in. Then, ever eager to impart information, she was off again.

"On each level of Helios, those working there can choose their own scents, sounds and colours to accompany their day." Sandra checked the computer terminal by the doorway.

"Rose, sandalwood and frankincense are today's choices of fragrance and the European Blackbird and our own Stellar Jay are the choices for sound. Mellow Peach, Venetian Red and Cool Slate are today's colours. These are reflected from the inner surface of Helios." Sandra moved to the head of the group and pressed a switch. An entire wall rolled away to reveal a tour-train with ranks of empty seats.

"Please step on board for the highlight of our tour."

The group shuffled forward. Carol sat down next to Murphy.

Sandra announced their departure. “A journey through the miracles of today to those of tomorrow.” She paused for a moment before providing the punch line. “A journey to the Outer Edge.”

As she pronounced the November mantra, the sound system produced an electronic flourish and the train moved off into a tunnel filled with an extravaganza of visual effects. They glided smoothly through holographs of 18th-century engravings. A voice with an echoing resonance spoke. “The English poet William Blake wrote of ‘A world in a grain of sand and eternity in an hour’. Our mission is to unite the timeless wisdom and ancient secrets of the earth with the wonders which our newly won knowledge of the building blocks of life can bring.”

“I guess this is the tunnel of self-love,” Carol said.

“I prefer the kind of bullshit you can smell,” Murphy replied.

The train continued its journey and the voice reverently highlighted the 3D images. “Already we have begun to heal our world. We are building new root structures that enable the rainforest to flourish again in places where greed has stripped the earth naked. We are engineering breeds of cattle that can thrive in arid areas of the world, bringing survivability to peoples who would otherwise face extinction.” The distant voice continued in ad-speak. “By travelling into the inner world of the human cell we shall create limbs and organs that can grow to replace those damaged by disease, destroyed by accident or in the violence of war.”

Suddenly, they were out into the light, gliding down a suburban street. Animatronic figures were performing Saturday chores; cutting grass, cleaning windows, washing cars. This time it was Sandra who spoke. “The things we do here at Dynamos are not confined to faraway issues; they touch every home in America.” The train trundled on.

"Glass so smooth that dirt doesn't stick. Car paints that self-heal scratches and grass that never needs cutting."

A chatter of identification rose from the group. Then small-town America was left behind and the train slid into a darkened tunnel. Everyone was silenced by images of famine, destruction and terrorism. The voice returned. "Now, more than ever before, we have the ability to empower the weak. To right wrongs, to eliminate poverty, to remove the need for violence and the motivation for terrorism." The train approached a point where Helios and Dynamos were closest – less than a hundred yards separated them.

"For a brief moment we're going to show you the engine of all these possibilities. The secrets of Helios are veiled by an electrical field that turns the surface of the dome opaque. On the panels closest to us, for twenty seconds, this will be reversed and we shall have a glimpse of what makes all of this possible."

The train halted and the nearby panels of Helios became transparent. Murphy started counting; there were twelve blocks of eight mainframe computers and a terraced area of workstations beyond. Between them was a small forest of tall plants. He was counting the number of people when the panels once more became opaque. There was a sense of disappointment among the tour group. The train moved on and as if sensing their mood, the voice returned.

"The wonder is that you see no wonders. Just as you see a person but not their mind, so you see the instruments of change but not the results. We hope that this tour will encourage you to discover such things in the world around you." The train passed through the portal of another tunnel, into a maze of holographs that showed faces from six continents. "The writer and seer H. G. Wells wrote that 'History is a race between education and catastrophe'. Our aim is to prevent that catastrophe. To do that we must learn from the failed systems of the past, for 'Those who do not learn from history are condemned to repeat it'."

"Who did they steal that from?" Carol asked.

"Steal what?" Murphy didn't get the point.

"That last quote: 'Those who do not learn from history are condemned to repeat it'. Who did they steal it from?"

"Voltaire or Marx, I don't remember," Murphy said impatiently.

"There's a difference," Carol insisted.

"Is there? French Revolution or Russian Revolution, they were both bloody disasters. Take your pick," Murphy said.

The voice returned. "We are voyaging through a landscape of failed ideas. They promised everything and delivered nothing but destruction."

The train moved into a cyclone of 3D images and surround sound: Nuremburg rallies, Pavlovian experiments in animal behaviour, Soviet May Day parades, Hippies in Sixties California, Napalm in Vietnam, tanks rolling across Wenceslas Square in Prague and in Tiananmen Square, Beijing. Tragedy turned to fantasy with Huxley's Brave New World and Orwell's 1984.

"I suppose they're trying to tell us that humans are crap at being human," Carol said.

Murphy didn't hear. He was shocked into silence by what he saw next. Charlie Chaplin, a boxing match and laughing gas.

As they left the train, he turned to Carol.

"How about we cut the tour, get out of this freak show and see the sun go down in the real world?"

* * *

Murphy was driving too fast. The heavy 4x4 threw up a plume of dust as they rattled and crashed across the virgin desert in the hills above the Domes. The terrain became impassable at the base of a sharp peak. Like a giant sundial, it cast a long shadow across the landscape. Carol was captivated by the endless horizon of mountains, canyons and plateaus, where the red earth was turned scarlet by the setting sun. She stepped down from the vehicle and stared into the distance.

"I love it out here. It feels as if you can see forever," she said.

Murphy stood alongside her and took in the same stark view. "If that's what forever looks like, I'll go right back to here and now."

"Why are men so cynical? Back there on the tour, everything you saw you trashed. And you're doing the same thing out here." She was more interested than angry.

"I can't answer for the male half of the human race, just for me."

"Okay, just for you then."

"Life's not like that, the human race isn't like that, he's not like that."

"Who?"

"The great and good Calvin November."

"Why would he give away all that money?"

"Good question, don't stop asking it." Murphy gestured towards the peak. "I'm going to the top."

"Do you always have to do that, go to the top?"

"Only when I want to see what's on the other side," Murphy said as he strode away. The shadows were visibly lengthening and he calculated that there were no more than twenty minutes of daylight left.

"Are you coming?"

"No, I'll stay here. I've got my book. I might find some snakes; it would make the trip worthwhile."

Murphy did not rise to the bait. "Take care."

"It's okay, I know about snakes."

The thin high desert atmosphere left Murphy breathless as he crested the peak.

Repeated gullies had lain across the route to the summit and the climb had taken a lot longer than he had estimated. Gasping for air, he did not at first hear the distant heavy diesel motors. Then he saw them, two large earthmovers. In the fading light it took him time to realise what was happening. They were shovelling a large number of animal carcasses into a long, deep trench. He started to move forward when he heard the helicopter. In the gathering darkness a spotlight traversed the dry riverbed where the 4x4 was parked. He scrambled down the slope. Three times he lost his footing and the sharp volcanic rock drew blood in several places.

It was completely dark by the time he negotiated both sides of the final gully that lay across his line of descent. Scrambling up the rising ground, he heard the helicopter engine stop and when the 4x4 came into view, the aircraft was parked alongside.

"Where the hell have you been?" A tall figure in Celestacom uniform shone a flashlight into his eyes.

"I've been to the Outer Edge," Murphy said contemptuously.

"You should have been right here." The guard snapped

"What are you, my social secretary?"

"Don't be a wise ass, mister. Your girlfriend is dead."

Murphy snatched the flashlight from the guard and ran forward to find Carol on the ground a short distance beyond the 4x4. The snake recognition book was alongside her. Her eyes were swollen and her face contorted. Murphy knelt on the earth and swung the beam slowly across the body. Her right ankle was swollen. He looked more closely; the inflammation spread from a small circular purple incision.

"Must have been a snake. With a Sidewinder you've got less than two minutes." The uniformed figure spoke over Murphy's shoulder as he looked down on Carol's body.

Responsibility for having involved an innocent outsider hit Murphy hard.

"You're right, I should have been here."

The second member of the helicopter crew appeared, carrying a stretcher. "We'll have to call this in, and we'll need a picture of you," he said.

"What for?" Murphy asked as the first crewman appeared with a digital camera.

"Video recognition." There was a flash and Murphy wondered whether he should make a grab for the camera, but decided against it. The crew strapped Carol's body onto the stretcher and loaded it into the helicopter. Murphy sat on a rock, knowing that he had overlooked something obvious but could not think what it was. From the flight deck there was the sound of an electronic printer.

"Godamn, look how this matches up," the pilot said.

Murphy edged closer. The two crew were looking at a printout. Murphy saw the picture of himself taken earlier in the day, at the start of the tour. To his astonishment he saw that it was set alongside pictures of him outside Goldman's apartment in New York, and at the airport in Bermuda. The radio crackled. Affirmative," the pilot said.

Both crewmen turned and stared at Murphy. "I have instructions to take you to Helios, by force if necessary," the co-pilot added, drawing a 9mm Browning Automatic from beneath his seat.

At that instant Murphy knew what he had missed. Two fangs, his whirring brain said; snakes have two fangs, and snakebites make two incisions.

21

A Journey East

Darcy was ill. Somewhere he had picked up the flu, and had endured a high temperature and the boiling resentment of his neighbours during the two crowded flights that had carried him from Bermuda, in the mid-Atlantic, to Washington and onwards to London. The woman banker in the aisle seat called a stewardess and insisted on being moved. But there were no other seats and the pair continued the flight in strained silence. In the transit lounge of Terminal 2 at Heathrow, Darcy was alternately sweating and shivering. Lloyd-Emlyn arrived exactly on schedule. He had an airport security pass and was a frequent visitor to transit lounges, delivering and collecting all manner of items that might be embarrassing at customs or during security searches at check-in. He sat one place away from Darcy and dumped a large padded anorak, a shoulder bag and a briefcase beside Darcy's raincoat that lay on the seat between them. Darcy appreciated the anorak; the weather forecast for Central Europe was bleak. He knew what the bag would contain: eight thousand dollars in cash, an amount large enough to be seriously useful but not so large as to attract undue attention; maps; a pair of winter shoes; a half-bottle of Scotch; and an automatic pistol with clip-on shapes to create an innocent X-ray image.

The pistol would be housed in a working transistor radio. Though a disguise for the weapon, it had a further use. In an emergency, it could receive and transmit over short distances. The field operative's Swiss army knife, it was often called. There would be no local backup. There was no time to arrange anything elaborate and in the complex uncertainty of the times, nobody could be sure who among old contacts might be compromised.

Darcy feigned a catnap. Lloyd-Emlyn opened the Financial Times and studied the unit trust pages. He took out a pocket calculator, made some notes, checked his watch and folded the paper. Then he looked at the bank of television monitors showing flights ready for boarding. It was an old routine; he got up and moved closer, as if he was short-sighted. He went back to the seat, picked up Darcy's raincoat as if it were his own and then shambled off towards one of the departure gates. He heard Darcy sneeze but did not look round.

"All aboard the Carpetbaggers Special," said a voice with a robust Manchester accent among the crowd of technical representatives, consultants and financial advisors who filed down the glass flightway for the LOT flight to Warsaw. There were only two women and no children on board. Darcy slept after take-off, but was wakened by the clatter of half a dozen laptop computers. He kept his eyes closed and tried to pretend that they weren't there. Two and a half hours later, he was coughing and sweating his way through customs and immigration. Nobody seemed suspicious of him and he found himself regretting the absence of the kind of challenge such moments presented in the old days.

The hotel, he knew from a dozen years before. The building was its old dreary self but a lot had changed.

Government bureaucrats from the provinces and travelling party officials from Moscow were long gone. The place was now largely filled with German and Japanese businessmen. Darcy offered a handful of Zlotys to the porter who had sullenly carried his bags from the lobby and dumped them on the threadbare carpet of the room. Saying nothing, he looked slowly down at the notes in exaggerated disbelief, as if he had been presented with a turd. Impatiently Darcy pulled a five-dollar bill from the roll in his jacket pocket. The man's eyes lit up like those of a child offered a bar of chocolate.

"Anything else I can get you, sir?" he added with a knowing gesture. "Anything at all?"

"Yes, peace and quiet," Darcy said irritably. The porter bowed elaborately and left. Darcy sank into the sagging bed and closed his eyes.

His temperature was still up and jet lag meant that by body time it was around three a.m.

He urgently wanted a long hot bath and a night's sleep but knew he had time for neither. His limbs felt leaden and seemed to weigh him down on the bed. It was more than flu.

Though he would admit it only occasionally to himself, and never to anyone else, depression haunted him with increasing regularity, and it was not something he wanted to have on his file.

Staring at the cracked plaster ceiling, he knew exactly what the problem was. The world, especially his world, had changed but he had been unable to change with it. This was the same job as ten years ago. Then, it had been important, or at least it had seemed important.

Now things were different. The future lay with Arabic speakers. The Cold War was over, and with it the purpose of his working life; the only life he had.

There were times when he felt his job was no more relevant to real life than that of toy soldiers changing the guard at Buckingham Palace.

Like them, he was acting out a tradition, doing something because it had always been done and nobody had thought of a reason to stop it. Despite the stress and possible danger of the task in hand, he felt no excitement, just a massive weight of boredom. This, he knew, was dangerous. Often the boredom gave way to anger at Thornhill. Yesterday's hero seemed diminished to the point of pathos and Darcy had serious questions about the judgement of the man of whom he had once been in awe.

His anger turned upon himself and he dozed off into a fitful sleep, dreaming of himself and Thornhill as two sad figures trying to capture fading shadows as the sun went down. He woke with a foul taste in his mouth and rummaged in the bag for the whisky. Drawn to the window by raised voices, he hauled himself off the bed. Two well-dressed young Germans were arguing with the driver of a rusty taxi whose smoky engine popped and spat impatiently as fumes drifted around the ankles of the protagonists. The argument was over the taxi fare but had quickly escalated into an exchange of ethnic abuse. The Germans were bewildered; for them the recent past was as long out of living memory as the barbarities of Attila the Hun.

One of them called the concierge to arbitrate. A number of euro notes were handed over and the voices dropped to a normal level; the driver roared off in a cloud of evil-smelling smoke and the Germans grumbled about the hopelessness of doing business with people so stupid.

Darcy forced himself into the shower and thought again about the various offers he had been made by industrial companies looking for what they called an 'Eastern European Representative', in reality, a glorified fixer's job; opening doors to people of influence for salesmen like the two Germans in the street below. And when things went wrong, to behave like the concierge, papering over contempt and ancient hatreds with as thin a veneer of money as possible. Self-pity was a weakness Darcy despised, and as he came out of the shower into the chill of the bedroom he realised he had been indulging himself too long. In an angry mood, he dressed, pulled on the warm anorak and set off for the Institute. He knew the city well and chose to take a tram rather than a taxi. Taxi drivers have memories, especially of foreigners. Despite the fast-food establishments and advertising for every kind of consumer product that had replaced the political posters of old, the city was much as he remembered it. For most people there was little to show for the arrival of the free market. In the Communist years, the main shortage was of goods, not money. As soon as anything worthwhile arrived in the shops, crowds with their hoarded cash rushed out to buy. Candles, jam, laxative, shoes, soap, whatever was spasmodically available. Now, under capitalism, their money was almost worthless and while the supply of goods had increased, their ability to buy them had all but disappeared.

Darcy's thoughts were interrupted when the tram arrived at the stop before the Institute. Habit once more took over; he got off and walked the remaining five hundred metres. At a distance, the main facade looked as he remembered it. But as he turned the corner to the East Wing he stopped dead. Wolski had vividly described it as being sealed off from the rest of the building, with guards at the entrances – an urban fortress. The reality before him was shockingly different. He surveyed the scene meticulously. There were broken windows on the ground floor and graffiti around a half-boarded-up doorway. 'The Peace Project', it said.

Crude flowers were painted among other slogans: 'Freedom and Shelter For All'; 'Peace and Freedom are Every Man's Right'. Looking for a way in, he walked across the courtyard where Wolski had described trucks secretly delivering state-of-the-art technology.

He passed through the doorway into the neo-gothic hallway. Broken glass crunched underfoot. On the far side of the hall, a group of youths huddled together under sleeping bags, old blankets and sheets of newspaper. As Darcy approached, he was hit by the distinctive smell of hash, overlaid with the odour of stale beer and unwashed flesh.

"Are you the iceman?" The voice of one of the teenagers collapsed from a challenge into a giggle.

Another of them shouted in halting Polish–American. He was not too far gone to recognise Darcy as a foreigner.

"You've got to have ice, man. Ice to shoot the pigs."

Fury hit Darcy; disgust at the insensible teenagers smoking their lives away, anger at being sent on a pointless errand and bitterness at an old fool's paranoid fantasies that seemed likely to finish the careers of a lot of good people in a terminally bad joke.

"Who are the pigs?" Darcy couldn't get sense from any of them. "The pigs, are they the police? How long have you been here?" he snapped.

"Since forever, man, since they shot the pigs. This place is ours; it was bequeathed to us. You know what that means, man, bequeathed?" He used the word with a sense of awe.

Darcy wanted answers. "Who bequeathed it to you?"

"Who else? The swineherds, man, the swineherds." The explanation seemed to exhaust him. He took another drag on the joint and collapsed into a fit of coughing.

Had Wolski been on drugs? Darcy wondered. That would be the most obvious explanation for the collection of rantings he brought across the Atlantic. Why hadn't he been tested? He cursed himself for the serious negligence.

Wandering through the corridors, he found that many of the rooms were occupied by squatters; some shouted obscenities, others were comatose. Shadowy figures cowered away in an instinctive reaction to anyone who might be an official. He came to the gym, the centrepiece of the Wolski horror story. The floor was littered with blankets, newspapers and a few camp beds. Everywhere there were empty beer cans and bottles. A few crumpled shapes were sleeping off the effects of alcohol or other drugs. He turned through the splintered doorway and into the corridor. His watch showed that there might still be time to catch the evening flight home and put this madness behind him. To salvage anything that could be recovered from the debacle, it was vital to warn London without delay. He pulled out his mobile phone but there was no signal. He needed to get into open space and looked for the back entrance, the one that Wolski had described as his escape route. Turning a corner, his way was blocked by an old woman sitting on the floor. She was dressed in two heavy coats that were held together by numerous safety pins. Her face was filthy, her fingernails broken and crammed with dirt. Darcy slid along the wall to pass with as much distance between them as possible. But she surprised him with a swift lunge, taking hold of his trouser leg. He tried to shake her free.

"Fascist!" she screamed.

Unable to pull away, Darcy reluctantly used his hands to uncurl her filthy fingers.

He began to run down the corridor towards the exit. She shouted after him. "You're too late, it's all gone. Serves you right, fascist bastard."

He froze and felt the hairs on the back of his neck stand on end. With a rising pulse, he cautiously turned back towards the old woman.

"Gone, what's all gone?" he asked gently.

"Gone, gone, gone," the woman repeated. "The man, the Russians gone … fascist Americans gone. Crazy pigs all gone."

* * *

An hour later, Darcy was at the bottom of the steps leading to Jakob's apartment. He had hurried from the tram stop but the flu, though pushed to the back of his consciousness, had slowed him down. He steadied himself for a moment and then began the climb.

The light was out on Jakob's landing and he had to use the flashlight one his mobile phone to check the number on the door. He knocked; there was no answer, yet he was sure there was somebody moving about inside. He tried several times more and eventually heard shuffling footsteps in the hall. The door opened slowly to reveal Jakob, but he was not as Wolski had described him. His eyes, reddened by lack of sleep, had a demented look. His spectacles were lopsided and thinning hair fell raggedly across his face. But his appearance made only a secondary impression. It was the large First World War vintage Luger he held in his left hand that was the focus of Darcy's attention. They looked at each other in silence.

"Come in," Jakob said, and Darcy complied; angry at his misjudgement of leaving his own weapon at the hotel.

"Sit," Jakob commanded.

Darcy was prevented from doing as he was told by the astonishing state of the room. The floor was covered with torn paintings, splintered frames, smashed porcelain and broken sculptures.

"Sit," Jakob repeated with shortening patience, and Darcy made his way across the room, treading canvases, splinters of wood and china into the carpet to reach the only chair not covered in debris.

"Who did this?" asked Darcy in amazement.

"I did." Jakob made the two words sound like a monosyllable.

Darcy asked the obvious question. "Why?"

"You have taken everything I love. All of this means nothing." It was not an answer that meant anything to Darcy, but with a weapon pointing at him it was not a moment to cause unnecessary antagonism.

"Why the gun?" Darcy wanted to deal with the most urgent question first.

"To kill you with."

Darcy said nothing. Jakob thought again. "Or perhaps to kill me with; you would be my witness. No man's death should go unnoticed."

A knot of fear constricted Darcy's intestines; he was certain that Jakob was mad and could fire at any moment.

"Don't you want to know who I am?" He asked.

Jakob seemed not to hear and became hysterical. "What have you done with her?" he screamed, raising the Luger so that it pointed between Darcy's eyes. Suddenly, Darcy understood. "I am a friend, a friend of Kloptik. Do you have any of his whisky left?" he asked quietly.

Jakob shuddered as if struck by a great blow. He collapsed onto a wrecked couch, his arm slackened and the gun dropped into his lap.

Darcy spoke softly. "Tell me what happened, I want to help."

"I saw them take her." Darcy waited, but Jakob said nothing more.

"What? What did you see happen?"

"In the street. We sometimes take coffee at Café Mozart. I had gone to meet her from her work." Jakob stopped again.

Darcy let him make his own pace.

"The car..." Jakob inserted a digression as if to avoid the heart of the matter. "One of those big black Russian Zils ... filthy it was. It used to be an offence in Moscow to drive a dirty car. The police would stop the driver and fine him on the spot. Did you know that?"

Somehow the irrelevance of the remark did not seem strange. Darcy knew Jakob was finding it intensely painful to get to the point. "I did nothing, do you understand that? Nothing," he said, driving the point home in bitter self-reproach.

"I was across the street when they grabbed her. She looked round desperately for someone to help. In our culture individuals don't kick and scream against those in power.

You need to be in a crowd to do that. Then she saw me, our eyes met. She shook her head, telling me not to intervene. But I tried. I tried but I'm old and slow. They'd taken her away before I even got to the kerbside."

"What did they look like?"

"Black leather coats, the kind of cheap leather that looks like cardboard. Russians, they were Russians."

"How do you know they were Russians?"

"I am a Pole. Poles can always recognise Russians."

Darcy paced around the room, oblivious to the sound of ceramics splintering beneath his feet.

"The car, the Zil, you say it was filthy. Why did you notice that especially?"

Jakob's mind seemed to be wandering again. "It was mud that saved Russia. Everyone thinks it was the winter but they're wrong." Jakob was trying not to deal with the issue of what happened to Anya. "It was the liquid mud of October that halted the Germans. They were bogged down long before the winter froze them into place. Otherwise they would have got to Moscow."

"Are you saying that the car was covered in mud?"

"Yes, mud. How often do I have to tell you?"

Darcy spoke quietly. "I think I may know where they've taken her. I'm going to need your help."

Jakob sat upright, removed his glasses and wiped his eyes. He ran his fingers through his thinning hair and straightened his tie.

"I am ready. Anything I have is yours."

"I need a car," Darcy said. "Not rented, not stolen. And somewhere safe that I can use as a base, somewhere they don't know about."

"Use this place, I have no further need of it," Jakob said without emotion.

"You would need to leave. They must think you've fled."

"Yes, I know."

"Where will you go?"

"To Ignace. You will know of the Night Watch. He was its most private member. Devoted to his books and engravings. He'll not even notice I'm there."

"How will I find you?"

Jakob made no reply but left the room, closed the door and picked up the phone in the hall. He spoke rapidly. Darcy couldn't make out the conversation through the heavy door, but Jakob returned looking satisfied.

"Look at those apartment blocks on the crest of the hill, the second one on the right. In a moment Ignace will flash his living room light on and off three times. You can identify where he lives."

A light appeared and disappeared as Jakob had predicted. Darcy counted the floors. It was on the fifth, to the left of the staircase.

"Why didn't I just give you the address or his telephone number, you wonder?" Darcy didn't answer.

"Because I thought it might bring him bad luck. I sense you carry a great deal of bad luck with you." It was not the kind of conversation in which Darcy wanted to engage.

"The car, what about the car?"

"I need to make another call. Do you have money?"

"I have dollars."

"Dollars are better than money," Jakob said.

* * *

Darcy parked the rusty Lada two blocks from the hotel. The small 4x4 Lada Nirva was more at home on a farm than in the city and he didn't want anybody to connect him with the vehicle. In the hotel lobby he sought out the sour-faced porter who had met him on his arrival. The memory of a tip in hard currency made him more attentive now. Darcy took a wad of notes from his anorak pocket. He wanted the man to see a large amount of cash. The porter's greedy eyes lit up as Darcy peeled off a twenty-dollar bill.

"I'm looking for some entertainment, I'm sure you understand what I mean."

The porter was eager to oblige. "I can arrange for entertainment in your room, sir, I'll make a call."

Darcy cut him short. "No, not here, somewhere with a choice of company."

"There is, I understand, sir, an excellent place on Miodowa Street, a very select clientele. Shall I call you a cab?"

"No, just write down the address."

Darcy took the piece of paper and handed over the twenty-dollar bill. He reckoned that the false trail would win him a couple of hours when the heavies arrived to trace him from the hotel. In his room he recovered his weapon and then scattered everything else across the floor to create the impression of a rapid search. The more confusion he could leave in his wake the better.

* * *

The feeble headlights of the Lada, and the slush thrown up by trucks on the potholed highway, made spotting any roadside feature almost impossible.

He would have missed kilometre post 121 if it had not been for the lights of a large Volvo road tanker whose driver chose that moment to overtake. Darcy pulled over and the Lada crashed and bounced across the deep ruts frozen onto the verge. For an uneasy moment he thought the car might bog down. He engaged the crude four-wheel drive and slowly reversed back towards a track that led away from the road and into the forest. The tough little Lada was on home territory. On the track there were tyre marks covered by snow. Nobody had arrived recently. He turned the lights off and waited for his eyes to adjust to the moonlight. After about ten minutes he started the engine and moved forward slowly. At the end of about two kilometres of slow advance, he saw light reflected in the upper branches of the birch trees. He drove slowly off the track and into the forest, got out and checked an impulse to lock the door; locks freeze.

He had expected to be immersed in the dense snow-deadened silence of the forest and was surprised to hear distant rock music. Moving cautiously through the trees, he came to the crest of a low hill. Below was a rambling dilapidated Dacha in the Russian style. The country home of some long-gone Soviet official, Darcy thought. At the front door there was a Zil limousine caked in mud. It had a heavy covering of snow on the roof and Darcy guessed it had not been moved for a couple of days. He stopped to listen again. The music was coming from the back of the building. From a distance it had masked the now unmistakable thumping sound of a slow-running diesel generator. He worked his way round the building. From the kitchen window, an unsteady brownish light spilt onto the snow.

Darcy calculated that the generator was past its best. He hid behind a pile of logs and waited to be sure that his presence had not been detected.

The brutally cold air made his head ache but he chose not to use the hood of the anorak, as it would cut into his peripheral vision and cost him the critical edge of his hearing. He crawled along the line of the logs until he found a gap that gave a view into the room. On the far side there was a large wood-burning stove. At a table in the middle of the room two men were playing cards. They looked like low-grade thugs. Rumpled layers of cold-weather clothing amplified their natural bulk. Both were unshaven and had vodka-reddened eyes. A pile of empty bottles lay in the sink. Close to them was a pair of Kalashnikov assault rifles.

There were more questions than answers. What did it all mean? Could they be holding Anya? Had she been taken elsewhere? Was his guess that this was the place just plain wrong? Should he wait for some kind of opportunity, try a diversion, a bluff or what? He retreated behind the logs and tried to think of what to do next. It was essential to search the house, but he was seriously outgunned and if discovered, would not survive a firefight. On the other hand, he had the advantage of surprise and the effects of vodka on his side. He was sufficiently confident of his aim to be sure that he could eliminate then both before they had a chance to shoot back. But he also knew he couldn't do it. It simply wasn't in him to commit cold-blooded murder.

One of the men got up from the table. Almost immediately the door on the veranda above the log pile opened and a shaft of dim light spread outwards. A pair of heavy snow boots stood within inches of where Darcy hid.

A wandering stream of urine made deep yellow holes in the snow. Through the loud music Darcy caught a fragment of a conversation that had begun in the kitchen.

"They seem to think she's important, the poor bitch."

"Let's hope neither you nor me become important to ex-comrade Golkov," the man on the veranda replied.

The door closed and Darcy felt a surge of exhilaration at the vindication of his judgement. A plan began to form in his mind. First he had to immobilise them. He made his way back to the snow-covered Zil limousine. Groping through his pockets, he found a couple of toothpicks from the hotel, split them into four and jammed one into each of the tyre valves. He knew that in the kitchen, the sound of the escaping air would be drowned by the music. The generator hut stood on the end of a well-trodden path on the dark side of the building. Careful not to leave any new prints, he moved inside and risked using the light on his mobile phone. He realised that obvious sabotage would betray the presence of an intruder. Instead, he pinched the flexible fuel supply hose closed.

It was an old motor of the kind that needed to be bled of air before it would restart after running dry. The motor coughed, spat and stopped. The lights went out and Darcy dashed for the house. He heard swearing, collisions with kitchen furniture and the sound of matches being struck. A butane lamp glowed into life, followed by the sound of tools being collected and thrown into a metal box. The two men appeared and set off for the generator hut. As they went inside, Darcy dashed across to the hallway of the house and ran up to the top floor. He reckoned that it would take at least fifteen minutes to find the problem and get the motor working again. But he also knew that his footprints would give him away to anyone coming into the house.

He went urgently from room to room, his eyes now well-adjusted to the darkness. Each was empty or contained derelict furniture. On the middle floor, he came upon a locked door.

The sound of distant cursing drifted across the snow. Darcy made a quick decision and put his shoulder to the door.
The centre panel pushed out and clattered into the darkened interior of the room. He paused and listened. The angry dialogue continued uninterrupted. He slowly squeezed through the gap. A kerosene heater by the bed created a small pool of light. He could make out a face, heavily wrapped in blankets. He moved closer. It was a woman with long matted hair. Her face looked numb and she stared at him, or through him, in the dim light; he could not tell which.

"Anya?" he asked. There was a slight inclination of the head. "I am a friend of Jakob's," he said gently, fearing she would cry out. But there was no response. It was as if her mind was switched off. He lifted her from the bed and moved towards the door. It was only then that he noticed the shackle and chain that ran from her left ankle to the wall. The lock looked primitive and Darcy struggled to remember how the tumblers lay in such devices. The search of his memory was interrupted by the sound of the diesel generator starting up. From the window he could see the Russians shambling back towards the house. He knew that as soon as they reached the hallway they would see his footprints. There was less than two minutes to stop them.

As he ducked below the windowsill an idea formed. He jumped up onto the bed and balanced on the iron frame.

In one of his pockets he found a US nickel. He reached up to the light fitting in the centre of the room, unscrewed the bulb and pushed the coin inside. Then he screwed the bulb back into place.

The Russians had reached the veranda by the time Darcy got to the doorway and tripped the light switch. There was a loud crack from somewhere below and the lights went out again.

The Russians swore and set off back to the generator. Darcy appreciated how close the call had been; the trick had only worked because the primitive wiring had a single fuse for the lighting circuit. The motor kept running and he knew that it would not take them long to realise that the fault was not with the generator but back in the house. Darcy tore at the Velcro fastenings of the hood on his anorak and forced the end of the metal hoop through the fabric. He bent the end of the wire in a segment of the bed frame and set to work on the lock. There were three levers and he managed two quite quickly. The last one he couldn't locate. Despite the cold, he felt sweat break out on his forehead. After what seemed like hours, the lock opened. He lifted Anya from the bed.

"I am going to take you home," he said.

It was a terrible journey. The open space between the house and the trees was a killing ground now fully illuminated by the risen moon. A short burst from one of the Kalashnikovs would cut them in half. Anya's cold corpse-like weight was staggering.

Darcy's breath came in great gasps, and by the time they reached the trees he had to rest. He lowered Anya onto the snow and collapsed beside her. He knew he had to regulate his breathing. Training told him that unchecked intake of air at this temperature froze the lungs, agonising and immobilising at best, and often fatal. Though hidden by the trees, their tracks pointed directly to their present position.

He could only rest for twenty or thirty seconds more. He used the time to knot one of Anya's blankets at both ends to form a crude sleigh. He got to his feet and pulled. With Anya's weight supported by the snow he was able to make much better progress.

As the Lada came into sight, there were sounds of confusion from the house. Two rapid bursts of fire were followed by the sound of the Zil engine. The battery was low and the starter motor struggled against near-frozen engine oil. It sounded as if the vehicle wouldn't start and Darcy's hopes rose. But the large truck-like engine began to fire, on three cylinders at first and then more evenly as the others came on stream. The Zil began to move and Darcy realised the flat tyres wouldn't slow it down in the snow. He pulled open the rear door of the Lada, raised Anya's dead weight and laid her across the back seat. Within seconds he had the darkened car back on the track and heading for the main road. In the mirror he could see the lights of the Zil weaving through the trees. If he could get to the road and merge with the traffic without them knowing what kind of vehicle he was in, there was a chance of getting away.

On the open road, with flat tyres, they wouldn't be able to follow either far or fast. It was a question of staying alive for the next kilometre and a half. The lights of the Zil came closer and the temptation to floor the throttle was almost overwhelming, but Darcy knew that if the wheels spun he would lose control and slide off into one of the snow banks that lined the track. If that happened, they were both dead.

With agonising slowness the main road came into view. The Zil was now closing on them, weaving across the track and throwing up clouds of powdered snow as the flattened tyres sluggishly responded to the steering wheel. There was a flash of gunfire but the unsteadiness of the vehicle sent the shots wide. Suddenly, they were at the road. Darcy turned on the lights and accelerated hard as the wheels hit the tarmac.

He swung the car in front of an approaching timber truck, anything to put space between them and the Zil. It was a near lethal miscalculation. The car's wheels spun on the loose gravel that covered the road, losing precious seconds of acceleration. The lights and horn of the truck came screamingly close. As the moment of impact came he closed his eyes and waited for the inevitable, but nothing happened; the truck had missed ramming them by inches. The car slowly pulled ahead and the gap increased. In the wing mirror he saw the Zil come barrelling out of the track and onto the road.

One of the flattened tyres rolled off the rim and the driver totally lost control. The heavy limousine spun sideways into the path of a container truck. The Zil took the impact side-on and spun off the road in an explosion of shattered glass and crumpled steel.

* * *

It was after three a.m. when they got to Jakob's apartment. Darcy parked the car a block away and opened the rear door. The car's feeble heater had been sufficient to release a fierce animal stench as he unwrapped the blankets that cocooned Anya's unconscious body. Her clothes were filthy and her face marked by smeared make-up and heavy bruising. As there was no hope of making a furtive entry to the flat, Darcy decided on a high-visibility disguise. He took her arm and hauled her from the car. He kicked the door closed and pulled her upright with her arm across his shoulders. With his other hand he held her round the waist. He launched into a loud patriotic drunkard's song and staggered towards the street door of the apartment building.

* * *

Later, Darcy was to look back on the next eighteen hours as the most important of his life. Yet the events were not spectacular and they took place in a simple, logical progression. It was the sum of their impact upon him that was remarkable. Jakob's apartment was cold, the result of another breakdown in the building's ancient heating system. The most urgent priority was warmth; without it he knew Anya would not survive. A hot bath was the fastest way of restoring body temperature. He turned the hot tap at the head of the bath but the water was cold. In the corner was an ornate water heater but he had no idea how to make it work. After several attempts, he gave up his efforts. Instead, he dragged the mattress from Jakob's rumpled bed, put it in front of the fireplace and lifted Anya onto it. He tore the pages of an old telephone directory and crammed them into the grate. Gathering a pile of torn canvases and broken furniture that Jakob had wrecked, he made a heap of them on top of the paper. But all his matches were gone, and he had nothing to start a fire with. In near panic he searched the flat, scattering Jakob's collection of pipes and tobacco onto the floor. Eventually, in a corner of the kitchen, he found a matchbox. There were only two matches inside and both felt damp. He knelt beside the fireplace and willed himself to move carefully. He tried to dry the matches on his shirt, but the only result was that they left long sulphur streaks on the fabric. Holding his breath, he struck one of them on the side of the box. It spluttered and seemed as if it would peter out, but the flame reluctantly grew, the paper burnt and the oiled canvases quickly had the wood blazing. The effect of the fire on Anya was near miraculous. In a few minutes she began to stir and then to shiver.

A half-hour later she slowly began to wake. What touched Darcy was that it wasn't an awakening from sleep, more a struggle to escape from captivity. His mind drifted back to a schoolboy memory of a butterfly fighting to be free of its chrysalis. Similarly, Anya began to metamorphose from a chemical carapace into a magical human being. Her returning circulation deepened the heavy bruising around her eyes. As time passed, he sat watching her by the light of the fire and tried to analyse what was happening to him. He had had plenty of women. Once, during a wakeful night in a bleak hotel room in some forgotten city, he had tried to remember them all. But it was like counting sheep and he eventually fell asleep. For many years it was the kind of thing he boasted about. Now he saw that most of these encounters had merely been matters of mutual exploitation. Two long-term relationships had nearly gone on to marriage but in neither case had there finally been sufficient devotion to make the commitment. Now Anya's struggle to be free of whatever she had been drugged with stirred a strange magnetism in him, something that was entirely new. He tossed more of Jakob's broken furniture onto the fire. As the flames lit up the room he thought how pitiful it was that the detritus of Jakob's life should illuminate the emotional wreckage of his own loveless past.

* * *

"Cold." The word jolted Darcy into activity. He twisted a piece of newspaper, lit it in the fire and carried it into the kitchen. The remaining match was too valuable to be used to light the gas stove.

He quickly made coffee and in a cupboard above the sink found a bottle of Napoleon Brandy; Jakob lived well.

When he returned, Anya lay gazing at the fire and appeared to be fully conscious.

"Jakob?" she asked as Darcy put the mug of black coffee down beside her. She seemed unwilling or unable to face him.

He moved closer and realised that her eyes were not yet focusing.

"I am his friend," he said.

"No." She said the word softly, her eyes trying to find focus. Then she screamed, "No! No! No!"

The shouting stopped, and she rose on one arm and stared at him. Her face came to life and her whole body was suddenly energised. He could not tell if her shivering was from cold or fear. Part of the answer came quickly. The slow pain of returning circulation caused her to sob convulsively. Darcy went to the kitchen, took a towel and dampened it with the remains of the hot water in the kettle. Gently he began to wipe away the mess of mascara, lipstick, tears and grime. It seemed to give her the strength to deal with the pain. She relapsed into a daze and Darcy took a pile of cushions from the sofa to support her back.

As they sat silently watching the fire, a wave of exhaustion swept over him. He knew he had to sleep and at last thought it safe to close his eyes.

* * *

When he woke, he was shocked to find that the sun was up and Anya was staring fixedly at him. She was icily calm, as if the cold from her warming body had retreated into her mind.

"Who are you?" She spoke as if from a great distance.

"You went to London. Jakob sent you to get help. Do you remember?"

She nodded slowly and Darcy continued. "You saw a man called Thornhill, on the steps of a church, after a concert. He's my boss."

She shook her head in disbelief. "But you haven't helped us. Look around you." Darcy couldn't find an answer.

Anya's coldness was suddenly transformed into fiery accusation. "Where's Jakob? What have you done with him?"

"You'll see him soon."

Her mood swung from anger to despair. "Away, they took me away," she said.

"Do you know why? Do you know why they took you away?" Darcy asked.

She ignored his question. "They did this?" Her eyes travelled slowly over Jakob's smashed treasures.

"No, Jakob did it. He was distraught when he thought he'd lost you."

She was unable to comprehend what had happened. "All these things, they were part of him," she said. Then her mood changed again. "Wolski,'" she said sharply, "they took me because they wanted to know where Wolski had gone."

"What did you tell them?"

"They gave me an injection."

"Anya, this is very important. Can you remember what you told them?"

She collapsed onto the mattress and her answer came in a succession of gasps. "I told them nothing … everything." She began to panic. "I don't know. I can't remember."

Darcy lifted her gently and cradled her head against his chest. "It's okay, he's safe. They can't get to him now," he said reassuringly.

"But I won't deceive you. The people who did this to you are still out there. They may be able to trace the car we used to get here."

Anya ignored the warning. "Find Jakob, bring him here. Bring him back to me, he's all I have, I can't live if he were…" She collapsed into sobbing which racked her whole body. Darcy held her closer. Slowly, the spasm subsided.

"Soon, very soon," he said in a whisper.

* * *

Darcy slept until mid-morning. When he woke, the grey winter light was still laden with the aggressive chill of the previous night.

"Clean." Darcy looked up to find Anya standing over him. She seemed unsteady on her feet, but her eyes were clear and she had a look of stern determination. Darcy, still half-asleep, did not understand her.

"I want to be clean, I want a bath."

"There's no hot water."

"You forget, this is my second home. I have clothes here. I know how to make hot water."

Darcy stifled a smile. Her English was excellent but occasionally an idiom sounded odd.

"I'll help you."

"No. Alone, I must do this."

She disappeared into the hallway, opened a number of drawers, returned with an armful of clothing and then disappeared into the bathroom. The door closed and Darcy heard the click of the bolt. He gathered up the filthy blankets and fed them slowly into the fireplace. They were damp with sweat and began to smoulder slowly. He crossed the room and opened a window.

The fire sucked in the cold air and once more began to blaze. From the bathroom there came the sound of the water heater coughing and grunting into reluctant service.

Darcy was still looking at the dying embers of the fire when Anya returned to the room dressed in a heavy Icelandic sweater and jeans. Her long hair was still wet. She seemed at peace with herself and spoke very formally.

"Thank you. Did you save my life?"

"I believe you may have saved mine." Darcy's words were out before he realised what he was saying. He was astonished. He'd never heard himself say anything of the kind before.

"What do you mean? I don't understand."

"Perhaps I don't either." He was now back in control.

"Let's make coffee and see what there is to eat, then there is something I need to show you."

The coffee was hot, black and bitter. They drank it with some dry toast made from stale bread, and caviar they found in the fridge. Darcy gathered more fuel for the fire and raked the embers into life.

"As soon as you are well, I am going to get you and Jakob to London. I promise you."

"How do I know you're not lying to me?" she said.

"Because I'm a professional liar and you're the first person who has ever made me want to tell the truth."

"That is beautiful," she said.

"You are beautiful."

"Why do you say such things?"

"Because they are true."

"Or because you're a professional liar?"

"You have my promise. I will get you both to London."

Anya stared at him as if trying to divine the truth. Darcy continued. "But first there are a number of things I have to do."

Her mind only seemed capable of one question at a time. "What is it that you need to show me?"

Darcy reached across to his anorak and pulled the automatic from an outer pocket. He glanced up at her. She was completely unmoved.

"Take it; the safety catch is on," he said.

She held the weapon uncertainly in her left hand. He moved behind her and held both her wrists.

"Are you left handed?" he asked.

"Yes." She nodded.

"Hold the weapon in your left hand and put your forefinger on the trigger. Use your right hand to support your left." He moved her hands into place. "Slide the safety catch off. Tuck your elbows in, hold the weapon level with your eyes and line the sight up with your nose. You aim by turning your whole upper body. Do you understand?"

She nodded again.

"If you need to fire, aim at the broadest part of the body and squeeze the trigger twice."

* * *

In the street, Darcy tried to reconstruct the profile of the building on the distant hill that Jakob had identified as housing Ignace's apartment. He had decided against using the car and waited for a taxi at the intersection two blocks away from Jakob's building. Traffic roared by but there were no taxis. He took out a wad of dollar bills and waved them at the approaching traffic.

A Polski Fiat swerved to a halt in front of him. The driver leant across the interior and wound down the nearside window.

"Where do you want to go?"

Darcy made a gesture towards the skyline. "Up the hill, to the top." He opened the door and got in without waiting for a reply.

"Ten dollars," the man said as the car moved forward. They drove in silence, each knowing that mutual knowledge might be dangerous. Then the driver saw Darcy catch sight of a medical bag on the back seat.

"Yes. I am a doctor. I endure indignities such as this for my daughter's education. Perhaps you would do the same."

"I don't have a daughter," Darcy replied.

"Then you are a poorer man than I," the driver said with a gentle shake of the head. The ugly concrete apartment block came into view. "Pull over here."

For a moment Darcy thought of giving the man twenty dollars rather than ten, but quickly decided that an expression of pity would be an unnecessary indignity.

He handed over the money, got out of the car and headed in a direction opposite to his destination.

When the Lada was out of sight he doubled back and began the long climb to the fifth floor. The block was crudely constructed, a relic of the quota system beloved of the Communist command economy. It was the sharpest of contrasts with the enduring 19th-century craftsmanship of Jakob's bourgeois home. There was a smell of excrement on the landings and graffiti on the doors and windows.

On the fourth floor he paused for breath, and began to wonder whether Jakob's choice in coming to hide in such a place was an act of contrition, a self-inflicted punishment for not being able to save Anya. On the landing above, the left-hand door was open. In Darcy's experience open doors were always a sign of bad news.

The flaccid body was stripped to the waist and had its hands tied. There were ugly burn marks across the chest. As he drew closer, Darcy saw that they had used the kitchen iron.

* * *

Anya looked at the large-boned Slav face over the sights of the weapon. She was puzzled by her own lack of emotion. If she moved her finger just three millimetres a human being would be turned into a corpse. It was a fact she acknowledged and understood without it being connected to anything else. It was a new feeling and she enjoyed the simplicity of it. Following Darcy's instructions, she held the weapon with both hands and kept her nose in line with the man's stomach. He had been caught unawares. She was sitting in the dark amid the gilt splinters of picture frames and 18th-century French gilt chairs when he burst through the front door and crashed into the living room. His mistake was over-confidence.

"Get up," he yelled in Russian. Her hand slid inside the sweater as if to clutch her stomach.

"Get up, bitch." He was used to people responding without argument.

She pulled the gun from the waistband of her jeans and pointed it at him.

"Sit," she said.

The man complied, more out of astonishment than fear. He grimaced as his heavy body came into contact with something sharp on the floor.

"You're mad," he snarled.

"Yes, I know," she said quietly.

For a long time they sat staring at each other. "You can't stay like this all day," the Russian said contemptuously.

"I know," Anya said in a whisper.

The man laughed, enjoying her dilemma. "Then what are you going to do?"

"I haven't decided yet."

* * *

Darcy picked up the phone and dialled Jakob's apartment; the speed of the warning was more important than the risk of a trace on the call. The phone rang for a long time. Darcy had almost given up when the call was answered.

"Anya?" There was no reply. "Anya speak to me," he said angrily. There was silence. He lowered the tone of his voice and spoke gently. "Anya, can you hear me? It's bad news. It's Jakob."

There were two shots in quick succession.

22

The Cabinet Office, London

The 747 from Washington touched down on time. It was half past six in the morning. The driver of the official Jaguar met Thornhill at the aircraft door. They were ushered through the VIP lounge and crossing Westminster Bridge before seven fifteen.

Thornhill smelt fresh Viennese coffee as he climbed the stairs to the flat. "Croissants are by the oven; put them in, would you?" Jane shouted from her study. "I'll be out in a moment." Thornhill opened the heavy oven door and slid the tray of croissants inside. The idiosyncratic cast-iron Aga was Jane's link with the country kitchen she had regretfully left behind when moving to a flat in London became essential. Thornhill heard the muted clatter of her word processor. The study was Jane's private realm, and even when returning home from another continent, he knew better than to enter it. After thirty years of marriage, she had developed a remarkable ability to predict his homecomings. The coffee was his favourite, a generous rounded taste with a hint of figs, which she had sought out from a small specialist importer in Covent Garden. He poured coffee for them both and checked the kitchen diary by the fridge.

At the weekend she was due to make a speech in support of the Third World charity where she worked three mornings a week. He guessed she was busy preparing. 'Making up for the greed and incompetence of the politicians,' she called it. Sometimes Thornhill saw his job and hers as different ways of trying to do the same thing.

He sipped his coffee and took a hot flaky croissant from the oven. Jane appeared in the doorway and gave him a kiss on the cheek.

"Going to sleep it off?"

"No. I've got a meeting, nine thirty sharp. The redoubtable Baroness Lathkill and committee. I've just got time for a shower and a change of clothes."

"I have to go to Church House, I'll walk across the bridge with you," Jane said.

From long experience, Thornhill knew that the Committee Office in Whitehall was a twenty four minute walk from the flat and added another five for Jane's shorter stride. "Must be away in half an hour," he said.

"I'll be ready," she replied, and disappeared back into her study.

* * *

It had become a beautiful morning. Even the London traffic was not able to spoil the crisp morning air. For Thornhill, the heedlessness of the crowds rushing to work reinforced the feeling of exhilaration that the possession of a world-class secret always produced.

He knew it was a childish notion, but it was one that he always enjoyed. Yet caution allowed him only a brief moment of satisfaction. Megalomania and paranoia were vultures ever ready to fall upon a stumbling sense of proportion.

"It's important, isn't it?" Jane asked.

He'd said nothing, but she knew, she always did. "I fear so." They walked on briskly in silence; all that could be said had been said.

As if the previous part of their conversation had never taken place, Jane said, "Mary Finch-Hatton called; they've asked us for the weekend after next. Thornhill's mind was elsewhere. He knew the meeting ahead would be of forensic intensity. Trying to concentrate, he took in the magnificent sweep of the river and the dome of St Paul's set among newly rising glass temples of mammon. Two co-existing realities, or was one real and the other not? Eventually, he replied.

"Good. I haven't had a good day's rough shooting for far too long and I expect you'd welcome a chance to ride again?"

Beyond the bridge they parted. She set off across Parliament Square towards the Abbey. He turned right into Whitehall and crossed the road outside Whitehall Palace where on a cold January morning in 1649 King Charles I stepped out to face the headsman's axe, wearing a second shirt lest he should shiver and the crowd think him trembling with fear. Thornhill wondered what kind of fate he might be facing. The door of the Cabinet Committee Office opened discreetly as he walked up the steps. He passed through the lobby to check the noticeboard that indicated the rooms assigned to the day's meetings.

"Hello, Jackie boy." Thornhill stiffened. Only one person called him that, the appalling Arnold Morgenstern, Resident Intelligence Liaison Officer at the US Embassy in the Eisenhower Platz, as Grosvenor Square was known in the trade. Everything Morgenstern did seemed calculated to annoy.

"On your way to golf, are you, Arnie?" Thornhill said with distaste at Morgenstern's pink cashmere sweater, yellow tie and blazer with gold buttons.

"Not anymore, and I've got you to blame for that." He drew Thornhill away from the traffic of arriving attendees.

"The way we see it, you've been using the good old Stars and Bars as toilet paper and you know how the folks back home hate crap on the flag."

"I can't think what you mean, and I have a meeting to attend," Thornhill said with calculated formality.

"Come on, Jackie, that's not friendly; you want me to jog your memory? The guys down the road seemed interested enough," Morgenstern said, pointing in the direction of the Foreign Office. Thornhill looked around to see who might be listening.

"This is not the time or the place. I'll meet you at my flat this evening. Eightish, shall we say?"

"Eightish it is," Morgenstern replied, in parody of Thornhill's turn of phrase. He passed through the tall double doors and disappeared among the tourists arriving for the changing of the guard in Whitehall..

* * *

Baroness Lathkill sat at the head of the long table. From her opening remarks, Thornhill knew that there was trouble ahead. "Sir Jack, you will recall that this committee was formed to carry out the will of Parliament concerning scrutiny of the intelligence services."

Thornhill looked at the faces round the table. Eight potential leaks, a multi-party mix of politicians; a random permutation of ambition, romantic good intention, avarice, duty and incompetence. The one thing they all had in common was a hunger for power. Or if power were not available, they would settle for influence as second best. The Baroness paused to put her remarks in context, another bad sign.

"As a matter of historic policy, keeping our American allies on-side used to be at least as important as keeping the Soviets outside. Many things may have changed but the central importance of maintaining the trans-Atlantic alliance has not, as we are all very well aware from our recent exertions in the Middle East."

It was obvious there had been a leak. Was it Morgenstern? The situation was serious, the rules of the treaty were plain and Thornhill knew he was in breach. He needed time to think. Attack seemed the best form of defence.

"Madam Chairman, my department is fully cognisant of its obligations under the Act," Thornhill said, aware that every word would appear in the minutes of the meeting.

The Baroness would not be deflected. "In that regard, Sir Jack, there are certain matters which require explanation. The committee has become aware of disturbing reports from Washington. I cannot stress how damaging this is, regardless of what good intentions you may believe you have."

Thornhill was appalled; he needed to find out the scale of the leak, and played for time. "Madam Chairman, I cannot respond to innuendo…" He was put off his stride by the appearance of an embarrassed uniformed messenger in the doorway. Everyone registered surprise. Interruption of Cabinet Committee meetings was almost unknown. The messenger handed the note to the Baroness, who stopped Thornhill in mid-flow.

"Sir Jack, it seems there is a telephone call for you. A most urgent telephone call," she added icily.

From every angle of the table, Thornhill felt shafts of resentment focus on him. The messenger led him to an empty office. "This is a secure line, sir," he said, and left.

Thornhill lifted the receiver slowly. He had no idea what to expect. It was Lloyd-Emlyn.

"There has been an incident," trade-speak for disaster. "I have Latchford on the other line; I'll put him through."

Latchford was suspiciously calm. "We've been hit. Bullivant is dead."

Thornhill felt the sweat break out on his forehead. He tried to use as few words as possible. "How?"

"A grenade launcher from among the rocks by the beach, that's what Morag thinks."

"Is Kloptik intact?"

"Yes, but badly shaken."

"Do you have Bullivant's gun?"

"I can get it," Latchford replied grimly.

"And Morag? How is Morag?"

"She'll be okay."

"Get her to deal with the local police, I'll arrange for someone to speak to the Governor to keep them off your back." The satellite link began to break up and Thornhill spoke with slow deliberation. "Listen carefully. Take Bullivant's gun and lock yourself and Kloptik in one of the rooms, close the shutters and shoot anybody who tries to get in. Anyone, whoever they are, do you understand?"

Latchford's was trying to cope with shock and disguise it with irony. "Not really my kind of thing; I'm more of a Hippocratic man myself."

"Make an exception," Thornhill said. "Just do it. I'll get Mantoni and a team down from New York. You only have to hold out for about four hours. Then we'll arrange evacuation to base."

Thornhill made a flurry of calls, shouting orders, calling in favours and covering tracks. When he returned to the committee room, the clock on the wall showed that he had been away for nearly twenty minutes, an unpardonably long time.

"My sincerest apologies, Lady Lathkill, but there has been a serious breach of security. A valued officer has been killed and others injured."

"What do you intend to do, Sir Jack?"

"The situation has been stabilised and an RAF aircraft will bring them home later today."

As ever, the Baroness cut to the critical issue. "Are these events related to the matters you have been called here to explain?"

"This is an operational matter, and in the light of current circumstances I must ask the committee to be patient," Thornhill said in a voice that he knew betrayed his anxiety.

"You mean be the last to know; to read about it in the Sunday papers along with everybody else," Sir Linton Ogmore, one of the Permanent Secretaries, said from the far end of the table.

"Worse still, hearing from Washington first," Patricia Lathkill said. "Do you understand the humiliation?" It was an accusation, not a question. "We, the committee, all of us, were put here precisely to prevent this sort of thing happening." She was now very angry and took pleasure in showing it.

David Maddox, one of the most ambitious members of the committee, felt it safe to venture an attack of his own. "What kind of outfit are you running, Sir Jack? First we hear about your doings from the Americans and now there's been some sort of cock-up overseas. Don't play games with us. What's going on?"

Thornhill did not explain. "I shall report to you in due course," he said, picking up his papers, and left.

"Does that constitute resignation?" Thornhill heard someone ask as he reached the door. He kept walking, down the long corridor and out into the crowded street.

* * *

"Do I have to feed him?" Jane asked.

"I rather think so," Thornhill replied.

"Well, I'll have to go to Sainsbury's," she said reproachfully. Entertaining was a duty which Jane Thornhill did not enjoy.

"Haven't you got anything in the freezer?"

"Only some goulash left over from the Canadians last week. I could do that with some rice."

"Yes, that and a bottle of red will do very well."

The meal was a disaster. The goulash hadn't mellowed with age and tasted thin and harsh against the watery rice. The coarse supermarket wine clashed with the peppery meat. Jane quickly withdrew to her study. Morgenstern did not seem to notice either her or the food.

"They're holding my feet to the fire over this, Jackie. I'll be straight with you. Your New York operation has been too quiet for comfort for a while now and we thought we should take a look. Then we got a lead, there was somebody who does the odd job for us at a party at Murphy's place. They were celebrating the son's graduation when there was a call."

"How very convenient for you." Thornhill knew that Morgenstern would not be giving away secrets unless he wanted something very big in return. "Thanks for the information." Thornhill was trying hard not to betray his rising anxiety.

"To save you searching, it was Largo Feingold, a cousin of Murphy's wife. Murphy left in the middle of the party. He'd only do that if there were something big going down. To cut to the chase, we put a tail on your man." Thornhill did not respond. The stakes continued to rise. "If you don't believe me, talk to him, ask him if he saw four black guys in a beat-up Caddy. They usually do a little street theatre to pass the time. He'd have noticed." So the story was well and truly out. But how much of it? Thornhill remained silent. "You're well aware that by rights you should have told us what was going on. Then your people get shot up in Bermuda. It doesn't look good for 'hands across the sea', does it, Jackie? Seems more like you're trying to snatch some big number for yourselves. You wanna tell me about it?"

Thornhill exploded. "No, I don't 'wanna' tell you about it. In the same way I didn't 'wanna' tell the committee about it this morning." The sarcasm bounced off Morgenstern.

"Come on, Jackie, you're among friends."

"Am I? Our people getting hit in Bermuda and cousin Largo are too close for comfort."

"Hey, come on, what are you saying? We may be pissed off but not that pissed off," Morgenstern said.

"Someone is." Thornhill got up and stood by the fireplace.

On cue, the clock chimed ten in synchrony with Big Ben on the other side of the river. Thornhill listened quietly, as if observing some personal rite.

"I don't give a shit," Morgenstern snapped. Thornhill didn't reply. "I don't give a shit that you think I'm some sort of colour-coordinated clown that is too tedious for your high intellect; someone you can snigger about over your Armagnac at the Reform Club. Neither do I mind, leastwise not very much, being served warmed-up food and poor wine. Allies don't have to be friends, they don't even have to respect each other, but they do have to have the horse sense to see where their common interests lie." Thornhill returned to his seat. He had severely underestimated Morgenstern and the man's passion shocked him. "Okay, Arnold, guilty as charged. You're right, but I won't patronise you with an apology."

"Thanks, I appreciate that."

"What do you mean, 'common interests'?" Thornhill asked.

"There's something big and bad going down. You've got a piece of it and you're not sharing."

"And what reason do you have for believing that, Arnold?"

"Okay, Jackie, let's cut the crap. This is a game where information is your entrance ticket, and there you're way ahead of me. I tried buying in with all I've got, but not enough, am I right?"

"You could be right about one thing, Arnold. 'Big and bad', perhaps very big and very bad."

"Then why keep me on the outside?" Morgenstern asked. Thornhill got up and crossed the room to the bureau beside his desk. From the bottom drawer he took a bottle of vintage Claret. He put the bottle and two glasses on the table.

"I've been keeping this for a special occasion," Thornhill said; "perhaps this is it." He drew the cork. "Let's give it a moment to breathe."

Morgenstern lifted the bottle and inspected the label as if recognising an old friend. "I was there," he said excitedly. Thornhill looked puzzled. "I picked grapes for this vintage. I was a graduate student doing my dissertation, working my way across France. That's how I came to be picking grapes that summer."

"Dissertation?" Another surprise – Thornhill had not thought of Morgenstern as a scholar. "What was your subject?"

"Post-revolutionary France. Year One and the Great Terror."

"See any kind of connection, Arnold?"

"Yeh, the kind of people who scare me crapless," Morgenstern replied.

"Enough of riddles, who do you have in mind?" Thornhill asked.

"Same guys as you, maybe," Morgenstern replied.

"And who are they?" Thornhill asked.

"That's what I need you to tell me."

"We're going in circles," Thornhill replied.

"Okay, let's try again," Morgenstern said. "Washington has been like a girls' school where a new clique has taken over. Familiar doors are closed. Old friends don't want to talk. It's not even like there's a new administration. There's something in the wind and it doesn't smell good. I've seen it all from Watergate onwards. Back then you always knew who was into what, and only CNN and the Washington

Post were surprised when it all came out. But this is different. For the first time in my life I don't know what's going on and that scares me like there's no tomorrow."

"Why do you think I can help?"

"I think you know who they are," Morgenstern said sharply.

Thornhill picked up the bottle and slowly poured the wine.

"Time to get your own back," Thornhill said. They both drank thoughtfully. "Worth the wait?" he asked.

"Yes." Morgenstern drank, took the bottle and refilled his glass. As host, the action jarred on Thornhill. "You know you have to tell me," Morgenstern said as he put the bottle down heavily.

"No, Arnold. If I know anything of that kind, I'm only supposed to tell you. There's no 'have to' about it."

"Okay, let's get naked," Morgenstern said. The phrase was new to Thornhill and his perplexity showed. "Metaphorically," Morgenstern said. "Metaphorically," Thornhill replied.

"Okay, hear me out. From the beginning, and never more so than now, America was, and is, so powerful that it can only work if power is defused. The Founding Fathers got it right and we have the Constitution and a Bill of Rights. The French Revolutionaries didn't and they got the Great Terror.

That's the genius of the American system, the separation of powers between the President, the Senate, Congress and the judicial system. Okay, year one civics, but it's ours and it works, or it has worked, for more than two hundred years. So if you had evil ambitions, how hard would you have to huff and puff to bring the house down? Any suggestions, Jackie boy?"

"I'd rather hear yours," Thornhill said.

"Well, how about fear? Good old-fashioned scared shitless fear?"

"Go on," Thornhill said.

"Until now, that was not much use as a weapon against the good 'ole USA, except during the days of the late and unlamented Joe McCarthy. Then along came terrorism, anthrax, SARS and thoughts of the unthinkable." Morgenstern faltered. Thornhill said nothing and Morgenstern carried on. "Got any unthinkable thoughts, Jackie boy?" Morgenstern barely waited for a reply. "Here's mine – a fear that you can play tunes with. A fear that invades the mind and drives the herd, a witchcraft for the 21st century."

"Whom the gods wish to destroy they first make mad?" Thornhill questioned.

"I remember that quotation, it's French," Morgenstern said indignantly, as if the language was a personal possession.

"Greek," Thornhill said. "The quotation is Greek."

"French, Greek, what the hell's the difference?" Morgenstern snapped.

"The real question is, is it accurate?" Thornhill asked.

"Like I said, 'big and bad'. And maybe you're right, maybe mad is the delivery system," Morgenstern said.

"Why are you so sure about all this?" Thornhill asked.

"I've been warned off. Me, on my own turf! Told not to ask the wrong kind of questions. Can you imagine how powerful they feel themselves to be to do that? I'm scared, not just for me, but for the Stars and Bars. Sounds crazy?

Dear God, I hope so. Well here I am, you see me naked and afraid, not a pretty sight."

"Ugly thoughts, Arnold; I should have liked to read your dissertation."

"Cut the crap. Will you help?"

Thornhill refilled the glasses before speaking. "The fact is, Arnold, you come with strings and neither you or I know who's on the other end."

"Is that a no? You won't help?"

"I'll make you an offer," Thornhill replied.

"Let's hear it."

"I need to judge for myself. I'm seeing your people in DC and I'll get back to you immediately afterwards."

"My people! Are you terminally insane? They'll fry you."

"I'm flying out tomorrow," Thornhill said. "I fixed it on the phone from the Cabinet Office. I still have some friends in Washington."

"Friends! Do you have any idea how things are on Capitol Hill nowadays? And me, what about me? I'm a liaison; I'm supposed to watch your ass. How does it make me look?"

"I'll tell them you sent me."

23

Washington DC

It was three forty-five a.m. when Thornhill woke. Despite decades of travel, jet lag was something he had never got used to. Before first light, he was striding the length of the Washington Mall, from the Capitol to the Potomac. His pace slowed alongside the reflecting pool that, true to its name, reflected a frosty full moon with magical clarity.

It was a walk that always touched him; the principles of the young aspiring republic simply set out in stone. It seemed to him that they were a more powerful expression of a human ideal than the worship of pomp and pride that the cities of Europe displayed, with their imperial statues and ornate ceremonial buildings. He climbed the steps of the Lincoln Memorial and let his mind wander across the skyline. The White House, deliberately built as the house of a gentleman, not an American Emperor. The Capitol, housing a Senate modelled on the Roman Republic, had no notion of a New World Caesar. The cold bore in on his thoughts as he walked on, across the river and up the hill into Georgetown.

The meeting with Morgenstern in London had established a lot. Crucially, it had shown what Washington officials did not know. It also demonstrated that it was difficult, to the point of impossibility, to know who could be trusted. By the time the sun was up he was in a side street with a row of elegant 18th-century houses. The one he was looking for had a blue door. He raised the heavy brass knocker and the sound echoed through the wood-panelled interior. He waited for what seemed like a long time and was about to try again when he heard footsteps on the tiled floor. An elegant grey-haired man in a tracksuit opened the door.

"Jack!" Harrison Waters exclaimed. "I didn't know you were in town," he said with amiable surprise.

"Almost nobody does," Thornhill replied.

"Then it can't be good news that brings you here," Waters said as he headed towards the kitchen, leaving Thornhill to close the front door. "Coffee or orange juice?"

"Coffee, almost black."

"You just caught me, I was leaving for the gym. I'm all alone here at the moment; Margaret is in Charlotte visiting the grandchildren." Waters was meticulous in not probing into the reason behind Thornhill's visit. "You haven't been here since the wedding. Must be all of five years."

As a young Senator from the mid-West, Waters had moved to Washington when Jimmy Carter was President, and after he retired had never moved back.

Their friendship went back to their time at Oxford. Waters was from a middle-class family in Missouri who had fallen on hard times after his father contracted tuberculosis. But Waters' outstanding abilities as a scholar and as an athlete brought him to the notice of well-connected local players in the educational power game that led eventually to a Rhodes Scholarship.

Their friendship was of the kind that did not suffer from irregular contact. Each time they met, it was as if their previous conversation had been days, rather than months or years, before.

"Did you ever think of going back when you retired?" Thornhill asked as he waited for the scalding coffee to cool.

"No, I used to be down there half a dozen times a month, but that's a past life. And despite what the song says, everything's not 'Up to date in Kansas City'. Everything that I love is right here." They walked into the living room. Waters drew the curtains and the morning light flooded in. They sat on either side of the large empty fireplace.

"This is unlike you, Jack, you're not usually impulsive. Why didn't you call?"

"I need your advice."

"Then you shall have it. I have plenty to spare; people don't seem to want it much nowadays."

"I have a meeting at ten."

"And?"

"I need to run the players past you."

"Are you going to tell me what it's about?" Waters said with rising interest.

"I'm hoping I won't have to," Thornhill said.

"I understand. I'll help if I can. But I'm retired three years, that's an eternity in this town."

"Distance may allow you to speak more freely," Thornhill replied.

"About what?" Waters was becoming cautious.

"Whatever the names suggest."

"Okay, let's hear them."

"Morgan Douglass, John Brightman, Henry Carlisle, Wilson McSweeney, Sean Harvey, Henry Petersen"

Waters slowly rose and paced across the room. Thoughtfully he spun the antique globe that stood in the window bay.

"These are not the kind of people you usually engage with in Washington, are they?"

"No, that's why I came to see you," Thornhill replied.

"What happened to the usual guys, the ones you trust and who trust you?" Waters asked.

"If your trade is deceit, trust is always conditional, Hal," Thornhill said, using Waters' nickname from Oxford days.

"So you called the people you usually liaise with and they were all busy or out of town?" Water asked.

"All except McSweeney, yes."

"Let's get this straight. You're the number one man on your side of the pond and nobody wants to listen to you?" Waters asked.

"You could put it like that," Thornhill replied.

"You're in trouble, Jack."

"Yes I know, but I believe they are in even more trouble than I am," Thornhill replied.

"In this town it works the other way around. However big a problem they've got, yours is bigger. They'll make sure of it. Hell, Jack, if you've forgotten that, you've been away too long."

"This is not about careers, it's very much more important than that," Thornhill said quietly.

"If you can't tell me enough for me to offer advice, you'll have to settle for speculation. My guess is that they've got the smell of something bad but don't know what kind of putrefaction is causing the stink."

Waters leaned back and put his feet on the coffee table. "Another explanation is that they, or at least some of them, do know, and want to stop you blowing the whistle."

"Incisive as ever, Hal," Thornhill said. "Now you see why I need the biographies. Not the stuff you can get on the Net, but the unwashed jungle nature of these creatures; the animals they prey upon, the camouflage they seek out, the kinds of ambush they might spring. Above all, any vulnerabilities they might have."

Waters looked at his watch and shook his head. "Your meeting's at ten, right?" Thornhill nodded. "Then let's get you a cab and have it waiting. I'd take you myself but it would do neither of us any good if you arrived in my car."

Waters disappeared into the kitchen and made a call. Thornhill closed his eyes and tried to get a grip on the wave of fatigue that threatened to loosen his hold on the hours ahead. Waters, by contrast, seemed full of energy.

"Let's get to work; I'll give you what I've got."

"Thanks," Thornhill replied as he poured another cup of coffee, entirely black this time.

"With these guys you've got the full set: State Department, CIA, National Security Agency, White House, Department of Defence. They're all heavy hitters. This represents more than mere curiosity at whatever message you may be bearing. They wouldn't put a group like that together at a first hearing unless they were seriously worried. How many of them do you know?"

"McSweeney I've met before, at the Joint Intelligence Committee. A disagreeable piece of work," Thornhill said.

"You're right, watch your back. He's got a lot to prove; he had a reliable track record until he made a big mistake about Iraq. Now he needs to re-establish his credibility. Henry Carlisle, he's a mystery man. The fact that I know nothing about him may mean he's dangerous."

"Morgan Douglass I know by reputation," Thornhill said.

"Then you'll know he's a Texan politician, a florid loudmouth who thinks he's LBJ reincarnate. He's got the vocabulary and he fools a lot of people a lot of the time, not least himself. But he's not got the mind of LBJ, or the heart for that matter. There's an election coming up and he needs headlines. John Brightman is a pallid little bureaucrat with some very nasty friends; our very own model of the banality of evil. Henry Petersen is the product of recent history. He's a guard fish for the White House. His job is to spot trouble while it's still far enough away to deflect onto somebody else. Publicly he's an idealist, and other than my innate cynicism about human nature and political life, I've no reason to believe him to be otherwise. In short, he's the only one of this pack who is halfway decent. Michael Harvey is ex Harvard Law School, an intelligence pro. He's Irish, rich and wants to make a political name for himself. He's very tricky, with the instincts of a sewer rat. He'd take that as a compliment."

"Sounds like an interesting morning," Thornhill said.

"You asked about vulnerabilities. There aren't many that I know of. These are some of the most powerful people in the country. They're an unstable mix of anger, fear and ambition. With that in mind, why do you think they've set aside a day of their lives to listen to you?"

"Because they've been told to," Thornhill replied.

"That's a very scary notion," Waters said.

Thornhill drank the last of the coffee. "I know," he replied.

"The only advice I can give you is to remember ego, that's what drives them. The loyalty of guys like that is not to their boss or to any institution but to the power that lies behind them. To some extent, they're all frightened of each other.

That's because nobody knows at any one time exactly where the balance of power lies. It changes, sometimes hour by hour. That's what makes them nervous and that's what makes them dangerous. You should bear that in mind."

"Thanks, Hal, you're a true friend," Thornhill said gratefully.

"I wish I could do more. Like I said, I'm out of touch these days."

"There is one more thing,"

"Shoot."

"What can you tell me about Calvin November?" In the silence that followed Thornhill felt half a lifetime of friendship slide into an abyss.

"I think I hear your cab arriving," Waters said.

* * *

At eight fifty Thornhill sat in a small deli with a large espresso, oblivious to the noisy crush of office workers ordering take-out breakfasts. What did it all mean? He felt like an archaeologist trying to piece together an understanding from incoherent shards of clay. The sharp jolt of caffeine helped focus the questions that crowded in on him. He shuffled the pieces around in his mind, trying to make them fit together. Suddenly, he got a match. A copy of the Washington Post, tucked under the arm of a man collecting a large bag of bagels, crossed Thornhill's peripheral vision.

A headline read: *White House Aide Accused of Corruption.* Underneath was a picture of Henry Petersen.

Thornhill hurried across the street to Union Station and bought a copy of the paper. Beneath the picture of Petersen was a damning story:

> White House special advisor Henry Petersen is due to face a press conference later today following last night's allegations of corruption at Carmichael Energy, one of the key partners in the Presidential Homeland Energy Development Programme, designed to reduce dependence on imported oil.

> Petersen, former Chief Financial Officer of Carmichael, is widely believed to be the controlling mind behind the controversial programme. He became a prominent White House figure when the project was launched two years ago…

* * *

It was a large room with a long table in highly polished American Walnut. The surface reflected distorted images of the arrivals as they took their places. Unusually for Washington, the meeting gathered in silence. There were none of the ritual enquiries about family and health. Morgan Douglass, a large, sweaty man in a heavy blue suit and yellow tie, sat at the head of the table. It seemed as if he was to be the chairman. Thornhill had no way of knowing if this represented seniority or self-appointment. Instinctively he sat at the opposite end and the others filled the places between.

Douglass opened the meeting. "We're all here, I believe.

Mr Petersen has asked me to apologise in advance on account of the fact that he has to leave ahead of any conclusions we may reach, so as to attend to more personal matters this afternoon." He could scarcely conceal a sneer, which, like a suppressed yawn, travelled round the others at the table.

"So I understand." Thornhill was astonished that Petersen was there. Why had he chosen to take time out from preparation for facing the world's press on the most important issue of his political life?

"I'll put it to you simply, Sir Thornhill," Douglass said, making the frequent American error about knighthoods. "What the fuck is going on?"

Thornhill did not respond and Douglass mistook his silence for weakness and his instinct was to kick a man who is down.

"Everyone round this table knows you've been operating here in the USA in breach of the inter-agency agreement. In Bermuda you had your ass kicked and now you're coming to Uncle Sam for help.

Same old Limey story we've heard so often before." He looked round the table for the silent approbation of others. "Boy, this had better be good." His sweaty palm slapped the table and left a grease mark as he sat back in his chair, waiting for a reply.

Thornhill's first reaction was relief. In Douglass he had thought he might encounter the kind of native shrewdness that had made LBJ's presidency so effective. Instead, Douglass was no more than a playground bully. He decided to counter-attack.

"Mr Chairman, thank you for your welcome. However, I suggest, amusing though it may be, we dispense with ritual abuse. It wastes time and clouds the issue."

For a moment Thornhill's icy ferocity put everyone off balance. Then John Brightman spoke. "As you say, Sir Jack, let's cut to the chase."

"What I have to say is not 'good'," Thornhill said, looking pointedly at Douglass. "On the contrary, I believe it's bad, very bad." Thornhill felt he was beginning to divide the opposition.

"Let's hear it," McSweeney said.

"I'm here not to tax the generosity of Uncle Sam," Thornhill said, while continuing to look directly at Douglass, who he believed was now holed below the waterline, "but because you have an even bigger problem than we do."

"How do you make that calculation?" Sean Harvey asked, as if expecting a mathematical response.

For the first time, Thornhill was unsure what to say next. He put both hands flat on the table and then spoke with slow deliberation. "I believe that a prominent American citizen, together with others in the Russian Republic, is conspiring to destroy a number of major democratic institutions, among them the Presidency and the elected government of the United States."

There it was, laid out on the table and with it a lifetime's reputation. Put coldly, it sounded barking mad. But there was no going back. Everybody seemed unsure of how to respond. It was Harvey who spoke first. "Is that what you Brits call understatement?"

"You're talking like we're facing the end of the civilised world as we know it," McSweeney interrupted sarcastically.

"Yes," Thornhill said.

"And you've fallen for this bullshit conspiracy theory!" Michael Harvey said contemptuously.

"Do you have any idea how many crank calls and conspiracy theories we have to deal with?" he continued.

"Yes, I do," Thornhill replied crisply.

"And you expect us to believe this?" Harvey asked.

"So who is this 'prominent citizen'?" Douglass had regained his confidence and was back in the game.

"Mr Calvin November," Thornhill replied.

There was a stunned silence. They were playing for time, each considering the implications for their own personal and political agendas.

"And how did you come to that conclusion, Sir Jack?" Harvey eventually asked, as if humouring a lunatic.

"I'm not ready to disclose that," Thornhill said flatly.

"Don't act like a virgin in a whorehouse, what have you got?" Douglass said aggressively.

"I've made my position clear. On the one occasion when you got close, one of my people was killed, others were injured and our prime source was put at serious risk," Thornhill said coldly.

"Fuck your source, you say our President is at risk and you won't tell us what you got!" Douglass exploded.

"Not yet," Thornhill said flatly.

"What this suggests to me is that you're out of your depth, Sir Jack," McSweeney said. "If you'd come to us earlier, all that stuff in Bermuda could have been avoided. The responsibility is entirely yours. We'd have provided a safe environment."

Safe for whom? Thornhill wondered.

"Where is your source now?" Harvey asked.

"Safe," said Thornhill, thinking of the tall building that looked like an apartment block, above Hampstead Heath on the ridge north of London. "How we derived this information is much less important than the information itself."

"Let's hear it," McSweeney said.

"It is our belief that the threat is centred on the forthcoming summit in Geneva."

"Go on," Harvey said.

"Let's hear it," McSweeney said. It seemed to be a favourite phrase.

"I believe that the lives or possibly the sanity of the principle participants are in danger."

The questions came rapidly.

"How?" Harvey asked.

"A chemical attack," Thornhill said.

"Chemical attack? What kind of chemical attack?" Brightman joined the questioning.

"A bio-chemical attack. Something entirely new, devised specifically for this purpose," Thornhill replied.

"Why? To what end? We have a study that lists more than three hundred chemical agents capable of killing any number of people in an environment like the Geneva summit," Brightman said. "Many of them could be made in any high school lab. Terrorism manual page one."

"Why go to the trouble of creating something new?" Harvey added.

"This is not about killing," Thornhill said.

"Then what the fuck is it about?" Douglass shouted down the length of the table.

"It's about control," Thornhill said coldly.

"Let's hear it," McSweeney said again.

Thornhill found the repetition of the phrase strangely irritating.

"I suspect it's intended to be a demonstration of power. The power to set world leaders at each other's throats; I mean that in the most literal sense, gentlemen."

"What could anybody possibly gain from attempting a stunt like that?" McSweeney said.

"Everything," Thornhill replied.

"That's preposterous," McSweeney said dismissively.

"Yes, it is preposterous," Thornhill said, and paused for a moment. Then he took a gamble, appealing to both reality and paranoia. "But you all know there's something going on. Invitations to important meetings are being cancelled or postponed. Key people are not returning calls. There are unexpected absences. I'll put it to you plainly, you're all big beasts in this jungle. None of you would have survived so long if you couldn't read the signs."

It worked. Round the table there was a silent interchange of glances.

"Hitler was elected to power." Petersen had not previously spoken; now he said something that seemed both bizarre and irrelevant.

"What!" Douglass shouted in annoyance.

Petersen continued without acknowledging the interruption. "The Nazis were elected because everything else was seen to have failed. The military had failed to win a world war. Money had failed; everyone remembered when a week's wages wouldn't put one meal on the table. Democracy had failed and there were private armies on the streets. Moreover, they had an enemy within, a revolutionary movement, much like the one that had taken over Russia just a few years before. Worst of all, they lost confidence in the system, in their history, in themselves as a nation.

They wanted their pride back, they wanted simple solutions. Then along comes Adolf who offers them everything they want, and more. He tells them they can stand tall and kick ass without impediment. A restoration of the natural order of things."

Thornhill checked his natural instinct to correct such a crude analysis.

"People will have anything but chaos," Petersen said. "Anybody hear echoes?"

"We don't need no history lessons, the future's got enough problems without importing them from the past. Let's move on," Douglass said irritably.

John Brightman's civil tone was overlaid with sarcasm. "May we hear your analysis, or should I perhaps say screenplay?"

Thornhill took a deep breath. "Mr Petersen spoke about echoes, a people no longer certain of who they are, with a longing for the security of simple answers, we must all admit he's right about that. Our system hasn't been able to deliver answers; it doesn't even want to listen to the questions. That's why the largest party in any election is the non-voting party. Now, Mr November arrives offering that same constituency a vast amount of money – a hundred billion dollars.
Give everyone with access to an Internet connection a direct say in exactly how it's spent , and you've got the makings of electronic mob rule."

"Sir Jack, I believe the argument is in good hands and I regret I must leave," Petersen said as he rose and gathered up his papers.

Thornhill noticed that there were no good wishes. It was as if the scandal Petersen had to answer for was a terminal disease and nobody wanted to risk infection. As the heavy door closed behind Petersen, Thornhill continued. "I believe that whatever is planned for the Geneva Summit is intended to be the first act in an unfolding strategy." Douglass did not seem to understand the magnitude of the argument. "Just exactly what are you proposing, Sir Thornhill?"

"That you believe me."

"And what should we believe?"

"That you have an urgent duty to restrain November and the power he represents," Thornhill said.

"You talk like he's some kind of home-grown Bin Laden," Douglas said contemptuously.

"The words are yours, not mine, Senator."

A secretary cautiously entered the room and put a note in front of Sean Harvey. He read it and slid it across the table to Douglass. The act had an air of theatre about it.

"I regret it is necessary for us to adjourn," Douglass said.

Though Thornhill had half-anticipated some manoeuvre of this kind, but the accuracy of his expectation did not reduce his sense of helplessness. Events seemed to be moving beyond any influence he had hoped to have upon them.

"We'll reconvene at nine a.m. tomorrow. That okay with you, Sir Thornhill?"

For the first time Thornhill realised that Douglass's misuse of his title was not an ill-informed error but a deliberate sleight. The realities of power were being spelt out to him.

"Nine a.m. it is then."

Douglass nodded as if not wanting to engage in further discussion. Thornhill remained at the table and waited until the group got to the large conference room door; then he fired a parting shot.

"A final factor to consider, gentlemen," he said. They turned to look at him.

He knew it was his last chance. "Remember the principles of judo. The aim is to turn the adversary's force against himself. In these new circumstances, the great power of the United States is its greatest vulnerability."

The group murmured an impatient acknowledgement and moved into the corridor.

* * *

Thornhill declined the offer of a car, and strode down the long flight of steps and immersed himself in the crowds of tourists and bureaucrats taking a lunch break. It was something that he would have severely disciplined a junior for doing in the same circumstances. Anything could happen. A man with a shared secret of this magnitude was a man with enemies. The advice of Hal Waters kept playing in his mind like a tape loop: 'They're all frightened of each other. Nobody knows exactly where the balance of power lies at any one time. It changes, sometimes hour by hour; that's what makes them nervous and it's what makes them dangerous.'

The satellite office was little more than ten minutes away. It had little to do with satellites in space. The name went back to the Cold War when there had been the need for a discreet venue for sensitive meetings. Its location was known to a few in the trade but not to outsiders, especially the media. The entrance was via a corridor in an apartment block to the rear of the main building. What amused Thornhill was that the front of the building, with its view of the Capitol beyond, was used daily by broadcast correspondents as a backdrop for on-camera reports of the major stories of the day.

Over the years, Thornhill had several times conducted discussions of some of the world's most critically important issues while the international press were plying their trade on the other side of the venetian blinds, two floors below. Thornhill commandeered the main conference room and made it plain to the staff that he did not want to be interrupted. He worked far into the night. For several hours, he repeatedly drew up courses of action and abandoned each of them as improbable or impracticable. Sometime in the early hours of the morning, the phone rang.

"Code Delta." The Communications Officer entered the office without knocking. Before Thornhill could complain about the intrusion, he added, "It's Mr Lloyd-Emlyn from London, sir."

Lloyd-Emlyn sounded grim. "They seem to be working late in Senator Douglass's office. They phoned a few minutes ago. The Duty Officer put the call through to me at home."

Thornhill hated long introductions." And?"

"Your meeting has been moved back forty-eight hours and the participants have changed."

"Who are they?"

Lloyd-Emlyn read the list. It was longer than before.

"Do you know any of them?" Lloyd-Emlyn asked.

"Enough of them to know that the whole thing has been downgraded, as well as delayed."

"Why would they do that?"

"They're stalling for time," Thornhill said.

Lloyd-Emlyn was indignant. "It's insulting to you personally, asking you to wait and then attend a meeting of assistants rather than principals."

"I have no intention of complying. I want you to call them back on a secure line. Tell them that I shall not be attending and that you will represent me. Get on the first plane in the morning. If you can't do that, call the diplomatic flight at Lyneham. Use my personal authority if you have to."

Thornhill returned to his papers and tried to clear his mind. After a few minutes, the phone rang again. The Communications Officer sounded hesitant.

"I'm sorry for a second interruption, sir, but it's Mr Morgenstern. He says it's a matter of the greatest urgency."

"Put him through," Thornhill said.

"Arnold?"

"It's bad, Jackie boy. Very bad. You've lit a fire under the ass of the establishment and you're the most unpopular guy in town."

"I'm glad to hear it."

"You won't be when you hear what I've got to tell you."

"I'm listening."

"Not on Ma Bell's line. I know where you're hiding out. I'm coming over right now and I'm bringing someone with me."

Morgenstern was never one to be inhibited by the lack of an invitation and fifteen minutes later, the Duty Officer was announcing his arrival. As the conference room door opened, Thornhill was astonished to see the tall figure of Henry Petersen follow Morgenstern into the room. Thornhill motioned them to the easy chairs around the little art deco fireplace. Nobody spoke until the door was closed.

"You've already met," Morgenstern said, making a gesture that embraced both Petersen and Thornhill.

It was not in Thornhill's nature to reply to a statement of the obvious. "You have something to tell me, Arnold?"

"The word I hear is that they only need to keep the cork in the bottle for a few days, then it won't matter. So they'll do anything to prevent disruption to whatever it is they have in mind. If it's as important as you say it is, they'll discredit any opposition and they'll silence any voice that they don't want Joe six-pack to hear. That's unless what you were saying this morning is no more than a fart in a thunderstorm. What's the reality, Jackie, fart or fact?"

Thornhill was appalled that Morgenstern should know what had taken place at a supposedly secret meeting just a few hours before. He stared hard at Petersen.

"Whose word, Arnold? You said 'the word is'; a telling phrase. Whose word are you passing on?"

"That's the final frontier, Jackie. You know I can't tell you that."

Petersen spoke. "That's why I'm here. Given time, the White House could deal with this through the usual channels but I've become convinced we don't have time."

"I fear you may be right," Thornhill said.

Petersen continued. "I began to get bad vibes on a number of people a few weeks ago. I started to turn stones over. I got a couple of PhD interns to check things like official travel patterns. There was a lot that didn't make sense and I began to ask questions. Then I got a visit from one of the elder statesmen. Alternative futures were set out for me. Money, tenure at an Ivy League college, the possibility of a world affairs TV show. All I had to do was stop."

"And the alternative?" Thornhill asked.

"Destruction of my career and credibility. Exile to obscurity in the Madlands of conspiracy theorists."

"What did you do?" Thornhill asked.

Petersen's composure began to crack. "You have to understand why I did what I did… There were once things I believed in." He turned away, took a deep breath and swallowed hard. "I remember looking out of my office window and seeing the flag. I remember it was hanging limply for lack of breeze." Petersen's voice faltered. "I threw them out, Sir Jack; it was one of the few wholly decent things I've done in a long career of political compromise."

"What happened?"

"You can see Act One on CNN right now or in the Post in the morning. I don't intend to resign, but my expectation is that I will be suspended from White House duties by the end of the week. They can't make any of it stick because it's all crap. But that's not the point. It's silence they wanted and silence they've got."

"Why have you come to me with this? You must know that I can't offer you any kind of political help," Thornhill said quietly.

"I'm going to fight back, but this thing is like an incubating plague. It's impossible to tell who is infected and there is no time to find out. You are the only person I know to be free of contamination. If things go wrong, I want there to be someone on the outside who knows me for who I am." Thornhill thought for a moment before replying. "How can you be so sure of me?"

"This morning told me what I needed to know, that's why I was there. You had nothing to gain and everything to lose," Petersen said.

"What do you propose?" Thornhill asked.

"A secure channel of communication," Petersen replied.

"That can be arranged. How will we contact you?" Thornhill asked. "You don't," Petersen replied. "That's too risky."

"I regret I cannot argue with you on that account," Thornhill said as he lifted the phone and spoke to the Communications Officer. "Mr Petersen is leaving shortly. He's to be given access to Channel Zulu. Prepare the paperwork; I'll sign the authority at the end of our meeting. What do you intend to do, Mr Petersen?"

"I'll contact you as soon as I make a move," Petersen said.

Thornhill realised that he wasn't going to get anything more and changed tack. "And Arnold? How can you be sure of Arnold?" Thornhill said, turning to Morgenstern.

"Much the same; nothing to gain and a lot to lose. Besides, he's too much his own man to be anybody else's."

Morgenstern cut the description short. "Enough already. So I'm an authentic American hero, that we're agreed on. I told you not to come to Washington. That was good advice. Now I'm telling you to go back to London."

"Not yet," Thornhill said.

"You know what Machiavelli said?" Morgenstern asked. "'Against a great evil, a small protest does not have a small effect. It has no effect whatever.' You're wasting your time here."

"Not yet, Arnold, I'm not ready to leave yet."

"Okay, I'll spell it out for you. These are bad guys. They mostly use three tools: manipulation, money or murder; they're not particular which.

They can't use the first two, like they tried to do with Petersen. So what option does that leave? Do the math. Thornhill said nothing and Morgenstern tried again.

"In the normal way of things they wouldn't dare do it with someone like you, but all they've got to do is hold the line for just a short while longer and then the questions won't matter anymore because there'll be nobody left to ask them. Clear and present danger, Jackie. Get your ass back to London, right now."

The door opened and the Communications Officer entered.

"I said after the meeting," Thornhill snapped, before he saw that the man was not carrying forms for signature but a single slip of yellow paper. It read: *Line 7 Murphy Code Bravo NYC.* He slid it into his pocket. "Please take Mr Petersen next door and brief him on Channel Zulu."

He turned to Morgenstern. "Arnold, please wait here. There's a good single malt in the cabinet by the bookcase."

He moved quickly to the Communications Office and was patched into Line 7. "Thornhill."

"It's Morag," the voice said. "There's a signal from Mantoni in New York. Murphy has been found in an alley in Tribeca. He's in a terrible state, ranting about dragons, Buddy Holly and the Hindenburg airship disaster. Mantoni got a call from an old buddy in the police precinct; they managed to get a phone number out of him. They think he's had a complete mental breakdown and were arranging to transfer him to Bellevue, but Mantoni got them to put that on hold. He's on his way there to take Murphy to the Hawkstone Clinic out at Westchester. He knows people there. It sounds bad, it's just not like Murphy."

"You're right, it's not. We're being sent a message."

"A message from–"

Thornhill cut her off in mid-sentence. "I'll call Mantoni. Go home and get some sleep. I'll contact you from New York."

Ten minutes later he was back in the conference room. Morgenstern and Petersen had a large glass of Scotch apiece. "I've signed the communications protocol. And now, gentlemen, I'm taking your advice and I'm leaving. Please finish your whisky before you go."

Petersen and Morgenstern went to the window and saw Thornhill hail a cab. It took off at speed, heading down the deserted avenue in the direction of Dulles International.

"Even the mighty are capable of being terrified," Petersen said.

"I'm disappointed," Morgenstern said. "I thought it would be much more difficult than that."

* * *

Thornhill waited until the cab had crossed the Mall. At Independence Avenue he spoke through the small grid in the Perspex barrier between passenger and driver.

"A change of plan – Union Station." The driver mumbled an obscenity at the loss of the thirty-mile fare to Dulles. Less than ten minutes later, Thornhill was using cash to buy a ticket to Penn Station in New York. Travelling by rail was more anonymous than a transit through two airports. With the new fast trains, the travel time was almost identical to the shuttle, plus the journey out to Ronald Reagan

Airport and the ride into Manhattan from La Guardia. He settled into a corner seat and closed his eyes.

24

The Refuge

Petersen heard the choir two blocks away, faintly at first, then the magnetic rhythm of Gospel music and clapping hands drew him across the street. He recognised the tall white spire of the church and knew he was in the right place. Opening the door, he slipped quietly inside and sat at the back. The congregation was small enough for an extra member to be noticed and he was immediately conscious of being an ethnic minority of one.

"Welcome, brother," the blue-robed speaker called. Petersen realised that the preacher remembered him.

"Welcome to our little light in this city of sin."

Petersen nodded in embarrassed acknowledgement. They had met a year previously when members of a Presidential Inquiry, which Petersen was chairing, visited inner city communities with severe problems. Among the angry, the greedy and the whimsically idealistic, Petersen remembered the Rev Jeremiah Newton as a man who stood out as comprehending both principle and practicality. The sermon began. "We live in a city of grimness and grace. We look to our majestic white buildings and what do we find? 'Whited sepulchres', such as our Lord cried out against, 'white on the outside and full of corruption on the inside'."

Petersen knew his life was in serious danger and he found strength in the preacher's clarity of vision. He had understood the risk as a possibility as soon as he began to investigate Celestacom and he knew it for certain less than an hour before entering the church. It had been a near miss.

Returning to his office for an all-night session to collate his final evidence, he had stopped to collect coffee from the café in the bookstore across the street. When he saw a light come on in his room, he left the coffee unpaid for on the counter and sprinted up the stairs to the top level of the store. From there he could look down into his office. Two figures in cleaners' coveralls were going through his desk while another was working on his computer. The bank safe deposit where he had cached copies of his computer hard disc would not open until the morning. He urgently needed a refuge, a place to work and a clean line into the Net. In those desperate few minutes, Jeremiah Newton was the only person he could think of.

"And where do we see God's grace? Not in the halls of government nor in the temples of high finance but in you, His people," the preacher proclaimed.

Petersen had lost track of how long the sermon had been going on; he was repeatedly checking over the precautions he had taken. He'd changed cabs three times and walked the last half-mile. Was it enough? Only by the most disciplined effort did he keep from turning to look at the door.

"On the outside you may be ugly, you may be broke, you may feel helpless, but by God's grace, on the inside you are handsome, wealthy and strong." There was an explosion of colliding 'Amens' and 'Hallelujahs' from the congregation and suddenly, everyone was singing.

Petersen sat with his head in his hands, trying to manage his fear. He looked up to see the church emptying and Jeremiah Newton standing over him.

"Being of the Baptist persuasion we have no confessional, but if you'd care to come into the vestry I'd be glad to listen."

"I may not have very long," Petersen said.

"That is true for all of us."

In the tiny vestry crammed with books and musical instruments, Petersen sobbed out the whole story.

"You must know that we get a lot of crazy people in here. What I have to decide is whether you're one of them," Newton said.

"I know," Petersen said quietly.

"What are you asking for?"

"A place to work for a few hours, somebody to collect computer discs from a safe deposit. Nobody knows about it, so it should be safe. Then I need to put the information in order. I need to use the Net and a phone, and I'd be grateful for some place to sleep after it's all over," Petersen said.

Newton stared at him for a long time before he spoke. "What you're asking me to participate in may be indiscriminate foolishness which could destroy my work here. There are many people who would like to see that; more of them than you might think are in the established church. On the other hand, if what you tell me is true, what terrors might you bring upon my people? Why should I take such risks?"

"What you were preaching about out there? Does it apply in here?" Petersen asked.

25

Tribeca, New York

Mantoni was waiting as the train drew into Penn Station in Manhattan. He held two paper cups of espresso and handed one to Thornhill.

"He's skipped."

"How?!" Thornhill spluttered as he swallowed the strong, tepid coffee.

"They were holding him at the precinct in Tribeca. There's no special security for the people they send to Bellevue. There's no crime been committed and most are glad to go; clean sheets and a hot meal. It took me ten minutes to call London and then another twenty to get to the precinct. By that time he'd gone. There were no charges to hold him on."

It was raining and they passed the cab ride in silence. The empty, dimly lit streets matched Thornhill's black mood. He had no plans, and no coherent idea of what to do next. When they got to the precinct, he was relieved when Mantoni took the lead.

"Leave the introductions to me."

Thornhill nodded and stayed a pace behind Mantoni. The sign at the desk said Sergeant K. C. O'Reilly.

Behind it stood a large, affable man with thinning red hair and a broad smile.

Mantoni spoke rapidly. "Hi, Kelly, this is Dr Blackthorn, he's a psychologist. The fugitive is his sister's brother-in-law and. He'd like to ask some questions."

"Okay," the Sergeant said cheerfully.

"This is how it is," Mantoni continued. "The family have been worried about him for a while. Then they heard he was acting strange; the doc's sister was worried; that's why he flew in from Dublin yesterday."

O'Reilly's smile faded as he wrote in the desk log. There was a slight shake of the head. He clearly didn't believe a word of Mantoni's clumsy cover story. Then Thornhill realised that the account of events was not intended to be believed, but was for the record. The underlying reality of the situation resided somewhere in the impenetrable world of New York traded favours.

The sergeant spoke directly to Thornhill with more than a hint of sarcasm. "So how are things in the auld country?"

"Is there somewhere we could talk?" Thornhill said.

The three of them went into an interview room furnished with graffiti and out-of-shape metal furniture.

"I need to ask you a few questions," Thornhill said in something between an assertion and a question, as he took a small notebook from an inside pocket.

"He's not a fugitive. We're not out there looking for him," O'Reilly said defensively.

"I appreciate that, but can you tell me how he came to be here?"

O'Reilly consulted the desk log. "We had a call. Anonymous, a disturbance in an alleyway, happens a lot; people call it in but they don't want to get involved."

"What did he say when you brought him in?"

"It was a quiet patch and he seemed different from the usual drunks, druggies and crazies. So I talked with him for a while."

Thornhill sensed a hint of an opportunity. "You said he was different, how different?"

"He was raving, saying the strangest things: 'St George and dragons', then things about Rock and Roll, Jerry Lee Lewis, Elijah and Lakehurst… that's over in New Jersey," O'Reilly added. "Then it was 'the wilderness' and 'James Baldwin'. We get a lot of this kind of thing. But this was different because, I don't know how to put this…" He paused and thought hard.

"It was like he was struggling, not just raving. He was trying to put these crazy thoughts in some kind of order. Then he began to give me the numbers."

"Numbers?"

"Yeah, lots of them; they seemed random at first. Then he grabbed my arm; he had a hell'uva grip. It was like I was his mind and he was trying to hold on."

"The numbers?"

"Yes, it took a while for me to figure out. I took down the sequences he most often repeated and read them back to him. It was like some crazy conversation. But in time we seemed to come to some kind of agreement. Then I recognised an area code. I read the other numbers back to him until I got it right. It was a Manhattan phone number. The effort seemed too much for him and he passed out. I called the number and Mantoni answered."

* * *

"Two Early Bird Specials," the waitress announced as the heavily overloaded plates clattered onto the table of the deli, which was crowded with breakfasting office workers. Thornhill was suddenly aware that he had not eaten for twenty-four hours. He consumed the eggs, bacon and waffles in mechanical silence. His mind was not engaged with eating, but with anger and inadequacy. Mantoni knew better than to make small talk. But it was not in his nature to keep quiet.

"What was all that stuff, those crazy-man things he was saying?"

Thornhill wiped clean a place on the crowded table and opened his notebook. Everything is connected. He wasn't rambling, he was trying to tell us something," Thornhill said.

"Connected, how in the hell is that?" Mantoni asked.

"St George and the dragon, Rock and Roll, Lakehurst, Baldwin, Elijah, the wilderness, that's the riddle we have to solve."

Turning the questions over in his mind, Thornhill lifted a cup of tea and stared through the steamy windows into the street. The rain was unrelenting and vehicles threw up huge sheets of filthy water that had collected in the deep potholes of the dilapidated roadway. Through the spray, Thornhill's vision locked onto a bank of television screens in an electronics store across the street. What he saw drove the riddle from his mind. There was a brief image of Arnold Morgenstern on CNN. It was gone almost as soon as he recognised the face. He slammed his teacup down.

"We need to get to the office, now. I need to use a computer."

"Okay, what do you have in mind?" Mantoni asked.

"The fate of an authentic American hero."

Mantoni looked puzzled but didn't ask questions. "There's no way we'll get a cab in the rain. I can call a car from base or we can take the subway."

"The subway; we can't wait for a car," Thornhill said.

By the time they got to the subway station they were soaked and joined the steaming humanity compressed into the Uptown Express. The dash to the office provided a second drenching. Suddenly, the cold, stress and fatigue hit Thornhill with physical force. He tried to stop himself shivering but didn't succeed. Mantoni was concerned.

"You look like you need a hot shower and a stiff drink."

"There are some weekend clothes in the operations room locker. That would help," Thornhill said.

In the familiar territory of the visitors' office, Thornhill began to change into the friendly warmth of a wool shirt and the shivering began to fade. He was still changing clothes while he switched on the computer and logged onto the CNN website. As he began to pull on a pair of rough tweed trousers, Morgenstern's picture appeared on the screen. The news story read: '*...a mugging that went wrong in a seedy part of Washington ... two shots to the head ... another digit in the statistics of a violent city...*'

The shivering returned and slowly Thornhill began to weep. Mantoni found him sobbing, with his trousers round his ankles. He quickly closed the door behind him and locked it to prevent intrusion by any of the staff. Mantoni mistook tears of cold fury for grief.

"What is it, boss?" he asked hesitantly.

"I was thinking of Machiavelli," Thornhill said.

26

Chelsea, London

Thornhill was in the club lounge at Newark Airport when he received an alert on his secure mobile phone. It was Lloyd-Emlyn.

"I'm speaking from the satellite office. Zulu from Petersen." Zulu status was given only to highly sensitive sources who feared a reply would compromise their safety. Code Zulu was one-way traffic; there was no means of replying.

"Seems that Celestacom have been buying up vast quantities of their own shares - blatant insider dealing. They're also stripping out their city offices in New York, Washington and LA. Just caretaker secretarial staff are left; computers, files, everything gone. Rumour is it's all going to the Domes."

Thornhill didn't react. "Thank you," he said as he switched off. His mind was racing. Another act of recklessness; first the shooting of Morgenstern and now financial irregularity on a huge scale. It demonstrated a frightening confidence in the future. And what of the removals to the desert? What did that foretell?

Thornhill opened his laptop and began carefully to compose an 'Eyes Only' message, outlining Petersen's warning, to Patricia Lathkill's secure email address. The message stressed that these new developments called for an emergency response. She replied just as the flight was being called. Reluctantly she agreed to see him.

* * *

"How was America, Sir Jack?" The uniformed driver of the dark-green Jaguar was in an irritatingly cheerful mood.

"Instructive," Thornhill said from the back seat as he tried to make sense of the psychiatrist's report on Murphy's behaviour that he had received on his mobile phone.

It had been dark when the aircraft landed at Heathrow and the sky was only a slightly lighter shade of grey when the car got to the handsome Georgian house close to the river in Chelsea. Thornhill mounted the short flight of Portland stone steps, rang the bell and waited. He was used to meticulous preparations for important meetings. Now there was no time. He felt shabby and unkempt. The flight had left him with a dull headache and a strange taste in the mouth. The toy razor from the in-flight goody bag had made little impression on his stubble and he was suddenly aware of the frayed edges of his ancient weekend clothes. He was about to press the bell for a second time when a buzzer sounded and the door opened. The hallway was empty. He stepped inside and closed the door behind him. "Good morning." The Baroness emerged from a doorway to his left. Despite the pre-dawn encounter she was dressed in her customary cashmere and pearls.

"You're early," she said accusingly.

"Sorry, tail-winds over the Atlantic."

"You seem to be propelled by a great deal of tail-wind, Sir Jack," she said as she led him into the large living room. It was starkly furnished.

The only concessions to decor were two French Impressionist paintings and a single Chinese vase on a mahogany stand. In the splendid Adam fireplace, there were the remnants of a coal fire, but the room felt cold. There was no offer of refreshment.

"You received the document?" Thornhill asked.

"Yes."

"I will come straight to the point," Thornhill said. "The Prime Minister must not be allowed to go to Geneva."

"Quite impossible, every other leader of significance will be there. How could he possibly be absent?"

"This is not merely a matter of protocol or prestige. You've seen the latest developments. This is much more than speculation, it's a threat of the first magnitude, to the Prime Minister personally, to the nation and to the international community."

"But you have no proof of any of that."

"I have the strongest possible circumstantial evidence. You've seen it in black and white."

"What I've seen is the alleged eyewitness account of an elderly Polish academic and your interpretation of subsequent events."

"You've also seen the Zulu message from an entirely new source. It shows that November and his people are behaving as if the world ends next week. Are you going to avoid facing that issue too?"

She did not rise to Thornhill's anger. "My point is that none of this creates any kind of convincing link with Geneva, let alone the personal safety of the PM. It's information that can be interpreted in a number of ways."

It was only at this point that Thornhill noticed they were both still standing. He had not even been invited to sit down.

"What about Bermuda? A rocket-propelled grenade attack is a matter of fact, not interpretation."

"Sir Jack, the world is full of RPG attacks. I don't doubt that the orbit you inhabit is peopled by ruthless characters. Nor do I doubt that it is your job, from time to time, to annoy some of them and to deal with the consequences of such activities."

Thornhill knew that only one option now remained open.

"Baroness, I must formally request an urgent meeting with the Prime Minister."

"You know I cannot agree to that."

"And you know that I have to ask."

"You went to Washington without consultation, and despite well-known American paranoia about the safety of the President, you failed to get past a first hearing. Now you come back with your tail between your legs and try the same thing here."

"So this is revenge for going over your head?"

"No, Jack, it's reality." To Thornhill's surprise her tone softened. "You'd do the same thing in my position, and I must warn you not to try a backstairs approach in Downing Street. I'm sorry, but that's how it has to be." It was clear that there was nothing left to say.

He moved towards the hallway and the Baroness followed him. At the front door Thornhill said, "Good people have risked their lives to provide us with these warnings and several of them are already dead."

She gently put her hand on his arm. "Jack, I am not your friend but over the years I have often been your admirer. Don't destroy yourself over this."

Thornhill stepped into the street. He looked at his watch. The most important meeting of his life had lasted less than ten minutes. The driver had been watching the house and the car drew up outside the door.

"Where to next, Sir Jack?"

"Home."

* * *

At the flat, Thornhill told the driver to get breakfast at the 24 hour café in The Cut, behind Waterloo Station and to pick him up at eight forty-five sharp.

Jane was away with Mary Finch-Hatton and he was surprised how much he missed the ritual of the warm croissants.

During the flight from Washington his anger had distilled into cold calculation. Now, in the bedroom, he laid out his clothes with the care of a mediaeval knight preparing for mortal combat. A suit, handmade by five – or was it ten? – years ago still fitted perfectly and the precision cut of the dark-blue wool was a renewed satisfaction. Alongside it he laid a Jermyn Street shirt and a silk tie from Florence. Though he appreciated the eccentricity of this often repeated ritual, somehow it was comforting. He laid out socks and underwear and then carried a pair of Lobb brogues into the kitchen for an extra shine. He took a long meditative shower and his thoughts were interrupted only when the water began to run cold.

When he had dressed, he sat at his empty desk and stared at the river. Big Ben struck eight and the clock on the mantelpiece was a chime late. He knew he'd been way too long and felt a flash of bitterness at his having achieved so little. He adjusted the clock, returned to the desk, picked up the phone and pressed the 10 Downing Street direct dial key.

"Private Office." He recognised the voice of Rebecca Brook, daughter of a friend in the Diplomatic Service.

"Rebecca, this is Jack Thornhill. Can you put me through to Sir Thomas?"

"Good morning, Sir Jack. I'll see if he's arrived yet."

Tommy Thompson, one of the Private Office Secretaries, came on the line immediately. "Jack, before you say anything, I've been warned that you were likely to call. The PM is absolutely off limits on this. You must drop it."

Without replying, Thornhill put the phone down and sat looking at the lightning sky. Emerging from the fog of circumstances he recognised a personal dilemma of a kind he had never before had to face. He dialled the combination of the safe buried in the concrete floor behind the desk. From beneath a pile of papers he took an unusual weapon, a small Russian pistol made of high-grade ceramics; a souvenir of less complicated times. Because it was not made of metal, conventional security devices could not detect it. It would not survive a sustained firefight but could accurately deliver a full eight-round magazine at close range. More than enough, Thornhill thought. He laid the weapon at the centre of the desk and closed his eyes.

He could hear himself, in his junior days, giving a familiar lecture to trainees: 'In our trade, the most common cause for the use of firearms is a failure of judgement.'

Though his sense of defeat was partly anaesthetised by anger, he knew the failure was not simply one of gamesmanship.

He was being manoeuvred into a course of action he believed to be immoral and the inescapability of it weighed heavily on him. Through his entire career he had remained aloof to dilemmas of this kind. Calvin November had changed all that. Wrestling with his thoughts, he took a single piece of paper from a drawer. On it he wrote a list of names. He began with Bullivant and Morgenstern, and then the catalogue of others whose deaths November had caused. After the briefest of pauses, he added: Murphy?

"The second thing to remember is that automatics jam at the slightest provocation," he heard his own voice say. Especially those made of china, he thought. "A failure of judgement might be survivable; attempting to retrieve it with a failed weapon would almost certainly be fatal. You must be sure: two to the heart and one to the head."

With great care he dismantled the weapon, then cleaned, lubricated and reassembled it. At eight forty-three the intercom sounded. He slid the safety catch on, locked the weapon in his briefcase and put the list back in the desk drawer. In the hallway he took a heavyweight Loden overcoat from the closet. As he closed the door of the apartment, Big Ben struck the quarter-hour and he heard the mantelpiece clock chime in synchrony.

* * *

The ponds at South End Green, at the bottom of Hampstead Heath, were unexpectedly frozen.

The sharp overnight frost had coated the trees and the rising landscape beyond with ice crystals. It was one of those rare events in London; a beautiful winter's day. Thornhill stopped the car.

"I'll walk from here. I'll meet you up at the house."

The wheels of the Jaguar slid, then the tyres bit through the slush and the car pulled away up the hill. Thornhill needed thinking time and knew that the exertion of a long, steady climb would help. It was a decisive mile.

Trudging across the virgin-white heath he resolved to kill Calvin November. Whichever way he confronted the issue, he could not escape the certainty that the viscous circle of November's power had to be broken. Because he had so far failed to achieve this through the system, he became resolved that it must be done by his own personal direct action. He tested each element of his conclusion: the names of the dead people on the paper in his desk drawer constituted the motive and the Russian automatic the means. The unresolved question was whether Geneva would provide the opportunity.

He reached the house and stood on the terrace for a moment, taking in the distant view of St Pails and the City.

"Earth hath not anything to show more fair." The ever-cheerful driver was keen to make conversation. The snow had muffled his footsteps and Thornhill had been unaware of his approach.

"Depends whether you believe Wordsworth or Keats," Thornhill replied as he climbed the stairs to the second floor. Outside the conference room door stood an unfamiliar heavily built figure.

"I'm Regimental Sergeant Major Hampton, Sir Jack; Sergeant Bullivant replacement."

"Welcome aboard, Hampton," Thornhill said as he shook hands. "How are you settling in?"

"Fine, sir; everybody's been very friendly."

Thornhill turned to leave.

"There is just one thing, sir. Please, no jokes about Cockney rhyming slang."

"What's that? I'm not sure I understand."

"My name, sir. Hampton. Hampton Wick, rhymes with pric–"

Thornhill interrupted. "Yes, I see. Not a word, Hampton, not a word. Tell me, is Mr Darcy in there?"

"Yes, sir, he was here at six thirty."

"Would you ask him to come out and see me?"

Darcy emerged from the conference room looking tense and sleep-deprived. Thornhill led the way to a pair of armchairs beside the picture window overlooking the heath.

"Tell me about Warsaw," Thornhill said.

"How long have I got?" The question was practical, not sarcastic.

"For now, five minutes. I need to know anything that may influence discussions in there," he said, indicating the conference room.

"Okay, here it is," Darcy said. "They've moved out and cleaned up. They covered their tracks by putting a group of druggies in there and giving them free dope."

"How can you be sure?"

"I'm sure."

"You know everything turns on this," Thornhill said gravely.

"They killed Jakob, Wolski's friend. It was him who set up the original meeting with you," Darcy faltered.

"Go on." Thornhill was conscious that Darcy was showing signs of serious stress.

"Then they kidnapped his daughter."

"Is she dead?" Thornhill asked.

"No."

"How do you know?"

"I got her out; you don't need to know how."

"I do need to know, I need to know everything about it, but not now," Thornhill replied.

"You said five minutes," It was clear that he didn't want to say more.

"Would I be wrong in suspecting that this has become a personal matter?" Thornhill asked.

"No, you wouldn't be wrong," Darcy replied.

* * *

Everyone stood up as Thornhill entered the room. For a moment he wondered whether Mantoni had leaked news of his emotional state in New York, but quickly realised his fear was groundless. Mantoni was not made that way.

"Sorry to keep you waiting. Everyone had breakfast?" he asked. There was a murmur of affirmation. The team had been assembled by phone during Thornhill's trans-Atlantic flight. There was no time to try out untested working relationships.

Morag and Darcy were part of Thornhill's inner circle. The others were specialists he knew personally: Angus McKenzie, a dour political analyst able to express complex ideas in very few words; Anwar Darzi, a criminal psychologist who had been with them during the attack in Bermuda; Winford Hicks, an expert in security countermeasures, a sly man in a trade where that was an advantage. The potential for a time-wasting clash of personalities was obvious. Thornhill decided to tackle the issue head-on.

"Gentlemen, let's establish the ground rules. First, no minutes or formal record of this meeting are being made. Whatever takes place in this room will have no place in history. Please remember that we have desperately little time. You're all here because your reputation precedes you, so there is no necessity for displays of ego or virtuoso performances. I'll try and apply the same rule to myself." The remark produced a couple of laughs. "Morag, is everyone briefed?"

"Yes, we've been over the ground as thoroughly as a couple of hours allows," Morag replied.

"Very well, I'll bring us up to speed on events in America and then we can get to work." Everyone made ready with laptops or notebooks. Thornhill went carefully through the chronology of events.

"I went to Washington for a high-level meeting; to warn and to trade information. There are two interpretations that can be put on the outcome. The first is that I was simply not believed. The second is that I was believed, and for whatever reason the news was too hot to handle. The follow-up meeting scheduled for the next day was both delayed and downgraded, which is why Lloyd-Emlyn is sitting in some Washington ante-room rather than being with us here this morning."

McKenzie raised his silver fountain pen and Thornhill paused to let him speak.

"A question, something I need to be quite sure about – you got the dead cat bounce?"

"Not my choice of phrase, but an accurate analogy," Thornhill replied.

McKenzie was still not wholly convinced. "You dropped this number on them and they did nothing. That's astonishing. How can they not respond to a warning of a threat on this scale? It's quite incredible."

"Credibility is exactly the point," Thornhill said. "Of course, they may have written the whole thing off as some kind of crackpot paranoia. But I'm minded to believe that, for some key players at that meeting, the news I presented them with was not news at all. The question is why? And of even greater importance, to whom do they report?"

"What leads you to that conclusion?" Darzi asked.

"Two things. The first is that I sought advice from an old and very well-connected friend. He was willing to advise on anything and anybody, but when November's name was introduced into the conversation he closed up like a New England clam."

"A slender basis for such large suspicions?" Darzi queried.

"I said there were two factors in my judgement," Thornhill said with a hint of rebuke at Darzi's premature interruption. "The second is much more serious. In Washington I was surprised to meet Arnold Morgenstern. He is, or I should say was, a US inter-service liaison officer based in London."

"Was?" McKenzie asked.

"I'm coming to that," Thornhill continued in a level monotone. Long experience had demonstrated that when briefing or debriefing, emotion could camouflage crucial detail.

It was essential that each listener should have an unobstructed view of the landscape.

"Previously, in London, Morgenstern had been sticking to me closely. It was much closer attention than usual and it became evident that he knew we were on to something important; he wanted to know what it was. He framed his concerns in terms of friendship. Of course, that was his job and I distrusted him because of it. He became very excited and at first was merely an irritation. Then there was a leak to the Cabinet Committee and just as I was receiving the wrath of Lady Lathkill, a code red message from Bermuda arrived. For those of you who were not with us during this incident, it was a rocket-propelled grenade attack on the hotel where we were holding our source. One of our colleagues was killed and we had to mount an emergency operation to extricate the source and the remaining members of the team to the UK. At that time I believed Morgenstern might have been complicit in both events, a judgement I have since come to regret."

Tension in the room rose. Everyone knew something critically important was coming and nobody wanted to be the person who delayed its arrival.

It was Thornhill who seemed in need of a pause. "Would somebody enquire whether the kitchen could be persuaded to let us have some tea, Darjeeling preferably?"

Morag and Darcy simultaneously reached for the phone. Morag got there first. The tea was ordered and Thornhill continued. "Just after the Washington meeting, Morgenstern turned up out of the blue. He was in an extraordinarily emotional state. On grounds of my personal safety, he pleaded with me to return to London immediately. At the same time, I got news of Murphy being found in a back alley in Manhattan. So I needed to leave with all dispatch. Not unnaturally he thought I was taking his advice to return home."

Thornhill couldn't remember exactly when he had decided not to mention Petersen; it had simply been a conviction that grew stronger as the briefing continued. "In Manhattan, my attention was taken up by the problem of Murphy, who had by now absconded from the Tribeca police precinct. Then, via CNN, I discovered that Morgenstern had been shot twice in the head. By muggers, the report said."

"Could it have been coincidence?" McKenzie asked.

"I wouldn't believe it was coincidence if he was struck by lightning with the entire Supreme Court as witnesses. The truth is that I totally misjudged him," Thornhill said fiercely. "A lifetime of trading in deceit ill-prepares you for the occasional encounter with honesty. I now believe that he was what he said he was, an ally. Events strongly indicate that he took serious risks in trying to warn us and it cost him his life."

"You can't be certain of that," Darzi said.

"No, in this business there's nothing that you can be certain of. Nevertheless, I am totally convinced."

"What about Murphy?" Morag asked.

"One thing at a time," Thornhill said.

"That's just the problem, isn't it?" Hicks spoke for the first time. "We can't deal with this one thing at a time, it's all of a piece."

"Let's get a grip," McKenzie said. "We need to assess the threat and define our options."

"That is why you are all here," Thornhill said.

McKenzie ignored the interruption. "We know that November plans to attend the summit in Geneva.
The Council for a New America has no official status but somehow he's managed to get a formal invitation. In the light of everything else, that shouldn't surprise us. Then he promised to make some epoch-making announcement at what he called a 'People's Summit' at Madison Square Garden twenty-four hours later. At his first appearance he offered a hundred billion dollars. He's going to need something spectacular to top that," McKenzie concluded.

"So on that timetable, he must be planning to pull some kind of stunt in Geneva." Hicks was someone who needed things to be spelt out.

"Does anyone dissent from that hypothesis?" Thornhill asked.

"The evidence allows no other conclusion," McKenzie said.

There was a general murmur of approval. Thornhill was relieved that time was not to be wasted by conflicting speculations.

"So we have agreement on motive, opportunity and timing. The question is, exactly what is he trying to achieve and how?"

"Do you believe he's mad?" Hicks pointed the question in Darzi's direction.

"That is not a scientific term. In my view there is no satisfactory definition of madness," Darzi said primly.

McKenzie interrupted. "The point is, what is he aiming to do and how do we stop him doing it?"

Darzi continued. "The first half of McKenzie's question is easier to address than the second. Consider the man – he needs a stage, a stage for his ideas, his ego and his ambitions.

We know that because, since childhood, he's constructed a succession of them. The most recent was Madison Square Garden. Now Geneva, it's the biggest so far – all the world's leaders in one place at the same time. Not just diplomats and bureaucrats like the UN, but presidents and prime ministers. He's over-reached himself; how can he possibly dominate a cast like that?"

"A comforting analysis," McKenzie said. "But what if the conclusion you draw from it is wrong? Look at it like a map. There are two roads leading to Geneva. One starts at Madison Square Garden with the emergence of November as a new kind of radical political figure with a spectacular offer: 'Power to the People' and a hundred billion dollars for them to spend. Too good to be true? You bet it is, because the other road begins in Warsaw with the development of a new kind of psychochemical weapon. Just the kind of toy a rich psycho might want to play with. But our man is very rich and very psycho, which leads to the question: what if he has no intention of playing on that stage as Professor Darzi postulates? What if wants to destroy the entire theatre?"

"Would anybody else like to develop that line of thought?" Thornhill asked.

"The timings support that analysis," Darcy said. "When the Summit is announced, activity suddenly quickens and serious mistakes are made."

Hicks interrupted. "So far we're just finding different ways of coming to the same conclusion. However many ifs and buts we want to insert, we all believe the same thing. November is going to try and use this stuff. Let's just concentrate on our options for stopping him."

"What do you perceive them to be?" Thornhill asked.

Hicks grabbed the opportunity to take the floor. "Go to the top. Speak to Downing Street and the White House."

"What do you imagine I was trying to achieve in Washington?" Thornhill asked coldly. "And Downing Street? As of this morning, nobody will speak to us."

"The central pressure is time," McKenzie said. "We have less than seventy-two hours to devise a strategy. That eliminates a leak to the press, or planting disinformation, the kinds of things that, in the past, have been effective in getting conspirators fighting among themselves. Even if we had the time, that line of attack would be impractical because we don't know who the conspirators are."

"You need to give us something else," Thornhill said.

Hicks made another suggestion. "Strike at his finances, his ability to deliver his promise of a hundred billion dollars."

Thornhill was anxious to move the discussion out of analysis and into action. "That's too diffuse a target; the money, if it really exists,

will be buried in hundreds of financial institutions, right around the globe.
A strike against that kind of capital base would be a strike against the global economy. It's just not feasible."

McKenzie spoke. "We're forgetting something – it's not just the money, it's the technology. We know that's been moved out of Warsaw. But where's it gone? My guess is the domes out in the desert. 'Hide in plain sight' is a well-proven strategy."

Darcy had not spoken for some time; now his frustration boiled over. "So what do you propose? We call the State Department and suggest they send the United States Air Force to bomb this techno-Disneyland. Or would you rather we ask them if we can send the RAF?" McKenzie spoke with slow deliberation.

"Then, Sir Jack, I must present you with the only workable strategy within the timescale. We strike at him personally."

"You mean kill him?" Darzi said.

"I would regard it as a counter-attack. He's already hit us, now we hit him," McKenzie said.

Darzi persisted. "But he would be dead at the end of this process?"

"Yes, I would very much hope so," McKenzie said.

"Thank you, Mr McKenzie, I just wanted to be certain of what we're talking about," Darzi said.

Everyone turned to Thornhill, and his thoughts turned to the automatic in his briefcase.

"I'm not going to ask anybody to do that," he said.

"Then what is our plan?" McKenzie asked.

It was Hicks who responded. "We've spent a lot of time considering the man and his methods. But in Geneva we're up against the deployment of a technical system capable of selectively delivering a chemical agent. Find the delivery system and disable it. That's our answer."

"But we have no idea how such a system might work," McKenzie protested.

"Then we need to find out, fast," Hicks said. "Sir Jack, I'd like to go to Geneva immediately. I'm aware that the Swiss and everyone else involved will have been doing inspections and threat assessments for months, but we know what to look for and they don't."

"That's the best idea yet," Thornhill said. "Darcy, I'd like you to go with him."

Without further discussion, the two of them moved towards the door. "With respect, Sir Jack, that looks like an act of desperation," Darzi said.

"Sometimes appearances are not deceptive," Thornhill replied.

"A strange moment for irony, Sir Jack," Darzi said. "So far every battle you have fought, you've lost." Form the doorway, Darcy heard Darzi's remark. It made him angry. "Remember our history, Professor; Britain has a tradition of losing every battle but the last one."

"Except in America. There we lost the last one as well," Darzi said.

Thornhill ignored the exchange and got up to leave. "I believe we have achieved all we can in this session; we need to move on." The others in the room began to engage in animated conversation. "Keep talking, keep thinking and keep in touch through my office." Thornhill said.

Morag followed him to the landing. "I must speak to you about Murphy," she said.

"Morag, I appreciate your personal concern for a colleague, but surely you must see that we can't afford to divert from the critical issues when we're under this kind of time pressure."

"It's much more than a personal concern," she replied.

"Morag, we've both read the psychiatrist's report," Thornhill said sharply.

"That's the point – it's not about psychiatry but cryptography. I believe he's trying to send us a message," Morag said.

"Remember what the police sergeant told you about the numbers? Whatever has happened inside Murphy's head means he can't communicate directly; he has to go through some kind of random access process. He knew the number he wanted to spell out but had to hide it among many others. The same goes for the words."

Thornhill guided Morag to the chairs by the picture window.

"Go on."

"Fire," Morag said.

"Tell me more," Thornhill said.

"That's what he's telling us."

"How?"

Morag read from her notes. "St George and the Dragon; dragons breathe fire. Rock and Roll. Who was the first Rock star?"

"I've no idea." Thornhill was in strange territory.

"Jerry Lee Lewis. And the song that made him famous? 'Great Balls of Fire'. Elijah, in the Bible, was taken up into heaven in a chariot of fire."

Thornhill thought aloud. "Lakehurst, New Jersey. That's where the Hindenburg – the airship the Nazis were so proud of – went down in flames." "It all fits," Morag said.

"The wilderness, the Children of Israel followed a pillar of fire," Thornhill added.

Morag concluded the list. "James Baldwin, he was a Sixties black activist. His best-known book was The Fire Next Time."

Thornhill sat silently for some time. "You're right."

"I hesitate to say this, but I also believe we're being sent a second message."

"A second message? From whom?"

"Calvin November."

"How so?"

"By returning Murphy to us in this state he's playing games. It's an act of contempt. He's showing what he can do to any of us."

"Oh God," Thornhill said quietly to himself.

"I think we should take Wolski to Geneva," Morag said.

27

The Hog's Back

"How long have I got?" Darcy asked as the Jaguar swung into the gravelled drive of the ivy-covered Jacobean House that sat on the Hog's Back, a ridge above Guildford on the Downs of Surrey.

"You can talk to her for as long as it takes me to persuade Wolski to come to Geneva. Not a moment longer."

"I understand," Darcy replied.

Mrs Rankin, the housekeeper, appeared in the doorway as they got out of the car. "Good morning, Sir Jack."

"Good morning. How is the Professor?"

"Quiet, sir, very quiet."

"Where is he now?"

"In the library, sir."

"And how is the lady? Is she comfortable?" Thornhill asked.

"Physically, yes," she replied.

"Where is she?" Darcy asked sharply.

"In the Wordsworth room."

"Thank you," Darcy said as he swiftly climbed the stairs.

"Fifteen minutes, no more," Thornhill shouted after him.

Anya sat erect by the fire and Darcy was reminded of the pain and magic of Warsaw. "You broke your promise," she said, without turning to see who had entered the room.

"How did you know it was me?" he asked.

"Liars have a special kind of footstep."

"I kept my promise to you," he said gently.

"But you broke your promise to us. Jakob is dead."

"I did what I could."

"Yes, you did," she said, slowly turning from the fire. They stared at each other for what seemed a long time and slowly Darcy thought he saw the ghost of a smile.

* * *

Wolski was hunched over a table of books set against a wall of lancet windows.

"What are you reading?" Thornhill asked.

"H. G. Wells, The War of the Worlds."

Thornhill was surprised. "I had thought it might be some weightier work." "Local colour. Did you know that Wells has the Martians landing here, on the Hog's Back?"

"I seem to remember something of the kind," Thornhill said.

"Thirty years later, the other Welles, Orson Welles, stole them and put them down in New Jersey and scared the nation to death, quite literally in a few cases; that's how he made his name."

"You know why I'm here," Thornhill said.

"I know how the Martians meet their end," Wolski replied enigmatically. "Superior technology defeated by microbes."

Thornhill changed tack. "How are they looking after you?"

"A beautiful house, good food, an intelligent library; the finest prison a criminal could ask for. But I am not a criminal."

"Others are; it's safer for you here."

"Time," Wolski said for no apparent reason.

"Time? What do you mean?"

"I brought you the precious gift of time. Have you used it wisely?"

"I'm on my way to Geneva."

"That means you haven't found a way to stop him."

"I need you there with me."

"Why?"

"We need your mind."

"What do you plan to do?"

"Plan A is to identify and neutralise the delivery system."

"And plan B?"

"That I can't tell you."

"A personal intervention?" Wolski asked.

"You've got to know me too well," Thornhill said.

Wolski began to pace the room. "I have pondered much on ultimate judgement while I've been here. Eventually, evil men must answer to God. In the meantime our task is to prevent them from spreading their plague. I have helped you with that. As to your personal matter, that I will leave to the Almighty."

"I need your answer. Will you come to Geneva?"

"I've already come too far. At first I was propelled by guilt and I believed I could achieve absolution by action. But it hasn't worked, my guilt is no less."

"How could you be absolved? You were complicit in creating this plague and it's your responsibility to help put the genie back in the bottle."

"You know that's impossible," Wolski said, avoiding eye contact. "You can't un-invent something like that. And my meagre store of self-delusion is now exhausted."

Thornhill realised that he could not win the moral argument and decided that anger was his last chance. "I had hoped not to have to tell you this in these circumstances."

Wolski looked up at him expectantly. "Tell me what?"

"It's Jakob, he's dead."

"How?" Wolski hid his head in his hands.

"They thought he had information. They used a hot iron."

Wolski's hands slowly slid down to reveal an ashen face. "When do we leave?" he said in a whisper.

"Now," Thornhill said.

28

Upper East Side, Manhattan

Fifty-five blocks to go; nearly three miles. Like a man buried by an earthquake, Murphy had slowly clawed his way back to a consciousness of the world outside his head. He knew he had to keep walking. Block by block his limbs were slowly becoming more controllable. Now his stride appeared no more remarkable than that of a survivor of an over-indulgent office party. Instinctively he realised that there was protection in an appearance of mild drunkenness. People gave him a wide berth. Yet even in the newly fashionable culture of zero tolerance, he was unlikely to attract the attention of the police. But such moments of clarity were brief. Ideas, names, fears, memories ricocheted around his head like broken crockery in a washing machine. Grimly he held onto the reality that Hunter College was now only fifty-one blocks away. How far was that at twenty blocks to the mile? His mind was incapable of making the calculation. He took refuge on a bench in the small, well-tended garden of a tall, dusty church. His strange appearance and the occasional incoherent phrase fortified his private madness against intrusion by others. A pattern seemed to be emerging. One part of his mind was struggling to gain control over the other.

He felt like a disinterested spectator at a riotous wrestling match; his was the only silent voice among a shouting crowd. "Hold on, hold on…" He sat motionless, blank eyes locked onto the passing sidewalk traffic.

"You okay, mister?" The kindly voice belonged to an elderly woman in a long red coat. She was clutching tall brown grocery bags. She took a packet from one of them and nervously approached.

"I'm just the audience," Murphy explained.

The woman took a cautious step forward and tossed the package onto the bench alongside him. Murphy made a convulsive grab at it. The sudden move frightened the woman and she quickly stepped back into the stream of pedestrians. The street scene turned Murphy's tangled mind to long-forgotten youthful explorations of the city. He heard his voice quietly singing. "Sadly I wander through scenes of my childhood… Hallelujah… Hindenburg… Fire and fishing line…" He opened the package – a pastrami sandwich. He held it at eye level – an object of awe. After an eternity that lasted no longer than a minute, he very slowly sank his teeth into it. The experience was psychedelic. The scent of the rye bread, the keen edge of the mustard and the texture of the meat crashed into his consciousness. How long it took to eat the sandwich – five minutes, half an hour – he had no way of knowing. How long had it been since he last ate? His memory refused to reply, but the renewed encounter with nourishment was energising, helping him climb through another layer of mental rubble.

'Onward Christian soldiers … onward … uptown-wards.' He got to his feet and found a distantly remembered steadiness to his stride. 'Marching as to war… We shall overcome…' Thirty blocks to go. "'This was their finest hour…' Just a mile and a half. With every block he passed, the images in his mental hall of mirrors were less distorted and he started to gain a grip on coherence.

The Four Leafed Shamrock stood two blocks from Hunter College; he faintly remembered Tad mentioning it as a student hangout. By now Murphy's head was clearer than it had been for what seemed like a decade. He sat on a fire hydrant and waited in the warm draft that drifted up from a subway grating. He spotted Tad at the edge of a rowdy crowd of friends.

"Hey, kid." His voice seemed not to penetrate their self-absorption. "Over here, kid."

The unexpected familiarity of the voice began to register. Tad's head turned; he stepped away from the group and began to cross the road.

"Dad?"

"Hi, Son. Tell them I'm a panhandler with a hard luck story."

"Dad, what are you doing here? You look terrible."

"Not half as bad as I feel. I need your help, kid. Get rid of those guys and meet me at the Campus Subway Station."

"You look like you need help right now," Tad said.

"No, don't raise any curiosity. I've got to keep on the move. An hour from now, okay? A hard luck story, just tell them that."

Tad reluctantly re-crossed the road. A train rattled beneath Murphy's feet and threw up a cloud of metallic dust as he shambled off into the shadows.

* * *

"Where's your roommate?" Murphy asked, sitting on the empty bed in Tad's tiny student apartment.

"In Ohio; his mother is seriously ill."

"Son, there are a lot of things to say and to do but it's important to get them in the right order."

Tad seemed not to be listening. "Three years I've been here and this is the first time you've paid a visit." Murphy nodded in acknowledgement. "Have you left home? Is that why you're here?"

"No, I've not left home, but I can't go back, not yet."

"I won't do anything to hurt Mom."

"Nor would I, Son, but sometimes knowledge is dangerous. That's why this needs to remain between us. I just need a place to rest up 'til morning."

"I don't understand any of this." Tad was scared.

Murphy breathed deeply in an attempt to expel the weariness that seemed to be soaking into his bones. He tried to get up from the soft bed and could only make it by reaching out to the doorframe and pulling himself up.

"I guess both of us never knew our fathers. Mine died doing what he loved."

Tad became alarmed. "Is that what you're planning?"

"What?"

"Walking back into my life to tell me you're dying?"

"You're only half right, kid. This is about living or dying, but I don't know which."

"I don't know what to say."

"Then just listen. I said I wanted to get things in the right order." It took a moment to find the words. When they came, they were very simple. "I love you," Murphy said.

Tad's astonishment was total. He shook his head in disbelief. "You've never said that, never."

"Not in words, but in every other way."

"Words matter."

"You remind me of your mother."

"I'm glad."

Murphy sank back onto the bed. "Are you sick?" Tad asked.

"I have been; I'm mostly better now."

"What's wrong with you?"

"With me? Nothing. It's just my head."

Tad didn't respond. Murphy tried to explain, but made things worse. "It's okay, kid, I'm not crazy. They got inside my head, that's all."

"Who?"

"That I can't tell you."

"You need to see a doctor." Tad reached for the phone. "There's a twenty-four-hour number; students have bad trips all the time."

"Bad trip? I guess I've been on a bad trip. But no doctor, no records. I just need a beer."

"I don't drink."

"Then what do you have?"

"Just herbal tea or water."

"Water," Murphy said without hesitation.

Tad filled a glass at the corner sink. "Is this about work?"

"Yes."

"Are you on the run?"

"Yes."

"Who from?"

"I don't know."

"You are sick, aren't you?"

Murphy took a key ring from his pocket. "Here's what I need to get me better, kid."

"What do you mean?"

Murphy held up the keys one by one. "This is a key to the house. This one opens the cellar. And this opens the safe in the old coal store. Nobody looks for safes among dirt," he added with a hint of self-congratulation.

"What do you want me to do?"

"It's Wednesday, your mother will be out at her literature club, then she goes out with the girls, usually to that Greek restaurant on 7th Avenue."

"Why are you telling me all this?"

"Because she won't be back until around eleven thirty."

"What are you asking me to do?"

"There are things I need. They're all in the cellar. There are some fishing clothes in the locker at the bottom of the stairs and I need my golf clubs."

"Golf clubs!" Tad was incredulous.

"Hear me out. Golf clubs; they're in an old Slazenger bag beside the wine rack. I need my fishing gear from the shelf above the workbench. It should fit into the golf bag."

"Dad, this is crazy."

"I'm not going on vacation." The heaviness of his tone silenced Tad's opposition. "In the safe you'll find all manner of things. I just need the zip-up wash bag and the Rox metal camera case. You can put the whole lot into the old leather suitcase in the corner cupboard." Tad took the keys and moved to the door. "Don't use a cab – drivers have memories. Take the subway."

Less than an hour and a half later, Tad was back. Murphy was in a deep sleep, draped clumsily across the narrow bed. Tad shook him awake. He took a can of Miller from the pocket of his jacket "Just the one; I didn't have enough money for a six-pack."

Murphy was angry at his own thoughtlessness. "Thanks. Open the case." Tad slid the catches back and Murphy took out the metal camera case. Turning his back to Tad, he opened it carefully. Inside was a hand grenade, an insane souvenir of an insane time in Beirut. He closed the case and zipped open the wash bag to reveal a passport, a driver's licence, credit cards and ten thousand dollars in cash. He split the wad of notes and handed half of them to Tad.

"I can't take that."

"Yes you can, you might need it."

"No."

Murphy ignored the protest and slid the cash under the computer on the table beneath a grimy window. "Regard it as a consultancy fee."

"A what?"

"I need you to do some work for me," Murphy said.

"What kind of work?

"Do you have any matches?"

"What for?"

"Just get them."

Tad went into the kitchen and returned with a matchbox. "Just three left," he said.

"One should do it," Murphy said. He opened the sunglasses case on his belt and removed the plastic sample he had taken from Helios. "They didn't find it; they looked everywhere else, but they didn't find it," he said.

"What is it?" Tad asked anxiously.

"It's best you don't know."

Murphy went into the kitchen, struck a match and held it to the sample. There was a sudden burst of flame. He dropped the plastic into the sink and watched it burn.

"I need you to do something else for me," Murphy said.

"What?" Tad asked cautiously.

"On the computer; work I can't do for myself."

"You want something from the Net?"

"No, I need your brain, I need you to do some calculations."

29

Geneva, Switzerland

In Switzerland, global conflict is good for business. A week before the Summit, every hotel room around the lake and within an hour's drive of Geneva was booked solid. Satellite uplink time was sold out. Only broadcasters with heavyweight clout could get a transmitter truck into the grounds of the Palais de Nations and those without such a facility were hiring dispatch riders to ferry tapes to transmission points as far away as Zurich and Basel. Organisation for the event reached into every part of life. Overtime rates were negotiated with sewage workers. Hotel staff were recruited everywhere from Bulgaria to Portugal. All road works were cancelled to ease traffic flow. Extra capacity was added to the phone system. Yet the biggest change – the transformation of the city into an electronic fortress – was almost invisible. The security plan had the structure of a mediaeval castle, with concentric rings of defence radiating out from the event itself. Airports, stations and border crossings were monitored with Swiss efficiency. Cameras, linked to image recognition software, observed the streets day and night. The city was on its best behaviour. Civic pride demanded that Geneva must be seen as the polar opposite of

New York. There must be no protests, no untidiness; everything had to work smoothly.

Crime fell to near zero. Even when camera equipment was stolen from the rooms of a dozen or more photographers during a welcome reception in the media hotel, there was a wholesaler's van on-site within the hour. While police meticulously recorded details, the victims were offered replacements. Canon, Nikon, Pentax; all were on offer against a signature on an agreement to pay when insurance claims were settled. As veterans of countless wars, frozen all-night vigils outside the boltholes of pop stars and threats of violence from their heavyweight minders, the photographers couldn't believe their luck as they checked out their new gear. Commercial opportunism went hand in hand with civic thoroughness. The international set of nomadic crack addicts, and the few rough sleepers native to the city, were arrested and discreetly moved out of town, or across the border to France or Italy. A specially chartered 747 freighter carried ATMs imported by the larger hotels to keep transaction commissions in-house. Huge additional quantities of everything from pomegranate juice to contraceptives arrived by truck. At the airport, the cargo terminal was converted into an ultra-high-security area to house and service the twenty-two vehicles in the motorcade needed to deliver presidents and prime ministers to the event with appropriate pomp. Everything was ready for the biggest event in the city's history.

* * *

It had been a mistake to expose Wolski to the endless succession of meetings with Swiss technical specialists. There were presentations on food and beverage security, air supply monitoring systems, explosives and chemical detectors, and skin wipes to reveal contact with threatening substances.

The coverage of every point of entry into the concentric rings of defence seemed flawless. None of the visiting experts had anything worthwhile to add, but they were made to learn a catalogue of acronyms and passwords so beloved of bureaucrats. Karl-Heinz Schneider was reluctantly coming to the end of his five minutes of fame.

"Finally, code words for states of alert, to be known only by those with access to the physical presence of the delegates."

"How many people is that?" Thornhill asked.

Schneider replied without reference to his notes. "Seven hundred and ninety-three." He hesitated for a moment and continued. "The code words are all the names of Swiss mountains, so they will be easy to remember. Jungfrau – think of virgin snow – is normal state. Dom is a perceived danger in the general area. Some of you will know that the word also means cathedral, so think of the fragility of the human condition. Eiger is an immediate threat to the safety of the delegates. As some of you may also know, the Eiger has killed more climbers than Everest."

"Who said the Swiss don't have a sense of humour?" Darcy muttered under his breath. The session ended exactly on time and there was almost half an hour in hand before the team meeting that Thornhill had called.

"Let's walk," Thornhill said as he guided Wolski towards the tall doors opening onto the gardens that led down to the lake.

Thornhill hoped that the catharsis of the damp ice-laden air at the margin of the water would somehow sharpen his mind and, more importantly, that of Wolski.

Across the lake, the city skyline of modest spires and discreet financial hideaways floated on a bed of pearly mist.

"If Michelangelo had been a banker, that is how he would have painted heaven," Wolski said.

"If you see a Swiss banker jump out of the window, follow him; there's money to be made on the way down," Thornhill replied. It was a mistake; the weak humour didn't connect with the intensity of Wolski's mood.

"You're thinking of Zurich. Things are different here."

"How so?"

"Geneva has a strangely magnetic quality about it," Wolski said.

"Magnetic? I've always thought of it as a pallid version of Paris," Thornhill said dismissively.

"And there you have the strangeness of the attraction. Geneva has drawn to itself the most unlikely collection of opposing notions. Calvin and the Protestant Reformation, Byron – 'Mad, bad and dangerous to know' – Frankenstein, the Red Cross, Carl Jung. So many competing theologies, and now we add to their number by seeking out our own special madness."

Thornhill listened carefully; he wanted Wolski to keep talking, to keep thinking outside the box. The old man turned slowly from the lake and stood staring at the grand building behind them. Thornhill said nothing.

"It's not only second marriages that are a triumph of hope over experience." Thornhill didn't understand and waited for an explanation. With a sweeping gesture, Wolski took in the whole elaborate facade. "Look at it, the architecture of failure." Thornhill did not to interrupt.

"At the very first world peace conference, much more than a century ago, the Russian delegate proposed the total abolition of all the world's armies and navies. Not a popular idea. Then, after the First World War – 'The War To End All Wars' – the League of Nations was born in there and, collapsing under the weight of its own indecisions, it died in there." Wolski sounded mildly drunk, but Thornhill realised that he was intoxicated by bitterness, not alcohol.

They walked close to the edge of the lake where the ice was frozen into a sea of aspirant icebergs.

The cold began to gnaw through Wolski's thin shoes and his feet felt numb. He stopped suddenly. "Ice," Wolski said thoughtfully. Thornhill knew him well enough to understand that this was more than a statement of the obvious and waited for him to continue, but he said nothing more and started walking again.

* * *

"Hicks, you were in Geneva ahead of us; what's your impression?"

The team were sitting at a conference table and Thornhill was starting his circle of questions.

"Can't fault it. Like I said in London, they've got it as watertight as a duck's arse," Hicks said reluctantly.

"Darcy?"

"I agree; they're doing all we would do, and more."

"Morag?"

"I've nothing to add." It was the first time in Thornhill's memory that she had not offered an assessment of her own and he wondered why.

The questions continued without getting any useful answers.

"Professor?"

Wolski, who had been listening intently, said, "I'm sure that all that's being done is necessary, but I'm equally convinced it's useless. November knows all these measures as well as we do; it's exactly what he would expect."

Nobody had anything to add and Thornhill spoke again. "Well observed, Professor. That leads us to try and identify what we know that he's not aware of."

Morag picked up the idea and Thornhill noticed that she seemed glad to be back in the conversation. "We must suppose that everything up to the Professor's arrival in New York is known to them, otherwise they wouldn't have taken such aggressive action in Bermuda. The main new factor since then is Darcy's visit to Warsaw."

Darcy took up the idea. "There was nothing there; it was only what the crazy old woman and the druggie said that stopped me from writing the whole thing off as a fantasy."

"Let's go over the ground again," Thornhill said. "What exactly did they say?"

"It's in my report."

"I'd rather have it from you than off paper."

"Okay," Darcy said, getting up and pacing to the window. The mist over the lake was thicker. "The place had been taken over by squatters; it looked like a hippie commune. In retrospect, that could be seen as camouflage. They asked me, 'was I a swineherd? Was I the Iceman? Was I going to shoot the pigs?' It was all crazy, in the most literal sense. I remember thinking that if I could find a cab, I could just about catch the afternoon plane home.

Then this filthy old mad woman grabbed my leg and wouldn't let go. She ranted on about them being 'all gone, the fascists, the Americans and the pigs'. She just wouldn't let go."

"Why was I told none of this before?" Wolski angrily sprang to his feet.

"It was secret," Darcy said.

"Secret!" Wolski shouted explosively. "Secret from whom?" His face was red and he was trembling with anger that he made no attempt to control. "They know about it because they set it up. You all know about it and you've kept it secret from the only person who may be able to tell you what it means. What kind of incompetents are you?"

Darcy snapped back. "Everybody thought you'd checked out after Bermuda."

"That's enough," Thornhill said quietly, and Darcy turned back to the view of the lake. Thornhill spoke to Wolski. "Be fair; remember our conversation in Surrey, you were less than enthusiastic."

Wolski nodded in acknowledgement and sank back into his chair. "Ice," he said. "This confirmed the suspicion I began to have when we were walking by the lake." Wolski hesitated.

"Take your time," Thornhill said.

Wolski swallowed hard. "As the disaster with the basketball team showed, the dose at which this substance is administered is critical. Ice could be a medium of storing exactly measured quantities. That is what I had begun to believe by the lake; what you've just told me reinforces my suspicion." He looked around the room, nodding in confirmation. "There is a strong indication that ice, as well as being a storage medium, could also be the delivery system, some sort of projectile. 'Iceman, swineherds, shooting the pigs', they could be experiments to test such a technology."

"Ice pellets?" Hicks asked.

"Perhaps."

"That would need some kind of explosive charge as a propellant," Morag said.

"Not possible," Hicks said. "I'm not a ballistics expert, but I'm sure that an explosive charge of the kind you get with a bullet would shatter ice."

The conversation came to a halt. Everybody wanted the idea to be practicable. It was the only possibility around which they could mobilise. Yet nobody could think how it could be made to work amid the most secure environment in the history of international events.

Eventually, Hicks continued. "In any case, an explosive charge would be picked up by the sensors."

It was Thornhill's turn to pace the room. The city across the lake had now faded into the mist rising from the water. The problem he was trying to understand seemed no less ethereal, yet he knew that twenty-four hours from now the last act would begin.

The team sat isolated from each other by their own individual sense of despair. They were among the best in the business, but could see nothing but defeat. Then Thornhill had an idea.

"Darcy, please ask Sergeant Hampton to join us." Hampton scanned the group. He knew the faces and the reputations but had no way of matching one with the other. He seemed nervous and welcomed Thornhill's gesture to sit down.

"Hampton, I believe you were in the Marines before you joined us?"

"The Royal Marines, yes, sir; twenty-two years."

Thornhill noticed the correction. Marines are American, Royal Marines are not. It told him a lot about the man. He was willing to offend his boss in defence of his own identity – a plus mark in Thornhill's book.

"You were squadron armourer, I believe."

"Yes, sir, for my last three years with 42 Commando."

"I'm going to ask Mr Hicks to explain a scenario to you and ask you for your suggestions."

Hicks quickly outlined the parameters of what they suspected. Hampton answered without hesitation. "Compressed air, sir, that's the most likely answer. Water doesn't compress, that's why landing in the sea from a great height is like hitting concrete. And it's why the sea smashes ships on the rocks. Ice, being frozen water, is the same. Air, on the other hand, does compress and if there is a controlled release it's much more like a spring than an explosion."

"Remarkable," Wolski said. "Why wasn't he asked to join us from the beginning?"

Thornhill didn't begin to explain the issues of rank, status and security, which were so often the enemy of effectiveness. "I believe we are beginning to understand," he said.

Morag spoke. "The most vulnerable moment will be the signing of the Grand Declaration at the very start. That's when all the heads of state or of government appear together to sign the formal document of intent. The Grand Declaration is a bland form of words, but it will be the media event of the decade.

Think about it; what more visible demonstration of the collapse of existing world authority systems could there be than to have its leaders quite literally tearing each other to pieces at the moment they are supposed to be signing up to peace and international brotherhood?"

The thought of such a bizarre possibility silenced everyone.

"There is something else you should know," Thornhill said as he stopped pacing and sat down. "I have information that there are major changes taking place within the Celestacom organisation. These suggest that November anticipates a future very different from the present."

"If this goes wrong there will be a huge number of innocent victims," Morag said.

"We should be more concerned about innocent perpetrators," Wolski said.

Everyone turned towards him, waiting for an explanation.

30

Morristown, New Jersey

"What do I say to anybody who asks about this?" Tad said, while he and Murphy waited for the Avis car rental office in Brooklyn to open. They had taken the subway across the East River; Brooklyn was an elementary subterfuge, a less obvious place to start than Manhattan. He needed to buy time, and the more confusion he could leave in his wake the better.

"You won't know who it is that's asking the questions, so tell them the truth; as little of it as you can get away with."

"And Mom, what do I tell Mom?"

"I'll speak to Mom."

The office doors opened and they went inside.

"I need to see photo ID," the clerk said mechanically.

Murphy handed over the driver's licence and credit card from the cellar.

"Do you accept or decline the additional insurances?" the clerk enquired, while looking at the computer screen. Irritated by the lack of a response, she asked again. "Collision damage waiver and life cover. Eighteen dollars a day, package deal price. Do you accept or decline?"

"You should accept, Dad."

Murphy still seemed muddled. "Life cover for eighteen dollars, how could I refuse? Accept."

The clerk pushed the form across the counter. "Sign here, and initial here and here."

They drove together to the subway, one stop from the connection for Kennedy Airport.

Tad took the train to the United Airlines terminal and then caught the shuttle back into Manhattan. Another cut-out in the trail. Murphy drove the rented Ford to the Shore Parkway beside Jamaica Bay and turned north. The final dregs of madness in his head had begun to drain away and islands of sanity started to merge into a recognisable landscape. The road changed to Leif Erickson Drive. Murphy's memory grappled with the name. Was he the first European to cross the Atlantic, five hundred years before Columbus? Or was Erickson not the first, but merely a successor to unnamed Irish monks who made the voyage in leather boats?

To part of him it seemed strange that he should be engaged by such trivia, yet in another corridor of his mind it seemed urgent to consider all questions, even irrelevant ones, in careful detail. The black skeletal shapes of Coney Island appeared against the lightening Atlantic sky. Images of sweaty youthful summers amid vast crowds of tenement escapees rubbing sand-covered shoulders on the world's most famous beach played through his mind. The car tyres thumped a regular pattern over the steel plates of the Verrazano Narrows Bridge. Fifteen miles away, across New York harbour, the lights of Manhattan looked like a distant fairground. He felt a stab of illogical resentment at such unknowing, uncaring normality.

The moment passed and he was soon in New Jersey, where the commuter traffic was beginning the daily process of clogging the highway into the city. He pulled onto the New Jersey Turnpike; then close to the lights of Newark Airport he turned off the highway to make a chain of purchases from small shops in small towns. He considered the mall at Paramus. It would have been quicker, but malls have security cameras. He bought duct tape at a garage, weed killer at a garden depot and a ski-suit and goggles in an outdoor store.

The successive stops added more than an hour and a half to the journey to Morristown Airport but it was worth it. An ITT company jet passed over the runway threshold as he drove through the main gate. Morristown had once been a rural airfield, but now it was busy with corporate aviation.

The flying club, housed in one of the original buildings, was small and unobtrusive and Murphy found this strangely comforting.

Arriving unannounced was a gamble. The security advantages were obvious but there was the risk that the aircraft would be rented out. He parked out of sight of the club office and walked across to the hangar. The old Cessna 180 stood in the open. He remembered the spare key taped inside a tail inspection panel – a precaution against the kind of embarrassing incident following a midnight swimming party in Key West a couple of summers ago. A key had been lost and a spare had to be couriered down from New York. A very expensive memory.

For a wild moment, he thought of simply taking the aircraft, getting as far as he could on the gas in the tank and putting down for a refill before the news got out.

Along with the idea came a parallel consciousness of the foolishness of such thinking. Once it might have worked; nowadays, a stolen aircraft would attract fighter jets.

* * *

Tad was in class when Mantoni arrived at Hunter. He had waited beside a vending machine that hid him from the doorway of the lecture room. When the students streamed into the corridor he stepped out in front of Tad. The class surged past in search of their next lecture.

"I'm a friend of your dad's."

"How do I know that?"

"You don't."

Tad began to follow his fellow students; he felt less vulnerable on the move.

"What you do know is that he's sick and he needs help," Mantoni said.

"He works in a sick business."

They were overtaken by another wave of students and loud conversations about relationships and rivalries. Mantoni was momentarily jostled aside. "It's a sick business that keeps all of you guys healthy," he said, with a gesture towards the crowded corridor. Tad kept moving and became alarmed at the realisation they were running out of corridor.

Mantoni tried again. "What did he tell you to say?"

"He said to tell you the truth."

They had reached the end of the corridor. Tad knew he couldn't walk back in the opposite direction, nor could he face the open campus beyond the double doors.

"Is that what you're going to do? Are you going to tell me the truth?"

"No," Tad said.

* * *

"Is Glen around?" Murphy asked the earnest-looking young man behind the clubhouse operations desk.

"No, he's skiing in Aspen. I'm Jason." He stretched out his hand and Murphy shook it. It was a relief – Glen always wanted to talk. They had known each other for years and last summer they had flown to the North Woods in Maine for a week's fishing. The last thing Murphy wanted was attention, even from a friend.

"Too bad; maybe we'll catch up when I get back."

"Sure; I'll tell him you came by."

"Is my aircraft available?"

Jason consulted the bookings log. "It's booked out to the Stephensons on Sunday."

"So it's free until then?"

"Yes, but don't be late back, the Stephensons have been good money earners for you. They fly down to their daughter in Savannah a couple of times a month. It's the only way the old man can get the old lady to fly. Are you sure you'll be back before the weekend?"

"Sure. I've just got to get some hours in to keep my licence."

"Where you headed?"

"What's with the weather?"

"Looks like we could be skiing here by tomorrow afternoon." Glen pushed the weather map across the desk. "There's this big storm system coming down from Canada."

"Guess I'll head south, get out of here ahead of it."

"Anywhere in mind?"

"Las Vegas maybe, work up a tan in the morning, Lady Luck in the afternoon and another kind of lady for the evenings."

"Skin cancer, bankruptcy and STDs. You sure you're coming back?

Sounds like a Kamikaze trip to me," Jason said with a leer.

"Is she gassed up?" Murphy asked as he filled out the flight plan. Jason resented Murphy for not responding to the joke. "Sure, just like always," he said.

Murphy parked the car on the far side of the Cessna and began to transfer the bags to the aircraft.

"Some vintage set of clubs; my granddaddy had a set like that." Jason had appeared unexpectedly and was much too close for comfort. "Can I give you a hand?"

Murphy spoke instinctively. "Sure. Will you put the car in the parking lot and put the key in my pigeonhole?"

"Sure thing," Jason said, and was gone.

Murphy slid the last of the bags into the passenger compartment, retrieved the hidden key and climbed into the pilot's seat behind the left-hand set of controls. The magic of the well-worn aircraft came flooding back. The tacky plastic upholstery, paint abraded through to the metal, the old-fashioned analogue instruments, the worn handgrips of the control column and that mystic smell of raw metal and aviation fuel that recalled memories of long flights accomplished long ago. He turned the key and the instrument panel came to life. The engine responded to the starter with a cough, then began to fire. Murphy rattled through the pre-flight checks and got taxi clearance from the tower. In his peripheral vision he saw Jason put down the phone in the clubhouse. He waved his arms and started to run towards the aircraft. Ignoring him, Murphy opened the throttle and the Cessna moved forward with increasing speed. Now the clock was ticking.

31

Golkov

The sleek hotel room was a prison to Wolski. Its digitally controlled double-security locked door, spotlights, polished surfaces and shiny leather offered all the comfort of a condemned cell. But he had nowhere else to go. Security demanded he remain locked away. He had no more insights to barter for conversation, no more suggestions to win him engagement with others. His sense of emptiness was acute; the need for human company was too great to resist, and he took a decision to rebel. In the high-speed lift, after a couple of false starts, he punched in the security code and seconds later was descending to the lobby. The hotel conference centre, with its set of interconnecting halls, was full of teams erecting exhibition stands. He wandered aimlessly among the feverish activity. Having been so long a focus of attention, he enjoyed the anonymity. To be among people whose priorities demanded nothing of him was liberating and he luxuriated in it.

Then, like lightning before thunder came the shock. The force of it hit him before his brain could fully grasp what he was looking at.

The largest of the cavernous exhibition spaces was devoted to the Domes: Dynamos and Helios.

He had heard them endlessly discussed but this was the first time he had actually seen what they looked like.

He stood frozen to the spot, taking it all in, powerful simplicity, pure technology, ambitions without horizons, it all seemed so completely achievable. He wandered among the technicians who were showing the combined stress of jet lag, last-minute technical failures and an unmissable deadline.

"Let's go for a laser and audio test," an impatient amplified voice said. The doors closed, the lights went down and Wolski was suddenly in a sea of holographic images and multi-track omni-polar sound. Ideas and images exploded around him. He was distantly conscious of yelled obscenities as he collided with hardware and tripped over cables. In a state of rising panic, he eventually found an exit. The crush bar yielded and like a drowning man coming up for air, he staggered into the hallway. Taking huge gulping breaths, he steadied himself against the wall.

"A glass of champagne, Professor?" It was Golkov. Wolski was transfixed, and Golkov took him by the arm. "I heard you were here and hoped to renew our acquaintance. The past is the past, come and celebrate." Wolski seemed devoid of any power to resist as Golkov steered him to the hospitality suite, where hotel staff were setting out trestles and loading them with bottles and glasses. Golkov guided him to a small round table covered by crisp linen. Wolski stared at the virgin-white weave and longed for innocence. A champagne bottle and two flutes appeared. He was faintly aware of a cork being drawn and the rising level inside the glasses. He heard Golkov say, as if reading his mind, "You did what you did, you made your contribution. Things that are invented cannot be uninvented.

You're a scientist, you know that is true." Golkov was enjoying himself and raised his glass in a parody of a toast.

The gesture touched a nerve and Wolski felt an infusion of anger, like a drowning man coming to the surface . With great deliberation, he raised his head and looked Golkov directly in the eye. He urgently wanted something memorable to say, some declaration of defiance, some expression of hope, but all he could manage was, "You will not succeed, you shall not succeed."

Golkov expelled air in something between a snort and a laugh. "Which is it, Professor, prediction or declaration?"

"Both," Wolski said without letting go of the lock he held on Golkov's eyes. When Golkov looked away, he realised he had won the tiniest of victories.

Something in Wolski's unflinching manner seemed to annoy Golkov. "You are wondering why I'm not alarmed." It was a statement, not a question.

Wolski remained defiant; holding on to the faint hope that Golkov could be provoked into an indiscretion, a weakness that could be exploited, but there were no obvious gaps in Golkov's armour of urbane superiority; he was taking joy in Wolski's helplessness. "When I was told you were here, I was delighted. I knew that your very presence demonstrated that you had failed. If you weren't so blinded by romantic notions of the human condition, you'd know how obvious your failure is."

Wolski felt his defiance deserting him, like a spent wave that rolled back to the open sea. He looked around for a way of escape. The room was slowly filling up with impromptu gatherings of officials discussing plans for the following day. Uniformed security guards patrolled the corridor.

Once more Golkov seemed to read his mind. "Test my hypothesis, call security. Who would believe you? Don't be too hard on yourself, the failure is not entirely your own. The people who believed you have failed you." Golkov poured himself another glass of champagne. "Use your scientific judgement, my dear Professor.

If you go public, the best you can hope for is to be treated as an elderly psychotic with embarrassing delusions, and be quietly deported. Of course, it might turn out to be very much less comfortable than that."

Wolski felt another welcome wave of anger. It was unanticipated and he was gladdened by its arrival; it allowed him to see a weakness – Golkov's need to strut and crow.

He struck back. "Do not preen yourself too publicly. Were you to succeed in this vileness, your usefulness would be ended and your existence terminated."

"How little you realise what the future looks like," Golkov said dismissively.

"How little you have learned from the past," Wolski snapped back. "Revolutions devour their children. You are a Russian, of all people you should know that."

At last Wolski had got under Golkov's guard, but nothing had prepared him for the reply that Golkov spat across the table.

"You judge everything by your tedious bourgeois sense of right and wrong. We are the new barbarians; we shall return the world to an earlier, purer time. We shall rule the strong and be ruthless with the weak – those like you who cling to the exhausted remnants of a collapsing world."

"You're mad." Wolski tried to find relief in the obvious insanity of it all.

"And if I were, would that be important?" Golkov said. "It is power that matters. Not merely the power of life and death but power for its own sake." Golkov poured himself a further glass of champagne. Was it the fourth or the fifth? Wolski tried to remember.

"You know what I say is true because you yourself are living evidence of it."

It seemed important to Golkov that his victim should agree with him. But Wolski had nothing to say. "Don't you understand?" Golkov continued. "You're a hostage of your own weakness. You hate killing but would dearly love to kill me right now, wouldn't you?"

Wolski remained stubbornly silent.

"You had the opportunity to kill me, but you didn't have a plan, and because of that you don't have the means. But most important of all, you don't have the resolve. Oh, and let's not forget, should you decide to act on impulse, you don't have the physical strength." Perhaps it was the champagne, but Golkov seemed to be behaving like an advocate before a jury.

"So, I rest my case; in every sense you are a prisoner of your own inadequacy."

At last Wolski understood why he was being subjected to Golkov's analysis. There was no other audience. A hermetically sealed existence in Warsaw had created a world where spoken thoughts were not permitted. Golkov was simply taking advantage of a newfound freedom.

"So Calvin November is to be King of this new world order?" Wolski asked.

He was astonished that Golkov seemed to agree with what he had intended to be a sarcastic remark. "We are led by a higher mind. He will be King in all but name and I shall be High Priest; the Director of Helios, source of our knowledge and our new power."

"If your Mr November is to be King, you realise he'll have to depose Elvis?" It was the first thing Wolski had been proud of saying for a long time.

Golkov slammed his fist onto the table and champagne slopped over the top of the glasses. "I controlled you in Warsaw and I control you still.
You made it so easy, you and your fellow carpet-slipper warriors: resistance until it becomes uncomfortable, then it's pass the vodka and black-market caviar. It was very convenient of you to keep all your vulnerabilities in such an accessible place." He paused and then rushed on in case Wolski might find some comfort in the possibility of his friend's survival. "Don't think you saved them, you merely made them irrelevant. And you, look what happened to you – once a scientific genius and now a moral bankrupt."

How strange it was, Wolski thought, that Golkov continued to need this kind of justification. All the words Wolski had been trying to find came out in a rush. "Morality!" he shouted. A few heads turned at the edges of the small groups absorbed in business and cocktails. They turned back, probably assuming a quarrel involving a woman.

"You dare speak of morality. You killed a team of young athletes, just because you were impatient."

"A result of the inadequacy of your work," Golkov said dismissively.

"Morgenstern was shot in the head."

"A tiresome little Jew. Not a racist's remark, you understand," Golkov added quickly, "merely a factual observation of ethnicity, personality and stature."

"You killed Jakob."

"A racketeer posing as a philosopher."

"You tortured him."

"The decision was his."

"He was my friend!"

"He made an unfortunate choice. The reality is that information can be expensive. The important thing is to make someone else pay."

Golkov looked at his ugly gold Rolex. "As enjoyable as it is to exchange reminiscences with an old friend, I have work to do. I will, however, leave you with one further thought. When this is all over you will be astonished at how simply it was done. Your self-contempt at not having seen it will be terminal. Goodbye, Professor."

It took all Wolski's strength to get back to his room. He sat on the large, soft bed and longed for the comfort of tears, but none came.

32

The Flight

At an airfield near the Utah–Nevada state line Murphy took a calculated risk; at least he wanted to think of it as such. In reality, he had no option. He had flown for sixteen hours, with refuelling stops at places like Covington Kentucky and Neosho Missouri, which he reckoned to be out of the way, yet with sufficient traffic for a casual arrival to be unremarkable.

The journey had, quite literally, been a nightmare. His rising fatigue allowed the residue of the drugs back into his mind. It was like flying through a vortex of distorted memories and fearful futures. Now he could go no further. He had to sleep. After signing the papers for the fuel he kicked off his shoes and sank into the seductive softness of the lumpy broken-springed sofa in the locker room behind the flight office. Nobody seemed to notice. Just an hour, he promised himself.

In normal times his mental alarm clock was accurate to the minute. Now things were different. It was the radio that roused him; he heard the words 'Cessna 180' and 'November Echo', his call sign, being read back by the operator in the flight office. It could only mean one thing. He grabbed his shoes and jacket and ran for the back entrance.

The aircraft was less than a hundred yards away. He opened the door and pressed the starter button in a single continuous movement. On the perimeter road he saw the red flashing light of a Utah State Police cruiser. The Cessna would not be hurried; it went through its normal routine of coughing indecisively before agreeing to fire on all cylinders. The flashing light was getting a lot closer. Murphy opened the throttle and roared down the perimeter track. On the radio there were urgent instructions to stop.

He swung the aircraft onto the runway and took off down wind, a dangerous procedure with a heavily laden aircraft, but he knew that the police would have time to block the runway if he taxied to the up-wind end for a conventional take-off. He cleared the hangar by no more than six feet. The shallow climb suited his purpose; he had to stay under the radar and that meant an altitude of sixty feet, or less. For the first ten minutes he flew a zigzag course in an attempt to confuse observers on the ground. His pulse returned to normal and he began to enjoy the thrill of flying under power lines and following the contours of the landscape.

He calculated that he had about an hour and a half of flying time to go. He could outrun a Highway Patrol helicopter but not any other type of aircraft. The night before, he had noticed on the flight office map that there was an Air National Guard base some two hundred miles away, so a fighter intercept was a serious threat. But it would have to be a visual search. He was now flying just fifty feet above the desert. He guessed it would take a half-hour or so for the State Police to contact the Air Guard and for aircraft to be scrambled. There was twenty minutes of flying time to reach the area, which meant they would have three-quarters of an hour to find him. Everything rested on what happened in those forty-five minutes.

The reduction of the problem to a single number was reassuring. He checked the compass heading and relaxed. It was then he realised that, for the first time in his life, he was flying in bare feet.

* * *

If a fleet of Martian spaceships landed at Noplace Nevada, Joe would have displayed neither surprise nor excitement. So Murphy's unannounced appearance raised no spoken questions. He ambled slowly over to the aircraft as it taxied up to the barn.

"Thought I'd drop by for old time's sake," Murphy said as he shut the engine down.

"Oh yeah," Joe said noncommittally.

"Golf," Murphy said, indicating the old Slazenger bag on the back seat. "Doing a tour of desert golf courses and had some engine trouble."

He reached inside the bag and pulled out a pair of two-tone golf shoes.

"Oh yeah." Joe used the phrase to express a variety of meanings. This time there was a distinct flavour of disbelief.

"Could I use the barn? Don't want to get sand in the works."

"Yeah," Joe said, and swung the doors open.

Together they pushed the aircraft inside. It was a tremendous relief; he was now out of sight. They each took one of the doors and swung it closed.

"Guess I'll get started." As Murphy spoke, there was a sudden roar as a pair of F15s flew over at rooftop height.

They both stepped outside to see the aircraft disappearing in a mirage of jet exhaust and heat haze.

"What do I tell them?" Joe asked. as the aircraft disappeared over the skyline.

"Who?"

"Any of your golfing buddies who happen by?"

"Tell 'em I stopped by, had a cheeseburger with fries and a chocolate malt. Then I flew on around sunset."

"I'll go fix the burger," Joe said, ambling towards the Diner.

"In a while," Murphy shouted. "I've got work to do first."

The barn had no air-conditioning. He dared not open the doors and the temperature rose rapidly as the sun got higher.

He carefully spread out Tad's pages of calculations on the bench and began work on the aircraft. He stuck measured lengths of duct tape on the windshield, as indicated on Tad's plan. Similarly, he measured out the fishing line, double-checking the length against Tad's calibration. He carefully opened the Rox metal case and removed the hand grenade. Then he tipped the clubs out of the golf bag and zipped the grenade into one of the outer pockets. With a rusty hammer from the workbench, he tapped out the hinge pins from the co-pilot's side of the aircraft and lifted the door off. He stood the golf bag in front of the co-pilot's seat and filled it with weed killer. Then he tied the end of the fishing line to the pull-ring on the grenade fuse. Carefully he wound the line back on the reel and lashed the mechanism to the seat frame.

It was a brutally simple idea. Flying at a known height and speed, when the target filled the gap between the tape marks on the screen, he would push the bag out. The carefully measured fishing line would pull the grenade pin and the bag would explode in an airburst immediately above the dome.

He calculated that the flammability of the dome's construction materials and the hydrogen in the recycling plant below should do the rest. Neither he nor Tad had been able to calculate whether the blast would tear the aircraft apart.

* * *

"Make that a double with cheese," Murphy said as he swung open the squeaking swing doors of the Diner. A fine layer of desert dust lay over the red cracked plastic seats that had started life in the 1950s. Perhaps it was because everything else in his life had changed so much that it seemed odd that anything from the past should remain unaltered. Joe tossed aside an ancient copy of Sports Illustrated left by some long-forgotten customer.

"You got it," he said as he began to rummage in the deep freeze.

The work in the barn had taken longer than Murphy had imagined and the sun was nearing the skyline of the desert hills.

"You got a payphone here?"

"Over by the restrooms."

Murphy pulled out a handful of change and fed the coins into the phone, dialled and waited. He had almost given up when Mary answered. "Hi, babe," Murphy said quietly.

"Oh God." She began to cry; it was thirty years since Murphy had heard her do that. "Where have you been?"

"I'm travelling," he said, avoiding the question.

"Mantoni has been here; he said you were sick, that you need help real bad."

"I guess I do, sweetheart, we all do."

"He said you'd call me; he wants you to tell me where you are."

"I can't do that."

"But they'll trace this call."

In the glass of the restroom door, the reflected sun was sinking below the horizon.

"I know," he said.

Mary became even more alarmed. "That means you don't care." Her voice rose in panic. "That means whatever you're doing has no future to it."

"It's going to be okay, babe."

There was quietness, and then she spoke with deliberate calm. “Don’t do it; whatever it is you’ve got planned, don’t do it. Come home, for God’s sake, if you love me come home.”

The glass panel of the phone door erupted into reflected light as the huge laser of Helios bore into the darkening sky. Murphy turned away from it. The last person had left Helios. It was time to go.

“Honey, I can’t tell you where I am, but I can tell you where we’re going. We’re on our way to Oregon. We’ll start again there, just like you always wanted.”

He heard a deep anguished scream and hung up the phone to shut the sound out of his head.

33

From the Rockies to the Himalayas

Network correspondents, journalists and anchors checked their hairstyles and, in a dozen languages, polished their phrases for the camera. Such a huge investment by the world's networks and newspapers meant that large amounts of coverage were essential to justify the expense. Every reporter wanted the line that history would remember, one with the staying power of 'Iron Curtain' or 'Cold War'. The current holder of the title, an anchor from NBC, who first coined 'From the Rockies to the Urals' to describe the scale of the conference, was now trying out 'From the Rockies to the Himalayas'. A woman reporter from the BBC was rehearsing. "The largest peace conference since Versailles 1919, which created new states from the Pacific to Czechoslovakia, from Africa to Iraq…"Fox News took an upbeat line. "This is an event of Olympic proportions and the difference between this and the other Olympics is that here everyone can be a winner; there are enough prizes for everybody…" ZDF from Germany were being cautious. "The lesson of Versailles must not be forgotten. Back then, the President of the United States stayed in Paris for three months to ensure America got what it wanted, but even so great an effort was not enough to get Congress to ratify the treaty…"

Everywhere there were officials, tireless as an army of worker ants. Technicians checked the lighting grid, the air-conditioning plant and the alarm systems. They calculated the humidification and temperature settings that would be required as thousands of bodies made their own individual contribution to the climate.

The sanitary staff were confident in the ability of the system to liquefy any quantity of waste, except the indestructible enemies of any sewage system: condoms and tomato pips.

Like sheepdogs, multilingual chaperones herded the children's choirs from rehearsal to commissary. Security teams ran their own checks for contamination of air, water and the voids under floors and above ceilings. Everyone was subjected to metal detectors and skin swabs for traces of explosives or toxic chemicals. Outside, as discreetly hidden as the shrubbery would allow, there were laser-guided missiles to enforce the air exclusion zone. The outer limits of the site were lined with a double rank of concrete blocks. Motorised access was limited to vehicles that had previously been checked and kept in guarded compounds when not in use. The instruments for the orchestra were shipped in overnight and security cleared before the players arrived.

* * *

How? Simple practicality had consolidated itself into the only question that mattered. It would not, could not, be allowed to go away. It was absolutely unyielding; the intellectual equivalent of concrete.

Thornhill felt an overwhelming need to speak to Jane. At the Tabac in the lobby he bought a phone card and a few minutes later was walking through the wealthy lakeside suburb that lined the busy road to Lausanne. He found a small, noisy bar with a card phone and called the secure line in the flat. Jane answered immediately.

"Sounds as if you're enjoying yourself," she said, hearing the conversation and laughter.

"I'm missing you." It was not the kind of thing that Thornhill had said in recent years. Over time, their closeness had become unspoken and the remark was out of character. Jane immediately sensed danger.

"Is it very bad?" she asked gently.

"Yes."

"Can I help?" There was a silence, and Jane sensed Thornhill was making a decision.

"There is one thing you could do." Jane said nothing, leaving Thornhill to make his own pace. "If you don't hear from me by one a.m. on Sunday there's an email on my laptop in the safe. Send it first and read it afterwards. It will tell you everything. Will you do it?"

"Yes," she said.

"I can't tell you anymore."

"I know."

To Thornhill, a loving absence of words meant more than poetry. "I'll be home for Sunday tea. "The ironic thought of a comfortable domestic ritual made them both laugh.

"I love you," Jane said.

Thornhill swung round, turning his back on the crowd to prevent others intruding on their moment of intimacy. The automatic in his pocket collided with the bar. 'Two to the heart and one to the head.'

* * *

Thornhill, conscious that the team needed thinking time, released everyone for an hour.

Wolski could not stay still; movement provided the illusion of coping with the stress. From past experience, he knew that he needed to let his mind wander. Occasionally inspiration had come that way. The increasingly urgent activity in the Great Hall of Nations took him back to Warsaw. A long time ago, ahead of the arrival of the Bolshoi Ballet from Moscow, he had been invited to the great Teatr Wielki. Ignace had a friend in stage management who let them in. It had one of the largest stages in Europe. How similar it all looked. This too was a performance of global scale with world players and an international audience, but a performance nevertheless.

Morag allowed herself a moment's amusement as she listened to photographers arguing in half a dozen languages about the placement of tripods and ladders. Everyone ignored the carefully drawn plans that were the Swiss officials' attempts to provide everybody with a clear line of sight.

Darcy watched intently for errors and omissions as the multi-layered security technology was put through a final succession of checks. Video recognition equipment was in place to scan the faces of all arrivals and check them in milliseconds against a vast database of images of known terrorist suspects, and others in whom the security services had an interest.

Next came chemical detection swabs across the palms of both hands and a retina scan to ensure that the person matched the pass they carried. Remote radioactive chemicals and explosives sensors operated in overlapping zones around the perimeter. Thornhill was one of a handful of senior officials who had an executive security pass.

It was this single flaw in the system that enabled him to get the automatic into the building. Everyone else had to go through metal detection, followed by an examination with the new generation of low-emission X-ray equipment that could see through clothing, shoes, briefcases and anything else capable of concealing a weapon.

For weeks there had been a bitter political row about the one-thousand-voice World Children's Choir. There had been endless arguments about the mix of languages and choice of songs. Decisions based on population favoured China, India and South East Asia.

Selections based on geography shifted the balance towards English, Spanish and French. Eventually, Mandarin, English, Hindi, Russian and Spanish had been agreed upon. Then there was a lottery for songs from smaller language groups. The winners were Serbian, Navaho and Welsh.

Thornhill knew that there had been an almost identical process of bickering about the order of precedence of the entry procession for the signing of the Grand Declaration, and places on the tiered seating to witness it. Arguments had been advanced on the basis of landmass, population and alphabet. After fierce wrangling, high-pressure lobbying, offers of aid and threats of withholding it, an order of precedence based on Gross National Product had been reluctantly agreed.

* * *

Thornhill called the team together for a final briefing. "Everyone knows that the period of maximum vulnerability is when the key players are in the open and the Swiss are well prepared for that. Our experience suggests that the threat is on the inside. Any questions?" Everyone wished they had some new possibility to discuss, but no one had anything to ask. "Then everyone to their places."

* * *

The procession began on wheels, with the longest line of limousines that anyone, even veteran journalists and diplomats, could ever remember. The whole thing had been timed with Swiss exactitude. The set-down points had been laid out to allow six limousines to disembark their passengers simultaneously.

Three lines of procession were marked out on the wide slowly rising steps leading to the huge glass-panelled doors at the entrance of the foyer. Inside, the Diplomatic Corps were allocated places on either side of the broad ceremonial staircase that wound its self-conscious way upwards to the Grand Hall. The diplomats had to be in place an hour and a half before the first delegates arrived. Thornhill chose a place on the outer curve at the mezzanine level. The position would give a clear line of sight as the great and good, presidents and prime ministers, captains of industry, Mafiosi, bankers, movers, shakers, stars of screen and science streamed upwards to the tiered seating reserved for those with the ultimate honour of being witnesses to the signing. At the apex of the curve, Thornhill calculated, there would be a moment when he faced November directly. He stood very still amid the diplomatic chatter that ebbed and flowed around him.

'Two to the heart, one to the head,' he kept telling himself. It had become a mantra in what had become a supreme crisis of conscience. Was he another Stauffenberg seeking to strike down a new Hitler or simply a failed warlord with nobody left to do his dirty work? With long-practised discipline, he forced himself to keep a mental grip on the sharp-edged resolution he had made, and it felt as if his mind bled.

Looking at Thornhill, Morag and Darcy knew that his cold isolation from those around him was no more than heavily disguised desperation. Wolski approached and stood quietly beside them. They turned simultaneously towards him, shocked at his appearance.

"You look terrible," Darcy said. "You need a drink, a large whisky."

"I've already been offered champagne," Wolski said. The trauma in his voice snapped Thornhill out of his introspection.

"Who by?"

"Golkov."

"Golkov, here?" Morag asked quietly.

"Yes."

"What did he say?"

"I've been told a terrible truth or a great lie."

"What did he say?" Morag persisted.

Wolski had difficulty speaking. "He said the simplicity of it all would drive us into 'terminal self-contempt'.

"Arrogant bastard," Darcy said.

Wolski was fighting tears as he looked towards Thornhill. "We have failed, don't you understand? We are no more than witnesses at the state funeral of civilisation."

34

Helios

'Laser, laser burning bright in the forest of the night…' A distorted Oxford memory of Blake's mystic poem The Tyger forced itself to the front of his mind. He was flying less than fifty feet above the ground, but the roaring air-stream from the open doorway isolated him from the shadowy moonlit hazards of the landscape below. Fatigue flushed incoherent horrors from the corners of his mind. '…what dreadful hand or eye formed thy fearful symmetry?'

With all the concentration he could muster, he hung onto the droning of the little Cessna's engine. 'It would be almost impossible to survive,' Tad had said. 'The size of an explosion big enough to ignite the canopy and set off the hydrogen would tear the aircraft apart – how fast will the aircraft be flying?'

Everything now depended on these last few minutes. Random thoughts collided like dodgems at a fairground. 'Half a league, half a league onward…'

The Domes came into clear sight. 'Sweet revenge and bitter regret…' He pulled on the stick and the aircraft climbed steeply and levelled out.

'The time has come to talk of many things, of ships and shoes and sealing wax of cabbages and kings…'

He lined up the tape marks with the curvature of the dome and the vertical column of the laser.

'…Government of the people by the people for the people…'

The shape filled the space between the edge markers. He kicked the golf bag into space. '…shall not vanish from the earth.'

The fishing line ran out and he could hear the cinematograph-like clatter of the winding gear above the roar of the wind. With the sound came agonising images of fishing with Tad in an Adirondack summer of long ago.

Then came the flash, vast piercing white, driven into his skull by Mary's scream.

35

The Summit

It was impossible not to be astonished at the sheer scale of the event as the world's most powerful leaders and richest players made their fan-fared entrance. For the sake of decency, aid workers, folk musicians, union leaders, artists and actors were woven into the procession. But it was the superstars with whom the distinguished crowd of watchers jostled to establish eye contact. In his place on the curve of the stairway, Thornhill was as unmoving as a statue. As the head of the procession crossed the wide hallway, the Global Children's Choir began their medley of world music.

On the balcony opposite, Morag, Darcy and Wolski stood among the sea of junior officials. Not far away, Golkov smiled at them like a contented snake.

Looking down on Thornhill, Darcy said, "He looks in a bad way. If I didn't know him better, I'd say he was in a catatonic trance."

"He is watching sheep going to the slaughter," Wolski whispered.

"Shut up," Morag said sharply.

Amid the crowd she saw only Thornhill and, like a mother unable to rescue a child from danger, felt only helpless desperation. By contrast, Thornhill's mind was strangely calm. As the procession began to make its way up the grand staircase, he knew he'd seen this picture somewhere before, but like a name on the tip of the tongue, he couldn't place it. Then suddenly, he had it. What he saw unfolding before him was a near replica of the earliest news-film ever shot; a procession of Kings, Emperors, Rajahs and Grand Panjandrums attending the coronation of the last but one Czar of Russia, the last glittering assembly of the old order.

He felt the warm shape of the hidden weapon. Everything seemed so beautifully simple. In fifteen paces the world would change, and he with it.

Morag was nauseous with tension. Shoot the pigs … the iceman… She swallowed hard against rising vomit. With her memory in overdrive, she swung round into Wolski and nearly knocked him over. "Innocent perpetrators. What did you mean by innocent perpetrators?" she demanded ferociously.

Ten paces. Thornhill counted each step. 'Two to the heart, one to the head.' He had no thought beyond the now inevitable event.

Wolski was at a loss to know how to answer Morag. All he could think of was Golkov's taunt: 'When this is all over you will be astonished at how simply it was done.'

At five paces, Thornhill's right hand was aligned with the pocket where the weapon was hidden.

"Think, for God's sake think," Morag shouted at Wolski. She was oblivious to the angry looks she was attracting from the star-struck crowd.

The security men closest to her discreetly closed in.

"Think!" she screamed incoherently. "'Water doesn't compress…', 'Shoot the pigs…'; you nearly had something." She sounded totally deranged.

Wolski looked around him with absolute desperation. For some reason he did not fully comprehend his blank gaze engaged with the crowded press enclosure.

The procession moved inexorably on. Calvin November was now three steps away from Thornhill, whose hand slid into the pocket and closed round the weapon. He slid the safety catch off.

* * *

Over the next two steps and five seconds the world changed, but not as Thornhill had anticipated.

He heard Wolski's thin voice shout, "The photographers, the flashguns."

Then Wolski's voice was drowned out by Darcy yelling, "Eiger!, Eiger! Eiger!" as he shouldered his way through a crowd of alarmed heads of state.

The emergency code word had temporarily immobilised the security team at the head of the stairs.

"Get everybody out of here!" Darcy screamed.

The procession stalled and there was pandemonium. The entire grand staircase was a mass of outraged egos.

Then Thornhill's mobile phone rang. Nobody who knew the number would call at a moment like this. It had to be Murphy.

"I've cut the bastard's balls off," the voice said. "The sun is down, Helios is out."

Those around him were incredulous at Thornhill taking a phone call. He felt a surge of energy; the icy calm was suddenly gone.

"Where are you?" he asked, trying to control the urgency of the question.

"Travelling."

"Where to?"

"You'll work it out. All you need to know is that Helios is out."

"Permanently?"

"Permanently, totally, globally."

"I'll pass your message on in person."

"In person?" There was stark astonishment in Murphy's voice.

"Yes, in person," Thornhill said as he ended the call.

"I know you." The contemptuous voice was that of Calvin November. Hemmed in by the crowd, he wanted someone to vent his anger upon.

Thornhill made firm eye contact and replied with measured aggression. "And I know you, Mr November, I know you very well. I know about Warsaw, I know about Cortexean and I know about Washington."

If November grasped the magnitude of what was happening, he didn't show it.

"And I've been asked to give you a message," Thornhill continued. "Helios is out, your sun is set – permanently."

Golkov had heard the conversation from a distance and was struggling through the crowd with a mobile phone to his ear. November saw him waiting for a reply. Golkov shook his head. Darcy was speaking urgently to the Swiss security team.

November's composure broke. "You're a dead man," he snarled at Thornhill.

"Thirty seconds ago, I was more dead than you could ever imagine. Now both of us are merely might-have-beens; you a wannabe colossus and I a squalid assassin."

It took the Swiss security team some time to reach them. Removing prominent world figures from a crowded stairway was not a contingency they had planned for and their natural deference to status slowed them down. As they closed in, the team recognised Thornhill as a colleague and tried to move November and Golkov away. But someone had taken the decision to move the procession on.

Enclosed in a bubble of self-importance and indignation at the delay, the crowd surged onwards, past November, Golkov, Thornhill they and the security team were pressed together by the shoulders and elbows of the rich, the powerful and the famous.

"You're merely an island in the stream, Mr November. History moves on, but now you're just a spectator, not a player," Thornhill said.

The Swiss, embarrassed by their slow response, wanted to establish their authority and began to hustle November and Golkov away through the crowd.

"I will destroy you," November hissed, as the distance between him and Thornhill widened.

"I nearly saved you the trouble," Thornhill said.

Wolski was oblivious to the high drama, pomp and circumstance of the event. For him, the moment was intimately personal.

"Wait." The loudest shout of which he was capable was almost lost in the surrounding hubbub, but his obvious frailty worked to his advantage. The crowd instinctively parted, allowing him to reach through the ring of guards and push a crumpled scrap of paper into Golkov's hand. It was the postcard of the Night Watch.

"This is your property; I no longer need it and it should be returned to you," Wolski said with formal politeness and the slightest of bows.

* * *

"How was it done? "Thornhill asked the group gathered in the security office.

It was Darcy who replied. "A number of the photographers had their gear stolen from the Press hotel. In an apparently generous gesture, it was replaced late last night

"Go on," Thornhill said.

Morag spoke. "The Swiss forensic lab have the gear and we'll get their detailed report in the morning, but it seems that in the replacement flashguns there was a tiny cartridge of compressed air and a projectile made of ice. The mechanism was to be activated by radio so as to avoid discharge before photography of the signing of the Declaration began."

"Why didn't the ice melt?" Thornhill asked.

"Ice doesn't have to be made with water," Wolski said. "This was some kind of synthetic ice within an outer casing with remarkable insulating properties. The friction of the projectile moving through the air would have caused the casing to melt. So, when the pellet hit the skin of the target it would have delivered a calibrated dose."

"That would have put them at each other's throats?" Thornhill asked.

"I'm sure they were confident of the technology after trying it out on the pigs," Wolski said.

"So only those being photographed at the signing of the Declaration would have been affected?"

It was Morag who answered the question. "Yes, that's exactly what they wanted. It was important that nobody else was hit. The whole point of the exercise was to create bloody mayhem among heads of government in front of the world's media."

"A workable madness," Thornhill said. "On the one hand, we have world leaders personally engaging in a display of violence not seen in public since Christians were thrown to the lions. On the other hand, Mr November is offering a hundred billion dollars for people to spend sorting out the world's problems. Who would you choose?"

"That's what his next appearance at Madison Square Garden would have been all about – to make the nation an offer it couldn't refuse," Darcy said.

Thornhill turned to Wolski with an outstretched hand. "Professor, how did you spot it?"

"I almost didn't," Wolski replied.

36

The End of the Beginning

There was a raw, clean cold by the slowly thawing lakeside. Thornhill stood alone beside the black water. Only the distant engine of a patrol boat troubled the silence.

"What are you doing?" It was Morag. The snow had silenced her approach.

"They're making history in there; you'll miss the show," Thornhill said without turning to face her.

"You're part of it, you should be in there," Morag said.

"No, I'm not. I nearly was, but I'm not, thank God,"

There was a moment of quiet.

"You're missing the event of the century," Morag said insistently.

"So are you. Why are you out here?" Thornhill asked.

"I wanted to be with you," Morag said.

The words swung Thornhill round, as he finally saw what he had missed for so long. Unsure of himself on unfamiliar ground, he couldn't find the right words. "Why?" he asked clumsily.

"You'd never understand," Morag said as she closed the space between them.

Thornhill replied gently. "Perhaps it's best for both of us if I don't try."

Morag turned to stare into the night. "Yes," she said in a whisper.

Thornhill stood alongside her. He took the ceramic gun from his pocket and hurled it into the darkness.

"What's that?" Morag said. For an instant, before it hit the water, the pistol was silhouetted against the looming lights of the city on the distant shore. "My God, you were going to..."

Letting her into his secret was a moment of intimacy. "Only you know," he said.

"Thank you." She turned to face him and stepped closer. "Will that be the only secret between us?"

"Yes."

"I'll keep it safe."

"I know you will."

He took her by the shoulders and kissed her on the cheek. "Thank you," he said quietly. They looked hesitatingly at each other. In the still air, a haze of frozen breath hung between them.

"I have to leave," Thornhill said.

Morag turned back towards the lake. "I know."

Thornhill's snow-muffled footsteps receded across the lawn.

Without turning from the dark water, Morag called, "Where are you going?"

"Home."

ABOUT THE AUTHOR

Julian Dinsell is a writer and filmmaker whose work draws upon encounters in Whitehall, 10 Downing Street, US Capitol, BBC, US Network TV, Hollywood Studios, The European Union, NATO, NASA, Moscow Media, Global Financial Markets, Aviation, Oil Exploration, Medicine and Surgery.

He is co-Founder TVC and former General Manager of Production at Reuters TV.

AUDIO BOOK

The Night Watch is also available as an Audio Book, read by **Nicholas Farrell:** *The Crown, Iron Lady, Hamlet, Legend, Chariots of Fire.*

Printed in Great Britain
by Amazon

65940403R00212